D1525189

THE CAR THIEF

V. REED

*To a Champion
for kids,*

[signature]

The Car Thief
By Vicki Reed

Copyright ©2020 by Vicki Reed
FIRST EDITION | Printed On-Demand

Cover photograph of boy: Anna Berdnik
Design: Kimber Gray

Softcover ISBN 979-8-63719-918-1
Hardcover ISBN 978-1-64338-098-8

24 Hours Books, Inc.
14 S. Queen Street, Mt. Sterling, Kentucky 40353, USA
www.reformationpublishers.com
Email rpublisher@aol.com
Orders 1-800-765-2464
Information 859-520-3757
Text 606-359-2064
Printed and bound in the United States of America

For all the resilient kids who persevere and prosper because of—or in spite of—their involvement in the System. And for all the social workers, juvenile staff, lawyers, judges, advocates, and reformers who slug it out every day on behalf of these vulnerable youth.

PART ONE

~

The Runaway

KELLY

1

It's a long way down. Like maybe die or at least break a leg or two down. For just a moment I consider ditching my plan, but then one look at the door locking me in and I decide yeah, I've got to do this.

Going into the bathroom, I take the sheets I stripped from the bed and put them under the bathtub spigot. The plan is to get out of here, but I'm careful not to spill any water on the floor. My grandfather wouldn't like that. I have a split lip, a black eye, and that locked door to show that it's not so good when he doesn't like something. When the sheets are soaked, I wring them out, freezing my hands in the process. If I'd been smart, I'd have used warm water. Usually I'm smart, but this is probably one of my less smart days.

I read once that sheets are stronger if wet and I want strong. I tie them together. I've been around horses all my life so I'm good with knots. If you can tie up twelve hundred pounds of horseflesh, you can tie up most anything.

After securing one end to the bedpost, I drop the rest of the sheet out the window, watching it tumble end over end before it stretches out and hangs there, like a ghost went splat against the bricks. I give it a few good pulls. Seems secure. I scoop the things on the bed into a pillowcase including a couple of T-shirts and a pair of jeans. I tuck the little bit of money I own into my pants pocket, and then consider whether to take my Oak Hill Military Academy ID with me or not. I give it a glance which is stupid, because I know what it says: Robert Kelly Morgan. I go by Kelly. Funny thing is I can't remember posing for it, but I must have. I stuff the ID in my pocket, not so much because I think I'll need it, but because it seems too personal to leave behind.

The last item is Buck, a little wooden horse no more than two inches high named after my first pony. He stares up at me. His little wooden eyes seem to ask, *Are we really doing this?* I give him a reassuring tap on his nose before zipping him into my jacket pocket. I remember watching my father carefully carve him from a piece of birch. The hunk of wood had come off a tree that had been hit by lightning. Dad told me Native Americans think this gives the wood extra power and I believe it. I pat the outside of my pocket. *Help me out tonight, buddy. Okay?*

In my head, I rehearse the plan one more time: Lower myself down until I reach the tree limb about ten feet below. Once on the limb, move to the trunk and climb down. Simple. I'm a good climber. Trees and I are good friends. Unfortunately, thanks to the diet my grandfather has me on—which for fun, let's call it *starvation*—I'm pretty weak. I hold up my hand and watch it shake. Here's hoping enough adrenaline kicks in to give me the boost I need.

I lean out the window and drop the pillowcase, letting my eyes follow it to the ground. My stomach plummets with it. I shouldn't have watched, but I have to be able to find it when I get down there. If I get down there. I crawl up and sit astride the windowsill. With my left hand, I take a good grip on the sheet just above a knot, chance one quick look down, grab a deep breath, and then, before my courage deserts me, swing out.

I grunt. The yank on my arms is worse than I thought. Only my death grip on the knot saves me from falling. I wrap my feet around the sheet and wait for the swaying to stop.

Cautiously, I lower myself hand by hand. The tree looked closer from the window. I keep looking down to see if I'm there yet. When my foot hits a branch, I breathe a sigh of relief. Okay, so far so good. But now there's a problem. It's not like I weigh much, but the limb won't support my weight this far out. Just a yard or so toward the trunk, it's thicker and should hold, but how to get there while holding onto the sheet? Looking down, I can see I'm twelve to fourteen feet up and if I take a tumble, there's a fifty-fifty chance I'll hit the driveway rather than the lawn. Not the best odds but nothing for it. I'll have to let go and fling myself to the thicker part of the branch.

I pick my spot and fix my eyes on it, before twisting in midair like one of those gymnasts on the high bar. I hang in mid-air for one terrible second while reaching for the limb. My left hand slips but my right one holds until I get a secure grip with both hands. The other good news is my friend Mr. Adrenaline has kicked in. The shakes are gone, replaced by my heart thumping so loud in my chest that anyone within fifty yards would be able to hear it. I scramble to the trunk where I can drop my feet to the limb below. From there, I shimmy down the trunk until I get to the last limb and then drop the remaining four feet to the ground. I pump my fist. I did it!

But there's no time for celebration. I grab up the pillowcase while I'm on the move. At the gate, I feel in the dark for the latch and hear it click open. I ease through and close it gently behind me. Time to run. My sneakers thud softly on the sidewalk. The cool air clears the sweat from my face. Eventually, I slow to a walk, keeping to the shadows as much as possible.

As my pulse returns to near normal, I think about this red-letter day. Once again, for the second time in less than two years, my life has drastically changed.

And I'm only twelve years old.

2

It takes hours to make it to the racetrack. I know it pretty well. It was near my boarding school and on weekends, when other boys went home or were busy with sports, I'd sneak out of the dorms to see the horses and be reminded of my home in Wyoming.

I arrive just before dawn. The rest of the city is still quiet, but here, it's buzzing with activity long before racegoers arrive to place their bets. Some horses have their heads hanging out of their stalls while others are being cooled off after exercise. Just the sight of them—their muscles rippling under their skin as they move, their hooves clopping in cadence on the concrete walk, the swish of their tails—calms me down after my long, stressful night.

I scan the grounds until I see what I've hoped for, a large horse trailer prepped and ready to go. I need to hurry before I'm seen so I slip up the ramp. In the front part of the trailer, there's a space at the top reserved for hay and equipment where I climb up and hide behind a hay bale. Sometimes it's good to be little.

It isn't long before horses are loaded. Their hooves clatter up the ramp. They snort as they start ripping into the hay tied up in nets in front of them. The grooms talk back and forth as they secure the lead ropes. The ramp creaks loudly as it's lifted into place and locked, throwing the horses and me into semi-darkness. I seem to be making a habit of getting locked into places. It's not a habit I want to keep. The truck engine cranks and roars to life and within a minute, we're rolling. Goodbye, Philadelphia.

In front of me are two chestnuts, one with a white star on his forehead. They fix their big brown eyes on me. "Hi guys," I whisper. They don't need me talking, of course, to know I'm here. They aren't afraid. They're used to people doing strange things. Their only interest is food.

I relax a little. I should be safe. It's unlikely my grandfather knows I'm gone.

He'll know for sure by breakfast. Will he call the police? I'm guessing that's a yeah. It would be the "proper" thing to do. He's big on proper. But the police won't have any idea where I am, and I know from listening to my father, that the smartest thing for a wanted person to do is leave the jurisdiction. Then it becomes the *next* cop's problem. My dad was the sheriff in Fort Dixon, Wyoming. He'd tell me about these things. That was before the crash, of course, and the court sent me to live with my grandfather.

As my eyes adjust to the light, I see a discarded fast food coffee cup. It's empty, half-crushed, and the black gunk at the bottom has long since dried but it'll do. The horses haven't drunk out of their buckets yet, so I lean over and dip the cup in the water, careful to avoid the fly floating on top. When you're really thirsty, you can't afford to be squeamish. I drink it all and dip again. The horse with the star dips his muzzle in his bucket, almost as if he's taking offense at my theft. The partially chewed hay in his mouth foams out over the top. I guess I've had enough to drink.

The hay smells like summer. I grab a loose strand from the horse's hay net and chew on it. Too bad it doesn't taste as good as it smells. I'm more than a little hungry but tiredness trumps hunger and there's nothing to eat anyway. I rub my eyes but stop when the bruised one lets me know it doesn't appreciate the attention. Exhausted, I stretch out as much as the space will allow, cradling my head on my bent arm. I hear the horses rhythmically chewing and close my eyes.

I have no idea where we're headed but we travel all day and it gets warmer and warmer so I'm pretty sure we're headed south. I sleep a good hunk of the trip but wake each time we stop for gas. The grooms refill the horses' buckets, so I get some more to drink but nothing to eat. I toy with getting out at one of the gas stations to try and find something but decide to stay in my safe spot.

The next time we stop, we've arrived at another racetrack. It's what I've been hoping for. I stay out of sight while one of the grooms unties the chestnuts. If I put my hand out, I could touch the guy's arm. I keep very still until the grooms lead the horses away, then I peek out between the metal slats and see the track office. I'm at someplace called River Bend Raceway.

There's a very dangerous moment when I leave the trailer, but no one spots me. Now what? Just hang around, I guess, drifting between the barns, trying to look like I belong, but most importantly, I need to find something to eat. My stomach aches.

I spot a bag of chips sitting on a table in the barn. I casually walk past the table and without slowing down, reach out to grab the bag. As soon as I'm in the clear, I rip it open and stuff a handful of chips in my mouth. God, they taste good. I'm on my third handful when I feel a hand clamp down on the back of my neck.

"Tu pequeno ladron!" You little thief!

A wiry guy with a mustache and beard has yanked my shirt halfway up the back of my head. I try to twist out of his grasp but although he may not be tall, he's strong. Stronger than my shirt which rips as he gives me a shake and lifts my feet halfway off the ground.

It's been a rough week and this is the last straw. My mouth trembles and my eyes fill with tears. The guy's hand grabs my chin. He pulls my face up and turns it from side to side taking in my black eye and swollen lip. He swears softly. Cussing is easy to recognize in any language. He eases his grip and sets me down.

Getting lucky is always a good thing around a racetrack and I've struck pay dirt. My captor's name is Rafa and he doesn't rat me out. He's illegal, so he and the authorities aren't good friends. When we talk enough for him to figure out I know horses, we work out a deal. Fortunately, with my dark hair and eyes, I can pass for his son. I help Rafa out with his work and he says we can split the money. Split might be too generous a word, but let's just say I'll get some. Money isn't a big deal for me anyway; it's not like I'm saving for my college education.

That first day I spend with Rafa, he lets me eat the rest of the chips, and later he gets us dinner from the track kitchen. We use a hay bale for a table.

"Thanks," I say, "It smells good."

"It ain't bad." Rafa pulls up another bale and sits. "Good thing too because they pay us crap. If they didn't feed us and give us a bed, none of us could afford to work here." He pops the top of his beer can and takes a long swig. "I sleep in the track dormitory, but you can't."

It's bad manners to talk with your mouth full, but I'm really hungry, so I chew while I answer him. "I found a hiding place in one of the barns." I wipe my fingers on my shirt.

"That's good," he says, "but don't be smoking in there."

"Oh, I don't smoke; it's bad for you."

He snorts. "Hey, some of the churches bring over clothes. We'll go look through the bags and get you some stuff."

And so begins my life at the track. In the next couple of months, my Spanish gets pretty good. I already knew some from when I was a kid back in Wyoming, when I used to play with the kids of Mexican workers who appeared each year to shear the local sheep.

Rafa is paid by the number of horses he can work, so with me helping out, we're doing pretty good. If we get his assigned horses finished, we can go to other barns and pocket thirty dollars for each extra horse we cool out. I notice that some new people start work, but then leave in just a couple of days.

"Why did they go so soon?" I ask Rafa one day, while we're washing down a horse.

"Happens all the time. It's hard work and shitty pay." He dips his sponge in the bucket and wrings it out. "But you and I, eh? We stay, don't we?" He puts his hand over his heart like he's acting in a Shakespeare play. "Because we have racing in our blood and the love of horses in our heart." He finishes and gives me a big grin, showing his missing teeth.

I roll my eyes. "I didn't know you were a poet."

He knocks me on the side of my head with his wet sponge. "Don't be a *mocoso malcriado*," he says, but he's just kidding around.

Considering that I was up before dawn scrubbing and filling water buckets and mucking out stalls, I don't think I fit the title of spoiled brat. But the other thing he said about me is true. I do have horses in my heart. I decide that would be a good title for a book I might write. *Horses in My Heart*, by Robert Kelly Morgan. It has a certain ring. I'm picturing it on a library shelf when Rafa whacks me again with a wet sponge.

I don't leave the track. Most of us don't. Hardly anyone owns a car and the nearest grocery store is several miles away. Most of my day is spent working, or resting up after working, but I'm not complaining. I don't have to go to school, no one is hitting me, and the good thing about working hard is I fall asleep exhausted, which keeps the bad dreams away.

The only thing I do for entertainment is read. The nice church people bring books as well as clothes. And I write. I can hardly remember a time I didn't put thoughts on paper. I made pretend books at the same time I learned to color. I wrote my first novel when I was eight. To no one's surprise, the book was about about a horse. My uncle lived on a ranch near me and my dad. He and I spent hours riding together. He taught me everything about horses there was to know.

I find a small spiral notebook in the church donation box and keep it in the back pocket of my jeans. I jot down random thoughts and things I notice. Little stories. One night, I get inspired and scribble until I fill up most of the pages. The fun thing about writing is being in two worlds at once.

The pretend one is better.

Sometimes I forget which one I'm in.

It's Friday morning, almost six months after I first arrived, and we're all scrambling, trying to get our horses ready for the afternoon's race card. My horse's official name is The Analyst, but in the barn, he's just called Ziggy. He's got a good shot at a win today. I take a rag and wipe his hooves till they shine. I'm not caring about how hard the work is; I'm just excited about watching him race. I don't plan on doing this forever, but hey, I can do it till I'm eighteen. After that, I can do whatever I want.

I take Ziggy's head between my hands and look him in his eyes. "Hey there, buddy, are you feeling it today? Are you gonna show the rest of these horses your back hooves?"

Rafa looks over Ziggy's neck and laughs. "He'd better. I put twenty on him."

I start to say something back but hear a commotion to my right. Everyone in the barn seems to be moving around all of a sudden. And then I hear it: "Inmigracion! Immigracion!"

I freeze but the rest of the place goes crazy. Everyone else drops their lead ropes and scatter, pushing through the horses and getting them upset. In another minute, it's a madhouse with bucking animals, dust swirling, and men shouting. I try to quiet Ziggy, but Rafa grabs me by my collar and pulls me along with him toward an exit. Before we can get there, we're surrounded by men in matching blue jackets.

Within the hour, we're loaded into vans. I want to go with Rafa but they don't let me. I get one last glimpse of him staring at me from behind the van window. We're driven to some building surrounded by razor wire then put in a big chain link enclosure. Me and a couple of other guys who are teenagers get separated from the others. One of the guys in an official looking jacket asks me my name and age. I just stare at him and don't answer. Another guy comes over and asks me the same questions in Spanish. I don't answer him either. I'm not being uncooperative as much as I'm confused. I don't know whether to lie or not. It's hard to tell which path is better; keep up the ruse or 'fess up.

Once when I was little, the family of two brothers made some threats of retaliation against my Dad after he arrested them. Just in case they were serious, he had me fingerprinted and entered the information in a national identification program. I'm guessing the immigration people just ran my fingerprints, because apparently the jig is up. A blond-haired man with a stern expression opens the gate, points at me, and says, "You. Come with me."

I give him my best stupid look, but he shakes his head. "Don't pretend you don't understand…" He glances at the paper in his hand. "…*Robert*."

No sense trying to fool him, so I do as he says.

He looks at me. "Really? Wyoming? Pretty far from the border, isn't it?"

I give him the *what-can-I-say* shrug.

He takes me to a little room where there's a black man and a woman with red hair waiting for us. They are standing by a desk and a couple of metal chairs. There's no window, just a light fixture with one of the two bulbs burned out. The man turns to the woman, says "all yours," then leaves the room with the guy who fetched me.

The lady smiles. "Hello, Robert. My name is Linda Hawkins. I'm with Children's Services. These gentlemen called me when they found out you're a U.S. citizen. Why don't you come over here and let's sit down and talk a minute?"

My mind is racing. I know I'm going to be shipped back to my evil grandfather. Maybe it'll be different this time. Maybe my grandfather will say, *I'm sorry I punched your lights out and practically starved you to death and I'm glad you're back*, but I wouldn't bet on it.

Ms. Hawkins has frizzy red hair that she keeps blowing out of her face. She looks frazzled. I like the sound of both of those words, frizzy and frazzled. If I wrote a book about two puppies, I'd name them that. Or maybe I'll make them into little alien creatures with electrical powers that keep zapping each other. Yeah. The Friz and the Frazzle. I like it.

Mrs. Hawkins clears her throat and gives me a sympathetic look. "Robert, I looked into your case and saw that the last place you lived was with your grand-father in Philadelphia."

Uh-oh, here it comes. Pack your bag. Circle the wagons.

"I'm very sorry to tell you this, but your grandfather died three months ago. Heart attack."

I just stare at her. What did she say? That can't be. How long have I even been gone? I'm surprised how upset I am. I didn't like him. He was a complete jerk, but with him alive at least I had family like normal people do. Now, like everyone else in my life, he's done gone and died on me.

The lady keeps talking, but there's a buzzing in my head. I nod here and there, which seems to be all that's required. Finally, the words *foster home* punch their way through the buzz. She goes with me while I'm processed out. As we're leaving the building, I overhear one of the agents say to the guy next to him, "He'll be out the back door before dawn."

We drive about twenty minutes and pull up in front of a house which looks identical to all the others on the street. A small red brick with white shutters. The red flowers in a pot on the porch are plastic. Mrs. Hawkins knocks and a lady with black hair lets us in. All her clothes are the color of oatmeal. Weird. I put my hand in my sweatshirt and hold on to my little horse. Good thing he was in my pocket this morning when I went to work, because everything else I owned is gone.

I look around. It looks very clean in here, but something seems off. There's nothing on the coffee table but the TV remote. The side tables have lamps but nothing else. It's like a burglar came in and stole everything but no one cares. There's only one picture on the wall and I'm not sure what it is. Some balls and triangles all stacked together. I turn my head, trying to decide if it would look better upside down.

I'm introduced to the woman, but don't catch her name so I just think of her as Mrs. Foster. Honestly, I'm not thinking real clear right now. This morning I got up at the racetrack prepared to live out my predictable day. Hours later, I'm told a family member has died and I'm shipped to people I don't know. It's like I'm living a flashback; I've been here before.

Papers are exchanged and Mrs. Hawkins and Mrs. Foster talk amongst them-selves while I keep looking around the room. It feels odd to be in a stranger's home. I feel like I'm trespassing. The lady looks at me and says, "Kelly, we're glad you're here."

It's the right words, but somehow, I don't think her heart is in it. She does seem nice enough, in a distant sort of way. Distance is good. More distance would be even better. Haven't I shown I can take care of myself? I really, really don't want to be here. However, my manners kick into autopilot and I say, "Thank you."

As soon as Mrs. Hawkins leaves, I follow Ms. Foster to the basement. It takes my eyes a minute to adjust to the dimness. The ceiling is low and the whole place smells damp and musty. Along the wall are three bunkbeds.

She grabs up a jacket off the floor and hangs it on a hook. "There are four other boys with us right now. They're all at school." She waves toward one of the bottom bunks, "That will be your bed."

She points to a TV in the corner. "Watch whatever you want. I'll fix you a sandwich in a bit and you can bring it back down. Do you have any questions?"

I'm at a loss for words, not a usual situation for me. "No ma'am," I say.

She gives me a slight smile and goes back up the stairs. It's sunny and nice outside, but I guess I'm expected to just sit here in the gloom and watch TV all day. I'm already missing the horses. Did Ziggy even get to race? And what happened to Rafa? I know that we had a business relationship, but still....

The immigration guy was wrong. I'm not going to make it till dawn. I find a bathroom, use it, and stall another five minutes before walking back up the stairs. Mrs. Foster is standing by the sink in the kitchen. She sees me and frowns, "Is there something you need?"

This time I'm ready. Making sure to make eye contact, I give my most charming smile. "I thought I'd go out and sit in the sun awhile."

Her lips narrow and she points to the basement stairs. "For this first day, I think it's best you stay in the house." It's not a suggestion. It's an order.

That does it. This sucks. All sorts of responses like that spring into my head, none of them good. "Oh, okay," is all I wind up saying.

I go back to the stairs and walk down the first three before walking back up on my tiptoes. I put my ear in the crack between the door and the frame. In a minute or two, I hear her talking on the phone from the dining room.

"Yeah, another one." A pause. "I know, I know, but the car bill is coming due."

I guess she's talking about me, but it doesn't matter. She sounds occupied. It only takes six strides to get to the back door. On the way, I grab an apple from a bowl. *Thanks.* I close the door quietly behind me and walk quickly till the house is out of sight. After that, I start jogging.

Eventually, I stop to catch my breath and take a bite of apple. What's next? I wonder, but no plan comes. I tuck the rest of the apple into my pocket along with my little wooden horse and keep going. There's only one thing for sure, I decide.

I'm getting really good at running away.

3

I know I can't go back to the racetrack. Maybe I can find one in some other city. The thing is, I lucked into Rafa, but it's doubtful lightning would strike twice, so I'm not sure that's a good plan. I sure hope he's okay.

That leaves me with two choices. Option number one: Roam around trying to kill time until I'm eighteen. Not appealing. So I go with option number two: Wyoming. Surely something will work out for me when I get back there. I so want to see the mountains and feel the wind. My family may all be under the ground, but I desperately want to be near them. More than anything, I just want to go home.

Now that I'm on fire to get back to Wyoming, it's getting there that's the problem. Hitchhiking is dangerous. There are perverts that might want me and cops that might get me, so I don't do much of it. I'm not moving very far, very fast, but I decide if given the chance, you can learn early in life to take care of yourself.

For the first couple of months, being on the run is exciting—a big game. I take pride in finding clever ways to survive. The mean city streets? Not for this cowboy. I learn the easiest thing to do is blend into the places a middle-class kid would go. After all, that's what I've been. Besides, being respectful, pleasant, and charming gets you a long way.

I also learn to lie. A lot.

"I'm just waiting on my mom."

"My dad asked me to get these for him."

I walk into a large church one Wednesday night and grab some food during some social thing. If I'm really hungry, I go to fast food places and find part of a meal someone didn't finish. I've eaten a thousand soggy French fries. When I run into some other homeless kids and stay with them a short time, they teach me the pizza trick.

"Man, just call in a pizza with weird shit on it," the oldest kid of the group told me. "When no one shows up to get it, not even the people that work there will want it, so you just wait till they toss it in the dumpster then go get it."

I hear them order an assortment of toppings that in less desperate times I wouldn't touch. Then I watch as they dive into the dumpster. Boy, do they look pathetic.

I try not to think about how I look when I do it.

The street kids look like street kids—dirty, with half-ripped clothes. Most of them have tattoos and piercings. If people bother to look at them at all, they either shake their heads in sympathy or look disgusted.

Dad always talked about the importance of appearance and I get it. To go to the places I want to go, it's crucial not to look too scraggly, so keeping clean and decently dressed is important. I learn to seek out the Ys, inventing stories to get past any gatekeepers. It usually works.

"I forgot my pass."

"My mom had me run back out to the car to get her towel."

"I have to pick up my little brother."

The Y's are also good places to find clothes. I can say I left something and be directed to the lost and found. I have no way to wash clothes so I change into anything I can find and stuff my old clothes in the garbage or toss them back in lost and found if no one is looking. No matter how dirty the clothes are I have on, I pass over the T-shirts that make you look bad. A black one with a skull and the words *Headed to Hell* is an instant reject. Polo shirts are good; a sport or dress shirt is a real score. The more respectable I look, the easier it is to blend in. I find a tie and consider putting it on, but decide it's too over the top. Not to mention I don't know how to tie it. I come across a used backpack and take it.

It's kind of a surprise, but I find sleeping is more challenging than finding food. In some towns, I go to the movies. I head to the bathrooms first and find a discarded cup or candy wrapper and act like I've been here and just went to get some food as I walk by the ticket takers. It's important to have the right attitude. Smile, nod, look confident.

I love the movies. Dark and cool when it's hot, warm when it's cold, and it brings back pleasant memories of when I actually went to them like a normal person. Sometimes I really want to watch the movie, but within a minute, I'm usually sound asleep and only wake up when the closing credits are rolling and people are shuffling past me.

My best go-to places are libraries where no one blinks an eye at a kid being there alone. They also remind me of my prior life. It doesn't matter where you are, if you're in a room full of books you're halfway home. I got my first library card when I was barely four. They didn't want to give it to me, saying I was too young, but Dad insisted. Never a week went by that we didn't stop to load up on a stack of books for me. I loved stories of fantasies and adventures and hoped one day I'd have a true adventure of my own.

Be careful what you wish for.

Basically, over the last few months, I've gotten by on luck and the goodwill and the gullibility of strangers. Lately however, luck hasn't been much of a friend and the constant looking for food and shelter is becoming exhausting. I don't know how cave men stood the stress. I bet some of them just laid down and let the saber tooth tiger eat them to get it over with.

I pass through West Virginia, which I can now add to my life list. Before my dad died, I had only been in Wyoming and Idaho. We'd go camping, but that was it as far as trips went. Dad often apologized about not going on vacations, but I didn't think much about it. I was happy and didn't care. When I get back to Wyoming, I'm going to be happy once again to just stay put. There are still a lot of states between me and there, but at least I'm further west than when I started.

April showers may bring May flowers but only if the rain lets up. It's been pouring for days so I'm sort of grounded and fall back on a library for refuge. I notice a place to squeeze in behind a bookcase that's next to a wall so when no one's looking, I slide back there to grab a nap. It's a shelf with oversize books and pretty much only old people read those, so they probably won't notice me even if they pull one out.

When I wake up, I find everyone has left for the night. I couldn't have planned it better if I tried. I decide this is a ploy I'll have to try again in the future. I'm in this wonderful space all on my own. I go look at the door and push gently on it. It's not the kind where you can push it open from the inside without the key. I'm locked in. For a second, I feel a little freaked out, but I could always crash through a door or window if I really needed out. Otherwise, I just need to hide out for a bit when they open up in the morning and make my escape when no one's looking.

I go exploring. There's a little kitchen with some food and drinks in the refrigerator. I rifle through the desks and find crackers and candy bars, which by my standards is a feast. Well-fed, I find it easier to leave the money I've seen in those desks alone. Stealing money from library people just seems wrong—not that all stealing isn't wrong, of course. I mean, I know that.

When darkness comes, I'm afraid to turn on the overhead lights to read, but I can turn on a light in the windowless bathroom without fear anyone outside will see. I grab some chair cushions, take in my drink and snacks, and hunker down with a book, sitting near the sinks and as far away from the toilets as possible. It's paradise. I feel lucky.

I should know by now that bad luck is free, but good luck comes with a price.

"You. Get up! You hear me? Get up!"

Still groggy from sleep, I squint up at a security guard. His gut hangs way over his belt and blocks my view of anything higher, so only when I sit up, do I see his red, round face. He looks like a troll. An angry troll.

He points a hammy finger at me, "What do you think you're doing in here?"

I think it's pretty darn obvious what I've been doing. Grabbing my backpack, I try to make a run for it, but the rent-a-cop has reflexes even if he doesn't have muscles and blocks the door. I retreat to a corner, feeling safer with walls on two sides of me. My eyes flick all around the confined space as I think of my options. Maybe he'll make a grab for me and I can dodge him and get to the door. I'll just slide past him on the slippery linoleum floor like going into third base.

But no, he blocks the door and cracks it barely enough to tell someone to call the police. I try to think up a Plan B but nothing comes to mind. So I just stand there, rigid with fear, and don't answer any of the questions he's firing at me until he gives up asking. We stare at each other until there's voices outside the door, followed by a firm two-tap knock. The guard opens the door to a cop, and I feel my heart rate pick up. Like a mouse pinned by a cat, I shrink back into my corner and try to dream up a good story. Yeah, a good lie, that's what's needed.

The officer looks like a father that could have kids my age. He doesn't look mean. He calmly looks me over. The guard is looking like now-you'll-get-yours so I'm glad when the policeman opens the door and motions with his head for the security guy to leave. The guard looks disappointed and shoots me one last nasty look before he goes. Now it's just me and the officer.

"Son, what are you doing here?"

I can't think of a good enough lie fast enough, so I go with honesty. "I accidentally got locked in."

Despite it being the truth, he looks skeptical, "How did you get *accidentally* locked in?"

My mind is spinning through possibilities. Maybe I should tell him some bad guy forced me into a closet. That might do it. I open my mouth to say it, but can't. "I fell asleep behind a bookshelf."

"What's your name?"

"Kelly Morgan."

He looks me up and down. "How old are you, eleven?"

It's hell to be short. "I'm thirteen!"

At this point, the door opens and a younger-looking officer joins our party. He's tensed up till he tosses one look in my direction and I watch all his muscles relax at once. He nods at the friendly officer who I see on his badge is Officer Clark. "What's up?"

"This young man spent the night here."

The young guy inclines his head to the world outside the bathroom door. "They said there wasn't any vandalism they could see. Some of them had money in their desk drawers and say it's still there."

Officer Clark turns his attention back to me. "Did you damage anything?"

"No sir." I gesture to the floor. "I borrowed these cushions, but I was going to put them back."

"Did you steal anything?"

Quick, tell a lie, but my father's face is in my head. "I'm afraid I did."

"What did you take?"

"Food from the refrigerator." My mouth has taken on a life of its own. "And some snack stuff from people's desks."

The officer squints one eye and tilts his head, "But you didn't take their money?"

I shake my head. "No. I thought maybe they wouldn't mind the food so much."

His radio is crackling with dispatch giving other calls. He reaches one hand down and adjusts the volume, then seems to make a decision and cuts to the chase. "Let's get you home. Where do you live?" The good news is they just want to get rid of me. The bad news is it won't be as easy as they think.

I put my hands behind my back and push off the wall a couple of times. "Nowhere really."

His face softens. "You're homeless?"

I like the way that sounds. Much better than runaway, and it's true, I am homeless. "Yes, sir."

"Are your folks in a homeless shelter?"

"No, sir."

"Do you know where they are?"

"Yes, sir."

"Can they come and get you?"

"No, sir."

"Can we call them?"

"No, sir."

The officers look at each other. I think they're getting tired of playing twenty questions. "Why not?"

Since lying didn't work out, I decide a little sympathy wouldn't hurt so I go for the puppy dog look and decide a few fake tears wouldn't hurt my cause either. I'm horrified when the fake tears turn real. I try to blink them back. "They're dead," I whisper.

Officer Clark says, "I'm sorry to hear that. Who has custody of you?"

Bounce, bounce. I'm pushing off the back wall a little faster. "No one."

"Come on now, somebody has to be responsible for you. Who was the last adult you lived with?"

"My grandfather. But he's dead now too."

"Are you saying you've been on your own since then?"

Bounce, bounce. I let my silence answer his question.

"You haven't spent a night in foster care or detention or any other kind of facility?"

I've learned leaving things out are the easiest lies to tell. And I haven't spent a *night* in foster care so it's technically true. "No, sir."

The officer reaches out and holds my shoulder. I'm worried he knew I was lying, but he just wants me to quit bouncing off the wall. He says, "Well, this is no good. You're too young to be out on your own."

"No really, I'm okay. Last night was just a fluke. It won't happen again, I promise. If you could just let me go."

I don't really expect he'll agree, so I'm not surprised when he shakes his head. "Not happening. You're going to get yourself hurt or killed. Just lucky it hasn't happened already."

There's a long pause while we all look at each other like we're deciding where we should go for lunch. The younger officer asks Officer Clark "Want me to take him to the detention center?"

My head is down, but from the top of my eyes, I can see Clark shake his head 'no.' "Let's take him to Oasis." He looks at me. "That's a shelter for kids. They can give you a bed and a meal and help you with your situation. How's that sound?"

I'll let you go would sound better, but since that's off the plate, Oasis has a nice ring to it, like swaying palm trees and tropical skies. It sure sounds better than *detention*. "That'd be swell," I finally say.

Good answer. Now they look pleased. Officer Clark reaches over and picks up my library book then gestures to the floor. "That backpack's yours?"

I nod. He picks it up and zips it open. I chew on my lower lip and bounce more off the wall while I watch him paw through my things. There's not much, a T-shirt, my ID, some loose change I found under a vending machine yesterday, and my little wooden horse. Oh yeah, and those stolen crackers I'd planned to take with me. When he pulls them out, I quickly say, "I'll put those back."

He smiles. "I doubt they'll want them. Let's see your pockets."

I oblige, pulling them out so they make bunny ears. They're empty.

He gives me a quick pat down, pulling up my shirt then taking his hands down my legs before making me take off my shoes. It's the first time anybody has touched me in a long time—other than hitting or grabbing me, of course. Finally, he says, "Okay, you're good."

The young officer reaches to his belt for his handcuffs, but thankfully my buddy Officer Clark shakes his head and they go away. "I think he's fine."

21

I look at him gratefully and nod. "I'm fine." I wasn't trying to be funny, but they both laugh. I join in like *hey, we're all pals having a good time.*

Officer Clark hands me my backpack, steps over, and reaches behind him without looking to push open the door, motioning me forward. When I get to him, he takes hold of my arm. I guess "fine" only goes so far. The library staff is gathered around the checkout desk and every eye turns our way. I hug my backpack to my chest with the hope it will somehow shield me from their scrutiny. Officer Clark addresses a woman who must be the librarian. She's a tall, skinny older lady who has those glasses that dangle in front with a chain around her neck. That screams librarian to me. If she put a finger to her mouth and said *shhhh* that would seal it. Clark hands her the library book. "If you're sure there are no damages, then the only charge would be trespassing. Are you wanting to press charges?"

She peers down at me. I don't have any trouble looking like I'm sorry.

"Not as long as it doesn't happen again." She looks at the book in her hand. *Bonecrack* by Dick Francis, an English jockey turned successful author. "Have you read other Dick Francis books?"

"Yes, ma'am, at least three or four. I like his style."

She puts her glasses on and her eyes skim the back. "Me too. His opening lines are always engaging. This was one of my favorites. How far have you gotten?"

"Not quite halfway."

She taps it with one of her pink painted fingernails, then extends it to me. "How about you keep it?"

Totally surprised, I meet her eyes, forgetting to be embarrassed for a moment. "But I don't have a library card."

She smiles at Officer Clark, and a corner of his mouth turns up. She turns back to me. "It's an older book and it's not our only copy. We'll call it a gift. I appreciate someone who enjoys reading."

A book I can keep. I'm thrilled. "Really? Thank you. I'd like to know how it ends." Then I remember myself and stand up straighter. "I'm sorry for the trouble I caused. Please forgive me."

She smiles at me as she hands me the book. "Consider yourself forgiven."

I would like to stay and talk to this nice lady about books, but Clark's hand is guiding me to the door. Guess it's time to go. I feel a bit less humiliated until we get outside. They haven't opened the library because of me, so people are waiting around, holding books in their arms, standing across from the two police cars with flashing lights. All their eyes zero in on me like a bunch of wolves that suddenly spot a fawn. I feel my face flush. I'm glad when the car door to the back seat is opened and I can escape their stares. Officer Clark talks a minute to the other officer before he gets in, but I can't hear what they're saying. Not that I don't try. I press my ear to the glass but zilch, nothing.

He looks at me in the rearview mirror as he pulls out. "So where are you from, Kelly?"

"Fort Dixon, Wyoming." I want to bond with him, so I add, "My father was the sheriff." I see it as a sign of progress when I can mention my father without bursting into flames.

"You serious?" He makes a turn onto the road.

"Yes." I look around. "He would have liked this car. His wasn't nearly this good." I think about it just a second then go for broke. "He was killed by a bad guy."

Now I have his attention. He turns part way in his seat to look at me again and says, "That's rough." I nod back at him.

In a few minutes we make a turn off a busy street right next to an auto shop. There's a sign, *Division of Children and Youth Services*. The first building is flanked with razor wire. I see another sign, *Coleman Juvenile Detention Center*. I quickly look up at the rearview mirror.

Officer Clark eyes meet mine in the mirror and he reassures me. "We aren't going there. The shelter is next door."

He pulls the car to the adjacent building which sure enough has its own sign, *Oasis Youth Shelter*. The building is smaller and looks far less scary than the detention center. I get the hand on the arm again as we walk toward it. He presses a gray metal button which buzzes and a man with a beard heads our way. That man presses a button to let us in and squeezes around a divider toward us. I lean in closer to Officer Clark.

The bearded man smiles at Clark and includes me in it as well. "Hi, I'm Al Flynn. What have we got here?"

"This young man spent the night sleeping at the library. He tells me he doesn't have a guardian or a home."

"Well then, this is the place to be. I remember most of our kids. You haven't been here before have you?"

I shake my head and Clark speaks up. "He says he's from Wyoming."

Mr. Flynn looks impressed. "Wow, long way from here, but we had a kid from California once, so you aren't the farthest. I'm trying to remember. What's the Capitol there in big sky country?"

He asks in a conversational way, but I recognize a test. Challenged, I find my voice.

"Cheyenne. Our flag has a bison on it." If they're going to test me, I'm going for an A.

"Nice." Flynn smiles as he and Clark exchange a look.

Flynn hands a form to Clark who leans over and starts filling it out. I get asked a few questions like my date of birth. Once he finishes, he hands it to Flynn and says, "He hasn't had any breakfast."

"We can take care of that." He looks at me, "You hungry? And you can call me Al."

I hadn't thought about food till they mentioned it and now I'm starving. I shrug and say, "Maybe a little."

Al is motioning with his hand for me to come with him. He looks friendly and he's mentioned food, but I move slowly, reluctant to leave Officer Clark who just might be reminding me of my dad. But now he's moving to the door, and I'll be left on my own in seconds. I want to say something to him, but all I can come up with is, "Thanks."

He gives me a thumbs-up. "Behave yourself, alright?"

"Sure," I say, not at all sure about anything.

4

Al makes me give up my backpack, although he assures me I'll get it back when I leave. I remember my free library book and ask to have it, but I'm told since it's a personal item, it's getting locked up with my other stuff. I sign a list of inventory form, then we go through a couple of doors and end up in a kitchen. It looks pretty much like a kitchen in a regular house, except there's gigantic cans and jars of baked beans, peanut butter, and creamed corn lined up on a shelf near the refrigerator.

Al opens up a cabinet door and brings down a loaf of bread. "We've already served breakfast. Would a peanut butter sandwich do you until lunchtime in a couple of hours?"

"Sure."

I take a seat at a scarred-up wooden table. On the wall next to me is something that says, "Chore Chart." The names Jeremy, Ben, Christie, and Pam are written in little cascading boxes down the left-hand side with checks in boxes to the right.

Al fixes me the sandwich and hands it to me with a big glass of milk. They both taste like heaven. I take a second one when it's offered to me and then, without asking, he hands me a third. I'd like to say I had too much pride to take the last one, but pride seems to have sailed on out of here. I glance at Al but his face is completely expressionless. I get the feeling he might be good at this job. After the last bite, Al takes me to a little office. He sits down and pats the chair next to the desk, so I sit.

He reaches over and grabs some papers and a pen and says, "Let's get a little more information on you, okay?"

I nod but I'm not excited. There are answers I don't want to give, so I trot out the shortest version I can of my so-called life, opting to leave out the Guiness

Book of World Records for shortest stay in foster care. I tell him I don't eat meat when he gets to the dietary questions and I'm happy when it doesn't set off the usual responses: *From Wyoming? What? That's silly. Surely you eat bacon!*

I expect the questions about school and where I've been, but some are unexpected.

"Were either of your parents incarcerated?"

"No." I scowl, insulted on behalf of my parents. I'd told him my father was a sheriff so why would he ask? But he's not done. His pencil hovers over the sheet, and he keeps asking bizarre questions with the same type of voice he'd use if he was asking me, *Would you rather have pizza or spaghetti?*

"Have you ever willingly performed or been threatened to perform a sexual act for money or goods?"

"No." I give Al a bit of a glare on that one.

He keeps at it. "Have you ever been the victim of sexual abuse?"

"Never." How many of these dumb questions are there?

Al's pencil lingers over the form. "Have you ever been the victim of physical abuse?"

My mind zips back to where I'd prefer it not go: The shock as my grandfather struck me with the flat of his hand—short, vicious, and hard. Before I could recover, his hand slapped my face again followed by his fist catching me smack in my eye. The left side of the world flashed white and, half-blind, I ducked and put up my arms. He grabbed the front of my shirt, smacking me on one side of the face and then the other before he dragged me upstairs and threw me in my room and locked the door.

I study Al's diploma hanging on the wall. "No."

I feel Al's eyes linger on me a moment. I play with my fingers because suddenly they seem real interesting.

When the question and answer period of our show is over, I get a tour of the building. There are kids of all ages. Mickey Mouse pictures down one hall where little kids are sitting on the floor pushing trucks and drawing with crayons. They're playing with toys, but I think they look kind of sad. I wonder how I look.

The unit for teens is on the other side. It's empty because everyone is next door at school. He explains it's an alternative school so there are kids from the community as well as the shelter. Al takes me to the bathroom and tells me to take a shower. He lays out some clothes for me to wear when I get out. Black sweatpants and a gray sweatshirt. Clean white underwear. That's not a bad thing because I have to admit the ones I'm wearing now have some mileage on them.

"Put your clothes in the basket when you're done. They'll be washed and returned to you later. Put your shoes in here too. Okay?"

"Yes, sir."

I pull off my shirt and Al says, "That's a pretty nasty scar on your arm. Did you get that in the car wreck?"

Suddenly self-conscious, I pull my arm in close to my body. "Yeah." For some reason, I add, "They told me the doctor had to work real hard to save it." I remember the nurse fluffing my pillow at the hospital, as she bragged about the effort the doctors had gone through. I think she was glad to tell me something had been saved. This was after the doctor told me my father and uncle were both gone.

I wait for him to leave before taking off the rest of my clothes and getting into the shower. When I step out, I put on the clothes he gave me. The basket with my things is gone. When Al comes back I say, "I don't have any shoes."

"You don't need any while you're inside. When you go out with staff, you'll get some." He says this in a way that implies we don't need to say any more about it. I'm not happy about this piece of news, plus it was sneaky how they took them away. There's also the fact I was planning on heading out of here later on today, and this complicates things.

I feel a little pissed and think it must show, but all Al says is, "Let's go back to the kitchen where I'll go over the point system with you."

This time Al joins me at the battered table and hands me a couple pieces of paper. I look at them while he talks. "Here's a list of the rules and privileges. Good behavior will earn you points, and bad behavior will get them taken away. The privileges you get are tied to how many points you have. You can buy a later bedtime, watch TV, play video games, and get snacks."

I read the rules and frown. I can never go outside on my own. Inside, I have to ask permission for pretty much everything including going to the bathroom. If I do, I'll get points. I can earn points by doing assigned chores, being respectful, being helpful, and following instructions.

As I'm studying the card, Al asks, "Do you have any questions?"

I feel an emotion I haven't felt in a long time. Irritation. It feels kind of good, a nice change from fear and sadness. What am I, a mouse in a maze? The whole thing is demeaning as hell.

"I don't get it," I say.

"You don't understand? Need me to explain it again?"

"I understand, but I don't get it. No offense, but it seems pointless." I just realize what I said, so can't help but smile. "Ha!"

"Funny." He smiles too. "The purpose is to train your behavior to be acceptable. To help you learn consequences."

"You've only known me for minutes. How do you know my behavior isn't acceptable? I'm here because I don't have anywhere else to go. I could be a saint."

Al's hand is smoothing his beard, and he's getting that look adults get when I ask a lot of questions. "I'm afraid we don't get many of those here. Just give it a chance. If you don't have a problem managing your behavior, it'll be easy for you, right?"

It's a reasonable argument, so I don't like it. I slump my shoulders. "I guess."

"Good. That's seven hundred points for being agreeable. You can look at this booklet and see how many other points you can earn. Or lose."

I skim over it. "Cussing someone out loses two thousand points?"

"That's a pretty serious infraction."

"Why not two hundred or twenty? Why two thousand? Seems like a lot of unnecessary zeros."

Al is still looking patient, but I suspect I'm beginning to get on his nerves. Not one to easily give up, I look at the rest of the card. "Bedtime at eight-thirty? It's hardly even dark then."

"Wake up is six o'clock, so you'll be tired by then. Besides, if you get your points, you can stay up till nine."

I want to say "yippee," but don't think it'd be appreciated. Al's standing up like discussion is over. I start to say "okay," but worry he might give me more damn points for being agreeable, so I don't say anything.

Al reaches in my direction. He has hairy arms. "Here's a marker and your points card. You'll keep your own points. And I'm going to add your name here on the chore chart."

There's nothing to do but take them.

Watching him write my name on the chart with the other kids makes it official. I'm a resident here. I don't like it. I'm not planning on staying long enough to do many chores, but I don't tell Al that.

Looking around, I ask, "So what do I do now?"

"You can hang out till lunch. There's books and games on the shelf over below the window. There's a good chance someone from Children's Services will come by this afternoon to talk to you. If not today, then tomorrow for sure. You'll go to court in the next forty-eight hours."

"Wait. What? Why would I go to court? I wasn't charged with anything."

Al's shaking his head. "You really are new to this aren't you? You're here under an emergency custody order. For a long-term placement, there has to be a dependency commitment. Or status offender commitment."

"Status offender?"

"Running away, not going to school, disobeying parents, that sort of thing."

I think of the foster home I left. It doesn't seem like that should make me any kind of offender. Offenders are criminals, everyone knows that. But all I say is, "Oh."

Al looks at his watch. "Look, you'll have a social worker and an attorney. They'll explain it to you."

He introduces me to a couple of other people who work here. After they say hi and leave me alone, I pick out a book and debate whether to sit in the critically injured chair or on the critically injured couch. I opt for the chair which is comfortable enough despite its abused appearance. The staff glance over at me from time to time like they know my plan is to hightail it out of here at the first opportunity. I smile and try to look wholesome and trustworthy.

Looking out the window, I can see the morning drizzle has given way to pouring rain, so there's no reason to hurry on my way. Plus, of course, there's the no-shoes problem. I grow sleepy and let my head fall back on the chair and close my eyes.

This immediately brings the red-haired staff guy named Marty. "Kelly? Sorry, buddy, but sleeping isn't allowed except when you're in bed. You're new so I won't take away any points."

I sit up and ask, "Can I go to my bed?"

He shakes his head. "No, not till bedtime."

Geez. This place is super dumb. Good thing I won't be here long.

I kill time till lunch. Once it's over, a lady hands me a cloth and spray bottle, telling me to wipe the tables down. I don't mind working, it's better than sitting doing nothing. The windows are dirty, so I use the spray bottle on them too. It's a good excuse to check out my surroundings and pick the best way out of here.

There's a big parking lot and a couple of basketball goals next to a playground with some old-looking swings and a rusty slide. Beyond that is a baseball field. I get a little pang looking at it. I've never been much into sports except for baseball. I liked playing in the outfield where it was less busy. I could smell fresh mown grass and look up at the clouds while keeping my ears tuned to the sound of a crack that meant a ball might be coming my way. My Uncle Jack was one of the coaches. He knew my ways and would scream, "Look alive out there," but even he'd have to admit I was good. I liked to run and loved the way the ball would drop down out of the sky and land with that satisfying smack in my glove.

The bookshelves below the windows are a mess which bugs me. I straighten them up putting the ones for the little kids on the lowest shelf. Marty comes over and acts like it's the greatest thing he's ever seen. He gives me a bunch of points I'm not going to write down. I thank him and he gives me more points for being polite that I'm also not going to write down.

The rest of the afternoon drags by. The other kids come back from school. Marty introduces us then walks away. A kid with a big tattoo on his neck brushes by me and asks, "Having fun yet?" Another kid looks to make sure staff aren't close, then leans in, "Got any smokes?" I tell him no and he sighs and says, "Figures." They drift away and I'm glad. I want to be left alone. I think of a quote I once read. *I don't hate people. I just feel better when they aren't around.* That definitely applies to me today. Most days.

In the late afternoon, the rain lets up and we are given shoes, but not our own. These have Velcro instead of laces. I'm surprised when we walk next door to the detention center, entering through a back door to their gym. I watch them lock the door behind us and my mind flashes back to my grandfather's when I heard that key turn in the lock.

Several basketballs are tossed out. We don't play a game, just take turns tossing the ball at the basket when it bounces our way. It feels good to move, but soon they blow a whistle and we line up to be paraded back. I have a fleeting thought of making a break for it, but suddenly remember all my stuff is locked up in the building. With a sinking heart, I realize I'm stuck here. I can't leave without Buck, my little horse. Even if they give me my shoes, I'll have to stay till I can rescue him from the back room. I wonder where they keep the key.

The evening goes better than the day. They show an Indiana Jones movie and someone makes popcorn. Several kids groan and say they've seen this movie three times since they've been here, but I sit back and enjoy. There's a moment of excitement when a couple of girls get into a shoving match. Staff break them up and in addition to subtracting a gazillion points, they threaten they'll be taken next door to the detention center if they do it again. The black kid on the couch next to me, Tyler, who looks about ten or eleven, leans over and whispers, "They ain't kidding. Cause trouble and you outta here."

I look at Tyler's feet. "Why do you get to have shoes?"

He's chewing his popcorn and talks with his mouth full. "It 'pends on what your papers say. If you're here 'cause you ran away or have criminal charge, they take 'em."

"Oh." Suddenly, I feel branded. Tyler is looking at me without blinking, waiting for me to own up. I debate whether I want to bother, but he smiles and holds out his bowl of popcorn. I already ate all mine. Won over, I grab a handful. "I ran away once. Well, maybe twice."

He's nodding like he gets it and doesn't judge, so I take another handful of popcorn. "I had good reasons."

Tyler gives an understanding nod. "I hear you."

I decide turn-about is fair play. "So why are you here?"

He looks like he expected it. "I was eating off plates at school. You know, when kids are done and put them up for the cafeteria ladies. The school people called social services and when they went to my house, the only food was a bottle of ketchup and some flour in the glass jar. There'd been sugar in the other jar, but I already ate that and some mini marshmallows for breakfast. They were kind of dried up, but they were good." He throws another handful of popcorn into his mouth. "They found out Mama hadn't been home in a couple of days or so."

This is so far beyond my upbringing, I struggle for something to say. "Well, it's nice of you to share your popcorn."

He tilts the bowl back to let the remaining kernels fall onto his tongue. "No problem. Lots of food here." He leans over and whispers, "I keep some hid in my room just in case it runs out."

As soon as the movie is over most of us are herded to the bedrooms. I don't use that word lightly. I feel like a cow getting nudged along. I almost moo. I was initially told I'd earned the privilege of staying up thirty more minutes. Marty asks for my book so he can check off the points. He frowns because he knows he gave me a bunch, but my book is empty.

"You have to write them down or it's like you didn't get them," he says.

I get some satisfaction by saying, "I don't really want them."

He gives me an exasperated look. "You're going to be difficult, aren't you?"

"I'm sorry. I don't mean to be." What a liar I am. "I just don't like it."

He goes all adult-faced on me. "Sometimes we have to do things we don't like, don't we?"

Doing things I don't like isn't one of my better qualities so I keep quiet. I'm given something to sleep in and they take away my clothes, telling me I'll get them back in the morning. I'm guessin' this ain't their first rodeo.

I'm put in a room with three other boys all older than me. They talk back and forth but I don't try to join in. This room suddenly seems very small for four of us. The mattress is thin and has the faint smell of pee. Given the choice, I'd prefer a barn. The lights go down but the door stays open, and the light from the hallway floods the room. A staff person looks in every few minutes. I hear sounds from the other beds and realize at least half the guys are jacking off. They seem to have the timing down to a fine art, starting after the man walks away and finishing before he comes back.

The day has been stressful and I'm tired, but my brain's on overdrive. I feel lonelier surrounded by all these people than I did when I was on my own. Without the distraction of trying to find food and stay hidden, there's too much time for thinking. Mainly about the long years stretching ahead of me till I'm an adult and can do what I want. This just can't be my life.

However, it's better to look at the bleak short-term future than it is the years behind me. I don't want to think about my losses. There's something else back there too, something from the past I can't quite put my finger on. Sometimes in my dreams it comes creeping out, but then, like a foal resisting a halter, it skitters away.

The guy on duty turns on a radio. He sits in a chair in the hall when he isn't making rounds. There's a country station playing Clint Black's "A Good Run of Bad Luck." I always liked that song.

Boy howdy, does it fit me now.

5

By nine-thirty the next morning I'm tired of school. There's endless work-sheets, things I did in third grade, but at least half the kids can't do the work. I zip through mine but should have known nobody likes a smart ass. The kids give me a nasty look and the teacher doesn't seem too thrilled with me either. On the next round I purposely answer about half wrong, which is kind of fun in a way. It takes the edge off of boring.

During the early afternoon I'm pulled out of class for a visitor. A younger looking lady, wearing her hair in a ponytail, smiles at me. "Hi, Kelly, my name is Mrs. Williams. I've been assigned as your caseworker. Mind if we sit over here and talk a few minutes?"

"Got nothing better to do." I slump into the chair.

She doesn't seem to take offense. "How are you getting along?"

"How long do I have to stay here?" Let's cut the chit-chat.

She gets that soft, sympathetic face. "Are you having problems? The staff told me you were doing fine."

Her earrings dance as she turns her head. I can't help but notice they're little hummingbirds. She's smiling and being nice, but for some reason there's a target painted on her forehead, and I unload. "Would you like to live somewhere that you had to get permission every time you went to the bathroom? Where you have to give up your shoes? Where you can't step outside except for a couple of times a day and then you're being watched like a hawk?" I slouch further into my chair and with a sneer, I say, "It's like being in a damn jail." I wait to be told to sit up, to watch my language, but she's still looking sympathetic. I appreciate that—really I do—but I want someone to know how miserable I am and it might as well be her.

She sighs. "Hopefully you won't have to be here too much longer. Tomorrow morning you have court. I'm looking right now for a longer-term placement for you."

Now I'm on alert. "What kind of placement?"

"That's something we need to talk about. Where would you like to be?"

I get to choose? Now we're talking. I sit up a little taller. "On my own. I can take care of myself."

"Has it been so great being on your own?"

She's got me there, but all of life is a comparison and I'm not admitting nothing. "Better than here."

"Then you need to be somewhere better than on your own or here, don't you think?"

She's tricky, I grant her that. I shrug.

Mrs. Williams nods at one of the staff walking by, then turns her attention back to me. "The options are foster care, a group home, or a residential facility that would be similar to this. From what you've told me, I don't think you want the last one."

Those are none of the choices I want to hear. I go back to slumping in my chair.

She toys with the silver chain around her neck and slides a colorful little charm up and down its length while she talks. It's a dragonfly. She must like things that fly. She could add hawks, eagles, and owls. Dragons would be cool. I mean, they fly in stories. I miss the first part of what she says but tune in to catch the last. "There are a few kids I work with who prefer a group home, but most want a foster home so they can go to public school, enjoy community activities, that sort of thing. So … which would you chose?"

This reminds me of that kid's game, where you ask each other questions like, "Would you rather slide down a razor blade into a vat of burning oil or be strung up by your neck with fire ants on you?"

"A foster home, I guess." It's the lesser of the evils and it's easy to run.

She smiles and nods like I got the question right. "Okay, I'll look into that. I've filed a dependency petition which means you don't have a guardian. There's also a petition as a status offender since you're a runaway. The court will decide which way to proceed or they can go with both petitions. The placement options are the same, so it doesn't make a huge difference, but a foster home is more likely with a dependent commitment. Behave yourself here at the shelter. That'll help. Can you do that?"

The target on Mrs. Williams is dimming. I like the way she's talking to me, like she's laying it on the line and also making me part of things. And she's got the animal thing going. My voice is still whiny, but nicer. "It's awfully boring here."

"I understand. But hang in there. It's important."

"So … and when do I get to leave?" I'm going with the broken record approach. Ask the same question till you get the answer you want.

"I'm not sure. Hopefully, not too long." Mrs. Williams is pretty good at playing the broken record game too. "I'll meet you at court in the morning. The staff here will bring you."

She starts collecting up her stuff, and suddenly I want her to stay and talk some more. After she goes, I feel a little guilty. She was nice and I wasn't. This isn't like me. I'm a nice guy. Or at least I used to be. I decide I'll be nicer to her tomorrow.

Next morning, I'm riding in the white Oasis van, on my way to meet Mrs. Williams in court. A brother and sister, barely school age, are in the van too. They're going to see their mom so they're excited. I'm not.

Our social workers claim us when we get to the waiting area. I thought this would take just a few minutes, but hours go by as I watch the door to the courtroom open and take someone in, only to spit them out a few minutes later like a monster swallowing its prey, then deciding it tastes bad. One sour looking teenager goes in with his mother, but only the mom gets spit back out. Maybe the boy got eaten.

"Robert Kelly Morgan," a gruff man's voice suddenly calls. I guess it's my turn in the monster's lair. Mrs. Williams guides me into the courtroom and has me sit behind a table before she goes to stand in front of the judge's bench.

The room is small—claustrophobic—and the walls could stand some new paint. The judge is wearing a black robe, and an American flag hangs on a pole behind him. There's a little plaque with his name, Judge Adam Donovan. It all looks very official. For the first time I start to feel nervous.

The judge reaches for the file Mrs. Williams holds out for him. That's my life in his hands, reduced to a few papers in a manila folder. "There are joint petitions for dependency and status?" he says, directing the question to Mrs. Williams.

She clears her throat. "Yes, Your Honor. Both parents are deceased. His mother passed away when he was a toddler and his father a couple of years ago. His uncle died in the same car wreck as his father. We can't locate any other relatives. There's a runaway petition on file from when he was living with his maternal grandfather who is now deceased as well."

She leans in closer to the judge and sounds less official as she continues. "His father was an officer who had been off duty when he responded to a call. Since the dad's brother and Kelly were with him, he parked somewhere that should have been safe, but their car was intentionally rammed by the suspect. Kelly is the only one who survived."

Everybody in the room turns and stares at me, including the judge. I try not to catch anyone's eyes, so I fix my gaze on the judge's hands and watch him read my file. When he finally speaks, his voice is softer than I thought it would be. "Where's he been since the grandfather?"

"As far as we can tell, on his own," Mrs. Williams replies. "There are no residency ties. He was just traveling through when he was picked up."

"He's been on his own for almost a *year*? At *twelve*?" He raises one piece of paper in his right hand to look underneath. "Well now, thirteen." He's flips through papers. "He's at the shelter?"

None of the questions are addressed to me. I feel like a bug pinned on a board in science class. An interesting specimen, but not one capable of speech.

"Correct," says Mrs. Williams.

"How's his behavior there?"

"He's quiet, polite, does everything he's asked to do but he stays to himself. He refuses to participate in the reward system. He earns all his privileges, but doesn't get to enjoy them because he refuses to carry the card."

The judge turns to me and I can feel my face get red. It's like he's just heard a litany of my sins. He beckons with his hand. "Come up here, son."

I go to stand by Mrs. Williams who gives me a reassuring little smile. The judge looks down from his bench. "You've been on your own a while, is that right?"

"Yes, sir."

"You know you can't keep that up, don't you?"

"That's what I'm told."

"So, you've been … what? Just running the streets?"

I'm not sure how to answer that. I look up at Mrs. Williams who saves me. "It's not really like that, Your Honor. He's been traveling the interstate before landing here. According to what he said during intake, he lived for several months at a racetrack."

"Why were you at a racetrack? Who were you with?"

"I worked there," I say it with pride. I want them to understand I can take care of myself if they'd just let me.

"You were hired at your age? What did you do there?"

"I was with this …um…guy. We cleaned stalls, groomed, hot-walked the horses. He paid me some of what he made."

"Hmmm. I bet he did." The judge raises his eyebrows at Mrs. Williams. "He stayed with 'this guy.' Any payment expected other than money?"

I'm wondering what he's getting at when Mrs. Williams replies, "There's no indication of that, Your Honor," which is when I figure out what he's asking.

Yuck.

"I didn't stay with him," I say. "I stayed in the barn."

"I see." He leans forward and rests his chin on his right hand. "I'm reading the report from the shelter now. It looks like you've done all right. Do you like the shelter?"

I try not to make a face. "Not really."

"Why not?"

"The worst thing is we're inside most of the time. I'm used to being out-doors."

The judge nods. "I can understand how that would make it hard on you. I take it you don't like the point system?"

This is dangerous ground. "I'm afraid not."

"What's your objection?"

I shrug. "It seems silly to get points for things you'd do anyway."

One side of the judge's mouth turns up. "Think of it like money. I get paid for coming to work. It's kind of the same thing."

"But it's not. Do you get money for brushing your teeth before you leave for work? Or get a few dollars off your paycheck because you tilted back in your chair?" The words fly out of my stupid mouth before I can corral them back in.

I'm thinking what a smart ass he must think I am when to my relief, the judge laughs and says to Mrs. Williams "He's got a point, you know."

I really can't help it. I give a little snort of laughter.

The judge catches it. "Something funny?"

"A point?" I say, looking up at him hopefully. I know I'm pushing my luck but apparently, I can't get enough of the point jokes. Fortunately, he chuckles and I smile. I like having someone important notice me. It makes me feels less like I've faded off the face of the earth.

He points his finger at me. "You're smart. Probably too smart for your own good."

Boy, I'd like a dollar for every time I've heard that in my life. It's a tossed aside compliment but I flush with pleasure.

He's still asking questions. "How's school out there?"

I'm afraid if I open my mouth, I'll say something I shouldn't again, so I keep it shut and go back to shrugging.

He looks sympathetic. "Is it hard doing the work?" Before I can answer, he turns to Mrs. Williams. "I take it he's not been in school for a long time?"

She shakes her head and today's earrings sparkle in the fluorescent light. Little bees. "No. And since it's near the end of the school year, they haven't done extensive testing, but the teacher reports his reading and writing skills are way above grade level."

"Really?" He reaches over and picks up a piece of paper and hands it to me. "Can you read this?"

I take a glance. It's a court document that's given to defendants about their rights. I'm on a please-admire-me roll and can't seem to stop myself. "Do you want me to read the English or the Spanish?"

His eyes narrow. "A little of each."

And so, I do. He raises his eyebrows. I bite my lip and can feel my face getting warm. I know I've been showing off, proving once again, I'm too smart for my own good.

He looks at Mrs. Williams. "What plan are you working on?"

"We'd like to find a foster care placement, Your Honor."

"I'd like to see that too." The judge looks back at me. "How does that sound?"

I stare at my feet. I got to wear my own shoes to court, but here in this official setting they look dirtier than usual. "Okay, I guess."

"Is there somewhere else you'd rather be?"

Unexpectedly, I feel a lump in my throat like I've forgotten how to swallow. "I'd like to go back to Wyoming."

"Is that where you were trying to run to?"

I give a little nod, and then a thought occurs to me. Why haven't I thought of this before? "Could I go to a foster home in Wyoming?" That would solve everything.

The judge raises one eyebrow at Mrs. Williams.

She sighs. "There's no jurisdiction for that. His last legal residence was in Philadelphia with the grandfather."

Judge Donovan asks, "Do you want to go back to Philadelphia?"

"No." It comes out louder and more forceful than I planned. The judge exchanges a look with Mrs. Williams. "Alright, Kelly." I blink with pleasure at hearing him say my name. He's scribbling something as he talks. "I'm going to set your case to be back in court for a disposition on the matter of dependency in just under thirty days. I'm assigning public advocacy to act as guardian ad litem." Judge Donovan gives me a man-to-man look. "You'll need to go back to the shelter. You can manage that a little longer, can't you?"

I want to please him. "I can."

"Good. You need to give things a chance, okay? These people are all looking out for you. Do you understand that?"

"Yes, sir."

The judge gives me a parting pep talk. "Running away means you could be up here on a status offender action instead of dependency. If that happens, your chances of ending up somewhere you don't want to be go up. You could have been prosecuted for trespassing and gone to detention. You don't want that, right?"

I shake my head.

"Okay then, hang in there. I'll see you on …" He glances at the lady sitting just below him who hands him a piece of paper. "… June ninth."

6

My brief time of being a regular person is over. There go my shoes and here comes my stupid points book.

I cave and start writing the points down. I don't want them talking bad about me in court again. Besides, I figure out that being good makes you invisible. Now that I'm walking the line, the staff back off. As they do, I begin to see opportunities to hit the road, even though I haven't solved the problem of rescuing my backpack.

While I'm waiting for the right time to grab my backpack and bolt, I figure out how to take the edge off my boredom by playing a new version of the points game. When I know I have more than enough credits to get the later bedtime and a snack, I purposely do things, little harmless things, to pull the staff's strings, and nothing seems to bring them swooping over quicker than if one of us is torturing the furniture. Last night during a movie, for instance, I tilted my chair on purpose and made the mistake of winking at Tyler, who laughed behind his hand. Marty's eyes narrowed when he looked at us. I lowered the chair legs and tried to look poker-faced, but a smile slowly forced my lips up against their will. For a second, I was afraid I'd gone too far, but after a few seconds of glaring at me, Marty smiled, reached over, took my card, and added points.

Well-played, Marty, well-played.

Now, it's the hour before dinner, so-called "free" time, and I'm sitting at a table reading *The Crystal Cave*, a book about Merlin the magician of King Arthur's court—I love anything about the Knights of the Round Table and quests and magic—and I'm trying not to tilt my chair back, when I see movement out of the corner of my eye. Someone has just plopped into the chair to the right of me. I immediately start to slide further left, but when I look, it's a girl I haven't seen before. And she's knock-dead pretty. Shoulder-length dark hair that swings

41

when she moves her head and vivid blue eyes that I find myself staring into.

"What do you think of that book?" she asks, more a command than a question.

"I … uh … like it … uh … it's a whole different take on Merlin."

My answer seems to pass muster. She inclines her head approvingly. "That's what I think too. Makes him more human, not just some creepy, hat-wearing, old man wizard. Spoiler alert. You know there are three more books after that one, don't you?"

"No, I didn't know that … but great. Means more to read. And, at the rate I'm going, I'll read everything on that shelf.

"The series is like ancient. People donate their old stuff here when they move to a different house or whatever, but I'm guessing the sequels aren't here." She looks a little sad about that. "How long you been here?"

"Five days, six hours, and …" I glance at the clock on the wall. "… forty-five minutes, but who's counting? How about you?"

"Just came in today … but I've been here before like …" She tilts her head and squints her eyes in thought. "… four times."

"That's … um …"

"Pathetic? Yeah, I know. My mom likes to …" She raises her hand up and down in that drinky-drink gesture.

"Oh, I'm sorry."

"Don't be. I'm used to it. She'll sober up soon and promise not to do it again and then I'll go home. She manages to be sober most of the time, but every six months or so it's …" The girl makes a whistling sound while moving her hand in a spiral downward. "I've calculated that at this rate, I'll be here about seven more times before I leave for college."

"Why do they send you here?"

She rests her chin in her hand. "Because the rest of my family are drunks too. Alcoholism runs in families, you know. It's not like it's a secret, but apparently my relatives aren't smart enough to figure that out." She says this about her family like she's talking about the weather. She chatters on nonchalantly. "I went to a foster home once but didn't like it. Way out in the country and really boring. This place is much more exciting." As if to prove it, she gives Al a big smile and a cheery wave as he walks by. "Hey, Al, I'm down the rabbit hole again."

"Hi, Mandy. Sorry to hear that."

I've just gotta say, this girl is amazing. And I like the sound of her name … Mandy.

She pushes her bangs off her forehead and says, "You look like a brooder."

"Pardon me?"

"Brooder. You know, the silent, tortured type that suddenly shoots things up. The kind the news crew interviews people about after they flip out and everyone says he kept to himself."

"Oh, gee, thanks a lot." I think she's teasing but I'm not quite sure how to take that.

Next, she asks, "So what's your story? Yucky parents, runaway, drugs, minor criminality?"

I think for a second. "No … yes … no … not really."

She looks at me and those wonderful blue eyes go large. "Oh, you have definite potential." Then she scrunches up her face. "So, you're running away from not yucky parents?"

"Your question is worded wrong. I don't have any."

"Oh … I'm sorry … that's sad. Now I feel bad."

"Don't." I switch the subject. "My name's Kelly."

"I know. I asked somebody. So where are you going from here?"

"A foster home," I reply, but all I can think is … she asked about me.

"Oh, I'm sorry I dissed foster care. I'm sure some people like it."

"Don't worry about it."

Mandy and I talk until dinner. She sits next to me and I try, and probably fail, at not hanging on her every word. Maybe this loner thing I've always had going on doesn't apply to girls. At least not this girl.

Mandy tells a story about a shopping trip with her grandmother that has everyone at our table cracking up, including the staff, although they try to hide it. She waves her fork in the air at her final line. "So Grandma, who'd had a few, mind you, says, "Well then, sonny boy, you can carry those bags to the car then get in the seat with them!" She rolls her eyes. "I wanted to crawl under a rock."

She doesn't look like she'd want to crawl under a rock. She's grinning, pleased at our laughter. She has a really nice smile.

I don't see Mandy the next day until late afternoon. She's one of the rare kids who goes to her home school instead of the school next door. Needless-to-say, she gets to have shoes. She tosses some snacks on the table and sighs before taking her finger and pushing them aside one by one. "Trail mix with raisins. Ugh. Granola bars, wheat crackers, cashews. Double ugh. Wouldn't you think they could get some Little Debbie's or Chips Ahoy or something?"

I pick up the cashews and open the bag. "I agree. War, famine, poverty, and bad snacks. Times are bleak."

I get one of her appreciative looks. She hands me *The Hollow Hills*, the Merlin book sequel. "Here, I actually found this at the public library. My school was there on a field trip."

When I take it from her, I end up holding part of her hand for just a few seconds before letting go. She smiles at me and I smile right back. "Thanks, Mandy, but I might leave before I finish it."

"That's okay, keep it. I'll just tell them I lost it. It's not a big deal. My mom will feel guilty after her recent fall off the wagon and will be happy to pay for it." She leans closer and whispers like spies might be listening. "We have money, but I don't tell most people because here it seems like bragging. You know, that's the reason I keep getting to go home. If we were poor, they'd probably haul me away, but they find my zip code intimidating. When Mom is sober, she looks like mother of the year."

It would be nice to move right into the sequel. I'm happy to have the book, even though it violates the Library Rules of the Universe to which I'm a huge follower. But hey, I throw those rules under the bus for swinging hair and blue eyes.

I hold up a foot. "Look I got shoes. Al told me since I've been good and I'm on my way to foster care, I could have them. But nothing seems to be happening too fast. I may be here months." That doesn't sound as awful as it did a few days ago.

"Sweet. But you can't stay months. Didn't they tell you? The maximum stay allowed here is thirty days. They move some kids out to temporary foster care for a weekend just so they can bring them back and start the clock over again."

"That's awful." I give her a closer look. "Gee, you really are an expert at this."

She shakes her head which tosses her hair the way I like. "Lots of kids here know that. But I pay attention to all the stuff that goes on, because I think I'm going to be a social worker someday. I consider this training."

That was on a Monday. On Wednesday, I'm standing around trying to not be obvious. I'm waiting for Mandy to come home from school. I scored her a chocolate chip granola bar out of the snack stash and can't wait to give it to her. She's running late today.

Al walks over with a Mountain Dew in his hand. "Hey there, Kelly."

"Hi, Al."

"Want this?" He holds up the drink. "I bought it, then decided I wanted a Sprite."

"Sure." I grab it before he can change his mind. The vending machine is for staff only. A soft drink is a major treat.

As I pop the tab and get that first cool swig, Al says, "Mandy was discharged home today. I thought you might want to know."

The drink hits my gut. I take another smaller sip and look sideways at Al who isn't looking at me. "Yeah, well, good for her." I'm pleased how casual I sound.

Al gives a little pat on my back and walks away. The room seems noisy and crowded. I want to go outside really bad, but oh no, *that's* not allowed. It's a stupid rule. The whole place is *stupid*.

I head to the chair by the bookcase, passing two of the preschool kids on the floor. They've been stacking blocks and have made a tall tower. My foot nudges their creation and it clatters to the floor. They howl in protest and I feel completely ashamed of myself. But rather than own up, I tell them it was an accident. They're little, but they aren't fools. The bigger of the two launches a red block at me and yells, "Dickhead!"

I'm glad when bedtime comes. I roll to my side, face the concrete block, and try to harden my heart to be as tough as that wall.

Why are people always disappearing on me?

Why don't I ever get to tell them goodbye?

7

Two days after Mandy leaves, I get moved to a foster home. Mrs. Williams calls the day before to let me know she'll pick me up in the morning. She explains it's a temporary foster home, but not just for a weekend like Mandy warned me about. I'll be there till my court date. The foster parents are older, she says, and they're in the process of moving to be closer to family, so I'll be their only foster kid, their last foster kid. Apparently, they usually foster younger children. Something about the way Mrs. Williams says that makes me think she had to do some begging to get them to take me. The good news is since the school year is almost over, I won't have to be enrolled. Yay.

After breakfast, I stay in the shelter instead of going next door to school. I'm wearing the clothes I had when I was admitted, and my backpack has been paroled from storage. I pull out Buck and he gives me a smile. It's good to have him back with me again. I return him to the backpack, and the book Mandy gave me joins him. I finished it, but I plan on keeping it forever.

I plop in the same broken-down chair that embraced me my first day here and watch for my social worker's car. I cringe. *My social worker.* Did I ever think I'd be saying that? She's become the most important person in my life, the one making all the plans for me. It seems strange to have someone I only met recently be in charge of my life. But I do like her. I hope I've made up for how I treated her that first day.

She's all smiles when she gets here. "I think you'll like the Haverly's. Al says you've been doing really well since you came back from court, so I think you'll do just fine."

Speak of the devil. Al, who always seems to be here, checks me out. We shake hands and he wishes me well. I thank him and find I mean it. I get to push the door open. Believe me, it's a fine feeling. If I'd done it yesterday, all hell would have broken loose. I hold it open for Mrs. Williams. Dad was big on manners. He'd be pleased.

I'm rewarded with a "Thanks, sweetie" and a smile. I return the favor. I'm in a good mood. It's like getting out the last day of school. Free at last. Mrs. Williams hasn't had breakfast, so we run through a McDonalds drive-through window to get her an egg biscuit and coffee and she buys me a cinnamon roll. They are a personal favorite, as long as they aren't contaminated by raisins which I personally think should be illegal in any breakfast food.

It doesn't take long to arrive at the foster home. I had hoped it would be in the country like Mandy's was, but it's in an older downtown area. The good news is the trees on the street are big, and there's a park right across the street so it looks a little like farmland. As we walk up the concrete steps, I see a ceramic basset hound wearing a hat and holding a *Welcome Friends* sign in his mouth. Mrs. Williams knocks on the front door. I jam my hands in my jean pockets as I hear footsteps approaching. I seem to remember doing this once before. One of the kids at the shelter told me he'd been in twenty-three different homes. He'd be an expert at this.

The man who opens the door looks pretty old and is kind of heavy, but he moves quickly. He shakes Mrs. Williams hand, then mine. "Hello there, Kelly," he says, waving us in.

Mrs. Williams does the introductions. "Kelly, this is Mr. Haverly."

A gray-haired woman, wearing stretchy kind of pants and a flowery shirt, walks in from the kitchen. She's even heavier than Mr. Haverly and is smiling as she wipes her hands on a red and white checked dishtowel. I'm told her name is Hortense, but she prefers Granny. Mr. Haverly says everyone calls him Pop. The three of them talk and exchange papers. As usual everyone is talking about me like I'm not here. I'm "he" and "the boy."

I tune them out while I scope out the room. It's clean but comfortably messy, like real people live here. A bunch of magazines are stacked on a side table, and a newspaper is trailing off the couch with one segment laying on the wooden floor. I like the floor. It's shiny and you can see the wood grain. There's a yellow and blue braided rug with frayed edges like something chewed on it. On the coffee table, there's a clock with a pendulum swinging back and forth. I feel an almost overwhelming urge to touch it. I stick my hands back in my pockets, so I won't be tempted.

Before leaving, Mrs. Williams hands me a card. "Here's my number if you need to call. I'll check back in a few days to see how you're getting along." She walks out the door, leaving me with strangers in a house I've never been in, on a street I've never set foot on, in a town I barely know the name of.

There's a very awkward moment for me once the door closes behind Mrs. Williams, but Pop seems comfortable. "Come with me and I'll show you your room," he says.

"Yes, sir."

He looks at his wife and smiles. "Polite. I like that."

We go up the stairs where I'm shown to a bedroom with white walls, blue drapes, and a red bedspread. I like the effect. Patriotic. The bathroom's in the hall and Pop shows me where the towels are, where to hang them up after showers, and where to put my dirty clothes. I try to remember everything, so I don't make any mistakes.

"Mrs. Williams tells me you're from Wyoming"

"Yes, Fort Dixon."

"We took our kids to Yellowstone years ago. Beautiful country. Granny is doing some cooking and I'm cleaning out the garage. How about you come out with me?"

"Sure."

We go outside into the sunshine. This alone makes this foster home better than my first one. Pop's cheerful good humor is catching. The garage door rumbles as he lifts it up. Whatever I was expecting, it isn't what I'm seeing. The entire garage is a very large table full of model trains. Not just trains, but bridges, tunnels, trees, and all sorts of miniature things.

He laughs at the expression on my face. "Well, what do you think?"

"It's amazing." I walk over and bend down so I can see everything at eye level. Little plastic cows stare back at me behind their little plastic fences.

"I've spent forty years collecting all this and somehow in the next month, I have to take it apart and pack it up. I'm giving it to my grandkids, but it has to be split to go to three different houses. I'm thinking maybe you could help me with that. First, I have to clean out all the rest of this mess in the garage." He winks. "Do you want to see the trains go?"

Who wouldn't? "Please."

He goes behind the big table to a set of switches. In seconds, two different engines are moving. As the train chugs along, I walk around checking out all the details. Cows and sheep around a barn. Cars, roads, and buildings for the city. He's pointing things out when he's interrupted by a barking Jack Russell dog standing in front of me. "Jasper, quiet!"

Jasper isn't very obedient. He keeps staring at me and barking. Pop shakes his head. "He'll quit in a minute when he figures out you're okay. Hope you like dogs."

"I do." I bend down. "Hi, Jasper." He quivers nervously. When I offer him my closed fist, he leans in for a sniff then begins wagging his tail. I scratch him behind his ears. He cocks his head and gives me the classic happy dog face with his tongue hanging out. For some unexplainable reason, I feel a little lightheaded and grab hold of the edge of the table.

Thankfully, the feeling passes, and I watch Pop reach over and tickle Jasper under his chin which sets Jasper's tail on overdrive. "He likes you. It usually takes him longer than that to accept someone new." A tennis ball appears in Pop's hand and when he tosses it, Jasper bounces across the floor to pounce on it. He brings it to me and drops it at my feet. I'm happy to oblige with a throw. And another. And another. Eventually, I have to hide the ball.

For the next couple of hours, I help Pop clean out the garage. We work mainly on tools. There's multiples of everything. A dozen hammers, a crazy number of screwdrivers, tape measures, and wrenches. I organize them by type. Pop winces when he sees how many of the same things he has. In the end, he pulls a few of the rattier looking ones out and says, "I guess I could donate these." I don't understand why he'd need the remaining nine hammers, but I keep my mouth shut.

I like Pop. I think the tool thing is kinda funny. I picture him at a Tools Anonymous meeting, standing up to give his "I'm an addict" speech with pliers and tape measures falling out of his pockets.

Granny comes out and calls us to lunch. "Y'all been working hard. I bet you're hungry. Kelly, Mrs. Williams told me you don't eat meat, but I think I have enough to fill you up."

I try to relieve her mind. "I know it's a pain. Don't worry about it. I don't need much anyway."

They both look at me like I said I could fly. Granny smiles. "Mmmm. We'll see about that."

We eat in the kitchen. There's a couple of shelves over our heads with what my Dad used to call knick-knacks and doo-dads. Dog figurines, a souvenir glass from Disney World, and a metal tin with the sun coming up over a field of daisies that proclaims *Chocolate Chip Cookies, they're not just for breakfast anymore!*

The table is loaded with more food than I've ever seen for lunchtime. There's a Jello salad, coleslaw, mashed potatoes, a bowl of peas. Cornbread. Ham. Sliced cheese, which I think was added for my benefit.

I look at Granny. "Gosh. I hope you didn't fix all this just because of me."

She waves her hand. "Oh, it's nothing, mostly leftovers. I save my big cooking for supper time."

Granny says a quick grace. I bow my head because it seems the polite thing to do. She reaches over, grabs my plate, then starts piling on the food. "I'll give you a little of everything, but you just eat what you like and if you want more, you dig right on in."

I stare at my plate. I'm not very hungry. I start picking at it while they talk about the weather, things to buy at the grocery, and where they can go to pick up some boxes. I feel movement by my leg and Jasper's head appears. He lays his muzzle on my knee and stares up at me. A small piece of cornbread accidentally slips out of my hand and he grabs it mid-air. I feel Pop's eyes on me. I risk a quick glance at him. He winks and goes back to eating.

I feel myself relaxing, my muscles going from tight to something closer to spaghetti. I like this shiny red table tucked into this corner, in full view of the pots sitting on the kitchen stove. I'm surprised a few minutes later to see I've eaten everything put in front of me. Granny sits back and picks up her iced tea. "So, tell me Kelly, what's your favorite thing to do?"

It's been a long time since I thought of doing something just for the pleasure of it, but the answer is easy enough. "I like to ride. Horses, that is."

"Well, I haven't ridden in more years than I can count, but when I was a little girl growing up on a farm, I had a fat little pony named Trixie." Granny pauses long enough to drop two more pieces of cornbread on my plate. "She was a terrible pony when you got on her, mean as the devil, but she was so pretty with a creamy mane and tail. I loved to braid her mane and put ribbons in it. She'd put up with that as long as I bribed her with carrots." She smiles. "Oh my, I haven't thought about that in years."

I put my napkin on the table like Pop did. "My Uncle Jack used to say ponies are like fairies. Cute, but not to be trusted."

Granny laughs as she stands up and takes away my empty plate. "That about sums it up."

Pop and I work for a few more hours on the garage before calling it quits for the day. I offer to take Jasper for a walk and I'm more than pleased when they let me go. I feel good knowing they trust me with him and it's wonderful to be outside, walking on my own again. Maybe foster care is okay after all. I feel the first stirrings of hope I've had for a long time.

Maybe I can get a foster home on a farm with horses. I play out the scenario in my mind. I'm getting along just fine and they tell me a new foster kid is coming. Wow, it's Mandy! I tell her living in the country can be great. We saddle up our horses and go for a long ride. At the end, when she's dismounting, she falls and I catch her. I smile at the thought, but it's interrupted when Jasper, tired of sitting, pulls on the leash. I didn't even realize I'd stopped walking.

The Haverlys are watching TV when I get back. After the ridiculously early bedtime at Oasis, I was looking forward to staying up later but out of the blue I'm so tired I stand there, blinking stupidly and going brain dead.

"This boy looks ready for bed," Pop says to Granny.

"I am a little tired," I admit. We say our good nights. At the top of the stairs I look at an old photo of them with their kids and grandkids. Everybody looks happy. I bet if they found out they had an orphaned grandson, they'd go to the trouble of meeting him at the airport instead of sending an employee like my grandfather did.

I bet they wouldn't decide they didn't like him just because he said he doesn't like football and doesn't eat meat.

I bet they wouldn't ship him off to a military boarding school two days later.

You can tell they've been good parents and grandparents. It's like I've been put in the hands of experts. I can hear their voices drift up the stairs over the blaring TV. "Well, isn't he the sweetest thing? We should have said we'd take teens years ago. Hopefully, they'll find someone to adopt him."

I like hearing compliments, but decide eavesdropping is a mixed bag. One thing I know for sure is I don't want to be adopted. I know who my parents were. I don't want any replacements. All I need is a place to live, nothing more.

I walk down the hall. There're more pictures on the walls including a really old one of when Granny and Pop were married. I had a picture like that of my parents, but it's gone. All the pictures I had are gone. My fists clench just thinking about it—me, sobbing and sobbing. The satisfied look on my grandfather's face. Who did he think he was fooling?

Next time you'll learn to be more careful with your things, won't you?

I was careful! They were right here! I know they were!

I shake my head hard, like that will purge the memory. I find the towels where Pop showed me earlier and take a shower. After, I'm happy to crawl between the clean sheets and turn off the light. But sleep, which seemed so close, is all of a sudden dancing away. When it was light out, being here seemed normal enough, but now in the dark, it hits me that I'm going to bed in someone else's house. More than that, it's the realization I'm somebody's foster child.

A memory floats into my head. Dad had to go see about this little girl, about five, standing in front of the gas station in the bitter cold, barefoot and without a coat. By the time he got there some people had brought her inside and put a pair of adult socks on her which went up way past her knees. They said the little girl's mom, who was already drunk, had come into the store to buy some cigarettes and booze and then drove off without her kid.

The mom was arrested, and arrangements were made to put the girl in foster care. I remember feeling sorry for her in that way you have when you know something like that could never happen to you.

Now, lying here in the dark, I picture the paperwork with my name on it, the phone calls from one person to another, discussions about me between strangers, decisions made without asking me what I want. It makes me want to be on my own again, even if it's a hard life. At least it would be *my* life. I look over at my shoes by the dresser. I bet the Haverlys sleep like logs.

8

For the next couple of weeks, I spend most of my time helping the Haverlys pack. Pop and I make daily runs to Goodwill. He always buys something, winking at me because he's supposed to be getting rid of things not getting more. I don't rat him out to Granny, but I kinda think she knows. Pop usually buys me something too. Books, a baseball cap with a bison on the front in honor of Wyoming, a T-shirt. I love Goodwill. It's like a daily treasure hunt.

Much too soon my court date is approaching and my time here is ending. Mrs. Williams picks me up the morning of my court hearing. My things are in a satchel the Haverlys gave me. One less thing to pack they joke, but I know they're saving me from foster child luggage, universally known as a black garbage bag. Foster kids are probably one of the best things that ever happened for Hefty.

We say our goodbyes. They both give me a big hug. I don't let on how sad I am to be leaving and I tell them, "You all are the best. Thanks so much."

"Oh darling, it was our pleasure," Granny says.

I give Jasper one last pat. Pop says, "You gained weight and Jasper lost some. He's going to miss those long walks you took him on."

Earlier, Pop had pressed three twenty-dollar bills in my hand and winked. "You earned this." I'm going to miss Pop's winks.

I wave out the window as we drive away. At least this one time, I've gotten to tell someone goodbye.

Mrs. Williams says, "I'm glad you did so well." She smiles but seems a little tense. It makes me nervous, so I ask, "Where am I going now?"

"To court."

I roll my eyes. Does she think I'm an idiot? "I know that. I mean, after. Which foster home next?"

"Well, let's just do one thing at a time, shall we?"

This doesn't sound so good for the next foster home. A week ago, she had discussed a few with me. One, I'd have had to go to church every Sunday and Wednesday night and dress a certain way and say prayers. That was a definite no. I'm not on speaking terms with God. The next one she mentioned was a single older lady which sounded okay. Now I'm worried I'm going to the religious people. Well, if it doesn't work out, I'll resume Plan A: Wyoming.

We drive around the courthouse three times looking for a place to park. Mrs. Williams tells me she has a government parking sticker for one lot, but it's full, so we have to find a meter. When she finally scores one, she fumbles in her purse for quarters and starts jamming them full force into the meter. One bounces out and she barks out "damn," as it rolls down the sidewalk. I run it down, feeling the heat radiating from the pavement when I pick it up. She takes it from my hand and says, "Excuse me, that just slipped out." Like I care. I was raised in a household of men. There are no curse words I haven't heard … or practiced.

Once inside the courthouse, we play the waiting game again. By the time my name is called about half the lobby is empty. I'm kind of excited to see Judge Donovan again. He waves us up right away. My guardian ad litem, a fancy name for my lawyer, comes up too. I met her a few minutes ago when she came out to the waiting area to talk to me. I think her name is Ms. Easton. Another woman I don't know stands up by Mrs. Williams. I don't pay her much attention, because my eyes are on the judge.

He gives me a smile. "You look good."

It's true. The mirror this morning didn't lie. Granny's cooking has filled out my face and I picked up a tan from my time outdoors. My clothes and shoes are better than last time, and Pop insisted on getting me a haircut. I just smile.

"So you liked the Haverlys?" he asks.

"Very much."

"You know they wrote me a note about you. All good things."

They hadn't told me they did that. I feel a warm rush of gratitude.

"So now you know there are good foster homes out there, right? You can go to the next one with a positive mindset."

The woman next to Mrs. Williams speaks up. "Your Honor, I'm Sandra Bridgewater, the new social services director for this region. We're looking at a different route for this boy other than foster care."

The judge quits smiling and leans back in his chair. "Why's that?"

"There's an opening coming up at Boys Ranch in a few days. We're pursuing that for placement."

The judge frowns. I frown. Mrs. Williams frowns, till the supervisor glares at her and she poker-faces up. I decide I don't like this woman. And I'm tired of being called "this boy." And I'm really tired of being talked to like I'm a stick of furniture. Why didn't Mrs. Williams warn me about this? I give her an accusing look, but she doesn't look back.

"What's Boys Ranch?" I ask.

Everyone acts like the wallpaper just spoke. The supervisor woman doesn't look at me but speaks to the judge like he asked the question. "It's a residential program for boys from twelve to eighteen."

Residential doesn't sound good, but I focus on the word ranch. "Are there horses?"

She gets that sound in her voice people do when you ask a stupid question. "No."

That was a little embarrassing, but I don't let it stop me from asking another question. "Is there a point system?"

"There are behavior levels the boys earn. Privileges are based on your behavior."

Now my radar is really up. "So that's a yes. How long would I be there?"

"The average stay is six months."

"And then what?" I demand.

For the first time, she looks at me. "I think that's enough questions. Mrs. Williams can explain it to you later."

"I don't want to go there." I surprise myself by how loudly I say it. Judge Donovan is looking at me and I look back, confident he won't let this happen.

But it's still the woman who speaks. "That's not your decision to make."

"Why not? It's my life. I'm not three years old." I hear my voice rising.

"Okay, calm down." says the judge. He looks at all of us. "I think a foster home is the best setting for him. Why would you put him somewhere he'd just have to move again in a few months?"

Yeah, judge, go get her. I knew you would.

Mrs. Williams has taken a step backwards leaving her boss, who I am now renaming Ms. Bitchwater, to battle on her own. Unfortunately, she seems up for the fight.

"Your Honor, Boys Ranch has a contract with the Department of Juvenile Justice as well as with social services. We believe he should be committed to DJJ. We would continue with the placement arrangements, and they could take over the payments once the boy is in residence."

My lawyer finally opens her mouth. "I strenuously object. This is not in keeping with the best interests of the child."

Bitchwater gives a mean look to my lawyer. "DJJ has substantially more funds than we do. This boy is not a resident of this county, or even of this state. There no possibility of family reunification and adoption is unlikely. Children's Services would accrue years of payments we believe should be DJJ's responsibility."

Ms. Easton says, "Your Honor, this is a pure dependency matter."

"He's a runaway and he was trespassing on public property," Bitchwater fires back, "... which is a criminal offense."

The judge holds up his hand, like a teacher in school stopping kids fighting on the playground. "That's *enough*. The trespassing charge was informally adjusted and I'm not reinstating it. Like it or not, Children's Services is going to be responsible for payment. And I want a foster home for this boy."

I'm back to being *this boy*, but the judge is stepping up for me so I'm not complaining.

My lawyer smiles, but Mrs. Bitchwater isn't going away. "As I'm sure you're aware, Your Honor, once commitment is given to us, you lose jurisdiction over placement decisions. Children's Services makes those as we see fit."

The judge stares at her, but she doesn't back down, and I'm left wondering, what does this mean?

I glance around the room and everyone is glued to our little drama. Judge Donovan's lips get tight. "Very well. I'd planned to have disposition on this case today, but instead I'm going to continue the emergency custody order for sixty days. I want a weekly report. What are the plans when you leave court for placement?"

I still don't know what's happening. I look at Mrs. Williams, but she's gone mute and won't even look at me. She leaves all the talking to her boss who says,

"He'll need to go back to Oasis for now."

The dismay must show on my face. Not the shelter again. But it gets worse. Mrs. Williams whispers to the supervisor who addresses the judge. "Your Honor, I've just been informed there isn't an empty bed at the shelter till tomorrow. We request a detention order until one comes available."

What's a detention order? Is it what I think it is? The razor wire around the building next door to Oasis pops into my mind. I feel my hands clench at my side.

Thankfully, the judge looks angry too. "I am not signing a detention order. He just spent almost thirty days in foster care and did well enough for the foster parents to take the trouble of writing a personal letter to me on his behalf. I'm not locking him up. What message would that send? Could you use a little common sense here?"

Now it's Ms. Bitchwater's lips that get thin. "We don't have a placement."

Finally, Mrs. Williams has something to say. "I can stay with him tonight at the office and take him to the shelter in the morning."

Mrs. Bitchwater nods a reluctant agreement.

The judge looks at them a few moments then says to Mrs. Williams. "Well, I hope you get overtime."

He turns to me. "Kelly, I need you to go back to the shelter long enough till another placement opens up, okay?"

I retreat inside myself looking for calm, but I can't find any. This is so unfair! I've been good. I did what everyone told me to do and look where it's gotten me. I should have known better than to get my hopes up that something was finally going right. *I should have run.*

Judge Donovan's voice goes quieter. "Look, I know this is a curve ball, but just hang loose a little longer, alright?"

"Whatever." I won't look at him. *Who needs you?*

"I'm going to set this for a review two weeks from now. I'll see everyone back here then." I can feel his eyes on me, but I still won't look. *I hate them all.*

The sixty dollars in my pocket is burning a hole in it. No way am I going back to Oasis. As we walk out, my head is so buzzing with my thoughts, it takes me a minute to realize Mrs. Williams is talking to me.

"I'm so sorry about all this, Kelly. Look, we'll go by McDonalds and get something to eat then I'll take you to my office. There's a TV and you can sleep on the couch in the waiting room tonight. There's a vending machine, so we can have drinks and snacks. You can stay up as late as you'd like."

I get it. She's trying to make it sound like a fun adventure. *Oh goody! I'm seven years old and will get candy if I'm good.* She rattles on while we walk to her car, but I don't say a word.

Ten minutes later, we pull into a McDonalds, get our food through the window, and she pulls over and parks while we eat. My mind switches over to calculating mode. I smile at her. "I know it's not your fault." *But I trusted you and you betrayed me.*

She looks relieved. "It'll all work out, just be patient."

"Hey, I need to use the bathroom. Do you want me to get you a refill or anything?" Clever, I think. Set the stage I'm coming back.

"No thanks. I'll just pull up and wait here by the door."

"Be right back." As I open the car door, I carry out my backpack since I've been holding it. The satchel with my clothes is in the back seat but there's no way to get to it without being obvious what I'm up to, so I'll have to do without.

Pushing open the McDonalds door, I end up holding it for a lady with a toddler in tow smiling at his Happy Meal. Once inside, I walk straight across, passing the counter where customers are ordering their Big Macs and filling their own soft drinks, then exit out the other side, walking across the back parking lot. It's beastly hot and there's a shimmer across the black asphalt. I can feel the heat through my tennis shoes. I just keep walking. I don't look back at Mrs. Williams. Will she really be surprised? If I was a betting man, I'd say she might be relieved. She can go home now instead of sitting all night in her office.

Within a minute of walking on pavement, my head feels like it's frying and a bead of sweat drips off my nose. I stop in the shade of a building, open my backpack, and take out the baseball cap with the bison on it that Pop bought for me. Before I put it on, I wipe the sweat from my forehead with my sleeve, then wipe it across my eyes. Sweat isn't the only thing dripping from me.

I take a couple of shuddering breaths and let anger build up inside me. It fills me up and stops my tears. *To hell with all of them.* My angry thoughts push my feet. They take on a life of their own. They know where they want to go.

9

Wyoming is calling me home, but it's a long way from here and no magic carpet is showing up. I break down and do a little hitchhiking, but it makes me nervous. Plus, there's a little problem; I don't know where I am. I just keep looking for interstates and go west. I sneak in the back of a farm truck, but it takes me off course when he turns north, and I'm lost all over again.

For the next few weeks, I spend most of my time in restaurants, gas stations, and hotels clustered at interstate exits, trying to find my next ride. Hotels are a bonanza with free breakfasts and cookies and fruit in the lobby. The secret is to always look and sound like you belong. Be respectful and friendly to the staff, mention your parents, sit near other kids.

Eventually, I find ways to get into the rooms for a quick shower. Being little and quick is good for zipping by maids who leave the doors cracked open while they're cleaning long enough for me to get into the closet. The first time I slept in a room was by accident. The bed looked so good I lay down for just a minute. When I woke the next morning, housekeeping was banging on the door. Fortunately, the room was near the exit door, so I just opened it, said *oh my gosh, my parents are about to leave without me*, and dashed out.

I've crossed another state line, but I'm having no luck catching a ride. I didn't find much for lunch or dinner yesterday, so I'm on my third hotel breakfast buffet. I ate at two on the other side then crossed the street to this one. It's the best of them; it has waffles. I pour the syrup on thick and dig in. This may be the last good food I get today.

Before I can finish the first waffle, my radar goes up. Two hotel employees are standing together, talking, and looking my way. The guy on the right was behind the front check-in desk when I walked in. The guy on the left was at the hotel across the street I just left a few minutes ago. Not good.

Casually, I pick up my juice glass and act like I'm going for a refill. I smile at the lady refilling the scrambled eggs and she smiles back. I'd told her earlier how fluffy they were, so she likes me. Her eyes go from me to somewhere over my shoulder and she gets that curious, what's-going-on look. I drop the glass and make a run for the exit door but two strides from freedom, my arm gets grabbed.

Within an hour, I'm handcuffed to a chair that's bolted to the floor at the local police station. I get asked a lot of questions, forms get filled out, hours go by. There's no way to get into a position to sleep, the air conditioning is cranked to the max so I'm freezing, the handcuffs are biting into my wrists, and the more I think about it, the more I'm sure I need to go to the bathroom. They must have forgotten I'm here.

"Hello, somebody?" No answer, so I try again. "Is anybody out there?" Still silence. "Hey, I could be dead in here!"

I'm relieved when the door finally opens. In comes an officer I haven't seen. He looks mean. He is mean. He points his finger at me. "Shut your mouth or we'll shut it for you. If you yell again, I'll come in here and Taser you. Do you understand?"

I nod and he closes the door. You wouldn't think it under the circumstances, but my gut reaction is my feelings are hurt. My father was a cop. I like cops. Cops like me. I've never had a law enforcement person yell at me, so I keep my mouth shut and sit shivering until finally my arresting officer sticks his head in and asks if I'm hungry. I nod, and in a bit, he brings me lunch and takes the cuffs off so I can eat. What else? McDonalds. A burger, fries, and a Coke.

I'm hungry, but I eat real slow to stay out of the handcuffs. The officer glances at his watch and says, "C'mon now, finish up." I finish the fries and the bun, wrapping the meat up in a napkin then stuffing it back in the paper bag. The Coke I drain to the bottom and make slurping noises before he takes it out of my hand.

He won't let me have my jacket, but he does let me have a quick bathroom break. When he locks me back on the chair, he assures me I'll be leaving soon. It doesn't seem soon, but eventually someone comes for me. I'm still looking for a sympathetic face, but I'm out of luck. I ask if I can have a drink. I ask if I'm going to a shelter. The officer ignores my questions and stuffs me in the back of a police car while telling me to be quiet. They aren't much on talking around here.

We pull into a drive next to a sign that says *Roscoe Garber Juvenile Deten-*

tion Center. It looks like the one I saw when I was at Oasis, but this one stands all by itself, no shelter next door. I don't have to ask to know where I'll be in just a few minutes. Not a happy thought.

We go in a door marked "Intake" where the officer hands me off to a guy who works here. After checking to make sure I have nothing on me I shouldn't, they put me in a room with glass walls on two sides and with three other guys. One's a little kid who's very worked up, pacing around the perimeter and muttering to himself. Another kid, about my age, tells me he's here because he missed some school. The oldest guy has to be at least sixteen. He whispers he should have gotten rid of the stuff he stole before the cops showed up. Oh, and he casually mentions he's already on probation.

I decide this third guy's bad news and should be locked up. It makes me feel better in a way. My crimes are so petty, surely I won't be here long.

They take the big kid out first, then come back for the little kid but he refuses to go with them. No one tries to talk with him to calm him down. Instead, two more guards come and he completely freaks out. He's fighting with everything he has, kicking and trying to bite them like a wild animal. I wince at how rough they are with him. They're grabbing his arms and legs which just makes him fight even more. His screams are so loud and shrill, I back into a corner and cover my ears.

It's scary watching grown men cuss and manhandle him like he's a calf at a rodeo. One guard glances at me, I think to see if I'm going to jump in and cause trouble, but I guess he figures out pretty quick I've claimed this corner and am not leaving it till I have to.

When they finally haul the kid out and lock the door, my nerves are shot. It reminds me of when Dad would take me to the doctor for shots when I was little. I'd watch that door waiting for the nurse to appear, all smiley and friendly, but I wasn't fooled. I knew what was waiting for me on the other side of that door.

When they do come for me, I try not to let them know I'm scared. Instead, I try to show how cooperative I am. To my relief, they aren't mean. They aren't friendly either. Just matter-of-fact. At Oasis, they tried to make you feel better about being there, but no one is trying to make me feel better about being in this place. After I'm searched and showered, they give me a uniform with DJJ Detention written on the back. I feel branded and shamed.

There's the usual questions and forms they need to fill out like name, address, where you go to school. They frown at my answers. I have no address, of course. I don't go to school. Even my name has complications. When he calls me Robert, I explain I go by my middle name. He tells me nicknames are not allowed and whatever is listed as my first name is what I'll be called.

He gives me an orientation handbook, and I have to take a written test to show I understand everything in it. It's really long and involved although normally that wouldn't be a problem. I'm smart, but my brain has sort of shut down and concentrating on written words isn't easy when your insides are going wild.

I want to skim over everything about parents: Your parents will be notified. You are allowed two calls a week to your parents. You will be given up to two stamps per week for mail to your parents. I have to memorize all this even though none of it applies to me.

The orientation book explains how they'll try to teach you to behave in a way so you don't come back here again and that it's your choice if you do. There's a complete presumption of guilt. That you're defective and in need of fixing. *Am I defective?*

There's a rule for every possible move you might make:

- Residents are prohibited from leaning against walls, doorways, or furniture.
- Other than when lying down to sleep, residents must have two feet on the floor at all times.
- Residents will not speak to any staff member unless they are spoken to first.
- Residents may not talk to each other without being given permission by staff.
- Residents must keep their eyes straight ahead and keep their hands below their waist.
- If resident movement comes to a stop at any location in the facility, residents are to turn their back to the wall, drop their chins to their chests, and look straight to the ground until directed otherwise.
- If staff are involved in an altercation with another resident, all residents who are not involved will immediately face the nearest wall, put their hands straight up in the air and on the wall until instructed to do otherwise.

There are a total of forty-six rules. No way could anyone remember all of these, but just in case they left anything out, at the bottom it says: *Be aware that any negative or inappropriate behavior will not be tolerated even if it is not listed in the brochure. Disciplinary action may be taken against you without warning for any violation of the rules and regulations.*

The man asks me if I have any questions. I can't help it, I do.

"How do you know if you've come to a halt and are supposed to put your back to the door or if you've come to a halt because of an altercation and are supposed to put your front to a wall? And, if you come just to a stop at first and have your back to the wall, but then find out it's an altercation, do you turn around?" I don't think he likes my questions, but I'm really not being a smart ass. I'm deadly serious.

After giving me a long look, he says, "You'll figure it out."

Since the handbook specifically says no warnings are given if you do something wrong, that's not reassuring. There is a long list of behaviors that put you in time out. They emphasize time outs are not given; they are *earned*. There's a whole page on how you do one. After I've finally finished the booklet and passed my test, the guy explains he will have me practice a time out so I'll know how to do it and can see how easy it is to comply.

I look at him like you're kidding, but he's not.

"You will stand facing the wall about six inches from it. Hands straight by your sides, your eyes straight ahead. Do not close your eyes. Do not talk. I will time you for five minutes. If you move your head, your feet, or your hands or if you talk, the clock will start over. That includes asking if the time is up. You'll be told when it's up, so don't ask. Do you understand?"

I nod yes and he narrows his eyes, so I quickly add, "Yes, sir." I have good manners and I usually say "yes, sir," but I'm feeling pretty overwhelmed and talking seems hard right now.

He scribbles something on the form in front of him then stands up with a stopwatch in his hand. "Okay, show me you know what to do." He points. "Use the wall right there."

I slowly get up while trying to remember the instructions and go stand. Apparently, I don't do a good job gauging six inches because he nudges me a little closer to the wall. Both of us stand there for five minutes in complete silence, me watching a three-inch square of wall, him watching me. I'm not sure what he thinks about, but my own thoughts aren't good.

These people can do whatever they want to me.

I have no one to call for help.

I feel like dirt.

The first half of the timeout I spend with tears about to come out of my eyes. The second half I spend making sure they don't. If I cried, would he say, *I know this is a difficult time for you?* Or would he say, *Don't be a big baby?* I don't want to find out.

After what seems an eternity, he says, "Time's up. See, it's not hard."

He takes my picture, and then booking is over. As we head toward a big metal door, he talks on a radio. There's a high-pitched whine before the door opens then slides back shut as we walk through, making a little thud when it connects. The sound might not be loud, but I know what it means. I'm officially caged.

My stomach is churning. The hall has doors all the way down spread out every few feet. Each door is solid metal except for a thin window looking into the hall. I glance in and the cells don't even have real windows, just a little slit at the ceiling way above your head. There's no way to see outside at all. I feel my chest constrict. It gets harder to breathe.

I get a break. They tell me they're overcrowded, so they have bunk beds in one half of the gym. That's where I'm taken. I can breathe again. The kid that missed school is in the bed below me. I don't know where the little kid went, but later, I find out he was put in an isolation room. I'm not sure what that means, but it doesn't sound good.

Turns out all of us "gymers" are considered low-level offenders. Most of us are younger and smaller than the other kids here. Not going to school seems to be a major crime in this town. The truant kid had been ordered by a judge to go to school every day. He missed because his mom was shooting up, and he wanted to stay home to call 911 if she overdosed. Of course, he couldn't tell anyone that was the reason. Just said he'd overslept. Now the judge is mad and locked him up.

There's a guy who shoplifted tennis shoes and another boy who got into a fight at school. They called his mother to come get him, but she said she couldn't miss any more work so here he is. I have a whole new appreciation for Oasis. All of us kids in this gym are the same type of kids I stayed with there. At Oasis, they acted like we were there to get their help. Here, they act like we're all bad. I don't feel like a bad person. Then again, maybe I am and just didn't know it.

In the dining area, the rules are posted on the wall. *Eat only your food. No offering anyone anything you don't want. No talking.* Turns out the no talking rule has to do with saving time. You have five minutes to eat before the next group comes in to eat and talking slows things up.

The guards stand around the room watching us eat and looking at their watches. As soon as the allotted time is done, one of them announces, "Everyone up." If you aren't done eating too bad. I don't dare say I don't eat meat. And even without the meat thing, the food is gross. There's no kitchen here in the building. The food is delivered on a cart in Styrofoam containers. I don't know where or when it was fixed, but the food is barely warm, old and mushy.

And of course, there's a behavior system. It's like the shelter's point system on steroids. It takes up four pages of the handbook complete with charts and explanation. I think it must be like calculus, not that I really know what calculus is, but I know it's math and it's hard. The last page states, *We are aware the rewards system is complicated and difficult to understand. Please ask staff if you have questions.* Oh, great, except the earlier rules say you aren't allowed to talk to staff.

At Oasis, we weren't outside a lot but at least when we were, it was like going outside for recess at school. The outdoor area here, however, is a concrete floor enclosed by four walls. With dawning horror, I realize there's nowhere in this place, inside or out, I can see a blade of grass or a tree. I remember old westerns I used to watch on TV with the bars on the jail windows. At least you could see something. My palms start to sweat. I wipe them on my pants then quick look around. I probably broke a rule. No wiping allowed. Or sweating.

The next day I go to school. I feel better here. There's desks and books and posters on the wall. Except for the fact the windows are all frosted over and you hear the door lock behind you, it seems like a typical classroom. We switch rooms going to English, math, and science.

The first teacher looks almost as bored as we are. Instead of trying to teach anything, she turns on the TV and gets out a magazine and starts to read. Half the kids put their heads on their desks and go to sleep. The math teacher is much better, doing a demonstration using little cubes that get multiplied then divided. He passes out a worksheet then comes around to us one at a time to see how we're doing.

I ask this teacher questions, just to have him stay with me a little longer. I play out a fantasy in my mind. *You seem like a really nice kid*, he tells me. *I can tell you don't belong here. Tell you what, you can just go home with me tonight. I live on a farm and you can stay in the barn. Did I mention we have a racing horse that no one has been able to ride? What, you think you can? Great. The horse turns out to be incredibly fast. I ride him in the Kentucky Derby. We cross the finishing line and the crowd roars!*

The fantasy begins to get vague at this point. Before I can head in my mind to the Preakness, I jump ten feet when some kid begins yelling and screaming. There are kids here with major problems, ready to strike out at any moment. I'd never cuss out a staff person or do the things they do, so I'm confident the practice time-out in my case was totally unnecessary.

I'm standing in the hall waiting for the line to move and staring at the rules posted on the wall. I think they could wallpaper the whole place with these rules, there are so many of them. I look at one of the letter O's in a rule at the top of the list and pretend a mouse is crawling out of it, that then tumbles to the top of one of the T's in the word below, before climbing to rest inside a W on the next line.

I don't hear my name being called because they're calling, "Robert." When I realize it's me they want, I jerk my head up.

"Robert Morgan, timeout for not following staff directions. Turn to the wall where you are. Five minutes." The guard pulls out his stopwatch.

Me? But I didn't do anything. I look at the guard thinking there's some mistake but no, he's staring at me. His hand comes up and his finger points to the wall. Turns out that practice timeout was needed after all.

I assume the position and feel a flush come up my neck and into my face. The other kids file past me. They aren't allowed to say anything to me and technically aren't supposed to look, but I know they do. I don't know if they're condemning me or are feeling gratefully spared.

"Okay, time's up. Now you need to tell me what you did to earn a time out or you'll have to start again."

I think I know what to say. "I didn't follow instructions. I'm sorry. I didn't realize you were talking to me, because I don't go by my first name."

I realize my mistake about halfway through. The stopwatch is coming back out. "Now you are arguing with staff. You have earned a 30-5 timeout. You will sit at this table for thirty minutes. Hands on your knees. Head up. Eyes ahead. During this time, you'll think about what you did wrong and what you'll do next time not to make the same mistake. When you are finished with the thirty, you will complete your original five-minute timeout."

I come so close to saying it was apologizing not arguing. What a mistake that would be. At least he doesn't stare at me the whole time. He talks to another guard and walks around looking in the windows at the kids in the classrooms. Normally, I could let my imagination go walking and kill thirty minutes without much problem, but I might end up in more trouble, so I do think about what I did wrong.

First of all, I was stupid. I need to learn to tell them what they want to hear and nothing else. I have to remember these people don't care about me. They aren't interested in anything I have to say. They see me as damaged goods. Like a horse no one wants to buy. If I admit it to myself, I've always been a little arrogant. Smarter than my classmates, not interested in the dumb things they wanted to do, confident in myself. To a fault. *Don't feel so confident now, do you?*

When the thirty minutes are up, I hit the wall, six inches away, to complete the original five minutes. The staff guy says, "Okay, time's up. What did you do to earn the 30-5? And do it right or you'll do a 60-5."

"I failed to follow staff instructions then I argued with staff." Jesus, I hope I said it right. If not, I might be here all day. I give him a hopeful look. And I try not to let him see while I'm parroting this back at him, that I really, truly, thoroughly, hate him.

"Alright, good job that time." He nods and smiles.

I despise myself for brightening up at his praise. And the smile. It's so rare for anyone to smile in here. I decide maybe I don't truly hate him. Maybe just dislike him a lot.

I'm taken to court for a detention hearing the following day along with the same two kids I came in with that first day. We get shackled at the ankles. A belt is put around our waist and our hands are buckled to it. I can't believe they do this even with the kid who just missed school, like it's some sort of dangerous crime. We're put in a room behind the courtroom and chained to the chairs which are bolted to the floor. We sit for hours.

When the three of us are finally ushered into the courtroom, the judge rants and raves at the truant kid but releases him to his mother with the threat of serving thirty days in detention if he's even late for school one more time. I wonder if the judge has ever been in the detention center. If he has, I can't believe he'd make someone stay there for thirty days for just missing school. The older teen, arraigned on a burglary and theft charge, gets released home on electronic monitoring while awaiting his court date. And then it's my turn.

I have high hopes I'll soon be on my way to a shelter or foster home. However, after my attorney makes a half-hearted plea for my release, it goes nowhere without, and I quote, *a responsible guardian*. I remember Judge Donovan saying my chances of a foster home were better as a dependent rather than a status offender. Now that I'm charged as a public offender, those odds have to be even worse. Besides, I'm the kid no one wants.

The judge orders me held in detention until *a plan can be worked out*.

I'm the only kid going back.

10

It's two o'clock in the afternoon, math class, and my desk is bathed in sunshine. A week has gone by since my detention hearing, but it feels like a year. Thank heavens for the skylights. I can close my eyes and pretend I'm outside. I do so, but only briefly, so I don't get in trouble. I'm glad the math teacher is good, because it's my worst subject. I've always preferred words over numbers. The best thing about this part of the day is I can suspend reality for a little while and pretend I'm a kid at a real school. With the future so uncertain, I find myself more and more looking to the past.

I loved books and learning but hated school. My father enjoyed telling the story about my first day of kindergarten. When he picked me up, he asked how it went. I said I liked the books, the colored paper, and the snacks. Then I said it was okay but I don't think I'll go back anymore. At this part of the story, he'd always laugh and say he didn't have the heart to break it to me that I had twelve more years to go. That was the beginning of my not-so-stellar school experiences.

In the early grades when I got bored, I just mentally checked out, letting my fantasies take me away. As I got older, I didn't rely just on my imagination; I let my feet do the talking, or in my case, walking. When I couldn't take it another minute, I just left.

My Uncle Jack accused my father of being too indulgent and volunteered to enforce the type of discipline my father couldn't bring himself to do. My dad, who like me loved to read and study things, said, "I want him to go, but in his case, I think school thwarts his natural desire to learn." They ended up in a big argument. I felt bad about causing them to fight about me.

So strong was my desire to avoid school, there was no punishment that was effective. My favorite school consequence for skipping school was getting suspended. It was like saying don't eat chocolate cake, then when you snuck a piece, they said okay, now you have to eat three more pieces.

My uncle tried to reason with me. *Don't you want to be at school with your friends? Don't you get lonely?* The answer was no. The kids at school weren't half as interesting as the books I could be reading or the places I could visit in my mind. I wanted to be outside, exploring and running free, not in a building walled off from real life.

The school authorities were at their wit's end. The real problem for them was my grades were good. I never skipped out when there was a test. I'd read my books at home, going ahead several chapters so I was always ready. I finished my written assignments and homework. If I could pass without being there, I wondered, why did I need to go?

Finally, the whole thing came to a head. One day, a couple of certified trouble-making teenagers who'd skipped out from school were thrilled to come across the sheriff's kid and beat the crap out of him. At that point, Dad pulled me out and homeschooled me.

Dad got a lot of grief from everyone about *letting him win*, but I overheard him telling my uncle there was no glory in fighting a losing battle. He said, "He learned to talk without a classroom teaching him, and he learned to read without one too. I'm betting if he sits out awhile, he'll be ready to go back on his own." Good plan, but then the wreck happened, and school became the least of my concerns.

How I'd love to be sitting at Fort Dixon Middle School right now.

The sunny patch has moved on and is visiting the guy sitting in front of me. I wonder if he even notices. Probably not. Nobody but me seems to care about being stuck indoors all the time.

Two weeks creep by until my court day. It's encouraging when I get a better lawyer, one who actually talks to me and seems to listen. It feels good just to have someone sit across from me and act like they care. She says I can call her Karen. She has wire-rimmed glasses and is wearing a blue suit. The glasses make her look intelligent which I think is a good thing. I need all the help I can get.

Karen says, "Kelly, let me explain where we are. We can plea to simple trespass. It's a Class B misdemeanor, a low-level offense."

Encouraged I ask, "That's good, isn't it?"

"Yes, it's as good as we can get at this adjudication hearing. It's the disposition hearing that's more important. Do you understand what that is?"

"Like sentencing?"

"Yes. I'm going to see if we can do both the adjudication and disposition today. I'm going to ask for a commitment to Children's Services. They'd have to find you a place to stay."

This sounds good to me. "A foster home?"

"That's one of the options. Or a group home with other teenagers. That's more likely."

My thoughts on foster care have changed considerably since my first encounter. Heck, I'd be happy to go stay in that moldy basement. Frankly, even a group home sounds good to me right now. Send me back to Oasis. If Al walked in the door right now, I'd run up and hug him.

"Foster care would be good," I say.

"We'll see. Our case should be called in a bit. Let me do the talking."

I feel stirrings of hope. Maybe in a couple of hours, I'll be standing in the real world again and this will be just a bad memory.

When my case is called, I think they'll take these shackles off me, but no, I wear them right into the court and stand there in front of the bench with Karen. This judge is a woman with long black hair. When I look at her, she kind of reminds me of someone. I realize it's this horse my uncle used to have. The judge's face is long like Black Rose's was, and her hair matches Rose's mane.

I thought all judges would be like Judge Donovan, but boy, am I wrong. This judge is not at all friendly. Her eyes skim over me and I don't think she likes what she sees. Geez. There's no way she could know I was comparing her to a horse. Besides, it wasn't an insult. I like horses. I don't mind her face at all. Except for, that is, her mouth. Tight-lipped and mean.

Karen speaks up. She gives a little talk about my situation and ends with, "Your Honor, we're asking for a commitment to Children's Services as a dependent child."

The judge frowns. "This is a public offense. I'm prepared to commit the minor to the Department of Juvenile Justice today until age eighteen."

Karen shakes her head and puts a hand up to push her glasses further up her nose. "My client has no priors. This child was alone and homeless and merely trying to get something to eat."

The judge is giving me the same look she did earlier, like I'm something that crawled in under the door and she wishes she had a newspaper to flatten me. She says, "Odds are he's committed other offenses and just didn't get caught." She shuffles some papers. "The minor has shown a pattern of running away."

A blond guy gets up from a chair along the wall and walks up to the bench. "Judge, this does seem more appropriate for Children's Services. At DJJ, our programs are generally completed within a year and he's going to need long term care until the age of majority."

A lady from Children's Services is on her feet now. "We have a difficult time just providing for children who are abused and neglected. A foster home for a delinquent teenager would be difficult to find and our group homes are filled."

I can't believe the same fight over who gets stuck with me is happening all over again.

The judge says to the lady, "I understand." She turns to the guy and says, "Mr. Anderson, you'll need to find an appropriate spot in one of your programs for the minor."

Mr. Anderson frowns. "Yes, Your Honor."

Karen isn't happy either. "In that case, we withdraw the plea and ask for a hearing."

The judge clenches her jaw. "That's your right, but all you're doing is increasing the minor's stay in detention when we could be done with this today."

"I think it's worth exploring his situation further to see if something more appropriate can be found. Maybe a private childcare facility."

The judge scowls at Karen but sets another hearing in a couple of weeks. My heart plunges into my empty stomach. I'm not getting out today. Or tomorrow. Or anytime soon. *Or ever?*

Before I can blink, I'm in the back room waiting to be transported. I never got to say a word. I guess the judge doesn't give a shit what *the minor* has to say. The first time she said minor, I thought she was talking about someone who digs coal.

The door opens and I think it's my ride, but it's that Mr. Anderson from the courtroom. He sits in the chair across from me draping his elbow across the back. After he formally introduces himself, he tells me, "I'll be coming to the detention center to get some information on you to help me determine where you might be placed if the judge commits you to us."

I'm so tired of people talking about where I'll be "placed." It's like I'm a framed picture to be hung on a wall somewhere. *Hmmm. Where should we put this? Over the couch? No, over there, next to the window.*

In desperation, I try a new strategy. "Couldn't I work it off? Like wash dishes or pick up cigarette butts in the motel parking lot or something?"

He gives me a little smile but shakes his head. "That's a nice thought but I'm afraid not."

I'm still clutching at straws. "Can't you put me in a foster home? I did really well the last time I was in a one. You can call and ask them."

"The Department of Juvenile Justice doesn't have foster homes."

I can feel my voice rising. "I'm sorry about what I did but this just doesn't seem fair! I'm going to go to prison for five years for this? I didn't hurt anyone. There's no damage. This is a first offense. Doesn't that count for something? Don't people usually get community service or probation for a first offense?"

"It's not really your first offense."

"It is!"

"No, you have two runaways on file."

"That's not a crime!"

He looks at me with what I think could be pity. "It is when you're under eighteen. This is for your own good. You need to be somewhere safe."

I shut up and look down. As usual, nothing I say matters to anyone.

Mr. Anderson keeps talking. "And it's not prison."

My plan had been to give this guy silence with a side of disdain, but I can't let this remark pass. "Yeah? They tell me juvenile detention isn't jail, but I'd like to know what the difference is. It sure feels like jail."

"Our treatment facilities are better than detention. There's a full school program and vocational training. It won't be so bad."

I look at him sitting there in his khaki pants and blue polo shirt with a crocodile on the pocket. After he leaves work today, he'll go to his comfortable home. He'll open the fridge and get food when he's hungry. He'll walk down the hall and use the bathroom whenever he wants, or he'll open the front door and just go out for a walk in the sun. He can raise his hands above his waist and look out a window. *Don't be telling me it won't be so bad.* I can feel myself glaring at him. The anger is so strong it scares me. It wells up in me and I can feel my eyes filling with tears of pure rage. I look down, hoping he doesn't see.

A few seconds go by before I realize he's staring at me. I think he might say, *I'm sorry, it's not fair.* Or maybe, *I understand why you're upset.* I'd feel so much better if he did. I wish he would.

"Hang in there," he says as pushes out of the chair and leaves.

Leaning sideways, I wipe my eyes on my forearms and wait for the return drive to detention. When I get back, I find out Mr. Anderson called to say I was upset about what happened in court, so I get locked in the isolation cell. I'm told I'm not being put there as punishment but for my own good, *so I can process what happened in court and calm down.*

The last thing this room does is make me calm. It's even worse than the cells. To my shock, when they put me in here, they put something over the window slit in the door so I can't see out at all. When that door slides shut and the lock turns, I panic. It's like I'm being sealed in a jar. The lid is being screwed on the top and no one is punching out any air holes. Logically, I know there's plenty of air, but I keep breathing hard like there's not enough.

Only pride keeps me from banging on the door and begging to be let out. Pride and knowing no one cares. For me, it's one of the worst days of my life, which is saying something because I've had some pretty awful days. To them, it's just another day in the life. A kid freaking out, ho hum.

I crawl onto the bunk and scrunch up, covering my head with my arms. I take deep breaths and will my body to relax, a muscle at a time. I pull my uniform sweatshirt over my head and escape by going to sleep.

When I get moved back into general population, my mood doesn't improve. No one asks what happened or how I feel. They only care that I don't give them any trouble. For maybe the first time in my life, I feel like doing something purposely bad. Something to get back at someone. I'd like to slug that Mr. Anderson but he's not here. Maybe I can slug someone else. I don't care who it is. Another kid, one of the staff, even the wall. Anything that would make me feel better.

It's time for the once a week art class. The lady that leads it is a volunteer and is very nice. She puts on some soft music and puts a bowl of blueberries on each table. We're making collages, using cutouts from magazines and gluing them onto our big sheet of paper. I'm not interested in art today, but I see a picture of a leafy tree and pull it out of the stack just to look like I'm participating so no one will bother me. Of course, it's only right a tree should have a bird in it, so I poke a few pictures around with my finger until I find one. In the process, I see a sailboat. I've always thought sailing would be fun. Gliding along on the water, kind of like riding a horse. I grab a blue marker and draw a lake for my boat. Twenty minutes later, my picture is looking pretty good. I decide to eat some of the blueberries. It seems to be a better thing to do than punching something.

On Thursday, I'm moved to a different detention center. The one here is overcrowded and since I have no family that visits, I'm one of five of us tapped to be moved. I hate the shackling, but the van has windows so my eyes, starving to see something other than walls, feast on the late summer scenery. The roadside flowers are dusty looking, and I can see cows huddled together under shade trees. A couple of times I spot horses and zoom my eyes in on them.

How I miss horses.

Turns out this detention center is brand new, only open for five days. I may be wearing underwear no one else has worn before. Nice perk. People come through on tours to see the new building. It's always a relief to have a distraction, so we look up until we're told not to. I hear one person say, "Some of these kids look awfully young to be in a place like this."

This detention center has more natural light and certainly smells better, like going from a dirty locker room to that new car smell. This time I get my own room, their word for a cell. Still no window to look outside. Who builds these places, anyway? Why did they decide windows were evil? I decide to dive deep into my fantasy life.

There was this place I'd ride my pony, Buck—a spot where the aspens made a circle and a creek flowed. I used to make-believe it was a portal to a hidden land, one with magic and amazing creatures who defended it from evil. I'd go there to write and dream.

I close my eyes tight and go there now.

The sky is above me and the wind's on my face.

I just escaped.

11

In the morning, the lights come on full force and all at once. It's time to get up and get ready for the day's monotony. Would it kill them to gradually raise the lights and give a five-minute warning?

Make your bed.

Step outside, put your shoes on, then stand in front of your cell with your hands clasped behind your back.

Wait for instructions.

Get marched to breakfast.

Don't talk.

Once a day, if the weather is decent and enough guards show up for work, we get to go outside. Like the other detention center, the outdoor area is just concrete surrounded by four walls. Against all odds, I keep looking for a way out.

There's one little area where there's a gate for deliveries. It's tall with razor wire on top. I can't scale the walls and I can't climb over razor wire, but I notice at the top, the gap between the brick wall of the building and the pole of the fence seems to be a little larger than the lower part. I slowly meander over and stand there trying to scope it out without being obvious.

I really think it's big enough that I could squeeze through. This is a brand-new building. I'm pretty sure a mistake in construction has been made. Perhaps it's my duty to point this out to them so a murderer doesn't escape. I'll be doing them a favor, right? I know from my trip here, this place is out in the country. There are fields and woods a short distance away. Good places to hide. I examine the fence and calculate where I would put my hands and feet to make it over. It's one of those things where you think about it, but you know you aren't going to do it. Not really. You just want to play with the idea.

Don't be an idiot, you're in trouble enough.

Yeah, but what do I have to lose? They're going to lock me up until I'm eighteen whatever happens anyway.

We're called to line up, so I begin to do as I'm told. Someone calls someone else a dirty name. When a fight breaks out among some of the biggest, baddest kids, the staff has their hands full.

I've got to admit, it seems like destiny.

All rational thought leaves my head, and my body takes on a life of its own. Before I can think twice, I'm making for the fence, putting my hands and feet where I'd visualized it minutes before. Spurred on by adrenaline, I scramble to the spot with the biggest gap. It's tighter than I thought and there's one horrible second where I think I'm going to be dangling here at the top with my head stuck. But one big painful shove and I'm on the other side.

From this point, there's no going back. One way or the other gravity is going to have its way, and I'll either be free or in big, big trouble within the next sixty seconds. I hit the ground and duck around the side of the building out of sight. The staff still doesn't know I'm out, but with the outside cameras, the control staff will let them know soon enough.

I run as fast as I've ever run in my life. I need to get to the hilltop where there's tree cover. I climb the slope, slipping on the damp loose stones that shift under my feet. The rubber sandals I'm wearing are not helping so I slip them off and carry them. I feel for toeholds and climb, pulling myself steadily upward. Gasping for breath at the top, I lean over with my hands on my knees.

I look down and see the roadway leading to the detention center. I walk along the top of the hill using the protection of the trees to stay out of sight. In minutes, one police car after another, sirens blaring, zip by beneath me. Wow, that must be some fight. They've called for reinforcements.

But wait. They aren't going to the building. They're driving around the building. Like a punch in the gut, I realize they're after me.

I can't believe it. I'm just a thirteen-year-old kid whose biggest crime is eating a few waffles. Surely, they bring out this kind of firepower for murderers and rapists. I've spent a lot of the past two years numb to any feeling other than sadness, but now I feel pure fear. And disgust.

Stupid, I tell myself. *What a stupid thing to do!* I'm in big, big trouble. Of course, what I should do is walk down there, tell them I'm sorry, and turn myself in. But fear wins out. My trust in adults has been shattered. Who knows what terrible things they'll do to me? I make a silent plea to the God I no longer believe in to please get me safely out of here and I'll never, ever do anything wrong ever again.

One police car stops not too far away. It's a K9 unit. That gets me moving. I head into the wooded area and almost weep with relief when I see a creek. I wade for some distance then climb up a tree on the bank. The trees are close enough I can move from one to another for several minutes. I get down and cross the creek and repeat the performance. Except this time at the last tree, I go up and wedge myself between two limbs.

For the next several hours, my heart rate goes out the roof while I watch the police and dogs comb the area. Two officers get close enough to me I can look down at the tops of their heads. Jesus, one of them has his gun drawn. My stomach lurches with fear. The one guy leans against my tree and lights a cigarette.

He blows out the smoke and says to the officer with him, "I'm allowed. Out of the public eye and all."

I try not to move a muscle. My lungs seem to have stopped working. Will he look up and shoot me?

Finally, some hours into the darkness, they all appear to give it up and go away. I worry someone stayed on the perimeter, so I wait what seems a long time and then slowly make my way out to the road. I stay well off it, as I follow it to the lights in the distance.

My feet are cold and squishy from getting wet in the creek. My stomach is growling. I'm good and scared. But despite the fear and discomfort, part of me is happy to be out. But I know unless I find a way to get out of town fast, I'm not going to be out long. What I need is transportation. That means a car.

Once again, my childhood as the son of a sheriff comes in helpful. I'd watched my father hotwire cars in demonstrations. He even let me try it once. The first parking lot I come to, I walk along pulling on car doors until I find one unlocked. In a few minutes, I'm on the road. Us rural kids from Wyoming all drive on ranch roads as soon as our feet can reach the pedals, so it all comes back to me. Part of me still can't believe I'm doing this. I tell myself I'm not stealing it, just borrowing it. Stealing is when you plan on keeping something permanently or selling it for parts or money or stuff like that. I'm just going to use it for a little bit. They'll get it back. It'll be okay.

I don't have a clue where I am, but I stick to back roads. If I was in town anyone who looked over would know I'm not old enough to drive. The sky is low and gray so night comes early, which means I can risk a stop at the edge of town where fast food joints line the highway.

Rummaging through the glove box and other cubby holes in the car, I score several dollars in loose change and hit Wendy's for a baked potato and a Coke. I get fries too, then worry when the lady who works there laughs about my two potatoes order. Not good. Now, if asked, she's likely to remember me. I take a breath and tell myself not to be so paranoid. What are they going to do, hit every fast food place in a hundred miles? I take my food back to the car but don't eat it until I drive a few miles and park again. Some part of my brain registers how good they taste, but I'm mostly too anxious with looking in the side and rearview mirrors to care if I'm eating worms.

It would be safer now to ditch the car but I keep putting it off. I like the car. No, it's more than that, I love the car. It's like sitting in a protective bubble, my own wonderful world with the radio for music and the feeling of absolute freedom. It lets me be in charge, does anything I want it to do, fast, slow, left, right. For the first time in forever, I get to be in total control of my life. With a turn of the wheel I can go anywhere. If I keep it, I could get to Wyoming so fast.

Two things hold me back. First, there's this nagging little voice in my head telling me it's someone else's car, someone who might need it for something important. I'd like to say that's the deciding factor, but if I'm honest—kind of funny using that word under these circumstances—the real reason is the tank is low and I have no way of getting gas. As much as I hate to, I'm going to have to ditch it.

I find a large parking lot that serves a whole row of stores. Maybe if I leave it here, it'll blend in and no one will find it for a while. I feel a little guilty about that voice in my head, so I dig around in the car again and find a piece of paper and a pen. With the end of the pen in my mouth, I squint my face in concentration, then lean over and scribble the owner a note.

Dear Car Owner,

Please forgive me for borrowing your car. It was an emergency. Hopefully, it didn't cause you too much inconvenience. If I had any money, I'd fill the tank back up for you.
Yours truly,
A Desperate Person in Fear for His Life

P.S. The brakes are squeaking a bit. You might want to get that checked out.

I read it over. I think it hits the right tone, kind of like some guy taking it because he has to drive his wife to the hospital to have a baby. Or maybe he got bit by a rattlesnake, and if he doesn't get to the hospital in minutes he'll die. The part about filling up the tank for them is a bit of a fib, but it'll have to do. I hope they understand I'm not a bad guy.

I stick the note halfway under the front mat and walk away with a great feeling of relief. I'm getting a do over, a fresh start. I've gotten away with the escape and the, *ahem*, borrowing. I make a vow to never steal anything again. Not even food. If it just wasn't so hard to get by without doing anything illegal. Heck, just being on my own is illegal.

It sucks to be a kid.

As if to prove my point, those dark clouds that have been sitting up there all day decide it's time to let loose their rain, at first in big heavy individual drops, bouncing off the pavement, before turning into a downpour. *Jesus, kick a man when he's down.* I look at the cars surrounding me and think about how probably one of them isn't locked and has at least a half tank of gas. *You just said you'd never do this again.* I'm cold, wet, and tired—and except for a few quarters and dimes in my pocket—I'm broke.

Oh crap. I remember this shirt says DJJ Detention on the back of it. I pull it off and consider just throwing it under a car, but I'd draw attention running around without a shirt, so I turn it inside out and put the wet, yucky thing back on. I'll keep my promise about no more cars, but I really have to have something else to wear. Yeah, I know. I said I'd never steal again but this is another emergency. This will be the last time. I swear it.

I walk through the lot trying to lift door handles, oh so casually. People leave clothes in their cars all the time. The first car that opens, I see something in the back seat, but it's a girl's pink sweater with *My Little Pony* on the back. I admire her selection but that won't do.

Anytime I've seen a car driving by, I pick up my walk to look purposeful. My eye catches one just turning in off the road. It's white. It's a police car.

Oh God.

I pray it's a coincidence.

I pray he drives up to a store and goes in to buy some new clothes.

I pray he's not looking for me.

I watch him out of the corner of my eye. He's driving too slowly to be a casual shopper. *Hide.* I need to hide. I crouch between two cars in the hope he'll pass on by. I wait what seems like several centuries with my heart thudding in my chest. Sitting there, my eyes go upward to a nearby light pole. There's more there than a light, there's a camera.

Oh God.

I make a run for it, staying low and trying to shield myself with the cars. Just get out of this lot. Find somewhere to climb. I see a motion on my left and it's another police car pulling into the parking lot, so I veer right. Doors slam and the sound of heavy footsteps ricochet in my ears.

No, no, no.

I know it's pointless, but like a rabbit just ahead of a coyote, I keep darting this way and that hoping somehow, I can find a hole to get through. Rabbits are smaller than coyotes. The one thing I have going for me is I'm little. Seeing a whole row of cars, I throw myself under the first one and roll and roll till I'm under the third. The cops are yelling at me now, but they are too big to join me here. They have to try and figure out which car I'm under by running around each one and stopping long enough to peek under it.

Even as we play cat and mouse, I know things aren't looking good. The one thing I'm accomplishing is making them mad.

Really mad.

"Get out here now or I'll shoot your fucking ass!" one of them yells.

That just spurs me to move faster.

The smell of oil fills my nostrils and my arms are coated in black slimy goo.

My hands are bloody from scrambling under cars, but I can't feel them for some reason. What I do feel is someone grasp my right ankle and jerk. The back of my head hits the underside of the car, and I must bite my lip because the metallic taste of blood fills my mouth. Worse yet, my face feels like it's being ripped off as I'm dragged across the asphalt.

All at once—while I'm there on the ground, rain pouring down—the cops yank my arms behind me, slap on the handcuffs, and tighten them painfully around my wrists. Once I'm bound, they jerk me to my feet and fling me over the front of the car—smooshing my face against the windshield.

It's cold and wet.

There on the front passenger seat is a blue sweatshirt.

It looks just my size.

12

Looks like no one's concerned about working out any plan for me now. At the police station, I'm charged with escape and car theft. At least I know the drill. After they get done with me at the police station, I'm loaded in a paddy wagon. I can't see anything, but the drive is long, so I guess they're taking me back to the juvenile center. The police were real mad, and I cringe when I think how angry the detention center staff will be when they see me. I'm not used to having so many people think so awful about me. Everybody used to like me.

When the doors open, I'm relieved to see that it's not the same detention center. But then I see it's not a detention center at all; it's an adult jail. *The Robertson County Jail.* The intake door gets buzzed open and a guard meets us just inside the door.

He says to the officer bringing me, "You've got to be kidding."

Transport guy holds up the paperwork. "Nope, he's all yours." He takes off the handcuffs and leaves.

Another officer, bald and built like a bulldog, walks over to join the first one. "Oh hell. Did he kill someone?"

Officer One looks at the paperwork. "No, just car theft. But there's a court order saying he's too disruptive for the juvenile center. Escape risk." He smirks at the other guard. "What is he? Eighty pounds? He glances at the papers again. "And only thirteen."

He looks me up and down. "What's that all over you?"

I look down at my shirt. "Oil, I guess."

"Did you drive the car or work on it?"

I shrug my shoulders. "I was sorta underneath it."

Two says to One. "His face is a mess."

I touch my face and feel the dried blood. One asks me, "Are you hurt anywhere else?"

"I don't think so." To be honest I'm kind of encouraged. They're the friendliest people I've seen in a while.

"So how were you disruptive? Are you like a real badass?"

"No sir, not at all."

"You in a gang?"

I give a little snort. "Hardly."

"Why hardly?"

I tilt my head and shrug my shoulders. "They're kind of dumb, don't you think? Wearing colors, secret handshakes, it all seems kind of silly to me."

Number One looks at Two. "God, don't let him talk to anybody. He'll get himself killed."

PART TWO

~

The Felon

HENRY

1

It's late in the day, but I still have work that has to be done before court in the morning. My boss comes in and plops some papers on my desk. "Here's a fun one for you. A kid the prosecutor wants to try as an adult."

I groan. "What did this one do?"

My boss laughs as he heads back to the hall. "It's one for the record book."

Oh, shit. That can't be good. Thankfully, juvenile cases aren't the norm for me. Like many of my public defender co-workers, I'd been assigned to juvenile court when I was fresh out of law school. Like prosecutors and judges, new attorneys are assigned to juvenile as a training ground to learn state law and trial techniques. When everyone gets enough experience, they're moved up to assignments considered more prestigious and of greater importance in the criminal and civil courts. Then the next inexperienced person comes in to take their place at juvenile. The physical settings also indicate juvenile court's status as bottom feeder. Often, juvenile courtrooms are in courthouse basements or portable buildings next to the actual courthouse.

It'd be good if the public knew what went on in juvenile court, but it's shrouded in secrecy. Supposedly, this is to protect the kids. Maybe that's a good thing, but I think it would serve the greater good for folks to know what goes on behind those closed doors. The system often protects the players more than the kids.

There was a national scandal a few years past. A kick-back scheme. A judge was paid by the private provider for every youth he sentenced to their detention center, so he sent kids who'd done next to nothing and ended up ruining countless lives. He got away with it for years because no one was there to see what was going on. Most scenarios aren't that dramatic, but with all the confidentiality, there's no accountability. One judge defied the law and opened his court up to reporters and the general public. The article in the newspaper the next day included pictures of the out-of-order signs on the bathrooms, the filthy walls, the crumbling floor tiles in the hall. Within a week, funds were allocated for new paint and carpet.

There are some dedicated individuals that find it their calling and stay to slug it out on behalf of the kids, but they are the exception not the rule. Initially, I thought I might be one of them. I threw myself into defending kids with a passion, but eventually the lure of more pay and less stress meant I followed that well-worn path up to Circuit Court where courtrooms looked like they do on TV crime shows.

Now I only handle juveniles when they're being tried as an adult. In this city, blacks make up sixteen percent of the population, but every kid I've represented in the past three years has been a youth of color. I'm a middle-class white guy, wife and two kids, house in the suburbs, and I know there's something wrong with that picture.

I pick up the arrest sheet hoping this is a robbery not a murder. There's a law that mandates any juvenile, at least fourteen, who uses a gun in the commission of a felony, must be proceeded against as an adult. In the days before everyone freaked out about juvenile crime, a judge looked at each child's case and decided whether he should be kept in the juvenile system or tried as an adult. Did the kid pull the trigger or was he waiting in the car because his older brother hauled him along? Did she kill her stepfather in cold blood or after he raped her for the past three years? Is the kid almost eighteen with a lengthy rap sheet or a fourteen-year-old first offender?

The mandatory waiver laws mean a lot of kids end up in the adult system, doubling their chances of becoming a repeat offender and tremendously upping the risk they'll become a violent criminal. Being tough on crime now doesn't help future victims. Many states have seen the errors of their ways and gone back to discretionary waiver, but not this one.

This state is also backwards because it mandates kids being tried as adults get housed in the adult jail. It's a terrible policy. Teens are more likely to be sexually assaulted, more likely to commit suicide, more likely to suffer long term health problems if they go there. It's bad enough for the guilty kids but how would you like it if your fifteen-year-old was falsely accused of something and subjected to that sort of trauma? Shouldn't we at the very least wait for a conviction? If all these other states can safely house all kids under eighteen in juvenile detention, why can't we? It makes no sense. It's the kind of thing that makes me want to beat my head against a wall.

Glancing at the paperwork in front of me, I groan again. This poor kid isn't even fourteen. Good news, he hasn't killed anyone. But this boy is my first case on an even newer law that states that any juvenile thirteen or older who escapes a secure facility and commits a felony is automatically tried as an adult. He's been in jail forty-eight hours, so I need to go see him before his upcoming arraignment.

With a sigh, I stick the papers in a folder, grab my briefcase and head on over to the jail to meet my newest client. He must be hard-core to have gotten out of a juvenile detention center. They're secure places. It's a good bet the juvenile justice people are pissed.

It's a short walk from my office and I swear I know every crack in the sidewalk. I go through the well-known protocols and get escorted to the small room reserved for attorneys visiting with clients. Hopefully, this initial visit won't take long because I'd like to get home in time to mow my yard.

I hear the whine indicating the door is about to open and put on my lawyer face. My mind knows what to expect. I've seen these juvenile offenders before, kids who have never known a word of praise or a friendly embrace, their minds hardwired to survive at any cost.

The boy walks in and meets my eyes. All I can think is, *Oh, shit.*

The law set a trap for a tiger. It caught a kitten.

KELLY

2

I focus on the man sitting across the metal table from me. Dark hair like mine but wavy. Maybe forty, it's hard to tell, and he looks like someone who stays in shape, like the runners in Fort Dixon who'd jog out of town till they hit the county line then turn around and run back in. Dad would roll his eyes when he saw them. He preferred hiking. I can hear him now, "If I'm moving my feet for exercise, it's not going to be on some damn road."

The lawyer is wearing a business suit with a nice tie that's bright yellow, blue and red. I fixate on it because it's nice to see color. The flag of Romania is those colors. I once had a thing for flags and memorized them all. I can remember the flag of Romania, but I've already forgotten the name of the lawyer. How many lawyers have I had now? They're all starting to run together.

This one is absentmindedly tapping a folder against the table. The folder has my name on the tab and my eyes watch *Robert K. Morgan* go up and down, up and down. The man's talking.

"...So, if you understand what I just told you, let's get started." He gives me a questioning look.

I bob my head like I understand completely.

"Do you go by Robert, Rob, Robbie?"

"I go by Kelly."

He smiles. "I have a niece with that name."

I hate it when I hear that. In first grade, I ran home and confronted my father after another kid said Kelly was a girl's name. Dad assured me the name Kelly had been strictly a male name for years until it was recently corrupted by the fairer sex. Those were his exact words. He said it was an Irish name that means "bright-headed." At six, I was easily satisfied with his answer, but I still don't like hearing about girls named Kelly. But I've got bigger problems, so I let it

90

slide.

"Okay, Kelly. Do you understand about lawyer client privilege?"

"I think so."

"What is it?"

Ah, a test already. "It means what I tell you is in confidence."

The man gives me a little finger wave. "Exactly right. That's important because I need you to tell me the truth so that I can try and help you as much as I can. And you can feel safe because it remains just between us." He opens the folder. "Let's talk about the charges." He moves the folder a little and I catch another name on it, Henry Galloway. Right, that's his name.

"So, you went to juvenile detention as a result of this charge at the hotel?"

I nod again. I'm like one of those little bobble-heads in the back of people's cars.

"I take it you weren't impressed with it."

Ha. Humor. He's keeping it light. "They'd already told me I was getting shipped off. I didn't think I had anything to lose. I see now the error in my thinking." *See, I can be funny too.*

Galloway shifts in his seat and leans on his elbows before looking across to me. "You have the distinction of being the first juvenile to escape from one of the Department's secure facilities in about twenty years."

I stick with the humor thing. "Yay, me."

He smiles. "Yeah, I doubt they're very happy with you."

I can't help but get a little defensive. "I really didn't think they'd get so upset."

He lays my folder down on the table, now my name is upside down. I wonder if he'd let me see what's in the file.

"Why would you think that?" he asks.

I'm pretty sure what he means to say is *how stupid are you*, but I do my best to explain. "I hadn't committed any big crime and I'm not from around here. I thought they might be just as happy having me gone."

Now he's giving me the you're-a-dumb-kid look, but I'm not offended. It's well-earned. "When did you figure out it was? A big deal."

"Oh, pretty quick. Then all I could think of was to get as far away as fast as I could."

"Did you ever consider giving yourself up?"

This must be where client privilege kicks in. Should I really tell him? Oh, why not? "Not really. I didn't want to go back." That came out kind of lame, so I say, "I felt like there was a miscarriage of justice." He's a lawyer, he might like that answer.

If he's impressed with my legal expertise, he's not showing it. *Tap, tap, tap.* He's back at it with the folder. "Okay, in the interest of time, let's skip ahead. I take it you stole the car?"

I inwardly wince. I hate the way that sounds. I prefer *borrowed* but the miscarriage of justice remark didn't go over so well, so I don't argue the point. "I'm afraid I did."

He's looking in the file and taps a spot with his finger before looking up at me and tilting his head. "You left an apology note?"

"I wanted them to know I was sorry for the inconvenience."

He gives a little laugh. "Well, that's a first. All right, today I mainly just wanted to meet you and introduce myself. Let me tell you where I think we are on this. Escaping from secure custody is always a big deal no matter how minor the underlying charge. It's a serious felony itself. Committing another felony after you've escaped from secure custody means an automatic waiver to adult court."

He pauses then looks at me and says very quietly, "The worst-case scenario is adult prison. I need to let you know that."

Mr. Galloway looks like he'd feel bad if that happened. That gives me some comfort, but if he's wanting to scare me, he's doing a good job. "I can't believe this is happening." My voice is shaking.

"Look, you seem like a pretty nice kid. You've done some dumb things no doubt about it, but I've dealt with people who do a lot worse and don't feel bad about it. I get the sense you do."

"I really do." My stomach is in knots. "What happens now?"

"Here's the thing. The juvenile justice folks will be pretty worked up right now. As some time goes by, everyone will cool off and hopefully, I can use your lack of a prior record to get the car theft amended down to Unauthorized Use of a Motor Vehicle. In this state, that's a misdemeanor so your case would get kicked back down to juvenile court." Now I get the standard question. "You don't have a relative somewhere?"

"No, I've run out of them."

"Okay, well hang loose and we'll see how it goes. I'll be back in touch soon." He's closing his briefcase but keeps his eyes on me. "They treating you okay in here? They haven't got you in isolation, have they?"

"No. I'm with others."

"Good. Here's my card. Just let them know if you need to call me."

I reach for the card like I'm sinking in quicksand and someone stuck out a branch for me to grab onto. My only hope before the ground swallows me up.

It's night now and I'm locked in my cell till morning. I have plenty of time to think. I've been here two days. When I got sent to juvenile detention, I felt like I didn't deserve what I was getting. Now it's different. I can call it borrowing, but I stole that car. Me, my father's son. How could that be? *I'm a good person, aren't I?* I always thought so, but now maybe I'm not so sure. The replay of what I did won't leave my head, filling me with shame and remorse.

Tonight, my situation begins to hit home. This could be bad, very bad. A spider is climbing up the wall. I read once there's always a spider within three feet of you. I watch him crawl up then disappear through a crack. If only I could go with him. The lawyer left me with the advice to hang loose. Glad I'm not having to pay him for that brilliant thought. But he seemed an okay guy. If he can get me out of here, I'd pay him anything. Of course, I don't have any money, but I'd pay him back somehow.

I'm hungry. I was too upset to eat dinner after he left. Although I wouldn't have eaten it anyway. It was a beef thing with this gross gravy that was slopped over everything. That's of no concern to anyone but me. The one thing I've learned here is the answer to any problem you have is "too bad" followed by its close cousin "deal with it." At least hunger is an old friend. I hold up my hand and watch it shake.

Hopefully, there'll be something decent at breakfast. Please no more of that awful oatmeal. Thinking about food just makes me hungrier. What time is it? No way of knowing, but I'm sure it's a long time till morning. I go to the sink and drink some cold water to try and ease my stomach before lying back down. The doors are clanging so probably someone new is being admitted. It's an awful sound. The tears I've held back are tired of waiting for permission. They slide down the side of my face and into my ears, but I'm careful not to make a sound. Crying quietly is a skill I'm perfecting.

I turn onto my side and curl up into a ball, wrapping my arms around myself. It's a more comforting position, but it's also because I'm cold. I wish the damn air conditioning would break. One other kid here told me they freeze us on purpose because if we're huddling under a blanket, we're less likely to cause trouble. I have one thin blanket and wish really hard for another one, but so far, no magical blanket has shown up.

This section of the jail is reserved for juveniles being tried as adults. The other guys here are all sixteen and seventeen. Although I was surprised to be put in an adult jail, at first it didn't really matter. After all, locked up is locked up. And some things are better. There's the commissary, nothing like that in juvenile. All the other inmates' families put money in their accounts so they can buy candy and chips. No family, no money, no snacks. *Too bad. Deal with it.* I see the other guys buy stuff and watch them eat, feeling like a dog waiting, watching anxiously for a crumb to be dropped. I did score a brown M&M that way. I watched it fall and roll away, unnoticed, the color blending into the floor. I waited until everyone had moved away before I went after it. Don't say I have no pride.

There's far less rules here than in juvenile. Nobody is marching you around, giving and taking away points or putting you in timeouts. If anyone is really bad, they go to solitary confinement. One of the other guys here makes that trip a lot. He gets a certain look and all of us move away and wait for him to explode. I feel sorry for him because, well, how can I put this? He's kind of crazy. But I feel sorry for the guards too. The guy does vindictive peeing and pooping, and they're the ones who have to clean it up. It's pretty gross. I'd tell him so, but I might get killed. Besides, none of the other guys care what I have to say.

There's a ranking in here. It's like horses. Put a bucket of grain in the middle of the field and the top horse gets to eat first, then the second. There may not be anything for the horse at the bottom of the pecking order. In jail, if you're one of the people toward the bottom, the trick is to appear non-threatening and dangerous at the same time. Some guys are good at it. I'm really good at the first and totally suck at the last. At first, I was worried everybody would be beating up on me, but it turns out my size and age make me less of a target. Nobody is going to up their tough guy reputation by thumping the little kid, and I can tell the guards are keeping an eye on me, which I do appreciate.

Out of sheer boredom fights are typical. The correctional officers hold a disciplinary hearing with themselves as judge. No one ever confesses of being guilty of fighting, of course. They're always *just goofing off or horse playing, and it got a little out of hand.* They either don't think the COs are smart enough to figure this out after the one hundredth time or just feel compelled to lie. Sadly, the person jumped on gets the same consequence as the attacker, usually days in solitary.

The worst thing about being here is my world has shrunk. When we aren't in our cells, we're in the living area, called the pod. Metal tables and chairs are bolted to the floor and there's the ever-present blaring TV. This is where we are most of the time. In juvenile, there was movement all day. We went to school rooms, to the gym for exercise. There had been chores to do, and most importantly there was an outdoor time every day, a chance to stand in the sun and see the sky. The loss of the outdoors is the hardest thing for me to take.

There's one good thing here. If I stand on my bunk, I can look out the four-inch window slit to the outside world. Funny, how juvenile cells don't have windows, but adults do. I can see trees. I can count the cars on the road or look up at the clouds in the sky. I spend a lot of time here. Without this, I think I'd go crazy.

Meals are the highlight of the day for most people. It's gobble and done, but it's a marker of the day's passing. Thankfully, today's lunch is something I can eat. Beans and rice are cheap so it's served often. At the end of the meal, the spoons are collected and counted.

Today, when lunch is over, there's excitement. Terrance, seventeen, is getting discharged. He's been here since he was fifteen. His trial on a first-degree murder charge just ended and he was found not guilty. I have to think, now what? Does he just walk back into high school and say, "Hey, everyone, I'm back, what's happenin'?" When they put me here, I was shocked to find out there's no school. It's like just being charged with something, whether you're guilty or not, is enough to strip you of any right to be treated as a kid.

I watch Terrance collect up his things and leave to get processed out. All I can think about is in a few minutes, he'll be walking outside. It seems an amazing transformation. Like he came in a caterpillar, was here in the cocoon, then turned into a butterfly that can fly away. We're all happy for him in an envious sort of way.

Every one of the other guys in here is looking at a lot more time in prison than I am. All of them are in a gang, so I don't share my opinion on that subject. I'm not *that* stupid

They don't really know what to think of me. Little, white, and I haven't hurt anybody, which according to them, means someone should take pity on me. They seem to be pretty sure no pity will be offered to them. They know I'm not in their league, of course, but the fact that I escaped from a detention facility gets me some respect. None of them has ever come close to pulling *that* off.

Wake-up time is four-thirty every morning. I used to think of that as night. Sometimes in the groggy time between sleep and wakefulness, I struggle to remember where I am. Like a home movie on fast forward, my mind spins through the possibilities. A hay loft, a bunk bed, a motel room, a library, some grassy ground, the Haverlys, Oasis, juvenile detention. Then, with a jerk, reality comes crashing in. On the rare days I wake before the lights all come on, I roll over, face the wall and try to fade back to sleep. Sleep kills time, but nothing has ever filled minutes or hours as slowly as this.

The monotony seems to magnify with each passing day. I dip deeply into my imagination to pass the time. I spend a lot of time in Aerdrie. It's a world I made up when I was a kid, named after a goddess of the air that loves to fly free and far above the earth. The land is full of magic and imaginary creatures. Other times, I'm a World War II downed pilot in a German POW camp. I do pushups and sit-ups in my cell, picturing my fellow captives beside me. We have to stay fit for our eventual escape and return to the war effort. The CO asks a question and I just give him a look. *Name, rank, and serial number are all you'll get out of me.* He narrows his eyes and asks again, and I hurry and answer. Best not to get too carried away.

Sometimes it's the Civil War. I read the Confederates kidnapped teens into their cause, so even though I'm against slavery, I'm an orphan who gets drafted onto their side. We get captured and are in a Union prison camp. Turns out the head of the camp is my long-lost father. I flatter the unknowing Officer Cooper by assigning him this role. My knowledge of the countryside and horses proves invaluable in averting further bloodshed. I make sure my Confederate friends aren't harmed. The war ends and I go live with my father. The end.

Other times I'm time traveling and landed here by accident. If only I can find the portal to get me home.

Each night, I'm glad another day is gone. I decide it's a sad thing to will your life's time away; it's not like you get it back. But night is bad because that's when I hear the cell door clanging firmly into place locking me in for the night. Putting my hands over my ears, I close my eyes and take myself away. It's early morning and the Wyoming sky is a vivid blue. I'm on my horse galloping and an eagle soars in the air above me. I concentrate on the sound of the hoof beats and Buck blowing air out his nose with every stride and on a really good night, maybe I don't hear that door as it locks.

I live for the library cart, but it only comes once a week and you can only get one book at a time. I ask one of the CO's what would be so awful about letting people have two books. He tells me inmates have ripped out the pages and stuffed them in the toilets to flood them. I make a face and shake my head in disgust. He nods like yeah, it's awful. It's a good moment because he's looking at me like I'm a person that wouldn't do something like that. He's right, I wouldn't. Ripping the pages out of a book? Unthinkable.

Since I'm stuck with only one book for seven days, I do two things to cope. The first is rereading the book several times. The other is to try and force myself to read slower, savoring every sentence, sometimes every word. I start noticing the construction of the book, the ebb and flow of the plot. Once I know how the book ends, I look for clues in the earlier sections that I didn't notice the first time through. I write down words, lines, and phrases I like.

I have paper and prison pens, soft round ones, thanks to Henry. He put money in my canteen account, so I can buy the pens and some snacks. Henry says his office covers it, but I know he's paying out of his own money. I want to think he likes me. I like him and the best time of the week is when he comes to see me.

I'm thrilled the first time I can buy a bag of M&M's. I arrange them in a row, ranking them by my favorite colors. Officer Cooper walks by and gives me an exasperated look. "What the hell are you doing?" But he's saying it like teasing. He's by far my favorite correctional officer.

I smile up at him. "I like to make it a process." I pop a blue one in my mouth.

"You're a weird kid, you know that, don't you?"

"I'm well aware of it." Now I throw in a green one.

I crunch it and slowly savor. It should bother me I obtained these through pity, but the pride ship sailed a long time ago. I know Henry has told them about my father. There was sort of a change after that in how they treat me. They've never been mean but now they go a bit out of their way for me. Henry said a lot of corrections officers come from the military and law enforcement.

I guess that makes them more sympathetic. Good to know. If it helps me get by I'm not against being a suck up. There's one last M&M. It's brown. I roll up the bag and use it as a bat, pushing the brown ball across the table then saving it before it drops off the edge.

One takes one's entertainment where you can get it.

KELLY

3

One day, I see a new flyer posted on the wall. A teacher from a university is going to conduct a writing workshop for anybody who wants to participate. No surprise all of us are in. To see someone from the *outside*? Wouldn't miss it. And what are we going to say? *Oh, I'm so busy with other things, I just can't spare the time?* It will be for six weeks for an hour every Tuesday afternoon.

The other great thing about the class is we get to leave the pod and go to a room down the hall. Still gray walls, but they are new gray walls, so yay.

And there he is. A regular guy. Not a prisoner, not a guard, or even a nurse or lawyer. An ambassador from the Real World, someone who hasn't forgotten we are here. One of the other kids tells me we are the *washed*. I didn't understand till he explained everyone has washed their hands of us. He's right. If a meteor was going to crash and the whole city got evacuated, we'd be the last to leave. Or maybe they wouldn't even bother.

Once we are all seated at a table, one of the jail lieutenants introduces the teacher. "Gentlemen, this is Mr. Hill. He's volunteering his time to teach this class, so I expect everyone to be on their best behavior."

At this point I notice him look at one of the other guards who rolls his eyes like that's not going to happen. The lieutenant turns to the teacher and says, "We're right outside the door if you need us." Mr. Hill nods and looks uncomfortable. He seems more at ease when it's just us and him.

He smiles and says, "Good afternoon," then waits.

We sit and stare till we figure it out, then half of us say "Good afternoon" back at him.

I decide he looks like a college professor, kinda old, probably in his fifties, mostly bald, and he wears those half glasses that people peek over the tops at you. But he looks friendly and as if to prove it, he says, "I'm happy to be here today. There are writing classes going on at other correctional programs in the state, and we wanted to try one here. I don't want you to worry about whether you're a good writer or not. This is about giving you a chance to find your own voice, so don't worry about spelling or punctuation or any of that right now."

I frown. I *want* to worry about spelling and punctuation. Hey, this is a writing class, that stuff should *matter*. I glance at the other guys and wisely keep my thoughts to myself. We're asked to introduce ourselves and give our age and where we're from. Everyone else in the room is from this city and they even all went to the same alternative school before their arrests. I'm last to speak and I can see Mr. Hill's eyes go soft when it's my turn, the pity flowing out of him and landing on me. All at once, I think I'd rather just go back to the pod, but I mumble, "Kelly Morgan, thirteen. I'm not from here."

Ian, who's a bit of a jerk says, "He's like a freakin' cowboy. You know, like Woody in Toy Story. From like Montana or something."

"Wyoming," I correct him with a scowl.

Ian isn't worried about my scowl. I'm just a bug to him. "Whatever," he says. "It's one of those cruddy states without a real city."

He's really getting on my nerves. I have to defend Wyoming. "We have cities. Cheyenne and Casper."

Ian's face splits into a wide grin. "Casper? Like the ghost?" He snickers. "Is it a friendly city?" The others join in laughing. Before I can say anything, the professor claps his hands and says, "How about we do some writing?" He starts passing out notepads and pencils.

Darnell immediately begins drumming his pencil on the table and Freddie spins his in circles. Jimmy makes a tent out of his notepad. I give a worried look at Mr. Hill, but he doesn't seem bothered. Darnell asks, "What we supposed to write about?"

Mr. Hill smiles and says, "Whatever you like. Well, except anything about your case. That's the one exception. And I can give you some ideas. Maybe start your essays with *I remember...* or, *What's important to me is...* It's up to you."

To my surprise everyone gets to work. Out of the corner of my eye, I watch them. Most of them hunch over their pencils with their faces inches from their papers. Freddie is doing serious chewing on his eraser. I turn my attention to my own paper and start writing. After about twenty minutes, we're told to stop, and Mr. Hill asks who would like to read what they wrote.

Shit. No one said anything about reading anything out loud. I don't want to and can't imagine anyone else will want to either. But I'm surprised again.

Darnell raises his hand, "I'll go."

He wrote about a fight at school and it's surprisingly entertaining. After that, everyone wants to read theirs. It's all about city stuff and I close my notepad and put my hands on top. After everyone else is done, Mr. Hill looks at me, "Kelly, would you like to read?"

I shake my head. No way. If I read the stuff I wrote, I'll never live it down.

It's time for the class to end and everyone jumps up leaving their pencils on the table, which the guards count. Mr. Hill comes over to me and says if I'd like, he can read my writing and return it next week. I hesitate but end up handing it over. As soon as we walk out of the room, I regret it.

When the next Tuesday rolls around, the class is about the same. For fear I could be made to read, I write something about the silly rules at juvenile detention centers, something that will make me popular. But he doesn't make me read. At the end of the class, Mr. Hill holds me back. I look at him and I'm glad his eyes no longer have that pitying look. He almost looks excited.

"Kelly, I read what you wrote last week."

I hold this week's notepad and tuck it under my arm. "Was it okay?"

He smiles. "Okay? It was fantastic, written from the perspective of an eagle, very creative. Where'd you learn to write like that?"

I flush with pleasure. "I've always liked to write."

He taps my notepad. "You have a vivid imagination."

I nod. "I do." This is not news to me. "Do you want this week's?"

"Yes, I do." I hear a throat clearing and the guard is looking impatiently at us. Mr. Hill apologizes to him for the delay and I hurry over to get in line, but look back with a smile at the professor as we leave.

The class becomes the highlight of my week. Everyone else writes about being locked up, life on the streets, or the horrible things that have happened in their past. It becomes a game of one downmanship. Who has the worst story? Who's the most miserable?

Not me. I'm writing to escape the walls, not dwell on them. So I concentrate on creating a whole different world and characters. Eventually, I start to read aloud some of what I wrote and the other guys seem to like it. After the fourth class, I'm so inspired I go on a writing blitz. For several days I pretty much write around the clock filling multiple notebooks. I almost forget where I am. At the last minute, I about chicken out and don't turn them in, but I go ahead and hand them over to Professor Hill, whose eyes get big at the sight.

I try to make it a joke. "I might have gone a little overboard."

As much as I love the writing class, it almost makes things worse because the rest of the week sucks in comparison. I find myself sleeping more and eating less. Hunger has become a constant in my life, almost like I'd miss it if it was gone. Food makes me sick no matter how hollow my stomach feels. This morning, I bite into a biscuit and can't find any desire to eat it. It's dry and powdery in my mouth. I chew and force myself to swallow, my stomach taking it reluctantly. I eat one more bite. On the next one, I spit it out without swallowing. I'm done.

Henry has begun to comment on my weight loss. The jail nurse comes to talk with me. The guards try getting me to eat more but I tune them out. It's the one thing they can't make me do.

A week crawls by until it's Tuesday again. Lunch arrives, some sort of chicken thing. I eat some of the bread and drink the milk and push the rest away. Mr. Cooper looks at my tray and picks it up telling me to come with him. We go in my cell and he motions for me to sit on the bunk then hands me the tray.

"Listen, you have to start eating your meals."

"I do. I eat what I can."

He shakes his head at me. "When you get out of here, you can be a vegetarian or anything you want. But while you're here, you need to eat what you're given for your own good. You're losing too much weight. You want to be strapped down and force fed?"

I look up in panic. *Would they really do that?*

"Yeah, that wouldn't be fun, would it? You want to go to that class today?"

I don't like where this is heading. "Yes," I whisper.

"Well, I'll make a deal with you." He reaches over and cuts the chicken into little pieces. "You eat three bites and you can go. You don't and you stay in the cell this afternoon."

I give him a look, wondering why he's being so mean, but he doesn't look mad and I think he really does want me to eat. I know they're getting grief from Henry about my weight.

He sits down on the bunk by me. "C'mon now, three little bites. The chicken isn't going to be any better off from getting thrown in the garbage can."

Sitting by me and being concerned works better than threats, and I really do want to go to the class. He's right; the chicken *is* dead through no fault of my own. I look at the tray. "Just three?" I ask, but it seems a lot.

"That's all."

I swallow, bracing myself. "Okay."

He leans forward and crosses his arms over his knees. "Great. Let me see you do it."

I pick up the fork. There's a piece of chicken on it from where he cut it. I lift it up to put it in my mouth and close my eyes as I open wide. I fight a moment where I think I'm going to gag, chew a few times, then decide to treat it like a wad of gum and just swallow.

When I open my eyes, Mr. Cooper is watching. "There, that wasn't so bad was it?" He's pleased he's done what no one else has been able to. "Come on, two more."

I quickly spear the next two bites, popping them in my mouth, and practically swallowing them whole before dropping the fork and pushing the tray away.

Mr. Cooper is smiling. "Good job. Maybe tomorrow, you can make it six bites," he says, as he picks up the tray. He thinks he has it all figured out. I've got some time before the class, so I stand on my bed and look out the window slit, still tasting the chicken in my mouth. I roll my tongue around my teeth.

I'd been seven years old when my Uncle Jack took me to the stockyard. Three hours later, he delivered me to my father. "I'm sorry, I should have known he'd react this way."

I sobbed in Dad's arms and had to sleep with him for the next several nights because of the nightmares. My mind kept returning to the calves taken from their mother's sides and put in a small corral. They all bawled for their mothers, which would have been sad enough if they were going to a place where they'd be bottle fed and live, but these were bound for the veal market. They'd soon be dead anyway, so no one cared if they were hungry and terrified.

The mothers went straight in to be butchered, shot in the head at the top of the ramp where they'd drop with a horrible thump. I was with two other boys, ranchers' sons, who took it in stride, but I'd sworn that day I would never eat meat again. Everyone thought it was a phase. *He'll grow out of it.* I lived in Wyoming for God's sake, beef capital of the world. But I never have. Even the thought of it brings the smells and horror of that day back to me.

I feel bile in my throat and barely make it to the toilet before everything comes back up. Grabbing my blanket off the bed, I hold it over my head to drown out the sound of my retching. I know Mr. Cooper will think I'm doing it on purpose. I try to hurry throwing up, which is not an easy thing to do. I finish and flush, quickly moving away and wiping my sweaty face with my arm. Glad no one seems to have noticed, I get a swig of water from the sink then suck on my wrist to get the vomit taste out of my mouth.

A few minutes later, it's time for the class. Mr. Cooper takes me himself. He comes out of the guard station and the others look at me and smile. He's obviously told them he got me to eat. There's going to be hell to pay when it doesn't work the next time.

KELLY

4

Several weeks later when the last class is over, we tell Mr. Hill thanks and goodbye. It's a big letdown and I stand in my cell and let the sadness fill me up. The only antidote is to let my imagination take me away, which I've been doing more and more. I can turn that switch on in my head and zoom, I'm gone, and the walls disappear.

One Saturday night, a new sixteen-year-old kid comes in. In the morning he sits by himself, hunched over, and stares at his feet. We leave him alone and so does the staff. Late in the afternoon, he hangs himself in his cell. Someone spots him and all hell breaks loose, guards running, their radios blasting the news to Control. One of the guards shoves me in my cell and the door closes.

I watch through the door window as they take the kid out on a stretcher. I hear a guard tell another one, "He emptied his bowels and wasn't breathing but CPR brought him back." The supervisor arrives and he gets on them for not keeping a better eye on the kid. He says most suicides happen in the first few days after admission. I know they work hard here to prevent suicides. For one thing, there would be lots of annoying paperwork.

It's only a few hours later, when they bring the kid back and lock him up in his cell. Now they're keeping a close eye on him. They post someone right outside his cell door to eyeball him. He's not going to get a second chance, at least not for a while. He was dumb. He should have waited till it was night when his odds would have been better. Maybe he didn't really want to die. If he did want to, I understand. Sometimes the walls close in and your body screams *get out*, but you can't. You can check out mentally like I do or try and check out for good.

All night I wonder how the guy did it. If he had had just a couple more minutes, he could have pulled it off. I think about the sheets I tied up to go out the window at my grandfather's. I look around the cell, but there doesn't seem to be anything good to tie them to. I get up and start feeling around, looking for the best spot. Just like I did when I stood outside at the juvenile center and studied the fence, I'm simply toying with the idea with no intention of really doing it.

But you did *do it, don't you remember?*

Yeah, but this is different—to die here alone? That's a scary thought. It would be like I never existed. There'd be no one to remember me. Well, maybe Henry would be a little sad. I wonder if he knows how important he's become to me.

The next day, as I enter the room, he sizes me up and I can read concern in his eyes. He's the one person out there in the real world who knows I'm behind these walls.

"How ya doing sport?" He gives me a smile as he opens up his briefcase.

"I'm okay." It's a lie and we both know it.

We talk about my court case a little while. It's now a destination, a marker that some change in this endless drip of time is going to happen. If there was a set end in sight, it would be better. I have no release date, just hearing dates that keep getting pushed back. I see the days stretching on and on without end.

I quit seeing myself as someone in a story who would rise above evil. I begin to see myself as what I am. A prisoner, someone people look at with contempt and disdain. I no longer belong to the world of ordinary folks. Nope, I have joined the fringe of society. The people within these walls are my people.

I remember an errand I went on with Pop Haverly. It was to the garbage dump to drop off some trash. The dump sat next to the County Jail. On the other side of the street was the Humane Society. Next to it was the juvenile detention center and good old Oasis. It was like the city had put everything no one wanted all together—for convenience, I guess.

Lying on my bunk in the quasi-dark, something catches my eye going past my window. I stand up and look out and I'm excited to see it's snowing, big quarter-size flakes, the kind that pile up quick on the ground. The kind that make for good skiing or snowshoeing.

There's something special about a first snow. It seems wonderful and mysterious before it becomes commonplace and wears out its welcome. It snows early in Wyoming. I couldn't believe here that Christmas could come and go with no snow. Shoot, it's February. At least I think it is. The days are so alike, it's hard to measure the passing of the days. The months. My initial excitement ebbs away. The seasons keep changing and it drives home my sense of confinement, a glimpse again of time passing.

I was thirteen when I came in. Now I'm fourteen. I picture the birthday cake I had when I turned eleven, not knowing it would be my last one, maybe ever. Dad got it from the Bootstrap Bakery. Everyone in town bought them from there. The Guthries knew everyone and would personalize the cakes without being asked. Mine looked like the mountains, blue on the top of the cake, with snowy peaks below and little green icing trees. I told Mrs. Guthrie how much I liked it. She said next year she'd try and add a horse, but they were hard to draw.

Time begins spinning through my head. I missed the entire fall, like it never happened. No changing leaves, no campfire on a crisp night, no geese flying south, no horses with their shaggy coats. I'm missing all of winter too. What about spring? Will I see any of it other than through this four-inch slit? Will I be out by summer? It's like time is moving on but leaving me behind, living this shitty half-life. I used to be miserable and lonely, but not hopeless. Now, I see nothing to hope for.

From here, it's a downward spiral, like pulling the plug in a bathtub. Swirling and swirling, down I go. The next morning, I try to enter my imaginary world, but with a growing horror, I realize I can't call it up. All day, I try to open that door, but it stays as locked as the ones keeping me here. I guess pretending is something kids do. I'm not a kid anymore. I picked a hell of a time to grow up. The fantasies that made my life bearable have left me. All I have now is the cold gray reality that's become my life. Every day gets a little harder to face.

The noises get louder and louder and become overwhelming. The constant sound of toilets flushing, bells ringing, metal food trays scraping across metal tables, clicks of the locks, the yelling. Even the crinkle of plastic being removed from commissary candy drives me crazy. The sounds, over and over, like the dripping of water on a rock, wear me down.

I look at the food, pick up my spoon, and feel my stomach shrink and close. *Eat something*, I tell myself. *You'll feel better if you do.* But I can't. I push my tray away, cringing at the noise it makes. And now, it's not just my own food. The sounds of other people eating, the look of meat on the plates, the trays when their food is gone is all nauseating. They say when you have your health you have everything, so no surprise, I lose that too. In the mornings, we are supposed to stand by our bed for the morning count, but today it doesn't seem like a good idea. I go back to sleep.

The CO isn't pleased. "Morgan, get your ass out of bed."

I slowly push up to half sitting, feel the world whirl around me, and quickly lie back down. Like through a tunnel, I hear him yelling. "Right now, Morgan, I mean it. Do you want a write-up?"

It's a matter of personal pride, I've never gotten a write-up, so I try to obey, but all I end up doing is rolling off the bunk to the floor. At this point, I give up. It's a mountain too high to climb. Write me up. I just don't care.

I hear voices and they're loud, so I grimace. *Please everyone, could you just be quiet?* Then the voices are quieter and they're from within my cell. There's two of them. I recognize Officer Cooper's voice.

"Kelly, are you okay? What's wrong?"

I want to answer but get distracted. His head is just above me. He has a brown spot on his face that looks like a mouse. Or is it a kangaroo? It makes my head hurt thinking about it, so I close my eyes.

"What's the matter with him?"

"I don't know, but something's wrong and he needs to go to the infirmary. Radio and let them know he's coming."

"Should I call for a stretcher?"

"Never mind that, I'll carry him."

There's the uncommon sensation of someone's arms around me. It feels good. My head falls back over his shoulder and I look at my bunk and toilet from on high, like when I rode the Ferris wheel at the Dixon County fair and looked down at things on the ground. Funny, what I'm seeing looks just like a prison cell, anybody's prison cell. There's nothing to mark it as mine.

After that I close my eyes. It makes me dizzy to keep them open while we're moving. But I like the moving. It's good to be going somewhere. I feel as much as hear the door locks opening, the pressure of the air changes. I smell a strong disinfectant, and as soon as my body is placed on a bed, I let myself melt into it. It's softer than my bunk. I drift in and out, answering questions in a whisper.

"Nothing hurts. Just tired."

"Yes, dizzy."

"No food. Please."

During the night and next day, there are whispers about forced feedings and psychiatric hospitals. The words don't touch me. I'm at the edge of a cliff with rocks below and they're calling me. I watch the nurses and guards as if it's a dream, a movie about someone that has nothing to do with me. My eyes close and I go floating somewhere, the pain and numbness gone. A delicious warmth steals through me. It's been so long since I've been warm.

The rocks don't win. I do get better, and on the third night, my eyes lock on the TV. I usually hate it, especially the way it comes on and goes off at preset times every day, like some evil little robot is toying with us. But tonight, there's a movie. It's *Castaway*. The main character is played by Tom Hanks. He's on an airplane that goes down and leaves him stranded on a remote island. I can't get enough of the beautiful scenery. Someday I'd like to see the ocean. Dad always promised me one day we'd go.

I watch the castaway struggle on his island for years. He almost commits suicide but eventually comes up with a way to leave and rejoin the world. After the movie's over, the evil robot makes the TV go off and the lights go down. I recite the movie's most memorable line over and over to myself: *I just keep breathing because tomorrow the sun will rise and who knows what the tide will bring.*

I stare at the gray of the ceiling. I feel so cut off from life, the one normal people live, going about their business, far from the world I live in. I think of them but know they don't think of me. Like the castaway on his island, I'm cut off and all alone. But he didn't give up. No sir, he made his raft and went out to sea.

My mind travels back to the time I was trying to catch my new pony, Buck. It was a big field and anytime I got close, he ambled in a different direction and went back to grazing. If I ran at him, he trotted away. I put oats in a bucket and tried to bribe him. He was interested but stopped a few feet beyond me, so I set the bucket down and backed off a few yards. He slowly walked over, dipped his head in, but as soon as I made my move, he jerked his head up and ran from me while still chewing his mouthful of oats. I threw the halter I was carrying down in disgust and kicked it. For good measure, I kicked the bucket holding the oats. Not done, I cussed a blue streak then threw a big clump of dirt, popping Buck on his butt before I left the field. My dad made me take a chair on our front porch. I sat there, with my arms folded across my chest, fuming.

Dad stood there until I looked up at him. I could tell I'd disappointed him. I went from mad to close to tears. He walked past me, went in the house, and came back out with a book in his hand. It was our dictionary. He gave it to me, tapped a word, then went back inside.

I looked at the word. *Fortitude. Courage in pain or adversity, toughness of spirit.* I sat there a few seconds looking up at the blue sky. A few minutes later, I walked back into the field. I picked up the halter and walked toward Buck. He walked away. I walked after him. He walked. I walked. It took almost an hour before he let me put his halter on and lead him to the barn. I was exhausted, but triumphant.

My dad came down and helped me put on the saddle. He picked me up, but before he sat me in it, he gave me a big squeeze and whispered, "That's my guy."

I feel a calm come over me. Where I am is bad. But will it last forever? No. One day, the door will open, and I'll walk out of here. I may not be tough, but I am a survivor. It's time to find out what I'm made of.

The next morning, I force myself to eat a piece of toast and drink a glass of juice. Two days later, I'm moved back to the pod.

A day after my return to regular housing, I ask about Officer Cooper, who I haven't seen since I've been back. Officer Bishop is scribbling on his clipboard and doesn't answer. I wait patiently. In here, there's no other way. As he hands his clipboard off to another guard and starts walking away, he says over his shoulder, "Oh, he's gone. Got a job over at UPS that pays better. They raised their pay and we lost six people."

For a couple of seconds, I just stand. I back up a couple of steps and go into my cell. I look down at my feet in my rubber sandals and chastise myself. Why shouldn't he get a better job? Even I can see being a correctional officer is tough. But couldn't he at least have come and said goodbye?

I put my head up. No, it's better this way. I was always sucking up to him, trying to get his attention, like a little kid. I'm older, I'm past all that. There's a power in relying only on yourself.

I don't need anyone.

I don't want anyone.

I stand on my bunk and look out the window. The sky is heavy and gray. The trees are bare. It's windy. I watch a plastic bag whirl around as it goes skyward before getting snagged by a branch. It hangs there, flapping in the breeze. The branch has a touch of green. Spring is coming.

HENRY

5

The visiting room is as cold as ever as I wait for them to bring in Kelly. It's stale air from being endlessly recycled. Kelly is probably breathing the same molecules as the day he arrived. I'd like to suggest they lock everyone in their cells for an hour and open all the outside doors just to refresh the damn place.

There's really not much to talk about on the case, but I know I'm the only visitor he gets. I'm worried about the boy. He's practically wasting away in here. After his recent infirmary visit, I demanded a face-to-face with someone in charge. We had a nice go-round about the boy's meals. They quote a policy that says diet adaptations are only for religious or health reasons. They say he's just trying to be manipulative and get attention and that he shouldn't be awarded for it. I don't think this is the case, but even if he is, so what? The kid has no control over any other part of his life. Let him win a little, I say. It went downhill after that.

The jail administrator quoted policies and laws. Blah, blah, blah. My blood pressure elevated with each passing second. I could feel my voice rising with every word I spoke. "Well then, do it for his health. You think it's good for him to eat almost nothing?"

The administrator got that irritating, patient-while-annoyed look. "I assure you, Mr. Galloway, he's given food. Nursing staff are notified anytime an inmate refuses two meals in a row. He hasn't totally quit eating, and if he does, we'll contact the court about force feeding."

I laughed out loud. "Tell me you're joking! Let me get this straight. You'd rather go to the trouble of sticking a tube down his throat than fix him a goddamn peanut butter sandwich? Well fine! You do that. And let me tell you if something goes wrong and he gets hurt, or he ends up sick from not getting the proper nourishment someone his age should get, I will personally sue your asses off."

Now the patient look is gone. "Don't be making threats."

"Call it what you want." We glare at each other and I leave. However, if there's one thing a good lawyer knows, it's words on paper mean more than a conversation. Call it documentation. Call it proof. Whatever you call it, they know if something happens, they can't say, "Hey, you're mistaken, I didn't say *that*." So as soon as I get back to the office, I write the jail a letter specifying my concerns and have it sent by registered mail. Now they know I'll have exhibit A if it ends up in court. That gets their attention. Within days I get a written response saying they will adapt his meals and *do everything they can to assure my client's well-being considering the special circumstances related to his age.* It's one small victory on his behalf, but I wish I could do more.

The door opens and Kelly comes in and takes his seat across from me. "Hey, kid."

"Hi, Henry. Nice tie."

The boy loves my ties. I make sure to put on my craziest one on the days I'm coming to see him. I hold up the bottom of the tie and look down. "Too wild you think?" It was a birthday gift from my niece. Lime green and red with jumping dolphins.

He nods approvingly. "It sends a message you're self-assured."

I chuckle. "Well, there's a message here somewhere. How're you doing?"

"Fine."

He always says fine. I know he's not, and he knows I know he's not, but we leave it at that. "Listen, I had a talk with the folks here about meals and they said they'd do better."

"Yeah, there's two cartons of milk and they quit putting meat on my plate, so it doesn't run over onto the other stuff."

"Good." I look him up and down. He's way too thin. "Maybe you'll pick up some weight."

He turns down one side of his mouth. "What I'd like to do is pick up some height. Some guy told me I look like I'm ten."

I wag my finger at him. "Someday you'll be happy to be told you look younger." What I don't tell him is that I'm glad he's so small. It helps our case. Appearances count as much as what's said in court. It's unfair, but stand a six-foot, two hundred pound fourteen-year-old next to a small, young-looking kid like Kelly, and who do you think gets the worst sentence?

Kelly gives me his hopeful look. "Is there any chance my court date might be sooner?"

I inwardly sigh. He asks this every time. "Probably not." I watch his shoulders sag. "Remember, time is our friend. The goal is to get this kicked back down to juvenile court. Okay?"

There's a long pause while he looks down at his hands, but then he looks up to me with a ferocity I have never seen from him. "No, Henry it's not. I don't care where I go, but I have to get out of here. I'll plead guilty. I'll do anything. Didn't you say wherever I go will be better than this? That it'll have places to be outdoors?"

I blow out a breath. "Yeah, I did."

"Then just do whatever it takes." He pauses a second. "Please, Henry."

I start to try and reassure him about court processes but abandon the idea and say, "Okay, Kelly. I'll see what I can do."

He sits back in the chair and looks grateful. Like I know what I'm doing. We talk a few more minutes and time is up. As always, he thanks me for coming to see him. I pick up my things and walk back to my office. The kid's eyes sit heavy on my mind.

The next morning, I hit McDonald's on the way to work for a coffee and biscuit. The idiot in the car in front of me has apparently never in her life ordered breakfast from McDonalds. She stares at the menu and keeps asking questions to the speaker. The line next to me moves up two cars. Why do I always pick the wrong one to get in? I glance at my watch. Dammit, order and move! I consider honking but figure that's going too far. Finally, she edges forward, and I order my first caffeine hit of the day. Certainly not the last. I get my food and pull over in the lot to woof it down. A slug of coffee first. The steam rises from the cup. This will likely be the highlight of my day.

Brain now engaged, I think about Kelly. Note to self, decline future cases of any big-eyed thirteen-year-olds. Well, now he's fourteen. I went to see him on his birthday, but they wouldn't even let me bring him a cupcake. He tried to cheer me up by assuring me that twelve and thirteen weren't great birthdays either, which made it that much more depressing. For me, that is. I can't imagine how it is for him. I wonder how much he thinks about it all. He's a smart kid, so no telling.

I'd paid the money to get a psychological report done on him. It put his IQ through the roof. What else had the psychologist said? *A good grasp of right and wrong.* The clinician who wrote up the report made sure to make it as glowing as possible, without sounding biased, which means he got to her too. The fact he doesn't *try* to get to you makes it all the more effective. Shit, he's keeping me up at night.

I thought I was hardened to the tragic circumstances in my clients' lives. His is sad but he doesn't win the prize. At least he had a stable and loving life for his first eleven years. Maybe that's why I identify. It's hard to picture yourself as a toddler with a crack addict mother, but when I picture myself losing my whole family at eleven, I feel the horror. Also, everyone else I deal with has somebody—a mother, a brother, a girlfriend. They might be dysfunctional as hell, but they've got 'em. Kelly's got no one.

Or maybe it's the damn pictures. I open the file on the seat next to me. I had an intern do some research and she found articles in Wyoming newspapers. I glance at the first headline. "Sheriff's son only survivor of horrific crash." There's a photo taken hours before the crash of the boy with his father and uncle. There's even a large black and white dog sitting next to him to wrench your heart a little more.

As gut-wrenching as the first photo is, the second one's worse. It's Kelly, with his left arm in a big cast and sling. His right hand reaches out to touch his father's coffin. The grief on his face is stark. No wonder it was on the front page of the newspaper. The photographer could have won a Pulitzer with this shot. It hurts every time I look at it. So why am I?

I close the file and unwrap my biscuit. I wonder if the kid ate anything this morning. I glance at the clock on the car dash. Pushing eight-thirty. If he ate, it was three or four hours ago. Institutional meal schedules are ridiculous. He used to be thin, but now he's skin and bones. And it can't be good for a growing boy to never be in the sun and get so little Vitamin D. And those eyes. I think it's those eyes that haunt me the most. They were so expressive when I first met him. Now, they're hollow and downright vacant at times.

I've got to get him out of there.

There could be an end in sight. The prosecutor, Bill Evans, is getting agreeable to sending the charges back to juvenile court. I think my nagging may have finally gotten to him. *Look at the kid. You want to send him to prison?* And then I showed him the pictures from the newspaper—my secret weapon. I think even hard-ass Evans was moved.

Getting his case back to juvenile court has been the plan, but now that it's about to happen, why do I have this bad feeling about the whole thing in the pit of my gut? Suddenly, the rest of my breakfast biscuit doesn't look so appealing.

Yesterday before I left work, I was mulling this over when my boss popped his head in the door. "Were you found in contempt or did you have a fight with your wife? You look like something the cat drug in. Oh, wait. Let me guess. It's that case with the kid."

I shrugged, which Charlie took as an invitation to come into my office and take over one of my two visitor chairs. He must have just come from court because he didn't have on his tie; I'm sure it was in his pocket. He's the only one here who gets more grief about his ties than me. He gets the cheapest clip-ons you can buy and yanks them off as soon as he leaves court. He looks like such a nerd, but he has one of the sharpest legal minds I've ever seen.

I leaned forward, putting both elbows on my desk. "How'd you know?"

"Because it's Thursday. You're over there every Thursday like clockwork. I thought you got it all worked out for him to go back to juvenile. Why so glum?"

"Because things for the boy are still going to be lousy. What's better, the frying pan or the fire? Did I ever tell you about the first kid I ever represented in juvenile court? A sixteen-year-old boy whose big crime was smashing a pumpkin on Halloween night. The wealthy homeowner caught him and was irate. Called the police and insisted they arrest him. They weren't excited but did it to shut the homeowner up. The kid's parents were out of town, so the judge ordered the kid placed in juvenile detention, said, 'a night or two in there won't hurt him.' How wrong he was.

"The school was notified, and the kid got kicked off the basketball team. His friends' parents told their kids to stay away from him, so he drifted to the kids he'd met in detention who introduced him to drugs. Three years later, he was on the way to prison for committing a burglary to support his drug habit."

"One night changed the whole trajectory of that kid's life, and Kelly's looking at four years. I just got off the phone with the Department of Juvenile Justice folks. They were nice enough, but they won't budge on where they're sending him. Because of the escape charge, he'll have to go to their maximum-security facility at McGee."

Charlie pushed his glasses up onto his nose and shrugged. "Better that than the adult state reformatory."

"Yeah, I know." I dropped my hands down on the desk. "But it's not without its problems. You've seen the recent investigative reporting from Channel 5, haven't you? About those kids who've been physically and sexually abused by the staff? The rampant use of pepper spray and solitary confinement? Oh, but wait, let's not worry because, guess what? A task force has been appointed to look into the allegations. Oh, *right*. Like the task force four years ago, and one three years before that. All wrote reports stating the problems are so ingrained that the place should be closed and the kids placed in smaller treatment-oriented programs like Kentucky and Missouri have. Great, right? But I wouldn't bet the ranch on that happening any time soon."

Charlie held up his hands. "Hey, don't yell at me. I'm on your side, remember?"

We both sat there in silence for a full minute, before Charlie spoke again. "It's a shame the kid doesn't have a suitable guardian, or he'd probably be out within a year. Without one, he probably won't be going anywhere fast. But hey, maybe they'll like him as much as you do and step him down to something less secure eventually."

"Yeah, I thought of that," I said, "but you know the other side of that coin. If he does have trouble getting along, he'll end up staying in a cell till he's eighteen. Then he'll walk out the door totally on his own after being institutionalized for five years. It happens to kids all the time. No wonder so many of them end up back incarcerated within their first year of release."

Charlie just sat there shaking his head. "Now I'm depressed."

I drain my coffee down as I think about my conversation with Charlie. If only Kelly were like my typical urban clients who worry about being shipped to the boonies. Instead, it's like he's a wild animal going crazy in a cage who needs to be set free in the woods. Too bad he couldn't go to one of the adult Department of Correction's forestry camps.

Out of the blue, a kernel of a thought nestles into my mind. I slowly chew my biscuit as the thought takes hold and begins to grow. *Could he? Is it possible?* Every kid I've ever represented in adult court went to prison when convicted, but none of them had Kelly's lack of a prior record and none were convicted of such a non-serious offense.

Excited, I rifle through papers looking for the Department of Corrections classification form. The magic number on the form determines how secure a setting the offender goes to. I grab a pen and begin calculating. I write down the points for the two felonies he's facing. He gets a zero for prior adult record. Since all his charges got sent up to adult court, technically he doesn't have a juvenile record so that's a zero. A zero for never escaping an *adult* facility. Ha, how funny, escaping a juvenile facility isn't on here. Zero for drug and alcohol issues. Zero for causing any problems in jail while awaiting trial. I keep scribbling down the form then add it up. *Holy shit, he does score for minimum.* That means he could go to a forestry camp which would suit him to a tee.

It gets even better. I do the mental calculations. If the charges are merged, he should pull about five years. As an adult, he can get credit for time served, and he'll earn good time, which will cut the sentence in half. Kelly would serve out by age sixteen, not eighteen. Legally, Corrections can't hold him one day past when his time runs out, regardless of whether he has parents or not.

I sober thinking of the downsides. Kids who are placed in adult facilities are much more likely to commit suicide or be sexually abused. And convicted as an adult, he'd have a true criminal record.

Maybe I should rethink this.

But then, I picture the last time I saw Kelly. The bony wrists, the flat voice, the dark shadows under his eyes. He looked terrible. Better to keep him alive and worry about the long-term issues later. Of course, I'll need to present the whole crazy idea to him first to see which way he wants to go. Last he knew, McGee was the best-case scenario.

I toss my last bite of food out the window to the starlings. I need to get to the office to make some phone calls.

Oh, *man*. The Department of Corrections is gonna love this.

KELLY

6

I remember reading an article about how amusement parks changed the way people wait in lines. They knew it was discouraging for people to see one long endless line, so they put up turnstiles you wind your way through. Every time you make a turn you are one step closer to the goal, so you're more patient. Is my upcoming court hearing the end or one more turn? I need to feel progress is happening. Henry comes to see me, and we claim our usual spots before he leans in and taps his forefingers together. My Henry is big on tapping.

"Okay, it's crunch time. I think the prosecutor is willing to send your case back to juvenile court."

"So, I go to McGee."

"Yeah, that would be most likely."

The ball in the pit of my stomach keeps expanding. I don't know why, since I've been pushing Henry to get things going. An hour a day outside, that's better than here, isn't it? I look down at my hands in my lap. "Well, it's what I expected."

Henry shifts in his seat and rests his arms on the table. "There is one other thing I've thought of." He drums his fingers on the table. He frowns and looks hesitant, but I want to know.

"Yeah?"

"Okay. This is pretty radical. You ever hear about rip tides in the ocean?"

"Yeah, I've heard of them."

"They say if you get caught in one, it's better to let it carry you out further from shore than fight it."

I have no clue where this is going. "So?"

"Well, maybe rather than fight being in adult court, we should go with it."

"Is prison better than McGee?"

119

"Absolutely not. But here's the thing. The way they determine where you go is calculated on a point system based on your charge and circumstances. I gave it a trial run and you'd score low, which means you'd be placed in a minimum-security facility."

"What does that mean?"

"No fence, no cell. A dormitory setup. Much more freedom as far as daily movement. Lots more being outside. In fact, most of the minimum-security facilities are forestry camps. I've done some calculations and you'd serve about two years. That'd be half the time you'd serve as a juvenile. Do you know what good time is?"

"Yeah, some guys here talk about it. They take time off your sentence for every day you don't get in trouble."

"That's right. It's a fairly substantial reduction. Adult corrections uses it, but you wouldn't get good time in a juvenile facility."

I feel a small door opening. A crack of hope. "So, I'd just leave then?"

"The facility, yes. Adult corrections won't have any legal hold on you. You'd still be underage so someone would have to assume custody, but we can cross that bridge when we come to it."

He doesn't need to do any more selling. "I'm in. Let's do it."

Henry holds up his hand. "Hold on before you jump. There are some down sides. You'd be with adults not kids. No one else your age to be friends with."

"I don't care about that. I don't need friends."

Henry looks uncomfortable. There must be a catch. I knew it was too good to be true. He smooths down his tie and leans in. "There's something else we should talk about. You may hate being here, but the staff have been good about keeping you safe. In a more open adult setting, there's a higher likelihood of an adult inmate taking advantage of you … sexually, that is … you know?"

I should be horrified even thinking about it, but for some bizarre reason I almost laugh. I see my Dad's face which morphs back into Henry. This is not how I pictured the birds and the bees talk would happen. The least I can do is let Henry off the hook. "It's not that I haven't thought about that, including when I was on my own. It's why I tried not to hitchhike. It's the one thing I've been lucky on. I'll hope my luck holds. It's not like it doesn't happen in juvenile facilities too, right?"

Henry sits back and sighs. "I wish I could tell you no, but it does. But it happens much more in adult programs. There's another thing. If this stays in juvenile, your record will be sealed after you turn eighteen, but as an adult, it'll be public record. A criminal conviction will reduce the types of jobs you can hold and even keep you from voting."

I conjure up an image of me writing a book in an isolated cabin in the wilds of Wyoming. I'm not even sure who the current president is, so voting isn't on my mind. I tell Henry, "I don't care."

"Are you sure? You probably should think on it."

"I'm sure. What do I need to do?"

"You'll just need to plea to the charges after I work out the details with the prosecutor. Here's the other good thing. It can all move fast from here."

"Fast would be good. I've had enough slow for a lifetime." Something occurs to me and I can't help but laugh.

Henry asks, "What?"

"It's nothing, just a thought, never mind." Henry wouldn't understand, but what has me laughing is I may be saved by a point system. Who knew?

The court date is set. I wait for it like a kid counting down the days to Christmas, and like a kid on Christmas Eve, I have a hard time sleeping before the big day. Here's where the comparison to Christmas ends, because I keep switching between excitement and dread. I ignore breakfast and shortly after my full food tray is taken away, they come for me. Other inmates are taken too, but they keep me separate and I get my own private holding room. I sit in a chair while they handcuff me to it. There's nothing to do but sit and wait. I look at the cracks in the wall and try to make them into something, but no magic happens. They just stay boring old cracks. At least there's a bit of window to look out of and the scenery is different than my jail window. I can see downtown stores and people going in and out of the doors, carrying bags and getting into their cars.

At last, the bailiff comes for me. Showtime. My breathing quickens and I tell myself to be calm, or at least look calm. Even with my anxiety, I can see this is very different from the juvenile courtrooms I've been in. Those were shanty huts compared to this courtroom. With thick carpet on the floor and nice paintings on the wall, it's like a mansion. I take a seat next to Henry near the front of the

121

courtroom.

My fingers go numb and I realize it's because of how hard I'm grasping the table edge. I let go and the blood flows back into my hand. *This is really happening.* I feel my palms getting sweaty but tell myself it's stupid to be afraid. Henry's gone over it with me and I know the script. Within minutes, I'll be back in jail, so why do I feel myself flashing hot and cold? I take a deep breath trying to steady myself.

Henry must know I'm freaking out a little because he takes hold of my elbow and leans over to whisper, "Try and relax. It's all just a formality now, okay?"

I nod. In a couple of minutes, we go stand before the bench. It's not like I haven't done this before. The judge is flipping through the papers in front of him. They must teach flipping at judge school because all my judges start things this way. And they all have those little plaques with their names. This one is the Honorable Richard Nolan. He looks at me for several seconds. I try to achieve a face somewhere between respectful and not sucking up. I can't read his expression. He looks sort of neutral, like he doesn't like or hate me. My mind goes to the three bears story. The first judge was oh, so friendly; the second judge was oh, so mean; the third judge was *juussst* right. I can only hope.

Henry, the judge, and the prosecutor go into legal speak. I don't look at anyone but Henry. I like seeing him all official and think with some pride that he's my guy, even better than the long ago Karen. After Henry finishes talking, he gives me a strange look and nudges me a little with his elbow. Oh right, the judge is talking to me.

"Mr. Morgan, do you understand the charges, and do you agree to plea as your attorney has stated?"

Here we go. "Yes, sir."

"Mr. Morgan, I need to ask you some questions before I accept your plea. I need to make certain you are competent to make this plea. Are you a US citizen?"

"Yes, sir."

"What was the last grade you completed?"

This is tricky. I was in fifth grade at the boarding school but failed. In this situation I decide it's best to go with total honesty. "Fourth."

He looks up from the paper in his hand, but instead of looking at me, he scowls at Henry and the prosecutor. "Who else is here with you today?"

I look at Henry. "Mr. Galloway."

"Besides him."

"No one."

He frowns and I try not to worry. These aren't hard questions. Surely I can't screw this up.

"Were you under the influence of drugs or alcohol during any of the offenses you have been charged with?"

"No, sir."

"How much have you used alcohol and drugs?"

"Never."

I can tell he thinks I'm lying. "You've never used drugs? Smoked a joint? Taken a pill?"

I shake my head. "No, sir."

The questions stop and the judge leans back in his chair. I'm hoping we are done but no, that's not it. He doesn't look happy. Unhappy-looking judges make me nervous.

The judge pushes his chair back. "I'm going to pause this right here. I'd like to see Counsel in my chamber. Mr. Morgan, you can have a seat." He motions to the bailiff who says, "All rise."

The judge leaves the room and I look at Henry. "Did I say something wrong?"

He puts his hand on my back. "No, you did fine. This happens sometimes. I'll be back in a few minutes."

The bailiff shows me where to sit. All the people in the room are looking at me. I stare at the table in front of me, like it's all of a sudden very interesting. I feel a little weak. Maybe I should have eaten breakfast after all.

HENRY

7

The boy looks panicked. I follow Bill Evans into Judge Nolan's chambers, and we wait while the judge hangs up his robe and takes his place behind his desk.

He temples his fingers and says, "Gentlemen, I don't like this."

I look at Evans who is giving me an I–told-you-so look, so I speak first. "I understand, Your Honor. I don't like it either."

He skewers Evans, which I admit I enjoy. "You really want to nail this kid? Looking at his file, I can sum up his entire criminal background as ate breakfast, climbed a fence, and borrowed a car. Okay, he stole it, but right here I have a copy of the apology note he wrote. I suppose that saved the police from extracting a confession. Why the hell hasn't this been remanded back to juvenile? Amend the theft down to unauthorized use. This kid doesn't even look fourteen."

Evans speaks up. "I was willing, Your Honor. The defendant's counsel wouldn't agree." I shoot him a dirty look because he only recently agreed, but he's acting like he wanted to all along. Suck up.

The judge's head pivots to me. "Is this true, Galloway?"

"Yes, Your Honor."

Before I can say anything else, the judge starts up. "This is what concerns me. I don't know how competent this boy is. He doesn't have anyone but you looking out for his best interests. Isn't there anyone else?"

"Afraid not. The circumstances lead me to believe it's not in my client's best interest to proceed as a juvenile."

The judge is looking at me like I'm a first-year law student. "Why ever not?"

I go on the offense, partly because I'm still not convinced that I'm doing the right thing. "The DJJ folks told me because of the escape, he'll go to their maximum-security facility. I'm sure you've been following their problems across the state. Two youth died in one facility this year, and sexual abuse was alleged at others. Kids have been locked in solitary confinement for weeks or months at a time. There's chronic understaffing and underfunding."

Hard to tell if my sell job is working, so I let more emotion come into my voice. It's not an act, I feel it. "Look, I'm really worried about this boy. He's a sensitive, unsophisticated kid, and he's having a hard time with confinement. I'm not kidding when I tell you I'm worried he might not make it out alive."

Evans surprises me. "He does look bad. Is anybody feeding him over there?"

"We've had issues."

"What issues?" Nolan asks.

"He won't eat meat. They wouldn't make any accommodations until it turned into a full-blown eating disorder. They finally made some changes, but I had to throw a bit of a fit."

Evans says out of the side of his mouth, "You? Who'd believe it?"

Judge Nolan doesn't look sold. "I'm not sure I follow your line of reasoning. You think adult corrections is better?"

"Not a prison, no, that would be worse. But he scores minimum, which gets him out of a cell. That's the most important thing right now."

Evans gives a sigh like he's failing at keeping his mouth shut too. "The jail has called me several times about him. Believe me, they want him out too. They said he's been no behavior problem but keeping him safe and healthy has been challenging."

I decide I'm going to have to buy Evans a lunch sometime soon. And it's time to rest my case. "I know there are risks with this, but there are risks either way."

Evans and I stare at the judge waiting. Like two middle school students waiting for the principal's verdict. After a pause, Nolan says, "Okay, I get it, but I still don't like it. And I'm not sure I can find him competent enough to accept a plea. A fourth-grade education?"

"Don't let that throw you. He has a sky-high IQ. That's the other reason I think we need to think out of the box. He's got so much potential. I'd hate to see all that intelligence channeled to a life of crime, if he got pointed in that direction."

"Jesus." Nolan leans back in his chair, tilting it so he's staring at the ceiling.

He comes back down with his chair squeaking in protest. "I want to talk with Corrections and see what they plan to do with him. And how soon they can do it. I know someone. I'll call for Bonnie Ziegler and get her over here. Put the boy back in holding."

We break up and I go back to the courtroom next to Kelly.

"It's okay. The judge just wants more information about where you'll go. They'll put you back in holding, and I'll see about getting you something to eat. Just hang loose a little longer. We're getting there." He looks at me and I see trust in his eyes.

Damn, I hope he feels that way a year from now.

BONNIE

8

I'm almost out the door when my phone rings. I hit the answer button and tell the receptionist, "I'm just leaving."

Teresa, who has been here at the Department of Corrections twice as long as me and is twice as jaded, says, "Someone wants you."

Uh-oh. "Is there a sheriff department coming for me?"

This happens more than I'd like. I work in the Classification department at the DOC which means pretty much nobody likes what I do. A judge gets mad at a DOC placement and issues a subpoena to haul my ass before him and *explain the Department's actions* i.e. rip me a new one. I give an answer the judge doesn't like; he or she gives me a lecture on how stupid the Department is; I say yes, Your Honor, and we part ways. Nothing changes, but the judge gets a perverse satisfaction from hauling my ass hours away and making me waste my time sitting on the bench keeping company with drug addicts and weeping mothers. They always wait to call my case last, the vindictive bastards.

Teresa, bless her warped heart, is good at spotting sheriff cars that pull into the parking lot below her window. She gives me a heads-up so I can duck out the back to avoid being served, which means the deputies wasted their time, not mine.

It's a fun game we play.

Teresa sounds bored. "Nah, it's Judge Nolan on line one."

I want to get out the door to my long-delayed dentist appointment, but I can't ignore this call. Judge Nolan is one of the good ones. I pick up the phone and try to sound pleasant rather than resigned. "Hello, Your Honor. What can I do for you?" *Please, let it be an easy twenty-second answer and I'm outta here.*

"Sorry to give you short notice, but I've got Henry Galloway and Bill Evans here, and we need your help on a special case."

127

Special case. I groan inside. These are the worst. My mind rushes to the possibilities. A six-hundred-pound offender, a guy on oxygen, a cross-dressing sex offender, or someone simply nuttier than a pecan log.

"We have an offender who scores for minimum. I'd like to confirm that with you and maybe know which facility he'd go to, if you'd see fit to let me in on it."

I breathe a sigh of relief. This is a bit unusual, but doable. I pick up two paper clips and play with them in my hand. "Shouldn't be a problem. The local probation office can handle that."

"Well, he's not a typical offender, so could you come over to my chambers to discuss it?"

I hear the voice of the dentist receptionist in my head: *This is awfully short notice.* Translation: *We're going to charge you.* I try not to sound exasperated. "I'll head on over."

Grabbing my purse, I stop by Teresa's station on the way out. I rest my hand on the edge of her desk, careful not to knock over her *Have a Nice Day* coffee mug. I happen to know that on the bottom of that mug is a big hand giving the finger. "Could you please call …?"

She frowns and shakes her head. "Don't ask. After the other three times, they're getting real snippy."

"I'll bring you a coffee and a Danish on my way in tomorrow." Teresa can be bought.

Teresa narrows her eyes at me and says, "Alright, but I'm about to start a diet, so you're going to have to work on some new bribes soon."

Teresa is always going on a diet. Tomorrow. I'm hoping she isn't pointing the bottom of that mug at my back as I leave.

At least it's a nice day for a walk to the courthouse, early March, but quite warm. After a cold, dreary February, it feels good to skip the coat. The metal detector stays quiet and I chat with Emmett, who's been here since I was playing basketball in elementary school. I punch the elevator button and hit pay dirt when the doors open right away. When I get on the second floor, I see Galloway and Evans outside the judge's office looking like best buddies. That sends up a warning flare.

"Hello, gentlemen. What are you doing to ruin my day?"

I get no answer. Galloway pushes off the door frame, rapping his knuckles on the door as he opens it and announces, "She's here."

Judge Nolan motions us to chairs in front of his large wooden desk. He's in his late forties with some gray just beginning to show in the temples of his sandy hair. I see him sometimes at the tennis club, where I've played doubles with his wife. She's got a killer forehand, but her backhand is for shit.

He waits till I'm seated before saying, "Thanks for coming over. This is rather complicated."

I pull out my trusty legal pad to make notes. "What makes this case special?"

"He's fourteen years old, barely." The judge holds up his hand, "About this tall. Looks like a stiff breeze would blow him away."

"Oh crap." My pen goes down on the legal pad. I try to recover. "Um, sorry, I mean…"

"It's okay." Amusement flickers in the judge's eyes. "I expected that reaction."

"I don't get it," I say. "We've gotten juveniles before for serious offenses or with extensive criminal backgrounds. How could a kid score for minimum?"

Now Galloway speaks up. "I ran the numbers. He does. Do you remember the newspaper story about the boy that escaped from the brand-new juvenile detention center last year? Stole a car?"

"Vaguely, it was juvenile, so I was just happy it wasn't us. This is the kid, I take it?"

"Yeah. The escape was just a dumb kid thing. An impulsive act when opportunity arose."

I point my pen at him. "That's exactly why our people groan about getting a juvenile. They do stupid things an adult has the sense not to."

Galloway continues like I said nothing. "The boy has sat at County for almost seven months. He's doing badly. Depressed. Has lost lots of weight. And he's a … I'm trying to think of the term … nature boy. Loves the out-of-doors and he's not taken confinement well."

Judge Nolan cuts to the chase. "Can you keep him safe? Where could you put him?"

Resigned, I hold out my hand to Galloway. "Let me see the score sheet."

He smiles and hands it over. I skim it. "What's the misdemeanor theft?"

"Survival crimes. He snuck into motels to get food, a shower, and a nap."

"Did he raid the mini bar?"

"If he did, only for potato chips. He's not a drinker. No tattoos or metal. His father was an officer killed in the line of duty." He opens a file folder and shows me a couple of newspaper articles with photos.

I glance and look up at him. "Crap again."

The judge reaches for the photos, takes them, and wrinkles his forehead. "Well if this doesn't tug at our heart strings, nothing will."

Galloway goes into bleeding-heart lawyer mode. "Look, you'll like this kid. He's personable as hell. Smart, polite. Oh yeah. And he's a vegetarian. Make sure you put him where they can handle that."

I lift one eyebrow. "That's not my job you know, making attorneys and their clients happy. Plus, you're the type to get suckered. You sure he's not just pulling the wool over your eyes?"

"You go talk to him and see what you think."

"Well, we have to get a presentence report done no matter what, so yes, I'll work it up. I'll need some time."

Galloway leans back in his chair and crosses his legs in front of him. "Sure, take half the afternoon."

I send an SOS look to the judge. "He's kidding, right?"

Nolan looks apologetic but doesn't give me the answer I want. "I would like to get this resolved today if possible. I asked specifically for you. My mother always said if you want to get something done ask a busy person." He gives a little grin. "That's a compliment."

Galloway reaches into his briefcase. "I've got a psychological report I did on him just a couple of months back. That'll give you the basic information you'll need. It's not like you have to report on forty years of crimes and wives and children. This boy's life fell apart at age eleven, so you only need to capture three years tops. The clinician who did the psychological sang his praises. Said he had a high moral compass."

I yank the folder from his hand. "Those mental health people are soft touches. You all may be suffering from the Bambi Syndrome. I'm immune. I say it could be a con."

Galloway continues looking superior, which is annoying. He says, "We'll talk later. The boy's in the back holding-room behind Courtroom A."

The bailiffs all know me and without asking, move to open the door to the holding room. The boy is looking out the window but there's not much of a view, since it's covered with heavy mesh. Yeah, he's small and to my consternation, looks like a fawn. I think it's the big dark eyes under that bad haircut.

A bit off kilter, I take a seat and launch into my official mode. "Hello. I'm Ms. Ziegler."

"Yes, ma'am." I wonder if he's really polite or just brown-nosing.

"I work for the Department of Corrections. I'm the person who will decide where you will go when your court hearing is done."

"Yes, ma'am."

His eyes are intent on mine. I've sat across from plenty of people where I can see the hate and anger blazing in their eyes, their stare their only vehicle to say, 'Screw you, bitch." Other times, there's a suggestive smirk that implies the offender is having less than pure thoughts about me. Neither is the case here. His eyes are warm and expressive.

Classification scoring is very important. Theoretically, we're supposed to look at the least restrictive setting possible. We look at the nature of the offense and the circumstances, the inmate's behavior and attitude following arrest, his prior criminal history. That's the easy part. I look down the presentence form and struggle to know where to start.

The form wasn't developed for a fourteen-year-old with almost no legal history or family. I can't ask about past and present employment status, his marital history, his children. I can't ask for the names of family or friends to verify the information given. I skip down past the financial information on bank accounts, debt, owned property. The only sections that apply are "education" and "future plans," which means I pretty much scrap my usual interview technique and talk like an adult who is awkwardly trying to engage a teenager she doesn't know.

"Did you like school?" *Lame, Bonnie, really lame. Next, you can ask him what he wants to be when he grows up.*

He pauses a second before answering. "Not really."

"I'm told you're smart. Is that true?"

He raises his hands, palms up, and looks around with a grimace. "Maybe not?"

I suppress a smile and move on to another question. "When you're released from custody, what are your plans?"

His voice is soft but emphatic. "Go back to Wyoming."

I set my pen down on my pad and scrap my professional demeanor. "So, tell me about Wyoming. I've never been there. All I know is it looks cold and bleak and the population consists of three guys named Bob and about a thousand cows."

He stares at me. I think maybe I've offended him, but he slowly smiles. It's a cute kid's smile. "You're funny." His eyes get big. "I mean …"

I can't help but return his smile. "It's okay. I try to be funny. You would too, if your last name was Ziegler. I'm always the last person to be called for anything."

He gives me a kindhearted look. "I can see that would be tough. Morgan's not too bad. It's before all those R's and S's."

I can't help but feel a little pang of sympathy at the sincerity in his expression and voice. He's sitting here handcuffed to a chair, facing confinement in an adult facility, and seems to feel genuinely sorry for my petty problems.

He nods and continues, "It's true Wyoming has less people than any other state in the country. But that's why lots of people like it."

His eyes go from mine to out the window, like if he tries hard enough, he can see his home from here. "You can climb to the top of any peak and see nothing but land and wildlife. It's incredibly beautiful. The wind never stops. On some days you can watch the clouds race across the sky, over the tops of the mountains, like ships with sails going over the horizon."

I look at the profile of his sensitive face and hear the wistfulness in his voice. A kid who wants to go home. His eyes drift back from the window to me. He looks slightly embarrassed, as if he realizes he got carried away. I've been somewhat hypnotized thinking about those clouds, so I shuffle papers to break the spell. Back to business. I work to extract more pertinent information on his background. It's not easy and being in a hurry doesn't help. It's a half-assed job.

I scribble the last bit of information and click my pen. "Okay, I think I have what I need. I'm going to go make some calls and see what's available."

"Thank you, Ms. Ziegler. I appreciate it." He sounds like I'm saying I'll check the back room to see if we have that shoe in his size. I tap on the door for the bailiff to let me out and glance back as I leave. He's resumed staring out the window.

I go back past Judge Nolan's office. Galloway is still sitting there, looking too sure of himself. He looks up expectantly. "Well?"

I shift my purse to the other shoulder. "I'll make some calls."

"Yeah? Where to?"

I start walking but turn and take two steps backwards. "The woods. I've got to find a good spot for Bambi." I stalk off with my nose held high, but I know he's laughing.

Hey, the kid's right. I can be funny.

Back in my office, I look over my notes. This kid is full of ACEs. In corrections, ACEs have nothing to do with poker. It stands for Adverse Childhood Experiences. Rack up four or more and your odds of an unfavorable adult life dramatically rise. You are seven hundred percent more likely to be an alcoholic, three thousand percent more likely to attempt suicide, and twice as likely to be diagnosed with cancer. There's a direct pipeline to the criminal justice system as well. A sixty percent higher chance of a juvenile arrest and thirty percent more likely to commit a violent crime.

I'm not even sure how to count with this kid. His mother's early death is clearly the first ACE. Do I count one for the car wreck or two, adding up both family members? Does he get a point for almost getting killed himself? Hell, even his dog was killed; shouldn't I count that? The way he evaded some of my questions, there's indication of abuse from the grandfather in Pennsylvania. That earns another point. Homelessness, foster care: cha-ching, cha-ching. And certainly, incarceration is an Adverse Childhood Experience in and of itself.

No matter how I add it up, he's way over the magic four threshold. And I easily could be missing some. I can't score for sexual abuse, but he's an awfully cute kid who's been on his own and then later, in an adult jail, so I have to wonder.

Despite his high ACE numbers, this kid is nowhere near the norm for what I usually see. There's the high IQ, yes, but more than that, there's something about him. It's rare, but I've seen a few like him before. Kids with an air of effortless self-possession that either makes the other kids and staff admire them or despise them.

There are lots of things about this boy I still don't know. What I do know is that I want to do the best I can for him. It's good he scored for minimum. It gives me decent possibilities. I pull up my directory and turn to the forestry camps. This shouldn't be too hard. I start making calls.

Thirty minutes later, I'm about to pull my hair out. Of course, silly me, no one wants a fourteen-year-old. They all tell me their woes.

We're a barracks set-up and have three sex offenders in residence.

You have to be eighteen to use power tools here.

We don't expect to have an opening for six weeks or more.

They've thrown up some good roadblocks, for sure, but as a woman who went into a field dominated by men, I'm not easily deterred.

I turn a few pages to another minimum forestry facility that's not usually used as a direct placement from court. It's located on the grounds of a state park where a religious sect once had a colony back in the 1800s. The park goes simply by The Village. The buildings have been repurposed as guest accommodations, and there's a restaurant that's well-loved by locals and tourists alike. The grounds are large, over three thousand acres, with a designated nature preserve. The inmates are housed at one end of the park and serve a vital role in maintaining the buildings and the preserve. It's located only about an hour away from here.

The Superintendent's name leaps off the page at me.

Oh yeah, now we're talking.

SAM

9

I'm looking forward to wrapping up the next forty-eight hours before leaving on a fishing trip with my brother and nephews. It's been some time since I indulged myself with days off. Friends joke that my idea of a vacation is coming back late from lunch.

The phone rings and I absentmindedly pick up. "Sam Murry."

"Hi, Sam. Bonnie Ziegler."

A voice from the past. Now I'm focused. At one time, Bonnie and I had a relationship. It ended amiably and mutually. I haven't talked to her in some time, but her voice brings back memories. Mostly good, now that I think of it. I really liked her.

"Hey Ziegler. What's up?" I wince. I tried to think of something clever, but that's what spit from my mouth.

"I need to talk with you about a referral."

"You still in the Regional office?"

"Yep, still there."

"You know we're a step-down program, right? The first call I usually get is from the referring facility, not Classification."

"This isn't a step-down. It's a front-end placement. Sentencing is today."

I lean back in my chair and switch ears so I can reach for my coffee. "Not our thing."

"But it's not prohibited. I mean... you can do it."

For some reason, I like annoying her. "Maybe. Why should I?"

"It's a unique case."

In corrections, "unique" is never good. "What's special about this guy?"

"His age."

This inmate referral must be ancient. The inmates here do manual labor to support the state park, so I don't want someone who isn't physically capable of putting in a good day's work.

"So how old is he? Is he ready for a nursing home?"

"You're still a smart ass, aren't you, Murry? You're at the wrong end of the spectrum."

"What do you mean?"

"He's young."

"How young?"

"Fourteen."

I laugh. "You gotta be joking. I'm not taking a fourteen-year-old."

"Listen we really need you to do this. He's got ..."

I cut her off. "No way. We're a step down. Most of the guys here are closer to fifty than thirty. We specialize in alcoholics. He's not an alcoholic, is he?"

"No, but ..."

I cut her off again. I can picture her fuming which brings a perverse pleasure. "Then find a spot for him that works. It's not here. Listen, I gotta get going. Good luck with that."

Fourteen years old. Geez. But it was nice talking to Bonnie. Hanging up on her probably wasn't the best move, but after she calms down maybe I'll give her a call. It would be nice to see her again.

Ten minutes later, the phone rings again. It's Thompson, my regional director. "Hey, Sam. Have you gotten a call from Classification?"

"Yes, and the answer is no. I need a fourteen-year-old here like I need a hole in my head."

"Well, I'm sure it's a shock to you, but that's what every facility says. Look, we're stuck with him, so somebody has to take him. You've got an opening, and after talking with Ziegler, you're the best spot we've got."

I make a mental note to kill Ziegler for going over my head. It's so like her.

"Who did he murder? And why in the world are you looking at minimum security? We don't even have a perimeter fence."

"He scores minimum."

"He must have a really bad lawyer."

"Regardless, he's ours now."

"Why me?"

"It's the work. You're the only minimum-security program directly affiliated with a state park. The nature-preserve folks y'all work with don't use power equipment. Even if we chose to overlook juvenile work laws, I wouldn't want to turn a fourteen-year-old loose with a chain saw or put him on a tractor mowing. Also, you're the smallest facility. Supervision should be easier, and you can make sure nothing happens to him. You don't have any sex offenders, right?"

"No one on a register."

"Tell you what, I'll make sure you don't get any while he's there."

"That's a small consolation. But we'd still have to make adjustments and move staff around."

"Okay. Do that."

"Easy for you to say." I scramble for some way to get out of this. Gene, my second in command, walks in and motions to the other line. I seize on the distraction to buy time to think.

"Hey, I got another call coming in. I'll call you right back."

"Make it quick. I need this resolved right away."

I pick up the receiver. "Murry here."

"Hello Mr. Murry. This is Judge Richard Nolan."

Uh-oh. Calls from judges are also in the not-good category. "Yes, Your Honor, what can I do for you?

"I've got a special case that Bonnie Ziegler is handling. She explained about your program and it sounds perfect for our situation."

I sigh. I'm beginning to see the writing on the wall. It reads, *you're screwed.* And by none other than Bonnie Ziegler. "So I hear."

"Yeah, I know. You don't want him, but I'd really appreciate it if you'd give the boy a look. I'm told you're a former policeman, is that right?"

"It is."

"Well, this boy's father was an officer killed in the line of duty."

I pause. "You're playing dirty."

He laughs. "I know, but the kid's been in the adult jail here too long, and we need to get him in a place more suitable. He's not hard-core by any stretch."

I ask the sixty-four-dollar question. "So, what's he done?"

"In a nutshell, he pulled off an escape from a secure juvenile detention center and stole a car while on the run."

A runner, swell. "You know he can book out of here any time. We're wide open."

"Everyone I've talked to seems to think he's ready to stay put. I believe he got more than he bargained for out of his little adventure."

"Does he have family close by? He might just take off and go home."

"Well, that's the other thing. He doesn't have family. Look on the bright side, you won't have to put up with family bugging you. I don't think he'll be much trouble."

I think to myself, *Oh, he'll be trouble.* But I know when I'm beat. "All right, I'll take him on a trial basis."

"Thanks. I'll owe you one."

"I'll remember that."

I call Thompson back. "That was the presiding judge. I can see I'm getting stuck with this."

"That'll be a relief to the other facilities. They've been calling all morning about why they aren't appropriate. And look, take him for now. I'll see if I can't get him moved somewhere else when I have more time to work on it."

"Better make it quick because I'm guessing he'll bug out within the week. I'll call Ziegler on the particulars."

"Great, now I can move to the next crisis of the day. Would you like a three-hundred-sixty-pound armed robber? Tried to escape in his wheelchair."

"Pass." I think a second. "But I'd take him over this kid."

"Nice try. Bye."

I take a deep breath and call Ziegler back to eat some crow. "Is there anybody else you've lined up to call me?"

She sounds smug. "That depends. Are you taking him?"

"I don't seem to have much choice, do I?"

She says in a sing-song voice, "Somebody has to take him, might as well be you."

A cartoon pops in my head of someone beseeching God after something terrible has happened saying, *why me?* And God replies, *why not?* "When is he being transported?"

"Tomorrow morning."

I'm shaking my head, even though I know she can't see it. "No."

"Tomorrow or the judge calls you back. Then Galloway, the kid's attorney."

"Him, I'd like to talk to. All kidding aside, give me to the end of the week before you ship. I need to get things lined up."

"Tomorrow. Hey, it's more than I got. I just heard his name for the first time a few hours ago."

"So, what is his name?"

"Kelly Morgan. I'm still working on getting all the paperwork together. I'll come out tomorrow before he arrives and bring the file. Maybe you can contact the local school system and see if they can set up something for him. He's smart. Oh, and something else you should know."

"I can't wait."

"He's a vegetarian. You'll need to make accommodations."

"You're pulling my leg."

"Afraid not."

"He's probably just yanking everyone's chains."

"I wouldn't bank on that. And they tried the old 'if he gets hungry, he'll eat what's put in front of him' thing at the jail. Didn't work. He almost ended up in the hospital."

"Okay. I'm sure we have the best food of any program in the state because we get it prepared by the same state employees that make the park's restaurant food. The Village folks are serious about their vegetables and corn bread. He won't starve. Any other medical issues?"

"Not that I know of. I can only give you a few other observations. He's a rural kid. He's ... I don't know ... *different.* He seems rather fragile. Think of Bambi. Try not to frighten him to death."

"What do you think I'm going to do to him?"

"I don't know. You can be kind of scary."

"Don't worry. I think I can handle this. I started out in juvenile work. I was just hoping it could stay forever dormant."

"I'm sure you've gotten worse folks through the door than this kid. You'll probably thank me some day."

"I doubt that. See you in the morning." I smile. "Wear that red dress you used to have."

"In your dreams."

"Oh, so you know about that?"

"Shut up, Sam. Or my next call is to Human Resources."

"Roger that."

I put the phone back in the cradle. Darn, if I'm not looking forward to seeing Ziegler tomorrow. I'd almost forgotten how feisty she is.

I make one more call. This one to cancel my fishing trip. My brother is going to be pissed, but no way can I dump this situation on Gene. We're a small staff, so second in command isn't saying much. Gene worked in corrections till he retired. He and his wife had big plans to travel and see the world. Within four months of his retirement date, his wife passed away. He says he came back to work after he got bored playing golf all day, but I'm sure other factors came into play. I bring him up to date on our expected admission, and we start planning how to pull this off.

"You want me to go next door and assign a bed to him? Should we pretend he's just another inmate?" Gene asks.

I rub my forehead. "Hell, if I know. I'm toying with the idea of putting him on the third floor to help us get a handle on what we're working with."

The first floor of this building is administration offices. On the second floor, there are apartments for Gene and me, split by a hall big enough to be its own apartment. Free room and board is a big perk for this job since the pay is lousy. The third floor is tiny, basically an attic. The stairs end at a small landing with a room on each side. Before corrections took over this building, they were Village guest rooms, so each has a bathroom. We've used them sometimes for inmate quarantine cases or corrections staff needing an overnight stay. The rooms are tucked up under the eaves with a slanting ceiling on two sides. Not a lot of headroom, but for our newest admission, that shouldn't be a problem.

Gene nods then says, "Not a bad idea, although I'm never excited when we have an inmate in the building right under our noses. Off time isn't as off."

"Yeah, I know. But this way we'll know he's safe. I'd like to keep him underfoot and watch for a few days to see if anyone shows too much interest in him. Plus, he's most likely to run when he first gets here. This way, rather than have him on the ground floor in the barracks, he'd be up there where it's way too high to go out the window."

"Alright, sounds like a plan. Let me grab some sheets for the bed."

We traipse upstairs. I stop halfway, thinking about the details. We already have motion detectors and cameras in the halls. I'll make sure and point them out to the little cretin, so he knows we have eyes on him. I use a key to open the door on the right. "Let's put him on this side. We'll make him leave the door open when he's in the room, and I'm going to get a monitor so we'll have ears on him as well."

Gene scratches his head. "Are you ordering through a corrections catalogue? That'll take a while."

I smile. "Nope, I'll pick one up today. I'm getting a baby monitor. My sister has one and it seems efficient."

Gene grins. "A baby monitor. Lordy, this is going to be interesting."

KELLY

10

Henry brings me something to eat. I'm nervous but also bored, so I nibble on it, as much for something to do than for hunger. After I've finished, the door opens, and a tall lady comes in. She's very pretty; I notice that straight away. There are women guards at the jail, but they're in uniform, so it's nice seeing a lady in regular clothes.

She explains she's doing a report for the court that will decide my placement. Henry told me about this. I know I need to be careful what I tell her, but when it's all over, I realize I wasn't careful at all. She wasn't just pretty, she was funny, and I let down my guard. I prattled on about Wyoming and she probably thinks I'm nuts. Now, I'll go to a place for mental patients. Good thing she can't read what I wrote for Professor Hill.

After she leaves, I sit forever. Henry comes back in to keep me company between his other court business and brings me a magazine. It's *Better Home and Gardens*. I take it and look up at him with an eyebrow raised.

"Sorry, best I could do. I ripped it out of the lunchroom."

"That's okay, I'm desperate." I glance at the guard at the door and turn the magazine to the side. It's got staples in it, so I'm worried he might confiscate it, but he looks almost as bored as I am and doesn't pay me any attention.

I'm glad I got to keep it. It's full of normal people doing normal things—gardening, going on trips, cooking. People, whose biggest concerns are if the restaurant is good and what to do if they get aphids on their houseplants. What would it be like to have a life like that?

Just when I think I'm going to be in here till nighttime, Henry comes and tells me it's time to go back in the courtroom. This time my plea is accepted. The judge looks at me with benevolent pity as he prepares the hammer blow and pronounces my sentence.

I knew what was coming, but when I hear him say, "five years," it's like I've been kicked in the gut. There's more legal talk, but the voices fade away.

There's a big window to my right. I can see a large section of downtown with people moving around. Somebody bikes by and I play the what's-the-last-time-I-did-that game. The Haverlys had a bike in the garage Pop fixed up for me, and I'd pedal through the neighborhood and around the park. I wonder how they're doing and if they remember me. Is it true once you know how to ride a bike, you always do? I wonder if they took someone who was eighty and hadn't ridden since he was six, if he really could?

Henry gives me a nudge and inclines his head to the bench where the judge is giving me an odd look. Can you be put in time-out for not paying attention in court?

The judge asks, "Do you understand what's happened here?"

I nod yes. The judge's eyes flick to Henry. "Well, I'm not sure you do, but I'm sure Mr. Galloway will explain it to you."

I leave the courtroom knowing I'll be a prisoner till I'm sixteen. That seems a long, long time away, but it sounds lots better than eighteen and I'm not going to dwell on it. The important thing is I'm getting out of jail. For a second, I think about Mrs. Williams and wonder where I'd be if I hadn't run away. I shake my head to get rid of the thought; it doesn't matter now.

Back at the jail, the officers want to know what happened in court, so I tell them I'm going to minimum security.

Mr. Rawlings looks satisfied. "Minimum is good. I'm glad for you. Did they give you any idea when?"

"Tomorrow maybe. Mr. Galloway said he'd know later today."

"That's unusually fast."

I give a faint smile. "I'm an unusual case."

They all smile. Apparently, that's funny.

I go to my cell and get the book I've been reading, but the lines keep swimming and I give it up. My thoughts keep churning. I'm glad to have one big hurdle, the courtroom, behind me. And I'm thrilled about leaving. But the unknown is a big gaping hole that's out there waiting to swallow me up. *Please let it be better than here.*

Time ticks by with no news. Maybe this means I won't get moved tomorrow after all. Another twenty-four hours sounds excruciating now that I'm all fired up to go. Thankfully, an officer sticks his head in and tells me Mr. Galloway is here. As soon as I'm in the visitation area, I zero in on Henry's face for a clue, as I pull out the chair opposite him. He looks relaxed. A good sign.

He gives me a smile. "Great news, buddy. It's all set."

I sink into the chair with relief.

Henry's smile gets bigger. "I talked to Ms. Ziegler and she told me where you'll go. She even gave me some things I can show you."

He pulls some brochures out of his ever-present briefcase and taps them on the table, reminding me of our first meeting. "It looks good to me and I hope you'll think so too." He puts them in front of me, side by side. "The facility is inside a state park. Inmates do the maintenance work there." He touches the two brochures on the right. "These brochures are about the park itself, so you can get an idea what it looks like."

The black and white pamphlet on my left has a state seal with the words *Department of Corrections* at the top. I read the title, *Guidelines for Minimum Security Inmates*. The first line states: *Minimum custody affords the inmate a more relaxed atmosphere.* I try to wrap my head around this. I, Kelly Morgan, will be a minimum-security inmate. I swallow and read on. *This classification requires the ability to work satisfactorily with minimal supervision.* There's lots more there, but the color brochures are what draw my attention next.

I pick up the one with *The Village* in bold letters across the top. One picture shows several big old stone buildings with a gravel road lined by stone walls and tall trees. Rolling hills form a backdrop behind the buildings, and everything is incredibly green. Smack dab in the middle, is a farm wagon being pulled by a couple of large draft horses.

My eyes fixate on the horses. How long since I sat on a horse? Since I even touched one? My breath catches in my throat. Henry is grinning like he just gave someone a present he knows they'll like, and he can't wait for them to rip off the wrapping paper.

He reaches over and squeezes my arm, "Yeah, sport. Pay dirt at last."

The other brochure shows a lake with geese. When I open it at the middle, it turns into a big map. The top is titled *The Trails of The Village*. Pictures run down the sides. A couple of people hiking. A waterfall. A group on horseback walking across a creek. My heart begins racing, but a cautionary voice pops into my head...

This is too good to be true.

Henry quits grinning and leans over the table. "It's a lot to take in, isn't it?"

I look at him and realize I'm biting my lower lip, so I stop, and try to say something but nothing will come. I manage to croak out, "When?"

"In the morning, a driver will come for you." He pauses and looks at me intently. "Kelly, I want to tell you something. You can do this. I believe in you. You need to believe in you too. I know at your age this seems an eternity but it's not. You have a whole life ahead of you. The most important thing is to stay there no matter what. If you leave, really bad things could happen. No, let me rephrase that. Really bad things *will* happen. You would get years added to your sentence and go to a real prison."

I start to speak, but he holds up his hand. "You need to plan ahead because at some point you're going to get upset or mad or terribly homesick and want to walk away. You're going to have to be sure to put the brakes on. I'm still your guy. Something happens, you call me and I'll be right there."

I hadn't thought about not seeing Henry regularly anymore. I feel the loss. Alone, again. A whole new set of people I don't know and who don't know me. Looking at Henry's concerned face, I know I can give him what he wants.

"I can't thank you enough for all you've done for me. I promise you I'm not going to run." I hesitate. "I just want to make the best of this. I'll think of it like going into the army and serving a two-year enlistment."

"That's a good way to look at it. And I'm not kidding when I say, I've still got your back. I'm going to come out there tomorrow afternoon to see you and look at the place myself."

"Really?" I feel a rush of relief.

"Absolutely. I'll see you in twenty-four hours, okay?"

After I'm taken back to the pod, Officer Bishop comes over. I hear you'll be leaving in the morning."

"Yes, that's what they told me."

He sighs and says. "Look, it's a rule that anyone who knows he's being discharged has to spend the last night in isolation. I'm sorry, that's just the way it is."

It takes a second for what he's saying to sink in. Now I know why I never got to tell any of the other guys goodbye. I thought they had all just walked out the door, but now I know most of them went to isolation like I'm about to. His being sorry doesn't make it any easier for me.

"Can I ask why?"

"If someone knows they're leaving, they might use it as a time to settle a score or sometimes another inmate wants to do the settling and knows it's their last chance. It's become standard operating procedure. I need you to strip down your cell, before we take you to isolation. They'll take you straight from there to the transport bay in the morning."

There's nothing to do but as he says.

My notebooks and pens are the only things I have other than one of the jail's library books. When I try to take it, he says no. "Only your personal things go with you." I drop the book on the bunk. It makes a soft thud.

We go to where a line of cells faces the hall, where there's no day room or common area. This is the mysterious security section where the troublemakers from our pod disappear to. A guy in one of the cells starts banging on the door. Mr. Bishop goes to the door on the right and I feel weak. I don't want to go in, but I have no choice. Once I'm in, I keep my back to him.

"Staff will look in on you. Dinner will be brought in pretty soon."

I can't help but feel betrayed, which is stupid because I know better than to think anybody cares about me. It's a job, nothing personal. Tomorrow, there will be a new inmate, then another. We're all faceless.

"I won't be here in the morning, so I'll say 'bye' now. Good luck," he says, and then he slides the door shut with that horrible sound like an axe striking metal.

I should try to just sleep away the next few hours, but I'm too keyed up to try. There's nothing to do but think. My mind wants to go back in time, but I clamp it down. Think about the future, this is where it begins. I picture myself as a hermit, a solitary writer, standing on a mountain. When I'm old, maybe none of this will matter.

I pull out the pictures of the brochures of The Village and wish I could enter them like I used to be able to. I can't do that anymore, but I can imagine in a day or so I'll be standing right there. I might touch those horses and put my hand in that lake. I squeeze my hand like I can already feel the water sliding through my fingers.

Then my mind jumps to other things. The faces of the guards, the other inmates, the things that can happen. My stomach lurches at the thought of the possibilities. Okay, quit dwelling on bad things. That won't get you through the night.

Dinner comes, pushed through the slit in the door. I have little interest but take a glance. It's tomato soup, some sort of sandwich, a blood red square of gelatin. Looking at it turns my stomach. I take the carton of milk and leave the rest.

I sit on the bunk with my back to the door. There's no window to look out of here. I try going to sleep but sleep just won't come. The place is strange and the guy in the other cell keeps screaming and moaning. Occasionally, I hear a CO hollering at him to shut the fuck up. And then a new thought enters my head. What if something happens tonight and screws up my release tomorrow? I think I'd just keel over and die if that happened, so I decide to remain awake at all cost.

A CO comes for the food tray. I have to pick it up and hand it through the slot. There's a congealed layer of red fat on top of the soup next to the dried-out sandwich, so I close my eyes to block the sight and keep from gagging.

"Don't you want to eat?" the CO asks.

"I'm not hungry."

"Okay. You alright?"

"Yes." Stupid question. I'm never alright.

The long night creeps by. A panicky feeling comes over me off and on. When it does, I lay on the floor and look up. The ceiling looks higher that way, like the space is bigger than it is. I take deep breaths. I count backwards from one hundred and try to remember multiplication tables and softly sing a few songs. The singing makes me sleepy so I quit, but just as I can't help but begin to doze, breakfast is brought. That's good, a time marker. I don't even look at it.

Sometime later, two COs come to my door. One voice sounds familiar. It's the higher in command guy. As the door opens, I hear him say, "Says on the log he didn't eat last night either."

He steps in a foot or two and asks, "You okay?"

I nod. Funny how not talking for hours makes you feel like you forget how.

"Don't you want to eat something? It's a long time till lunch."

I shake my head no. He gives me a considering look then steps back out and talks quietly to someone. I worry I'm in trouble. They can't make me stay here because I didn't eat, can they? My heart starts thudding. I always manage to get in trouble without trying to.

The guy talks to someone else, then walks in and sets something down on the bunk next to me. I see an opened plastic bottle of Pepsi and a bag of potato chips, like from a vending machine. I look up at him in surprise and he says, "It'll still be a few hours till transport gets here. Someone will be in to start processing you out in a while."

As he turns to go, he places his hand on my upper arm for just a second. I wish he hadn't. It almost causes me to come apart.

I sit back to continue waiting. I raise the bottle of Pepsi and take a long drink. It's ice cold and tastes great. So my stomach says, *I'll try those chips.* I lick the first one thoroughly, tasting the salt, before I bite a small corner off and chew. And then, I chew a lot more before swallowing. I eat about half the bag this way but quit when I start to feel queasy.

I put my back against the wall, my feet on the bunk, clasp my arms around my knees and rest my head on my legs. All of a sudden, I feel very tired, but stay sitting up so I can't go to sleep. I catch myself a couple of times before I almost fall off the bunk.

Finally, the door opens, and a CO tells me it's time to get ready. They hand me some clothes none of which match, but they are real clothes, not a uniform, so who cares? The CO sees me looking and says, "Yeah, I know. They aren't the best, but you weren't admitted with street clothes, so these are just for the trip. I'm sure they'll have something else when you get there. Go ahead and get changed."

I finish getting processed out then get put in a small holding room near the car bay to wait. Waiting means thinking and that leads to being scared. I remember my favorite line from *The Crystal Cave* book: *The Gods only go with you if you put yourself in their path. And that takes courage.*

I decide to be brave.

KELLY

11

The door opens and the CO is standing with a man in a different uniform who has on dark sunglasses. The new guy says, "I'm Officer Mullins. I'll be transporting you this morning. Bonnie Ziegler told me to take good care of you today. You ready to go?"

I nod. I'm not sure I'll ever talk again.

He pulls out a pair of handcuffs but thankfully cuffs me in front. As I hear the clicking noise and feel them tighten around my wrists, I wonder if maybe, just maybe, this will be the last time for this. It's a humiliation I've never gotten used to.

We step into the big bay area where my carriage awaits. No pumpkins or mice. Just a white sedan. The thought of getting in the car makes me so excited I feel almost dizzy. He opens the back door and I settle in behind the wire cage. "Put your seat belt on," he instructs me.

Officer Mullins gets in the front seat and scribbles on a clipboard, as the garage door slowly rolls up and light pours in. Last night's nerves are gone, lost in the thrill of being on the move for the first time in almost seven months. The car moves forward and turns onto a road. All I can think is, *I'm out, I'm out, I'm out.*

It's a sunny day. I want to look but it hurts my eyes, so I'm forced to look down. Eventually, they adjust, and I can look out the window as we wind through town. At a stoplight, I see kids about my age walking down the street wearing team shirts. They have soft drink cups in their hands. They're probably coming or going from a ball game.

Looking at those kids, I think that should be my life. I shouldn't be in this car that belongs to the state. My gaze moves to the car next to ours and I notice a lady looking at me. I realize she can see the state insignia on the car door and

149

the wire cage between the seats, so I immediately look down at my feet. I'm glad when we leave the city and get on the interstate. No more prying eyes. I enjoy going fast and watching the guardrail as it ribbons by.

Moving, moving, moving. Going somewhere.

The sky is vivid blue with big white fluffy clouds—the kind where you imagine God took a straw and blew in a vanilla shake to bubble them up. It's early spring, my favorite time of year, when the earth comes alive. It's coming alive much earlier than it would in Wyoming.

Everywhere I look, it's green. The sunlight streams in the window, and I put my hand in the beam where it shows all my veins. This is real light, not the fake stuff I've been enduring. For the first time in months, I revel in the feeling of being truly warm. It feels so good I find myself nodding off. I don't want to arrive dead tired, so I speak for the first time since yesterday afternoon. "Is it okay if I sleep?"

To most people, this might seem like a stupid question, but I've gotten used to having to ask permission for most anything. The driver looks at me in the rearview mirror. "Go ahead. I'll wake you when we get close. It'll be about an hour."

I lean against the door, trying to find a spot the seat belt doesn't get in the way. I have to pull it down with my handcuffed hands and hold it to keep it from cutting into my neck as I lean into that special space where the window meets the back of the seat. The hum of the car's wheels on the road is hypnotic. It feels like the times I slept in the back seat while my father drove, feeling safe in his hands.

Now I know there's no such thing as being safe. At any time, something bad can happen. If he hadn't gotten killed, I know I wouldn't be here. At the same time, I'm glad he doesn't know what's happened to me, because he would be so horrified. He'd feel really guilty.

Well, maybe he should.

My fingernails dig into my palms as my hands clench. It's a horrible thought and I don't know where it came from. *No, no, no, I don't mean it.* I squeeze my eyes tight and turn my face into the sunbeam. In my head, I sing *Here Comes the Sun* by the Beatles.

"Hey, kid?" My eyes fly open and I bang my head against the window.

"We're just a few minutes out," Officer Mullins says.

I work hard to shake off the sleep clinging to me. My eyes adjust and the world comes into focus. The scenery is still great, but I think less about it and more about the next few hours.

I'd gotten a pep talk from another inmate a couple of days ago. Antonio was an expert. He'd been in five different juvenile facilities starting when he was twelve. "They like to mess with you on arrival," he told me. "Break ya down, ya know? Get up and holler in your ears. They'll ask you some questions, but whatever you answer will be wrong and they'll holler some more. They'll tell you 'sit up, put your shirttail in.' Better not be smiling, they don't like that, say you're not taking the program seriously." It sounded unpleasant, but it's a small price to pay for getting out of lock-up.

The road twists and turns, so I'm glad there's no food in my stomach. When I peer out the window, there's only a few yards of road between me and an incredibly steep drop off. I can see the tops of trees waving in the breeze. A river winds and bends through a steep gorge.

"Wow," slips out.

Mullins smiles. "Pretty isn't it?" He doesn't wait for an answer and says, "This is the first time I've ever had a juvenile go to minimum. How did you manage that?"

I give a half grin. "I had a good lawyer." I close my eyes and take a deep breath.

The driver glances back a few times "Are you nervous?"

Why lie? "Yeah, I guess so."

"The guys that run the place are good. Just do what they tell you and you'll get along fine."

"That's my plan."

I start to mentally rehearse the intake to come. I've been through enough of them to know they aren't about you; they're about making sure you're going to cause the least amount of trouble for staff. It's the place to make a good impression, to figure out what they want to hear and give it to them. It can be a little tricky. Too little eye contact and you look shifty, too much and you look defiant. In between, you have to look like you aren't sucking up, especially if you are.

Brown signs appear that announce *The Village State Park, 2 miles ahead*. My heart rate picks up as the driver turns in the big gate with stone pillars on either side. The butterflies that calmed down during the talk with the driver start fluttering again.

We come to a stop in front of a tall stone building with lots of big windows which are gleaming in the morning sun. The driver grabs his clipboard and steps out slamming his door and walking back to open mine. Out of the blue, time stands still. I become hypersensitive to everything I see and hear, and for one horrible second, I worry I'll burst out in tears. It's more than fear of physical harm. It's the fear that who I've been to this point will fade out of existence, like I'm going to be rubbed out.

I've lost everybody else in my life. Will I lose "me" too?

SAM

12

I've been in a foul mood all morning as I make accommodations, shifting schedules and revising plans. My well-ordered world got a wrench tossed into it. What makes it the most irritating is it's probably all wasted energy. The kid is likely to hightail it out of here before the week is out. Kids are by nature impulsive and he's a runner, a hard habit to break.

I just hope when he leaves, he doesn't try to take someone's car with him. I need to remind Village staff to keep their cars locked and keys safely stowed away. I'd given them a heads up and they weren't too happy about the change in the type of usual inmate. Over my years here, I've built up some credibility with the park staff. This kid better not ruin it.

Ziegler arrives and helps herself to some of my just-made coffee. She didn't wear the red dress, more's the pity, but she looks good in the black pants and boots that show off her long legs. Her hair's a little longer than the last time I saw her, but it's the same warm auburn color. She'd once threatened to go blonde and I'm happy she didn't. My favorite part of her is her face. Not the way it's put together, although I have no complaints, but the way it constantly moves, going from teasing to serious to exasperated and back in two seconds flat. She'd be a lousy poker player.

I try to keep my concentration on business. "So, where's the file?"

She stirs in three packs of sugar, slowly, making a production of it. "Give me a minute for a caffeine fix and I'll get it."

I know her. She's stalling. But if I push, she'll just push back, so I opt for patience.

I try and busy myself with routine paperwork, but I've got one eye peeled on the road waiting for the car. It's easy to see when it appears, the standard white Crown Vic with the state insignia. The driver, Steve, has delivered here before.

He opens the car's back door and I get my first look at our newest inmate. Bonnie joins me at the window.

I turn to her. "Good God, what does he have on?"

She grimaces. "Obviously, they had some trouble finding him something to wear."

Everything the kid has on is at least three sizes too large. What's worse, everything is completely mismatched. He has a pullover soccer shirt that's blue and yellow swirls. The gym pants are green with a bright red stripe running down each leg. He doesn't have any shoes. I wonder if they took them, because he tried to run. He does have on socks. One black, one white.

Gene walks over for a look. "Little kid in handcuffs. What a world we live in."

They start up the steps, the boy's head down watching the stairs, so all I see is his shaggy dark hair. I turn from the window to look at Bonnie. "What have you done to me?"

She smiles that vicious smile of hers. It's a turn on. "Nothing you don't deserve."

When they reach our room, the driver waves the boy on in before nodding at me and raising the clipboard. I know the drill and sign for the "package."

I'm a big guy. Six-four. My nose is crooked from being broken at least twice when I played college baseball. I have a scar on my chin from my police force days when I was on the wrong end of a broken beer bottle. I know I look intimidating and I've cultivated it. I expect the boy to look away, squirm, or put on a show of bravado. But no. All I get is his steady quiet gaze fixed on my face.

He's a cute kid, even with these ridiculous clothes and lopsided haircut. Big brown eyes. Crap, if Bambi doesn't pop into my head. Damn that Bonnie and her word association. But the look I'm getting is like a cornered animal waiting to see if the hunter is going to pull out a gun. I've been in this business long enough to see other things in those eyes. Pain and fear. Like the adult inmates next door, he's someone who lives in constant anticipation of life's next blow.

I wipe the frown off my face, because I can tell I'm scaring him. I rock back on my heels as I peer down at him, trying to look non-threatening. "Hey there."

He manages a smile, a timid one that doesn't hold. "Hi."

Steve pulls out a key and removes the handcuffs. The boy never breaks eye contact with me. His hands, now freed, drop to his sides.

"I'm Mr. Murry. This is Mr. Simmons. You can go with him a minute while I sign some things." Scribbling my name on the form, I glance at Steve. "Any trouble? No shoes. Did he try to run?"

"He was fine. I think he's kind of scared, but I told him he'd be alright." He gives me a look that seems to seek assurance he didn't lie. This kid seems to stack up allies left and right. Either that or everyone has a lower opinion of me than I ever knew.

"Considering he's our first juvenile, we plan on foregoing the usual beatings."

That earns a grin from Steve. "No shoes because they couldn't find him any. They thought with today's weather, he'd be okay without them. In other words, they decided to let you worry about it."

"What did they do, dress him from a dumpster?"

"I think they raided lost and found as well as their own lockers."

"Personal things?"

"Only these." He hands me notebooks. Usually family will provide supplies from our list of allowed items that help inmates live a little more comfortably. This kid is coming in blank, not even spare change.

After Steve departs for his next trip, I flip open the top notebook. I do it without a qualm. There's no privacy in corrections. The pages are filled with writing but it's in Spanish. The other booklet has lots of little notes and drawings, the pages filled with horses running, standing still, jumping. What makes them different from other horse drawings I've seen is the expressions on their faces. That and they have little conversation bubbles coming out of their mouths. I find myself smiling down at them and wanting to know what they're saying. *Shit, Sam, what does it matter? Get back to business.* With a grimace, I shut the notebook and go join the others.

Usually I talk with new admissions, then have them change into a uniform but his outfit is driving me crazy. "Gene, I can't talk to him while he's dressed like this. See what we've got for him."

Gene gives a little one finger salute and heads down the hall. The boy won't quit staring at me. I'm saved by Bonnie. "Well, Kelly, this is a better place than our last meeting, wouldn't you say?"

The boy slowly smiles at her. It completely changes his face and suddenly he looks less like a wounded animal and more like what he is—a young boy. The smile reaches his eyes, temporarily erasing the pain. Those eyes shift from Bonnie to out the door where the sun illuminates the new spring greenery.

"It's beautiful," he says softly.

Bonnie's eyes go to mine and she makes a little *awww* expression. I can see she's let this kid get to her. She should know better.

Gene shows up with the clothes. I wave the boy over. "Come on in here." I open the door to a smaller room with a bathroom on the side. "Do you need the restroom first?"

He nods yes and passes in front of me, giving me a wide berth.

I look to see Ziegler is making herself comfortable. "Are you heading on or sticking around?"

She smiles. "I think there might be a free lunch at the end, so I'm hanging here."

"That's *not* why you're staying."

"True. I wouldn't miss this for the world. I think there's a good chance I can get an 'I told you so.'"

"Don't get your hopes up."

Before I can say more, the kid emerges. I tell Bonnie we'll be out in a minute and shut the door. She understands the process. The boy came straight from the jail, so odds are he doesn't have any contraband, but we search all new admissions. I can tell from looking at him, the kid knows the drill, so I don't bother with explanations. "Get undressed."

I'm shocked at how he looks once those way too big clothes come off. Every rib shows. Underweight doesn't begin to describe it. Unlike most of our inmates, he has no tattoos, but I can see the very visible scar on his left arm.

Gene's eyes meet mine. He's as appalled as I am but manages to sound matter of fact. "I've got two pant sizes. Let's try the smaller of the two." No shit, Sherlock.

Still too big for him, but better than what he had. We have nothing else, so it'll have to do unless we wrap him in a towel. I take a shirt in my hand, but before I give it to him, I open the door and motion to Bonnie with my head. I want her to see what she's giving me. She takes one look and gets her "I'm going to kick-ass" face. Some people have some explaining to do.

I hand the kid the shirt. It's a short sleeve button down which takes him forever to fasten because his hands are shaking so much. Is he that scared?

Although too large, the new clothes make a big difference in his appearance. Khaki pants and a button-down polo shirt with "The Village" written on the pocket. We had to get female sizes from The Village staff inventory. The only difference between the staff's uniforms and inmates is the color of the shirt. Green for staff, gray for inmates. I'll have to special-order a uniform.

I wonder if he feels some pleasure being in regular clothing. You'd think it would have been embarrassing for a teenager to stand there in that ridiculous outfit, but he hadn't acted like it bothered him at all.

"Here's some boots. They'll have to do for today." Female staff again. Fortunately, they are a close enough fit. As soon as he gets them on, I tell him, "Come on over here."

I put him into the chair beside my desk chair with him on my left. I don't want the desk as a physical buffer between us. Gene and Ziegler take seats where he'll be aware of them but won't be in his direct line of sight. Turning to Ziegler, I pin her with a look. "Do I get the file?"

"Oh sure, here you go." She gets up and takes a few steps then leans over to hand it to me. She has a very innocent look on her face which sends up a red flag. She never looks innocent. What's she up to?

To the boy, I say, "Since you came so quickly from court, I haven't had a chance to look at this, so give me a moment, then we'll talk."

"Take all the time you need," he says, and for a moment I think maybe he's being a smart aleck. But no, he looks at me apologetically, like sorry you were inconvenienced.

The information contained in the pre-sentencing report, together with what I learn from talking with a new admission, should assess their strengths and problems as well as gauge the person's readiness to change. I flip open the file. It should be arranged chronologically, with most recent entries on top. At a glance, I can tell this one is reversed. The first pages are newspaper clippings. *Sheriff's son only survivor of horrific crash*, reads the headline. There's a picture of everyone taken hours before the wreck. The next picture is the boy at the funeral with his arm in a cast from shoulder to wrist.

I look to where Bonnie is sitting and shoot her a condemning look. She gives me a bright innocent smile and cocks her head like, *yes, something wrong?*

"This seems to be out of order."

"Oh, yeah? New secretary. I'll have a talk with her."

"You do that." I tilt the file to make sure the boy can't see what I'm looking at. I don't think he's moved a muscle since he sat down. "So, do you want us to address you as Mr. Morgan, like we do the other men, or Kelly because you, well, are younger?"

"Kelly."

I nod. "Okay, Kelly. What brings you to my door this morning?"

He pauses and I think for a second he might say a Crown Vic, but he doesn't say anything. I know how to ask a question and wait, so I say nothing. He stares ahead frowning then looks at me and says apologetically, "Sorry, I'm thinking."

"Take all the time you need."

That gets a fleeting half-smile. "I have lots of that, don't I?"

Funny, but not like he's trying to be. Bonnie's hand comes over her mouth and I work to ignore her. Thirty seconds roll by. The silence doesn't seem to cause any anxiety for him. I hear the steady distant drone of an airplane. I continue to wait him out. The clock ticking on the wall sounds especially loud.

He wrinkles his brow and his eyes roll up, then seeming to come to a decision, he focuses on me and says, "I'd have to say poor impulse control." Then as an afterthought, he adds, "And a good run of bad luck." He gives an assessing look, like, *is that okay?*

"Where did you come up with poor impulse control?"

"One of the officers at the jail was taking college classes in criminology. I saw his text book. It said most prisoners exhibit poor impulse control. I'm afraid that describes me. I guess I'm a typical inmate."

I want to laugh. Typical inmate? God help us. "I see." What I think is, what fourteen-year-old boy doesn't have poor impulse control? "So how about the bad luck thing?"

"Oh, that. Maybe it's a sign I'm not accepting responsibility..." Surely another quote out of the textbook. "...but it's kind of a surprise to me I'm here." He shrugs as if his story doesn't matter. But of course, it does. It has shaped his life.

"Well, I'm glad to hear you say that. I'd hate to think this was your life plan."

He gives a tentative smile, like he's not sure if I was kidding or not.

I thumb through more pages of the file trying to stay one step ahead of the conversation. The boy continues to sit like a stone with his hands in his lap.

"You know the purpose of this report that Ms. Ziegler prepared, and the reason we're sitting here talking now, is so I know more about you. That's important since you'll be here for some time. It will help us make decisions that can help you in the long run. Do you understand that?"

"Yes, sir."

"I know things in the past can be painful to talk about but necessary."

He nods and for the first time looks down. He knows where this is heading.

"I want to ask you about the accident. You know about dominos, don't you? How you stack them up and knock one over and the others all fall?" A nod. "So, the accident is the first domino, the one that leads to you sitting here with me right now, do you agree?"

Faintly, "Yes, sir."

"Have you talked about it with anyone before?"

"Not really." He hesitates. "There was this lady, a counselor at the boarding school I went to after the accident. We talked a little."

"What did she say?"

"Honestly, I don't remember a lot." Another hesitation. "Just this thing about a box."

"A box?"

"Yes, she said that sometimes it's too overwhelming after something bad happens to deal with it at the time, so people put it away, like in a box on the top of a closet. They put it up there and one day when they're ready, they take it down and open it."

"That's interesting. I think I like this counselor."

"Yes, she was nice. She said it was okay to put it away for a while, in fact maybe better in the short run."

"And in the long run?"

He takes a breath. "That someday you have to open it, because if you don't, it'll find a way off the shelf and open itself when you least expect it."

I pause a second and this time I'm the one initiating the eye contact. "So, where's your box?"

The pain has returned to his eyes. "Still on the shelf."

"I can understand. I'm sorry for your loss. That was a terrible thing." He looks at his hands, studying them. I wait a few seconds. "Maybe now's not the right time to talk about that day... unless you want to?"

"I don't, and anyway, I don't remember any of it."

"Okay, let's talk about after that. You went to, let's see, a grandfather in Philadelphia, right?"

"Yes, sir."

"Tell me about that."

He doesn't say anything. He stares at the pencil holder on my desk as if there might be some comfort there. Again, I wait. And wait. I get the idea he thinks I'll start to hurry things along, so he won't have to answer these questions. But if it takes all day, we'll sit here. Lots of people in this business don't understand how important a good intake is. It's the critical hour.

Eventually, Kelly says, "I've never talked about it with anyone before. What do you want to know?"

"Had he been involved in your life before this?"

"No. I'd never met him till I was sent there. My father told me he and my mother didn't get along."

"How did you all get along?"

"Badly, I'm afraid. I flew there right after my father's funeral. My grandfather had someone who worked for him pick me up at the airport. I didn't see him until the next night at dinner."

I keep my face blank. *What a bastard.*

Kelly's still talking. "It was a Saturday night. He told me Monday morning I'd be taken to this prep school that was very prestigious, and he had to pull strings to get me in. He said he could because his family went back to the founding fathers and that meant something. If I was asked, I was to tell people I'm from Maryland and not mention Wyoming."

"Why not?"

"That's what I asked. He said it was a heathen state with heathen Indians. I got a little defensive, I guess. I told him my other grandfather had been half Cheyenne, which made me part Cheyenne too, and I wasn't ashamed of it."

"Yes?" I prompt.

He meets my eyes "He said he was... ashamed."

I slowly rest my chin on my hands. "That wasn't very nice."

"Yeah, I kinda knew right then and there we weren't going to be pals."

I watch him closely. I know he wants this to end. And part of me feels like I should let him off the hook. There are dark shadows under his eyes. It's his first day. He's stressed. He's tired. But the flip side of the coin is he's vulnerable, and now's the time to pry everything out of him before he can shut down.

I press on.

KELLY

13

Well, my earlier hope about blitzing through the intake was wrong. Mr. Murry acts like he has nothing better to do than talk to me all day.

"So how was the school you were sent to?"

I don't want to talk about it, but either the lack of food, the excitement of the last few days, or those quiet, non-judgmental eyes on mine, have me spilling my guts. "I don't remember much about the first weeks. Or months. I'd be sitting in class, and suddenly I'd realize where I was and didn't remember anything from earlier in the day. Not getting up, or getting dressed, any of that stuff. But I must have. Sometimes I'd look down and see a half-finished test, but I didn't remember writing anything. My grades weren't so good."

"Did you talk to anybody about these memory lapses?"

I pick at my thumb. "No."

"Why do you think you had them?"

I shrug.

Mr. Murry leans back in his chair, clasping his hands behind his neck, and looking up at the ceiling. I think he might finally be getting bored with this. *Good.* "No clue?" he asks.

I shrug again. Maybe the tactic will work this time.

Slowly he lowers his arms, looks at me, and sharpens his voice. "Make a guess."

It's a command, not a request. Alert to the sudden danger, I scramble for an answer that will satisfy him. "I guess I just sort of checked out."

Mr. Murry pins me with his eyes. "And why would you do that?"

I look out the window, like maybe the answer might be out there. "I don't know." It's a lie but now's not the time or place for the truth.

He leans in closer. "Sure, you do."

He hasn't raised his voice, if anything it's quieter, but the answer is yanked out of me. I whisper the words to give them less power. "Everybody dying."

Now he leans back and I'm glad to have my air space back. He says, "Sure. The mind can only process so much grief, right? Spacing out is a way of coping. I know if it was me, I'd be very sad. Weren't you sad?"

His x-ray eyes are on me. This is new territory. I'm used to being looked at but not really seen. This guy sees too much. I swallow and try to think how to answer, but suddenly he switches the subject.

"Did you make any friends at the school?"

Relieved to be on safer ground, I answer quickly. "Eventually I did. My arm was in a cast so I couldn't do the activities at first. Nobody paid much attention to me. Things got better with the other kids by accident."

Mr. Murry rotates his coffee cup with his hands, but his eyes stay on me. "How's that?"

"One day a teacher was yelling at this kid who was new and homesick. He'd spilled something on the floor and the teacher was going off on him. He called the kid up to the front of the room to get hit."

"Hit?"

"Yeah, he had this baton-like thing, like for conducting music. Kids would hold their hands out with the palms up and get strokes. Usually three. The kid was starting to cry. I asked, 'Is that really necessary? Couldn't he just clean it up?'" I give Mr. Murry a questioning look. "Wouldn't that make sense?"

"It would to me," he says.

"The teacher asked if I'd like to take the strokes in his place. I'm pretty sure he thought I'd say no, but I said okay. I wasn't being heroic; I just didn't really mind. It was better than watching the kid cry. "

"So, you did?"

"Yeah, but it wasn't the usual three. It may sound weird, but I didn't really feel it. I believe I smiled. That made him mad. Well, madder than he already was. Anyway, I lost track of how many times he hit me. My hand swelled up so bad, I couldn't do any work in the next class so that teacher took me to the nurse. The headmaster came in and by the time the day was over, the teacher had been fired. I usually sat at dinner by myself, but that night a bunch of kids came to eat with me."

Mr. Murry smiles. "I can't say that surprises me. You became an instant hero."

"I guess. It was kind of nice. It made school a lot better. The cast came off and I started playing baseball and made better grades. But I began at like sub-F, so even A's didn't mean I could pass but I kept trying. Then I got in trouble again." I look up at Mr. Murry. "Do you see a pattern here?"

He gives a little grin. "Maybe. Go on. What did you do?"

"It's what I didn't do. I wouldn't eat meat. The other kids asked me why and I explained how it's an animal with feelings, trying to live its own life, and how sixteen thousand animals are killed every second for food. I guess I did a good sell job, because a bunch of kids decided to quit eating meat too. We were like a club.

"The Lieutenant got mad at me, said I was setting a bad example. When the school year was over, I went back to my grandfather's, and a letter came saying I wouldn't be accepted for the next year. They suggested some other school that would be more suitable. My grandfather made fun of it. He said it was a school for sissies. He said what I needed was a stricter military school."

"Was that the end of it?"

"More or less." There, a quick and easy half-truth. I'm good at those.

But no, this guy's like a pit bull. I feel his eyes boring into me. I look away but he taps the desk with his fingers, drawing my eyes back against my will. Once I force myself to look at him, he asks, "What happened?"

I sigh. Might as well get it over with. "He got more and more worked up. He... he said I was a faggot. He yelled about how I was raised and said really bad things about my father. I told him to shut up, that my father was three times the man he could ever think about being."

I hear my voice get louder and higher, so I stop. I've said too much.

Mr. Murry is looking at me with a thoughtful expression on his face. "Go on," he says.

I wonder what he'll do if I just refuse to say anymore. I try to look clueless but know right away that strategy isn't going to work. His eyes are reaching into my brain, dissecting what I'm thinking.

There's no escape.

SAM

14

The boy gives me a please-don't-make-me look which I ignore. I press him. "I take it that didn't go over well."

"No."

I can hear a mower outside in the distance, but in here, it's deadly quiet. Gene and Bonnie aren't moving a muscle. I keep my tone conversational. I use the reporter technique. Act like you have a microphone, and you're interviewing someone for the six o'clock news.

I make a calculated guess. "How bad were you hurt?"

"Oh, nothing that serious." He waves it away like it's nothing. "A bloody nose, cut lip." A pause like he's remembering. "A black eye. After he was done, he locked me in my room."

"How long until he let you out?"

"He never did. He sent up food, but it was nothing but meat and sometimes a piece of bread. He said when I ate for three days straight, he'd let me out. So, I went out the window."

I lean a little closer in. "I'm surprised he hadn't sealed it up."

"It was three stories up, so I don't think he thought he needed to."

Oh, shit. My eyes flick to Gene's and we share the thought. Third floor? I gotta know. "How'd you manage it?"

"There was a tree right outside the window."

No trees outside his window here, but I'd still like to nail it shut even though the fire marshal would have my ass. "Where did you go?"

"The racetrack."

We inch our way through the rest of his life story. The racetrack, the juvenile detention centers, the escape and stealing the car. When we get to the crime, he looks down. "I feel bad about doing that. The old me would never have done it."

165

I toy with my pencil as we get to the crux of things. "So how else is the old Kelly different from the new one?"

"I don't know. I get confused because I'm not that person anymore. I used to be very honest, like annoyingly so."

"You're not now?"

Fatigue and the relentless questioning make him incautious. "I've become an accomplished liar. I guess it's true, practice makes perfect." He looks straight at me. I figure he's trying to determine how I'll take his confession.

"You seem to be pretty truthful with me right now."

"I'm trying to turn over a new leaf. Part of my rehabilitation to rejoin society someday."

I raise my hand to my mouth to cover a smile. More Criminology 101. "Okay, so you're going to be truthful. That's good. I'll try to be truthful with you too. I can help you by calling you out if you lie, because I'll let you in on a secret. I've been in this line of work so long, I can pretty much always spot a lie. It's like a superpower."

Kelly smiles. "One of the guards at the jail said he didn't believe ninety-percent of what he heard and fifty-percent of what he saw."

I laugh. "It's an occupational hazard. What else do you want to work on while you're here?"

"Doing what I'm told. Keeping my mouth shut." He glances up apologetically. "I've been told I talk too much."

I watch his eyes get droopier. I bet he didn't sleep at all last night. I should wrap this up. I lean toward him and rest my elbows on the desk forcing him to look at me. "I know something you can add to your behavior change list."

He gives me a wary little grin. "Just one?"

I don't smile back. I want to be sure he gets this. I wait till I capture his gaze. He nervously blinks a couple of times. Now that I know I have his full attention, I say, "It's an important one. You have got to stick around. No running away."

He nods solemnly. "I know. Mr. Galloway said the same thing."

"I'll say it anyway. We don't have a fence. There's nothing to stop you from just walking away. Running away from your problems can get to be a hard habit to break. But Kelly, the stakes are very high. If you leave here, there won't be a second chance. You can't say, oh, I didn't mean to do it. You'd be charged with escape. That'd be a whole new felony offense which would add years to your sentence. You would instantly go to a locked facility. You don't want that. And I don't want that for you."

He gives me a solemn look. "I promise I'm not going to run away."

"Does a promise mean something to you?"

He nods. "I don't have anything else, but I have my word."

His earnestness tugs at my sympathy. "Good. I'll take your promise and hold you to it. If a problem comes up while you're here, then you come to me, or Mr. Simmons, or another staff person, and we'll work it out. Okay?"

"Yes, sir."

"All right, this is probably a good spot to talk about how things will work here. Then I'll show you where you'll stay for now and we'll get some lunch."

I open the right middle drawer and pull out one of our tracking devices, looking for the smallest one, and lay it on the desk between us. The boy looks confused. Man, he's a baby to the system if he hasn't seen one of these. All of a sudden, I feel like a guy about to kick a puppy.

"This is an electronic monitor. It tracks your movements, so we know where you are and where you've been. You can shower in it but no baths. No swimming or anything else that would immerse it in water. For the next couple of weeks, you'll be sticking close to the building while we get to know you. In addition to security, this is for your safety since some of the terrain here is pretty rugged. "This," I tap the device, "will be your safety net." There, I put a positive spin on it.

I reach under the desk and pull out a stool. "Set your right foot up here." There's the slightest pause, then he does as he's told. He looks away as I fasten it on his ankle. I knew he wouldn't like it.

I blaze on, happy to change the subject. "Mealtimes can change with the seasons, but right now they're at seven-thirty, noon, and five-thirty. You need to be in the dining hall next door whether you eat or not, because we do head counts then. Do what staff tells you. That's pretty simple, isn't it?"

"Yes, sir. "

"You need to be sure you don't accidentally leave the property. The boundaries are clearly marked but I'll show you too. I pull out some forms. "I've got some things I need you to sign. This first one explains your rights. You need to sign you've received them."

I give him a pen, but his right hand is shaking so bad he can't write. He reaches over with his left to try and steady it, muttering "traitor" under his breath. If it wasn't so sad, it'd be funny.

Reaching over, I take the pen out of his hand. "We'll do these later."

He looks sheepish. "Sorry."

"Don't worry about it." I lean my arm on the desk and shift my weight, letting a few seconds go by before my next question. "Did you have breakfast this morning?"

"Yes, sir."

I put my other arm on the desk, steeple my fingers and lean in, narrowing my eyes. He looks apprehensive, as well he should. "Kelly?"

"Yes," he whispers.

"Let's try this again. Did you *eat* breakfast this morning?"

His eyes shift a fraction. "Yes."

I do a slow count to five and wait for him to squirm. He doesn't, but his shoulders are disappearing into his body. I keep my voice level. "I have to disagree with something you told me earlier. I don't think you're a good liar at all. In fact, I think you're pretty bad at it. Try again."

His cheeks flush. "They brought it, but I didn't eat it all."

You little shit. Give it up. I ask slowly one more time, "Did you eat any breakfast?" I hold up one finger before he can answer and make him look at me. "Don't lie."

His breath catches and he says in a rush, "No, I didn't eat anything."

You'd think he'd just confessed to stealing the crown jewels. I lean back. "Better. We definitely will have to work on lying. Especially when the lying seems pointless."

He blushes red. "I'm sorry. It's just my eating has been kind of a big deal to everyone. I haven't been very hungry lately."

"I'm thinking once you're outside, your appetite will come back. No one's going to try and force you to eat anything you don't want. I do think it's important you gain some weight. There are activities you can't do if you aren't in decent physical condition. Would you rather wash dishes or go outside and work in the woods?"

That gets a smile. "The woods."

"I thought so. Let's try another one. Did you sleep last night?"

His eyes lock on mine. "Not much. I dozed off some this morning after they brought breakfast, and I slept a little in the car."

There you go. I reward him with a smile and a nod. "Much better. See this honesty thing is already catching on."

His eyes soften. My smile and a hint of praise have struck the mark. That tells me tons. This boy is looking for approval. That will make things so much easier.

"Were you worried about coming here?"

He hunches his shoulders and his eyes drop down. "That was part of it, and I got moved to isolation for the night. I don't know..."

I feel a surge of pity because in those few words I know last night was hell for him. I'd forgotten about that as standard operating procedure in some jails. Couldn't they have made an exception?

He looks up at me and says quietly, "These were kind of big days for me."

I give him a slow nod. "I understand. Do you have questions for me?"

That catches him by surprise. I just handed him some power, and I'm sure he hasn't had any for a long time. He's up to the task, although I have to hide a smile when he asks, "Aren't there more rules?"

"I think that's all we need to go over right now. I'll let you know others as they come up."

There are a slew of rules about contraband and visitors, but none of them apply to him. He has no money and it doesn't look like any visitors will be dropping by, other than his attorney who Bonnie warned me is coming later today.

"This afternoon we'll talk about work assignments. And we can discuss how else you can occupy your time here in constructive ways. You don't have to wear the uniform when you're on your own time, so tomorrow we'll hit some stores and get you some regular clothes."

"I'm not sure my sizes."

"That's okay, you can try them on while we're out."

He looks confused like he heard me wrong. I smile. "Ah, I didn't explain that very well. When I say *we'll* go shopping, I mean you and me."

His mouth drops open and he blinks.

I'm enjoying the reaction. "What? Did you think you'd never leave the property while you're here? As long as you're with a staff member, you can go where we take you. So, you aren't going to be stuck out here all the time. Good news, huh?"

He smiles, nods, and a little bit of light comes into his eyes.

"You're also going to need a physical and a haircut. When was the last time you saw a doctor?"

"I saw a nurse at the jail."

"How about a dentist?"

He scrunches up his face and closes one eye. I can tell he's having to think way back. "In Wyoming. Dr. Pleasant."

"You're making that up."

He gets that earnest look again. "Really, that was his name. Walter Pleasant. Everybody joked about what a funny name it was for a dentist." He sounds wistful. And homesick.

"So, you haven't seen a dentist in at least three years?"

For the first time, he makes a kid's face. *Relaxing a little, are you?* "I'm not complaining."

I counter his kid-face with adult-speak. "You will if your teeth fall out." I reach over and pick up the notebooks that the transporting officer gave me. "These are yours, right?"

"Yes." He looks at me hopefully. "Can I have them?"

"Most likely." I use my thumb and flip through one. "This is Spanish, right?"

He scrunches down in his seat. "Yes."

"So only you can read it?"

He nods.

"I understand. Privacy can be hard to come by, can't it? But I need to know you aren't writing things that would be disturbing. Even in another language."

He hastens to reassure me. "Oh, it's nothing like that."

"Then, what?"

"Just, um, stories and stuff." He's aware Bonnie and Gene are within listening distance. He gives them a glance and looks uncomfortable.

"That's cool." I give him the book on top. "Read me a line or two."

He gives me a deer in the headlights look.

I tap the book. "Any lines, you pick."

Resigned, he slowly flips it open, scans, and looks up from the top of his eyes. "Would you prefer weather or horses?"

I can't help but chuckle. "Horses sound more exciting."

He looks down and reads. He may be a reluctant narrator, but his voice is clear even if it's not loud: "You hear him before you see him. Nothing else is like the sound of hooves beating the earth. As he crests the hill and barrels past, you think nothing could look freer than a horse in full gallop, mane and tail billowing in the wind. Riding is as close to magic as you can be on this earth, but only because the horse allows you to join him in leaving the earth's boundaries behind. It's the ultimate escape."

When he finishes, he looks up. "Was that okay?" Then he looks concerned. "Should I not have said 'escape?'"

There's this file that says he's smart, but this is the moment it really hits me. He's not your average kid. *What have I gotten myself into?* "Yeah, it's more than okay. It makes me want to take up riding."

He smiles. "I've been riding—and writing—since I was a kid."

I feel the corner of my mouth turn up. *Like that was long ago.*

His eyes get fierce as he proclaims, "I'm going to be a writer. For a living, I mean." For the first time he looks somewhat defiant, like he expects to be told it's a pipe dream.

I give him a serious look and nod. "Sounds like a plan."

His eyes soften. "It's a job where having a felony conviction doesn't matter."

I'd wondered if he knew all the ramifications of what's happened to him. "So, you know about that?"

He nods. "Mr. Galloway explained it when he asked me if I wanted the case in adult court."

"Let's hope your record can be expunged when you're older. Did he explain how that could happen? It's a recognition people make mistakes."

He scrunches up his mouth. "Don't I know it."

I have to lecture a little. "It's important that you recognize when something's a mistake and try not to make the same mistake again. To do better."

Quietly, he says, "I'm trying."

"I believe you. Here, you can have these." I set the notebooks on the desk by him.

He puts his hands on them protectively. "Thank you."

I'm remembering one of the reasons I left juvenile work. I hear tragic stories from adult inmates and feel sympathy. But it's not the same as having a kid with his whole life in front of him, right here in front of you. A kid who made a mistake at age thirteen that has already severely limited his future employment. Who is already banned from voting, four years before he's even old enough to vote.

I feel a need to give this boy some hope as I wrap this up. "You know what else?"

He looks expectant, like the stern, you'd-better-behave-yourself lecture is finally coming.

"Ms. Ziegler told me this would be the best place for you. And you know what? I can tell she was right." I give Bonnie a wry look. Maybe if I say it first, I might get spared *I-told-you-so*.

Reaching over, I cover his clasped fists with my right hand. Mine easily engulfs his as I give a little squeeze. "I think this is exactly where you need to be right now. We're going to take good care of you. It's time you got a break from taking care of yourself. You took that on when you were too young. You can tackle some of those things on your list and we'll help with those. You've had hard times, but you can get beyond all that. None of this has to define your life. Can you see that?"

He stares at me, his breath hitches, and he looks down. He doesn't answer, but I didn't really expect him to. I give his hand a final little pat as I stand up. "Alright, let's go look at your room." I reach in the middle drawer and pull out the key. The boy isn't moving, and he's gone pale.

"I ... I thought it was a barracks," he whispers.

"Well, it is for everyone else. Because of your size and age, we've made other arrangements." My words don't seem to bring him any comfort.

I see his gaze drop to the key in my hand, then I get it. "It's not a cell; it's a room. This is to open the door, not to lock you in." He still doesn't look convinced. "C'mon, you'll see." I turn to Bonnie. "You coming?"

"Sure." She stands up.

Oh, those long legs.

BONNIE

15

The ceiling in this old building is tall and the wooden stair treads are narrow with about thirty steps to each level. It's a decent workout. Sam leads the way and I bring up the rear. Halfway up, I see the boy obviously struggling.

I say very quietly, "Sam?"

He turns and I nod my head toward Kelly, who is looking unsteady and holding tightly onto the rail. The boy knows we're looking at him and says sheepishly, "I guess I'm a little out of shape."

Sam and I exchange a look, both of us thinking a fourteen-year-old ought to be able to sprint up these stairs in five seconds flat. "We'll take it easy," Sam says. He starts pointing out architectural details of this hundred-year-old building to cover our slow progress. When we reach the third floor, the landing is bathed in sunlight, compliments of the non-historic skylight illuminating the woodwork and the colorful rag rug.

Sam unlocks the door on the right then holds up the key to Kelly. "This is yours. Lock the door when you leave. When you're up here, I want you to leave the door open so we can hear you, or you can hear us if we holler up to you."

I smile as I watch the boy's eyes get wide with surprise, and I think, delight. But the light in his eyes dies out when Sam says, "Oh, and don't lose that key or you'll have to pay for a new one."

Sam reads him like a book. "Ah, more good news. Unlike juvenile facilities where you work for free, adults get paid for their labor. Not much, mind you, but you can spend it on snacks and other things on our approved list including lost keys if you have to."

Sam pushes the door open, motioning Kelly and me in ahead of him. Kelly goes completely still, except for his eyes. They are taking it all in. I'm doing the same. The space isn't plush, but it's darn cozy. There's a double bed with a col-

173

orful quilt. A small desk and chair sit in one corner, with a rocker and side table occupying the other. A three-drawer bureau is next to the bed. The bathroom is through a door on the left. I love the vintage sink. Pegboards line the wall on both sides, functional for towels but also decorative.

Kelly clutches the key in his hand. "Really? This is my room?" The look on his face is hope, relief, and gratitude all rolled together. He looks and sounds like someone who was just told the lab made a mistake and they aren't going to die after all.

The look on Sam's face is priceless. It screams, *Oh, shit.* He hadn't thought this through. It was supposed to be temporary, but now if he takes it away, it'll be like handing a little kid a kitten before saying, *just kidding,* and yanking it back. I watch Sam glance at Gene in panic. Gene's shaking his head, giving him a wide-eyed, don't-spoil-this-for-him look.

I'm amused at the two of them. Sam cops out by saying, "This is your assigned room for now." He hands the boy a plastic bag. "Here's some shampoo, soap, and other things you'll need. Why don't you put all this away, wash your hands, and in a few minutes come back downstairs and we'll walk next door for lunch."

"Yes, sir."

We leave him and return to Sam's office. Sam shuts the door part way before turning to me with a scowl on his face. "Okay, you can start the I-told-you-so's."

I'd planned to do it.

I wanted to do it.

I can't do it.

This past hour, my heart simply melted as I watched Sam reassure, challenge, comfort, and discipline this needy, young boy. I also have to face the fact that I didn't really have to come here today. I could have sent the file with the driver. To be honest, I wanted to see Sam again. But I wasn't prepared for the effect this has had on me.

"Lord knows I want to tell you 'I told you so,' but sadly, I cannot. You've taken the fun out of it. You were so good with him." I cock my head, taking in all six-feet-four inches of him. "I may have to alter my whole opinion of you, darn it all."

He gives me a half-grin, half-scowl. "God forbid."

"Your lie detecting abilities were spot on. You even knew he didn't eat. Impressive"

He squints one eye and tilts his head sideways. "*Wellll*, maybe a small confession. A supervisor at the jail sent a note telling me he hadn't touched a bite this morning or the night before."

I cross my arms and lean back against the doorframe. "Now this is the Sam I know. Devious." I lift my head toward the ceiling. "I think Kelly's realizing this is a lot better than he thought it'd be."

"Keeping with the confessing, I have to say after hearing his story, I'm happy to give him a break. It's not like we haven't heard horror stories before, but he's sure been through the wringer. And despite what you and Judge Nolan told me, I had the perception any kid tried as an adult was going to be hardcore, but he's a baby. Beyond that, he's different in a way I can't explain."

"You like him."

"Yeah, I like him. What's not to like? Other than of course the fact he lies and steals."

Paranoid, I glance out the cracked door making sure the boy's not in hearing distance. "He may not be the norm, but he does match the typical juvenile offender in some ways. More than half the kids in the juvenile system have been physically abused and involved with child welfare first. He fits right in the profile." I peek out the door one more time. "Okay, so kid-wise, what are your thoughts?"

Sam puts an arm up on the door frame and leans in. "Good news or bad news?"

"Bad first. I'm hoping there's more good than bad."

He shrugs. "The bad is obvious. He just became an inmate in adult corrections and will be an ex-con at sixteen. He's in a world of pain, plus his confidence and self-worth have been shot to hell. He's a runner, a definite pattern of avoidance as a solution to problems. In fairness, some of that is age typical. And situational. But I still see it as an issue. Physically, he's in terrible shape although that should be the easiest thing to fix with a good diet, fresh air, and sunshine. His emotional state should improve once he feels stronger."

I give a big sigh. "That was more bad than I thought. Tell me the good."

"Easy. He's bright and articulate, well-mannered. All the social skills are there. He has zero drug and alcohol issues. That's unusual and huge in itself." He drops his arm off the door frame. "The most important thing is during his first decade of life all the foundations were built. He grew up trusting and respecting adults, something many kids in juvenile justice never got to do.

"So... I did good, huh?"

He pins me with a look. "Is that an *I-told-you-so* in disguise?"

I give him a little poke on the chest. It's shameless, this flirting on work time. "I like flattery."

He reaches up to grab my hand before it can leave his chest and holds on maybe a little longer than necessary before releasing it. "Much as it pains me to say it, you were right. He can get a lot here. Three hots and a cot, safety, the outdoors, our time and attention. The bad thing is we have an older population than any other state program, so he won't have anyone else his age around. And I'd like to know what we do as far as planning for his eventual release. When he leaves here, he'll have no family, no home, not even any old friends to fall back on."

I think about that a second and realize he has a good point. "I still stay in touch with kids from my old neighborhood and some of my best friends are from school days. These kids that grow up in institutions don't get to make those life-long connections. But I guess you have to concentrate on what you can do. Get him healthy and make sure he stays put."

At the sound of footsteps coming down the stairs, we stop talking and Sam pushes the door fully open. The boy looks at us with that shy look he has. I can tell he's in awe of Sam.

"All situated?" Sam asks.

"Yes, sir"

"Okay, Let's go get something to eat. You're hungry, aren't you?"

He opens his mouth, stops, gives Sam a long look. "Maybe."

I grin as Sam laughs and says, "Good answer."

KELLY

16

A room of my own. Not a cell, *a room.*

I reach out to tentatively touch the bed, fearing when I touch it there will be a poof and it'll disappear. After sleeping for months on a thin mat on a concrete bunk, where you roll over and hit a wall, the idea of sleeping in a real bed is a thrill. I want to crawl up and lie down right this instant but have to resist the urge. There's only one window, but it's large with a view of the hills and the trees in the spring sunlight. In the morning when I wake up, I'll be able to see this view instead of looking at a toilet. Hours ago, I was staring at four gray walls. It's like I fell through a magic portal.

The intake went way different than I thought it would. I wince, remembering getting busted for lying. I can see Mr. Murry's tough, nobody to mess with. I kind of like him, even if he is scary. I pull up my pant leg to look at the tracking monitor again. Two years of wearing this. Ugh.

Suddenly worried that I'm taking too much time, I put up my things, an easy task if there ever was one. I set the shampoo, soap, and stuff on the bathroom sink and put my two notebooks on the desk. There, all done. It feels good to be claiming this space as mine. I feel a sharp pain when I wish I had my little horse to set on the shelf. The pain of losing him hurts more right now than my bigger losses. It's more recent, and unlike the car wreck, it was my fault this time. I thought only of myself and left him behind when I went through that fence. I get a picture in my mind of some person at the juvenile center tossing the most precious thing I owned in the garbage. I cringe.

I reluctantly go downstairs where Mr. Murry and Ms. Ziegler are waiting. They've been talking about me, I can tell. I'd like to know what they said. Then again, maybe I wouldn't.

We head next door and I hear them talking, but I don't pay much attention to what they're saying. I walk with my head partly down, loving the sight of green grass under my feet instead of concrete. When we get to the building, I experiment with the idea of being hungry.

Once we get inside, there's a large room with tables and chairs. Now *here's* the institutional look I'm used to. The smell of food hits me like running into a wall and my stomach goes into full revolt. I want to spin around and walk right back out the door. But no, I'm sure that wouldn't be allowed. Mr. Murry could get mad if he thinks I'm being uncooperative. If only my lie about eating breakfast had slipped by him. I could just claim I wasn't hungry. Maybe Ms. Ziegler will distract him enough he won't pay much attention to me. He's looking at her a lot, so I can hope.

Lunch is lined up like a buffet—you choose what you eat—a big change from getting handed exactly what you can have and no more. I'm going to have to make choices. My stomach clenches up even more. There are men eating at some of the tables, prisoners like me. They glance my way, but I avoid eye contact. They're all full-grown men and there's a sea of tattoos. One guy has a big red scar on his face that runs from the top of his left ear all the way to the side of his mouth. I move a step closer to Mr. Murry.

He motions for me to step in front of him and hands me a plate. I clutch it with both hands, terrified I might drop it. He bends down by my ear and says so quietly I know no one can hear but me, "You eat what you want. Don't worry about having to clean your plate. If you take something and decide you don't want it, that's okay."

The knot in my stomach loosens a little. I look at the line-up of food and automatically hold my breath for several seconds so I can't smell it. With my shaky hands, I don't want anything that requires a fork so that eliminates some choices. The cold food doesn't smell as strong as hot, so I zone in on that. I pick up half of a pimento cheese sandwich.

Further down the line, there's fresh fruit and vegetables that shine up at me in all their bright colors. I take a couple of apple and carrot slices, a few grapes, and some of the bright red strawberries. The aroma hits my nose, but my stomach doesn't object. It seems to remember strawberries in a good way. At the end of the line, there's only tea and water but from somewhere Mr. Murry comes up with a carton of milk and puts it on my tray.

The three of us go sit at one of the tables. Mr. Murry sits next to me and Ms. Ziegler sits across from us. I'm glad she stayed so I'm not sitting here with him by myself. I feel the eyes of the other inmates looking at us but relax a little when I figure out they're looking mostly at Ms. Ziegler. They quit immediately when Mr. Murry looks their way and narrows his eyes.

I stare at my plate and try to use my imagination to dream up an appetite. The apple slices seem safest. I take a bite and hear the crunch in my mouth and in my head. Cold and sweet, not bad. I chew for some time before swallowing. It seems to go down okay. Encouraging.

After I finish the apple slices and the carrots, I focus on the sandwich. I set a goal of ten bites. After bite seven, my stomach seems to ask, *what are you doing to me?* but I force it to take in three more. I try a grape, but the texture doesn't feel right, so I push it under the remains of the sandwich to hide it. I glance sideways from the tops of my eyes to see if Mr. Murry is looking, but he's still busy talking to Ms. Ziegler.

I save the strawberries for last. They're wonderful, but two are enough.

When we're done Mr. Murry points to where everyone takes their dishes. I start to pick up my tray, but Mr. Murry says, "Here, let me get that."

I think he doesn't trust me not to drop it. Probably a wise move. I press my hands together to keep from showing any tremors. I'm glad when we leave the building to go back out. We stop on the large back porch. Mr. Murry waves to some chairs and says to me, "I need to check on something. Have a seat a minute." He goes back in the building and Ms. Ziegler goes with him. I settle into a wicker chair with a high back. The view is great. I'd be happy to do a 30-5 timeout right here in this peaceful spot.

Robins are on the lawn looking for worms, tilting their heads then swooping in for the kill. A red cardinal flies into a nearby tree and starts singing, *cheer, cheer, cheer.* Some ants walk by close to my boots. I'm careful not to move my feet and squish them. Ants are cool. If you lift up a rock and disturb a colony, they won't run away to save themselves; they'll start grabbing up their eggs and young first. Self-preservation is not their thing. The colony always comes first.

Sometimes I'd see an ant on my Dad's truck and know that by hitchhiking into town with us, the ant had doomed himself to die, that he'd do nothing but wander around trying to find his colony again. He wouldn't eat or sleep. He'd just go till he couldn't go anymore. Sad, really.

I'd like to follow these ants by my feet to see where they're going, but I'm not disobeying what I was told to do. Unlike them, I *am* into self-preservation.

I could sit here forever. As I lean my head onto the high back of the chair, I feel every muscle turn to jelly. I let my body soak in the warm sunlight and feel the breeze gently sweep across my face. I jerk up just as I'm about to tumble out of my chair. Good thing I didn't, because Mr. Murry comes back with a coffee cup in his hand. But there's no coffee—just vanilla ice cream with a spoon.

"Here, you might like this. Made here at The Village, not the store-bought stuff."

When I take it from him, he goes back inside. My hands have settled, and I think I can handle the spoon. I take a tentative bite and hold it in my mouth till it melts. It's heaven.

Legally, I'm just as much a prisoner here as I was at the jail, but this is so much better. For a long time, it's like I haven't known who I am anymore, but at least for the moment, I feel a bit more like Kelly Morgan with every bite of ice cream I take.

Still, I remind myself not to drop my guard. Some dangers I can see. Others are still unknown and could be out there waiting for me. I look down at the cup and realize the ice cream is all gone.

I wait for whatever happens next.

SAM

17

I hit the fridge to get the ice cream container, grab a spoon, and put a small scoop in a coffee cup. Bonnie peeks at it. "Kinda stingy with it, aren't you?"

"I'm afraid anything bigger would spook him. Let's see how this goes."

We position ourselves to spy without him knowing, and I'm pleased to see him eating.

Bonnie whispers. "He didn't eat much for someone who hasn't had hardly any food in a couple of days."

"Best to take it slow. I don't want to make a big deal out of it. That might backfire."

After he's finished with his ice cream, we collect the boy and return to the administration building. At the bottom of the steps, Bonnie stops. "Much as I hate to leave the party, I'd better get back to the office." She puts her hand on Kelly's back. "You take care of yourself, okay? I'll check back on you from time to time."

He gives her a shy look but straightens up to address her. "Thanks, Ms. Ziegler... for working this out for me."

She smiles at him as she pulls her keys out of her purse. "I think Mr. Murry has it pegged. This is going to be a good place for you."

I ask Bonnie to hold up as I walk the boy inside and return to where we did the intake interview. I hand him the forms he was too shaky to sign. "Sit here on the couch and look these over while I tell Ms. Ziegler goodbye."

The boy takes the papers and sits. He's nothing if not obedient.

Out by Bonnie's car, I find myself hating to see her go. "You've done all the damage you can do, so I think you owe me."

She opens her car door. "Is that so?"

I lean into the door she's put between us. "Yeah, like maybe dinner. One without inmates staring at your legs."

She pushes a lock of her hair behind her ear and smiles. "Yeah? I guess I could do that. You have my number, right?"

I give her one of my slow smiles. "Yeah, it's filed under 'pain in the ass.'"

She laughs. In the driver's seat, she rests her hands on the wheel. "Good to see you too." She puts the key in the ignition, then gets serious. "Keep me posted on the kid. I've got my fingers crossed. It's the first case in a long time that's gotten to me."

I rap on the roof then watch her drive away before heading back inside. I'm about to tell Kelly we'll go walk, but the boy is sound asleep, slumped over with his head on the back cushion. The forms I gave him are askew on the floor.

Gene walks in. "Ziegler gone?"

"Yeah, she left us this."

"Poor kid," he whispers softly. "You gonna wake him up?"

"Naw. He's dead on his feet. Let's get him more comfortable."

I gather up the papers and set them aside, then move his head onto a pillow. Gene slides his boots off and lays his legs on the couch. The only movement from the boy is to turn a little to his side and curl up.

Standing back up, I stretch to work out the kink in my back. "Gene, why don't you go on next door and make sure the work details are set up. I'll do some paperwork and keep an eye on the kid, although I don't think he's going anywhere today. His lawyer is supposed to be coming sometime this afternoon."

After Gene takes his leave, I shuffle some papers around, but my eyes keep going to the boy on my couch. Now that the distraction of Ziegler is gone, the reality of the situation is hitting me. I've been preoccupied with the practical matters of housing him, staff ratios, and other logistics, but what I didn't plan on was the emotional burden of caring for a hurting kid. There's a lot more at stake here than with the adult inmates. He's a work in progress, far different then the men who come here already formed in their second half of life.

My prior experience with juveniles was at an institutional setting. I worked an eight-hour shift and went home. Even then, I often felt the weight of the responsibility. Here, the boy's right under my nose. Kind of like having a kid. I'm divorced with no children, so I'm way out of my league. I guess half-raising my younger siblings should count for something, though.

It's a miracle we three kids came out as good as we did. Early pictures of my parents show a happy couple. I always wonder, when did it go so wrong?

Just before college graduation, my father began having what was termed by the relatives as "nerve trouble." Now it's termed "bi-polar disease." They say it's the only mental illness you can enjoy half the time, and for my father, that was true. When he was in the manic phase, he was the ultimate fun dad, running up huge expenditures on shopping binges. Ultimately, he'd crash into depression and end up in the VA hospital undergoing electric shock treatments. He'd return home in a week or so with half his memory gone.

During the times my father was completely off the pendulum one way or the other, my mother was stable and functioning. As soon as Dad stabilized and was able to work, Mom picked up a liquor bottle. My father took away her car, so she got creative in her quest for anything containing alcohol. She drank the vanilla extract used in cooking then downed my father's aftershave lotion despite the fact it made her sick as a dog. Ultimately, she got smart and simply took taxis to the liquor store, leaving us home alone while she did.

One memorable day when I was twelve, Mom greets my dad as he comes home from work. "Dinner's ready." The table's set and a pot of vegetables is simmering on the stove. I can see my father's pleased expression, but I'm nervous. I know she's been drinking off and on all day.

We sit down to a dinner of fried chicken, and fried it is. Make that, almost completely black. My brother cuts into his and blood oozes out. Apparently, she hadn't thawed the frozen pieces before cooking them.

Dad throws his napkin on the table. "What the hell is this?" My little sister starts crying.

"It's fried chicken," my mother proclaims in a voice a little too bright and cheery, the slur noticeable to all of us.

"It's goddamn raw!" my father roars.

Mom starts to cry. "I try and make a nice dinner, and this is the thanks I get." Even drunk, she knows tears work on my father.

He deflates before our eyes. He sees my sister crying and our downcast eyes. "Go on. Get in the car, kids. We're going out for dinner." Mom isn't invited.

I skirt past her, sobbing there in her chair, without sparing her a glance. To anyone who hasn't lived with an alcoholic parent, that might appear callous, but I've seen enough crying jags in my life that I no longer care. Plus, I'm old enough to have switched from that little kid mode of worrying about mom to an almost-teenager who feels disgust, not pity.

As soon as we get seated at a local diner, my little brother says, "Man, am I hungry!"

The tension is broken, and we enjoy ourselves. We've had a lot of practice at pretending everything is fine, plus it's a rare treat to have dinner out with just our dad. After we finish, we drive out in the country with the windows down enjoying the night air.

Everyone is happy and content, but we grow silent as we pull into the driveway. It's well after dark. The kitchen is just as we left it but to all our relief, Mom's in bed, fully clothed, sleeping it off. Dad cleans up the kitchen, while we kids watch TV, then go to bed like everything is fine and our mother isn't passed out in the next room.

Hospital visits, periods of calm interspersed with vicious fighting, shake and repeat. One up, one down on their marital seesaw, with brief moments where they'd intersect in the middle. For those glorious times, we gave the illusion of a typical family. We'd go on camping trips, have cookouts, they'd come to our baseball games and cheer us on. You'd think maybe, just maybe, *this* time it was going to last, but inevitably, one of them would make the turn back to crazy or drunk. My parents did this give and take for the next thirty years until my father's death. My mother died soon after.

Of course, it doesn't take a therapist to know why I'm here running a corrections program with alcoholics. I could have taken my police pension and gone to work at Home Depot, but like a moth to the flame, I was drawn back into trying to fix things for people who often don't want... or can't be fixed. But here and there you see a success, and like a slot machine that pays one out of a hundred times, it's enough to make you keep playing the game.

I push aside food bills and open the file on Kelly, taking the time to read it more thoroughly. As crazy as my parents were, I never doubted they loved us, and between them they cobbled together a stable enough life for us. We had one house we lived in for our whole childhood. With that house came friends from the neighborhood, school, pets, basic stability. We were never hungry or lacking heat. And we kids had each other. Never once did I feel all alone.

I look at the boy's face deep in sleep and wonder what it must have been like to have had a happy life, to wake up one morning with everything fine and by the end of the day find your whole life has gone to hell. Everything gone. Because if that car hadn't plowed into them, I'd bet good money this little guy would be sitting in junior high right now wondering about whether Suzie Smith likes him, or whether he studied hard enough to pass his history test.

But it *did* happen, and none of us in corrections can play the what-if game. He's here now whether he likes it or not, and whether I like it or not. But damn it, it doesn't mean I can't feel sorry for him.

Late in the afternoon, as forewarned, Kelly's attorney shows up. I watch a dark-haired man in a suit and tie climb out of a maroon Honda Accord. No one around here wears a tie, so he might as well be holding up a sign proclaiming, *I'm an attorney.* This guy, even more than Ziegler, is responsible for this fiasco with my name written all over it. I glance at the boy who has only moved enough to scrunch further down into the pillow and feel a scowl come onto my face. Honestly, this whole thing is *ridiculous.*

The screen door gives a loud thwack as it closes behind me. If it wakes the kid so be it. The sound gets the attorney's attention. Meeting his look, I cock an eyebrow. "The famous Mr. Galloway, I presume? Bonnie Ziegler said you'd be coming. I'm Sam Murry, the superintendent here."

The lawyer holds out his hand and we shake as we size each other up. He loosens his tie and says, "I see my reputation precedes me. I know it's the first day, but I'd like to talk to my client."

Given that this guy is responsible for getting me into this mess, I feel like yanking his chain a bit. "Well, you can certainly see him. I'm not sure he's up to talking."

He gives me a perplexed look. "Okaaay, so … where is he?"

Without answering, I turn and walk into the building knowing he has no choice but to make like Lassie and follow. When we get to the office, I point. "Exhibit A."

Galloway looks down at the sleeping boy for several seconds before slowly raising his eyes to mine. He looks me up and down. The wariness leaves his expression and is replaced by an annoyingly superior look, like he just figured something out and likes it.

This wasn't the effect I was going for. Folding my arms across my chest, I try to wipe that smug look from his face. "This is probably the last rest he'll get. He'll be working eight hours a day from now on." Much to my irritation, Galloway gives me a half-grin and doesn't rise to the bait, so I clear my throat and continue. "For the record, we didn't drug him. I think it's an understatement to say he was tired. I do need to get him up soon, but maybe we could talk a few minutes first. Want something to drink?"

He drops his keys into his jacket pocket. "Sure."

In the kitchen, I grab a drink out of the fridge and hold the door for him to pick his poison. He takes a Sprite, pops the tab, then gets right to it. "I guess you're wondering why I'm here. No offense, because I don't know you, but my main concern is Kelly's safety and I want to know what safeguards you've put in place."

I can't help but laugh. "No offense, because I don't know you, but that seems rich coming from the guy who helped put him into the adult system instead of juvenile."

He gives me a piercing look. "Have you seen juvenile facilities? If so, you'd know they aren't summer camps. This state's whole system is under court-ordered monitoring right now. Hell, I just read that at one facility, the washers broke and they don't have the money to fix them, so the kids are washing their clothes in a bucket."

I kind of like poking at him, but he's got a point. "No need to get defensive. I used to work in juvenile justice, and I've seen some awful places. Some of the men here tell their juvenile prison horror stories and call it the hardest time they ever pulled."

I guess I should offer Galloway a chair, but he leans his elbows on the counter behind him and seems comfortable enough. "Taxpayers and politicians aren't keen on sending state dollars to support kids no one much cares about. They wait till some kid dies, then committees get appointed and some attention is paid, at least for a while, until they lapse back into neglect."

It's like we're two guys trying to one-up each other with horror stories from our neck-of-the-woods, but I can't help it; I have to put my two cents in. "I hear you, but the adult system has its own nightmares. Extreme violence. One staff to a hundred inmates, so little supervision. Rapes. I think it's easier to get illegal drugs in prison than it is out. It's a horrible place to put a kid."

Galloway drapes his jacket over the back of one of the chairs, making himself at home. His bright purple and yellow tie stands out against his white shirt. Jumping frogs, for Christ sake. I wouldn't be caught dead wearing that. If I was a judge and he wore that in my court, I'd find him in contempt.

"I don't disagree," he says, "but sadly there seem to be more safeguards for adults than kids. There's more legal representation, and adults can take it upon themselves to sue someone. Kids are powerless."

"Philosophy aside," I try to say with an even-tempered voice, "we're taking every precaution to assure your client's not harmed." He looks satisfied, so I add, "I don't suppose you worry about my overtime costs related to staffing."

His eyes light up and he smiles, showing all his teeth. "Not a bit."

I crush my can one-handed and toss it into the blue bin next to the counter. "Didn't think so. The easiest thing would be to isolate him."

Now he's staring daggers at me. Saying the word *isolate* is like a bullfighter waving a large red flag. Just the reaction I was aiming for. "I don't like the sound of that," he says.

"Stand down, counselor. I didn't mean we were locking him in a supply closet. We're housing him in this building away from the general population."

Galloway stands straight up. "I'd like to see."

Cardio work out time again on the steps. Galloway walks into Kelly's room and gives a little whistle. "Now we're talking. Has he seen it?"

"Yeah, he seemed pleased."

The lawyer breathes a big sigh, like he's been holding back a heap of worry. "I bet. I know I'm going to sleep better tonight." All the joking leaves his voice. "I've been really worried about him. He's put on a brave front, but this has about done him in."

Now he's gone and done it. I can tell he truly cares. "So, tag I'm it, huh? Now *I* get to stay up nights making sure nothing bad happens to him."

He smiles in confirmation.

I walk past the bed to gaze out the window, taking in the vivid blue sky and the greenery below. "Here's a question. What happens when he's sixteen and his sentence runs out?"

Before he answers, he reaches over and gives the rocking chair a little push, setting it in motion, then looks up with a grin, "I'm channeling Scarlet O'Hara. I'll think about that tomorrow."

I put my hand on the rocker, stilling it. "Is that a legal term?"

"Should be. The only plan I have is to call Children's Services on the day before he's released and say, 'come get him.'"

I give a little snort. "You'd better hide quick if you do that. They won't want to deal with a released prisoner, no matter what his age."

Now it's Galloway who walks over to take in the view out the window. "Believe it or not, I've done it before. The legislators pass these get-tough laws and never consider all the ramifications. I represented two adults and a juvenile on a murder case. The juvenile was in the car when it went down, but he saw it happen. Each of the adults was fingering the other as the shooter so only the kid could give the scoop on who did what. The prosecution tried the kid as an adult but offered a plea deal if he'd testify.

"The boy got a one-year sentence on an accessory charge. His parents disappeared during the year he was incarcerated, so a couple of days before his release, Children's Services was notified to come claim him as an abandoned child because the prison couldn't open the door and turn a fifteen-year-old onto the streets. The social workers screamed bloody murder, but they did it. I have no idea what they did with him."

This lawyer may wear the ugliest tie I've ever seen, but I'm figuring out he knows his stuff. "I have some sympathy for them. Theirs is a tough-ass job. As a police officer, I went and knocked on doors in bad neighborhoods, knowing I had a gun and a radio for backup. Child protection workers have nothing but a cell phone, clipboard, and good intentions. I wouldn't do their job for anything."

"I agree, but I get annoyed sometimes about how they treat teens. They forget they're kids too. And so does everyone else. It's like Christmas toy drives where the cutoff age is twelve. People donate toys to give a one-year-old, who would be happy with an empty box. Meanwhile, a thirteen-year-old, who knows all too well he's having a shitty holiday, gets nothing."

My mind goes back to the time I was on the police force and arrested a man who killed his fifteen-year-old stepson. The boy had been getting beaten for two years and had outright told several people but no one reported it.

I nod. "Yeah, teens don't get much sympathy. An eight-year-old reports his parents hit him and everyone jumps right on it. If a teen reports abuse, the first thought everyone has is, what did you do to deserve it? That's only if they believe them in the first place.

My phone buzzes in my pocket and I take a glance. It's no one I want to talk to, but I see it's later in the day than I thought. "Let's go wake the kid. Maybe you should do it in case he comes up swinging."

This time, Galloway leads the way. When we get back to the office, he kneels down and gently shakes the boy, softly saying his name. The boy's only response is to roll over to the other side. Galloway looks up at me. "You sure you didn't drug him?"

On the third try, Kelly starts to rouse. He rubs his eyes with his fists, which makes him look terribly young. "You came."

Galloway pulls up a chair. "I said I would, didn't I?"

"Yes, you did. Thank you, Henry."

I walk a distance away, giving them some space. Galloway says, "So Mr. Murry showed me around before we woke you. I think it looks good, how about you?"

"I'm still taking it all in. What time is it?"

Galloway glances at his watch. "Almost four o'clock."

The boy furrows his brow, trying to put it all together. "I've been asleep since *lunch*."

"Yeah? But that's good. You needed it."

I walk a little further away and grab my jacket. I come back in time to hear Galloway ask something interesting. "Listen, I was thinking on my way here. Were you ever told anything about your father's will?

"I don't think so."

"I would be surprised if everything wasn't left to you. There could be insurance money, pension funds. Maybe your uncle left you something too. I didn't want to look into it before. It might have complicated having a public defender assigned, but now that you're here, it would be a good idea to investigate. It might take a while with my current workload, but I'll get on it when I can. Sound good?"

"Sure, it would be great if I had some money to pay you," Kelly says.

"Hey, I keep telling you not to worry about that. I get paid. You just worry about yourself, not me."

Kelly sticks his foot in his left boot and looks around for the other one. "You know what's funny?"

Galloway fishes around under the couch and comes up with the right boot. "What?"

Kelly slides his foot in, looks at both his feet, and knocks them together, seemingly admiring his boots. I can't help but smile. He says, "When I'm released, this will be the second longest place I've lived and I don't even know where I am. Is there a city near here? I'm not sure about the states around this one. Eastern states are squiggly. Out west, ours are mostly boxes."

"Tell you what, I've got an atlas in my car. I'll show you before I go."

My smile is gone. I shoot Galloway a nasty look, which he doesn't see. I'd prefer keeping the kid in the geographical dark. In fact, if I could spin him around three times till he was completely disoriented every time he walks out the door, I'd do it. Anything to keep him from running.

As I leave Galloway and Kelly to their little meeting, I think about what we have in place to keep the kid tethered. The ankle bracelet is essential, and yeah, putting him upstairs was a good idea, even if it means having him underfoot. He's much more contained up there. Tonight, when I throw on the alarms, he won't be going anywhere.

How can you be so sure of yourself? He's climbed out a third-floor window before.

What I have I let them get me into?

KELLY

18

It's spring in Wyoming with the sky the most vivid blue. I've been riding for hours and I get off Buck to let him graze a minute. Once the reins are dropped, he lowers his head and rips at the grass. I stretch out on the ground and look up at the sky, trusting him not to step on me. Buck's face is above me. He's pulling on my arm and saying my name.

Opening my eyes, I have a moment of disorientation before I realize I'm looking at Henry. Memory comes flooding back and I want to go back to the dream. Henry's smiling down at me, and as happy as I am to see him, I don't tell him I'd rather be looking at Buck.

"You came."

He gives me that Henry look. "I said I would, didn't I?"

I sit up fast, trying to get rid of the grogginess. I'm worried I broke some rule, but no one seems upset with me.

Henry doesn't stay long because he's coming back tomorrow, but before he leaves, he shows me on a map where I am. Boy, I did a lousy job of going west after I left the Haverlys. I'm a long way from Wyoming. Out of curiosity, I looked at the interstate numbers that would take me there. It still hasn't sunk in that I won't see it again, at least for a long time. It just doesn't seem right.

After Henry leaves, I must still look zonked, because Mr. Murry tells me to go wash my face before we take a walk. Patting my face with a towel, I look at myself in the mirror. The face looking back at me is pale and pinched and I don't want to look at him long. I linger another few seconds, torn between the desire to go outside and the anxiety of being alone with Mr. Murry with all the dangers of what I could say or do wrong. I picture him on the phone with Ms. Ziegler. *This isn't going to work out … He won't quit running his mouth … He's too quiet… He won't look me in the eye … He stares too much … I caught him in another lie.* I shake my head to dislodge the thoughts.

I gut up and step out. He's waiting for me and extends his arm, holding a jacket. "The sun's about to go down and it's cooling off, so put this on. It's a loan from Mr. Simmons. We'll get you your own tomorrow." He also hands me a baseball cap with The Village written across the front. "The sun's low and bright so you'll appreciate this." And it's true, looking west is blinding.

The hat brim helps, and I find it a pleasure to have it on. Even better, he tells me it's mine to keep. I own the notebooks and a hat. I've doubled my personal possessions. But possessions don't mean near as much as smelling the earth and hearing the sounds of the wind through the trees. There's a stone wall with build-ings stretching down the road. I recognize this scene from the brochure Henry showed me back at the jail.

Mr. Murry points in that direction. "This is the tourist part of the Village. It's okay if you are here with staff, but otherwise it's off limits. In the next week or so, I'll take you down some of the trails. I know you like horses. Want to see what we've got?"

I nod. I've decided to keep my mouth shut as much as possible. Partly to keep from doing something wrong, but also, I don't want to break the spell. This is the golden hour when the sun is near the horizon and about to set. Everything glows. My Uncle Jack dabbled in photography. If we were out this time of day, he'd suddenly pull the car over and leap out to photograph something that would catch his eye. He would have loved it here with all the greens set against the sun.

Mr. Murry and I come to an old weathered barn, more or less red, depending on which part of the faded boards you look at. In the paddock are two huge black horses. I've never seen horses this big before. That's all it takes for my vow of silence to fly out the window.

"Gosh, they're huge." And just like that, I start running at the mouth telling things no one needs to know. "Horses are my thing. That's another thing that's bad about … um … leaving the detention center. I'd forgotten I was leaving something important behind."

"What was that?"

Now I'm embarrassed. I feel childish, but I can't not talk about it. "Oh, it was this horse thing … that my dad made for me … out of wood. It was the only thing I owned from, you know, *before.* But I left it behind without a thought …

until later … I remembered it." I can't bear to look at his face, to see what he's made of my silly rambling.

Keeping my eyes on the horses, I'm pleased when the biggest one slowly heads my way. They must associate people with food even though there's a prominent sign that says *Please don't feed the horses.* The taller of the two puts his head over the fence and snuffles hopefully. I give his forelock a little pull, before laying my hand flat on his massive face between his eyes.

Like an electric shock, a flood of memories flies through my head, as if someone is flipping a deck of cards: My father laughing as he forcibly pulls me out of a saddle, when I was about four years old. Me, kicking and screaming and him laughing, saying, *he'd rather ride than eat.* My uncle, handing me the reins for my first solo ride. Alone, standing on top of a ridge mounted on my pony Buck with the whole world beneath me. I drop my hand like it's been scorched and turn away.

Mr. Murry's eyeing me up. I worry that he's got more superpowers than spotting lies. I'm going to need to be extra careful around him. He starts walking and I fall in beside him after jamming my hands in my jacket pockets. Well, Mr. Simmon's jacket pockets, to be accurate.

We reach a gate where Mr. Murry shows me the trail sign and says, "This is where one of the best trails begins. It goes to a really nice waterfall. You'll have time for hiking on your free time, but I have to warn you, we do a lot of work here."

This is safer ground. "I like to work."

He leans back and squints one eye as he looks at me. "Really?"

"Honest, I really do." I'm not lying; surely he can tell.

He smiles. "Good deal. I'm looking to put you in the stables. You'll have a secondary assignment rotating among all the jobs. We do building maintenance, landscaping, and work in the nature preserve maintaining the trails among other things. We'll need to get you some boots that fit better and some sneakers. I called the doctor's office while you were sleeping today, and they said they could squeeze us in. And you need a haircut, so we'll have a busy day tomorrow. Plus, soon we're going to have to do something about school."

This comes as a surprise. "School?"

"Sure. You're fourteen. You need to get an education. What did you think?"

193

"I didn't go at the jail. I was tried as an adult, so I thought it meant I wouldn't have to."

"Being tried as an adult doesn't make you an adult for everything else, to be honest, for much of anything else. You can't drink alcohol, operate power tools, get a job, or a driver's license, among other things."

I frown. "That doesn't seem fair. Either you're an adult or you're not. Who makes up these stupid rules anyway?" The instant the words are out of my mouth, I want to suck them back in. But it doesn't make him angry. He even laughs.

"Yeah, it's a contradiction for sure."

KELLY

19

I'm in my room about to spend my first night as a state prisoner, but the gamble of going to an adult facility seems to have paid off. Thank you, Henry.

I'd asked to come up here right after dinner and got permission. The rule is once I'm up here, I can't go back downstairs till morning. Fine by me. I couldn't wait to be where no demands are being made of me.

Mr. Murry turned on the alarms to the outside doors, while he pointed out the motion lights and cameras in the hall. He emphasizes the cameras are for my safety as well as for security reasons. I understood what he meant, that anyone would know they'd be on film if they tried to get at me. There's also some little voice monitor thing on the dresser. I'm so happy to be up here, I don't care about any of these things.

Going to the window, I open the curtains all the way. No city lights. I turn off the overhead light so I can look through the glass and see the stars outside. It'd be better to see them without the glass. Looking over my shoulder at the open door, I quietly slide the window open, then glance back at the door one more time as I slide the screen up too. It squeaks a little and I grimace. Surely, this is one of those rules Mr. Murry should have gone over with me. But he didn't, did he?

Way to go Kelly, turning over a new leaf? That lasted a whole half day. Is that a personal record? But all I want is to feel the night, to be part of it again after so long away. I really don't see the harm. I lean out and take one deep breath of cool night air, while I look up at the moon and stars. I'd lost them for a long time and it's good to have them back.

When I look down, all I see is a very long drop. It's much higher here than the window I went out at my grandfather's and there's no tree nearby. I can still recall that moment I almost fell to the pavement below. *Maybe it'd been better if*

I had. I push back the thought. This is the first day of my new life, and I'm going to try and stay positive.

I glance back at the door, and even though I believe I could hear anyone coming up the stairs, I get nervous. Which is why I oh-so-slowly lower the screen, wincing again at the same damn squeak. The glass quickly follows. I flip on a lamp switch and dart over to the rocking chair and grab a book. *Look, I'm just reading.*

Pushing with my left foot, I close my eyes to set the chair in motion enjoying the novelty of having one that isn't bolted to the floor. I picture a guy walking in with a drill and a large bolt. *What's this? A chair that moves? This can NOT be allowed. The universe will rotate backward on its axis. The chair throws up its arm rests. Please, I mean no harm. I just like to go back and forth. I hold up my hand to the man. Away with you. I'll take responsibility for this delinquent chair. I'll make it give up its evil rocking ways.*

I smile at my thoughts then stifle a yawn. I'm feeling thick-headed but don't want to go to bed before enjoying my new room. My chair keeps on rocking a beat or two after I get up, and I let my feet take me into the bathroom. I close the bathroom door, presuming that's allowed. Standing in the middle of the room, I extend my arms. I can reach each of the walls, but every inch of space is well used with little shelves and peg racks.

The sink has a rubber stopper on a chain like the house my old babysitter used to have. Sticking it in the drain, I pull the chain to hear the satisfying little pop it makes. I do it twice more. *Snap, crackle, pop, Rice Krispies.* By the third time, I'm leaning over the sink silently laughing all the way down to my stomach. I could stand here making this pop noise all night but tell myself to knock it off. *Nut job.*

I reach in the shower to turn it on, then quickly strip off my clothes and get in. The water feels wonderful, hot and strong. I let it blast me till I feel clean and calm. No need to rush. No one is standing just feet away telling me my five minutes are up.

Turning off the water, I grab the white towel to dry off, smushing it to my face to take in the flowery scent. After I step out, I get a glimpse of my body in the mirror. Gee, I look awful. I remember a game Dad played with me when I was a little kid. *I'm going to count your ribs. One, two...* I'd dissolve into giggles. But this isn't funny. I look like an addict or something. I've got to start eating better.

The shirt is in the bureau like Mr. Murry said it would be, but I have to pull out a couple of drawers to find it. The blue lettering on the front says, *The Village 5K Run*. There's nothing for it but to put my jail underwear back on. I hate it, not because of any big cleanliness issue, but because it's my last tie to that awful place. I guess I'll get new ones tomorrow. Buying underwear while I'm with Mr. Murry. *Ugh*. But I'll be happy to get new ones. These will hopefully go in the garbage. I'd burn them if I could.

Pulling a chair over to the window, I sit looking out. I spent hours looking out that window slit in the jail and can't seem to break the habit. This window is way better, so much bigger. I can see all the way to the main Village road where I walked with Mr. Murry. The old gray stone buildings gleam against the white, old-fashioned streetlights.

A motion catches my eye and I realize it's a raccoon walking across the broad lawn in front of my building. *My building*. I'm wrapping my mind around the concept that this isn't temporary. I live here now. I'm enjoying my view, but before long, the bed cannot be resisted, so I turn off the lamp and climb in practically groaning. It's bliss to be in a real bed again, to lie warm and fed and safe.

The feeling of safe is unexpected. I'd thought I'd be sleeping with adult convicts all around me, and safe would be the last thing I'd feel. I close my eyes and sense, as much as hear, the quiet. No slamming doors, no voices, no toilets flushing.

Tomorrow for the first time in a long time, fear and boredom don't appear to be on the agenda. Shopping and a haircut. The gift of an ordinary day. I pray my luck is changing for the better, but best not get my hopes up.

With that thought, the worries roll back in. I picture an angry Mr. Murry and don't like the image. I imagine him explaining to Mr. Simmons: *At first, I thought he wasn't such a bad kid, but after spending time with him, I can see this isn't going to work out.* My stomach clenches and I wish I hadn't eaten so much at dinner.

The sleep I felt so close to minutes ago vanishes. I tell myself it's better to focus on the here and now, a comfortable bed and best of all, an open door. It doesn't matter I'm not allowed to leave this room till morning. There's a huge difference between a doorway you aren't supposed to cross, and a door you physically cannot open.

I watch the shapes of tree limbs dance across the ceiling from their shadows cast by the moon. Out of long ago habit, I reach into my mind for a story, a creature, an adventure to occupy my thoughts, but nothing comes. Even with my real life's improvements, I miss my fantasy life. For one thing, it helped keep my head occupied. It kept out the pain.

All the talk this morning about my past has opened the door I've kept slammed shut, and I'm having a difficult time closing it. At first, the door is opened just a crack, back to the boarding school and Mr. Farley, who the kids referred to as Mr. Fartley behind his back. I see me standing in front of him as he raises his baton and brings it down across my palm. There's a sharp sting but the pain is distant and strangely, almost enjoyable. There was a girl at Oasis who would cut on herself and I understood completely. That pain was a break from numbness, a chance to feel something, a welcome distraction from what really hurt. That kind of pain gives you power.

After revisiting that scene, other memories flash before me like a curtain has been ripped aside. They zip past in glimpses until I land on *that day*. I got up that morning, had breakfast, got dressed, with no idea of what was coming—that the life I knew would soon be gone forever.

Lying on my back, my hand slides over the scar on my arm. In a way, it's a comfort, a tangible reminder of my former life. I can't stop myself. I squeeze my eyes and fly back to Wyoming. I open the front door and walk through our house ending up in my bedroom. I can remember what's on the walls, the treasures on my dresser, the view out the window. I can walk down the stairs and into the kitchen. There's Banner's dog basket he loved so much. I see it all exactly like it was, and I want to be there so badly it feels like desire alone can physically pull me there. Pull me home.

Dear God, I just want to go home.

I miss my family so much. And I don't want to picture the people I loved lying under the cold ground. *Rotting.* How long does it take to rot? It's been years now. Are they done rotting or is it just half over? I picture their bodies in their caskets and groan as their clothes and skin fall off, leaving just their skeletons. I fling my arm over my eyes, as if doing so will block the sight, and just like that,

I'm crying.

I turn my head into the pillow to drown out the sound. The best day I've had in such a long time, and I end it blubbering like a baby.

SAM

20

My original plan was to take the kid next door for dinner and leave him there until I collected him at bedtime. That way he'd only be underfoot for sleeping purposes and nothing else. Yesterday I'd prepped the inmates on our new arrival and laid down some ground rules. Thankfully, we have a pretty decent bunch of guys here right now so with supervision he should be okay. But at the last minute I decided it would be better to wait till tomorrow. Give him a chance to settle in. One more day won't hurt. But I'm glad when he has asks to go upstairs early. I'm ready to be shed of him and go up to my own quarters.

It's hard enough to draw boundaries when you live at the same place you work. I'm always on-call as long as I'm on the property. That's the downside. The upside is the commute is great and I save all the money I'd have to pay to rent or own a house. And I love this historic building with its tall ceilings, original wood flooring, and the large windows with their phenomenal views. Gene's quarters on the other side of the large hall are identical to mine. The religious sect that built this dwelling was big on symmetry.

The living room and bedroom are decent sizes. I don't have an official kitchen but tucked a microwave, hotel sized refrigerator, and a coffee maker in a corner of the living room behind a screen. If I want real food I use the full size kitchen downstairs or eat out. It's simple living and it suits me. No clutter or complications. The one new thing I've added tonight is the baby monitor which sits on a table near "the kitchen." Thankfully it isn't pink or blue, just a simple white square with three buttons that could be any number of electronic devices if you didn't know what it was.

TV reception is almost non-existent here. On a good day, if the airwaves are just right, we pick up a few channels the old-fashioned way, with an antenna. There are no TVs in The Village guest rooms. It's part of The Village experience for visitors to "unplug and get away from it all." I listen to a ball game on the radio and clean up the place a bit. It doesn't take me long to tune out the random sounds from upstairs. When the game's over, I click off the radio and the room goes quiet, except for what's coming out of that five-inch square box. A kid sobbing.

Shit.

I hear Gene coming up the stairs. I open my front door, knowing it's an invitation for him to stop by. He stands in the doorway and says, "Hey, I talked to Riley and he got the truck fixed for tomorrow. I'll take it since you'll be with the boy." He leans in and lowers his voice. "I'm still coming to grips with the fact there's a kid upstairs. He sure pulled at my heart strings today listening to his story."

"Yeah, well then don't come in here."

At his puzzled look, I motion him in and point at the monitor.

He listens a second and grimaces. "Oh, no."

I fling my arms up. "I'm over my head here. Should I go up? Please tell me no. I don't think he understands how powerful the pickup on that device is."

"Maybe it's just relief to have everything over. I'd leave him be."

"Yeah, I thought the same thing. I'd like to turn the damn thing off, but I feel compelled to listen in case it leads to him trying to leave or something worse." I lean my head back and run my hand through my hair. "Damn, why couldn't he be the kind of kid who snarls and cusses us out. I could deal with that."

We stare for a minute at the monitor like it's a TV set. The sobs get quieter and fade out. With a big sigh, Gene says, "I think he's winding down. Hopefully, he'll go on to sleep. I'm turning in myself. Call me if you need me, otherwise we'll take it a day at a time."

"Good plan. Goodnight."

An hour later, before I turn in for the night, I go up to peek in on the kid. His crying unnerved me. Hadn't I been pretty gentle with him? He'd seemed fine the whole evening. Why the melt down? Christ, I hope he's not going to make a habit of this.

I stick my head in and see him curled up on the bed, perfectly still and obviously sound asleep. Lying in the bed he looks frightfully young and fragile. His hands clutch the sheet up under his chin; his head is burrowed half under the pillow. Quietly, I back out a couple of steps then turn around and tiptoe back down the stairs. Once back in my apartment, I unplug the monitor and take it into my bedroom and set it on the nightstand. I sleep fitfully, one ear listening for sounds I hope I don't hear.

KELLY

21

I wake with a jolt. Somebody is shining a flashlight in my face. Then I realize it's only the light streaming through the window. I've forgotten what it's like to wake when the sun is already up. It's a good thought and I try to hold on to it. I feel my face flush thinking about last night. Crying. What a stupid thing to do. No more looking back. Or forward. One day at a time. This is Day Two. When it's over there's about seven hundred and eleven more to go.

I'd love to stay under the covers but want to be ready before Mr. Murry calls, so I get dressed and carefully make the bed. There's the thud of footsteps coming up the stairs. I stand up by the wall near the front of the bed, not sure what to do with my arms and hands. I clasp them behind my back like they made us do in detention but worry that maybe it looks like I'm hiding something, so I drop them by my side.

Mr. Murry has to bend his head as he comes through the door. He's in jeans with a black T-shirt and black jacket. He looks cool and kind of dangerous, but in a good way. His eyes look me up and down and go around the room. I'm worried maybe I didn't do something I should have but he says a friendly, "Good morning."

I clasp my hands behind me and wait for instructions.

He gives a smile. "You made your bed. Good."

I reach over and pull the bedspread tighter on the righthand side. I can feel myself biting my lower lip. "Is it okay? This one part wants to wrinkle."

"It looks fine. This isn't the army. I'm not going to try and bounce a quarter off it. I'm not sure they really do that anyway. Well, let's go downstairs and get you some breakfast."

I follow him to the kitchen, and he reaches up and opens one of the cabinet doors. "Here's cereal Mr. Simmons bought. I hope you like at least one of them."

"I do. I like them all." And I do. It's a smorgasbord of animals. Tony the Tiger, the Cheerio's honeybee, and the Trix rabbit. I line them up and mentally greet them as long-lost friends. I rotate them so the bee is in the middle since he's the only insect. They all look happy and why not? They're on these cheery boxes and they never age. I feel Mr. Murry's eyes on me, so I snap out of it and grab the bee box.

"Bowls are behind that first shelf and spoons are in this middle drawer. Help yourself. I'm going to pop some toast in. Do you like orange juice?"

"Yes, sir."

I pour the cereal in the bowl and get milk from the fridge, enjoying opening the door. I sit at the kitchen table and find I'm actually hungry. Mr. Murry puts a plate with a couple of pieces of toast next to my cereal and sets a glass of juice down.

It's nice eating in the kitchen and looking out the window. Clouds have mostly swallowed up the sun, but it pops out now and again while I finish eating. I rinse my dishes off and put them in the sink like I'm told. Mr. Murry pulls a big wad of keys out of his pocket and hands me the jacket I used last night. "Okay, let's roll."

We go out to the car and I freeze up, not knowing which door I should head to. Would I actually sit up front? There's no metal cage divider, but shouldn't I be in the back seat? I shift my weight from one foot to the other and twist my right foot in the loose gravel while I think about the options. Mr. Murry slides in behind the wheel then uses his hand to motion me to come around the car and ride shotgun. As I get in, he leans over grinning and says, "I don't want to look like a chauffeur."

I get it. He's teasing me. I slide in the seat next to him and reach for the seat belt. The last time I rode in the front seat was when I bailed on Mrs. Williams. With that thought, I steal a glance at the man beside me. He's much scarier than Mrs. Williams. Nope, if I'd leave it wouldn't be by trying to jump out of this car. And something tells me he won't be dropping me off to go by myself into a Mc-Donalds. No, if I bailed it would have to be in the middle of the night. I'd have to be very careful.

SAM

22

The Village is deep in rural America. It takes at least twenty minutes to get to a gas station, and any retail stores are in the next county over. I glance at the boy who seems engrossed in watching the passing scenery. He seems okay. No signs of the emotions that brought on tears last night.

Target is in the middle of a strip mall. Kelly points to the store next to it. "Can we go there?"

"Goodwill? Really? That's where you want to go?"

He gives a serious nod. "It's cheaper. And everything is broken in already."

I smile at his reasoning. "I'm game. Is this where you shopped in Wyoming?"

"No, I went there with a foster parent I had."

I give him a quick glance. I can see there's more to his story than what I learned yesterday. I keep my tone conversational. "Were you in a lot of foster homes?"

"No. I was supposed to go to a long-term home, but they couldn't find one." He grins and tries to make a joke out of it, as we get out of the car. "I've gotten kind of used to people not wanting me." Thankfully, I have a good poker face, while inside I cringe. If he only knew how much I fought having him come here.

I've managed to live this long without ever setting foot in a Goodwill till now. Kelly's right. It's easy to find about everything he needs, and it costs next to nothing. He goes for plain shirts, solid colors, no logos. With the permission of a clerk, I tear off the tags so he can wear the clothes now. Dressed in jeans and a T-shirt, he looks more like a kid, which of course he is, regardless of what the law has said to the contrary.

At Target, it doesn't take long to get underwear, socks, sweatpants, and footwear. He doesn't care what sneakers he gets. My nephews always have to have

205

the expensive, big-name brands, but Kelly seems oblivious to them.

I box up the shoes. "We got done quick. I thought we'd be shopping most of the morning. Is there anything else you need or want? Besides clothes, I mean."

He looks uncertain. "I don't have any money yet."

"I'll front it to you. You can pay me back later. Do you have something in mind?"

He makes a little square with his hands. "Those notebook things?"

"Show me." He heads over to office and school supplies and picks up two different sizes of spiral notebooks. He looks up at me with a questioning look. "They have wire."

"Not a problem." Wire notebooks aren't allowed in jails, or magazines with staples for that matter. Wire can be made into a weapon, and staples can be used for people to cut on themselves or others. A lot of people think prisons are restrictive, but in reality, it's jails that get that prize.

I take them from him. "It won't take you long to get the money to cover these. Anything else?"

He chooses a box of colored pencils and some pens which he also holds up for my inspection. "Are these allowed?"

"Sure." I'll be glad when he gets past this first day paranoia.

We make our purchases, then I take him for a haircut. We have a barber who comes to the facility, but he was there last week, and I can't stand looking at the kid's lopsided hair another month. The barber who cut his hair at the jail must have been half blind, drunk, or both.

I take him to where I go. Annie cuts just about every man, woman, and child's hair in town. I'm thankful she doesn't ask Kelly who butchered him. By the time she's worked her magic, the kid looks so much better. Annie keeps up a running chatter, and I can tell he enjoys the attention, but he barely meets her eyes except at the end when he tells her thank you.

We take a little walk through town to kill some time, then go in to grab some lunch at a local sandwich shop. It's right out of central casting and screams cute small-town café. Gingham curtains, waitresses with aprons and attitudes, black and white linoleum flooring with metal round tables lit by the sun streaming in the large front windows.

I pick a spot but there's a crisis moment when the boy tries to decide which of the two remaining chairs he should take. Freeing him from his agony, I point at the one on my left. I hand him a menu. He stares at it and chews on his thumbnail before handing it back to me. "Could you pick?"

Geez. He's exhausting me. I consider forcing him to choose something but decide to humor him this first full day here. I look over the selections and skim past burgers, ham sandwiches, and five things with bacon. "Grilled cheese?"

He nods then stares at the table when the waitress comes over for our order. What the hell, I get a grilled cheese too. Fries and Cokes round out our meal. No fruits or veggies, so not the healthiest food outing, but he's eating so I chalk it up to progress. There's not much conversation though. I think he's said ten words all day, and I have to do all the initiating. I can tell this being out and about in the community is an adjustment for him. I've seen this with adult inmates and expect it's even worse for a kid. How easy it is to get institutionalized.

After he drains his Coke, I lay my napkin on the table. "You ready? On to the doctor?" He curls his lip. It's the kind of face a kid would make and I grin at him. "Yeah, not the most fun part of our day, but you'll like Dr. King. He's a good friend of mine. That's how I got you in at the last minute. I had to explain your situation. He needs to know so he can handle your medical exam the right way. Do you need a restroom first?"

He nods.

I point along the far wall. I've been here before and know there aren't any windows in the restrooms. Let's not have any temptations this first day.

KELLY

23

Today I'm doing the kinds of things normal people do. But I don't feel normal. I feel disconnected from these people going about their lives, like I don't belong. Looking out the window, I see a couple of rough looking guys standing by a beat-up truck. I think I'd feel lots more comfortable if I was out there with them instead of sitting in here with these nicely dressed people laughing and eating their lunches. The only person that ties me to this world now is the man sitting a few feet away from me eating a grilled cheese. I like him, but his ability to see into my head makes me nervous.

As if to prove it he asks, "How ya doing?"

"Fine."

He gives me one of his super-power looks. I bite my lip as I reach for some safe words to say. "I don't feel real." That's *not* what I meant to say, and I expect him to look at me like I'm crazy.

But he doesn't. He says, "Don't worry. It's normal. That feeling will fade."

I sure hope he's right. He seems like the kind of person who is right a lot. It's strange sitting with him like we're just two people out to lunch. I play the *what's-the-last-time* game, and it's with some shock that I realize the last time I sat in a restaurant having a meal was with my father at the diner in Fort Dixon. I always went through fast food windows with Mrs. Williams, and Granny Haverly liked to cook so we never ate out.

This is the most time I've spent with just one person since Pop Haverly. This feels different because unlike Pop, this guy is going to be in my life for years. Wait a second, what am I thinking? *Duh.* Mr. Murry might get a new job at any time. He's probably just temporary too. Doesn't matter anyway. Nobody's in my life anymore unless they're paid to be. Now that I look back on it, I see even Rafa was in it for the money.

I walk through the restaurant to use the bathroom giving a wide berth to the people of this planet on my way there. I'm kind of surprised Mr. Murry lets me leave his sight. When we get to the car, he stops me before I close the door and has me stick my right leg out so he can take off the tracking device before we see the doctor. I'm glad to be rid of it, even if it's just for a little while.

The nurse has me step on a scale. She writes down my weight and looks out the side of her eyes at Mr. Murry. I follow her down a long, narrow hall into an exam room. The doctor arrives and after he and Mr. Murry say some kidding things to each other, he turns to me.

"Hello, Kelly. I'm Dr. King, but you can me Dr. Mike if you want. How are you doing?"

"Fine." It's the automatic response. After I make it, I turn and stare at a picture on the wall of a lighthouse. This is the first person on the outside to know I'm an inmate. It's embarrassing.

"Let's have a look at you." He pats the paper-covered table. I climb up and pull off my shirt like he tells me.

He takes my blood pressure, listens to my chest with his stethoscope, then takes hold of my left arm turning it. "That's a pretty serious scar. Do you have complete mobility with this arm?"

I pull my arm from his grasp, maybe a little harder than I meant to. Worried, I flick a glance at Mr. Murry while I answer, "Yes, sir."

The doctor feels up under my throat, then has me lay back and pushes around on my stomach before reaching down to a more personal level. By now, I'm used to having my privacy invaded but it doesn't mean I like it.

"Okay, you can put your shirt back on," Dr. King says. "How's your appetite?"

I try not to look over at Mr. Murry. "Okay." My appetite is fine *today*, so it's not a lie in my book.

Mr. Murry says, "He's a vegetarian." Like it's a disease.

"A vegetarian from Wyoming. Bet that made you popular." This joke wasn't funny the first one hundred times I heard it, and it's no better now. I'm proud of myself when I don't roll my eyes.

As he looks in my ears, Dr. King says, "You can be a vegetarian and be perfectly healthy. I'll give you some written information to help you with your choices. You aren't going to be surprised if I tell you you're too thin, are you?"

It's like he's naming one of my many sins. I don't answer, spending time checking out my new shoes and thinking about how great it is to have a pair of sneakers again.

He scribbles something, then looks at Mr. Murry. "How about giving us a few minutes, Sam?"

Once we're alone, Dr. King rolls his chair over to me and sits down. "Mr. Murry told me about your situation. Kind of a tough spot for someone your age. How are you getting along?"

How do you think I'm getting along? Life's just grand, isn't it?

"Okay," I say.

He leans back and puts his hands behind his head. "So? What do you like to do for fun?"

It's an unexpected question. I almost laugh. Fun? *What the hell is that?* "Not much."

"You like to be outside I'm told. Me too. Do you like hiking?"

I love hiking. "I guess it's alright."

"That's something you can do plenty of at The Village. Exercise would be a good thing. You know a lot of your physical health is tied to how you're feeling about things in general." He looks at me but I'm looking at his shoes. I bet he doesn't know one of his socks is dark navy and the other is black.

"Let's try this. On a one to ten scale with one being crawl in a hole, and ten being a happy camper, where are you?"

I mull the question trying to decide, despite myself, what number I might pick.

"Have you hit a ten any time in the last three years?"

It would be rude not to respond, so I whisper my answer. "Hardly."

"How about an eight?"

The floor has a big crack between two of the square tile pieces. "I don't think so."

"Six?"

I'm kind of getting into the game. I think back. The days at the Haverlys were pretty good.

"Maybe."

"Good. How much of the time are you at one?"

I don't want to play anymore because the truth hurts, so I say nothing. Crawling in a hole describes a good hunk of my life these last few years.

"How often do you feel nauseous? None, occasionally, most of the time?"

This guy is sure big on measurements. "Closer to most of the time."

"I'm thinking being depressed has a lot to do with that."

Is that what I am? I feel like shit all the time. Somedays I can ignore it. Other days it's almost overwhelming. If that's depression, I have it. For a second I think back to the kid in jail who tried to hang himself. Was he depressed?

Dr. King keeps talking. "A lot of people don't understand that grief and depression can make you physically sick. I think when you get settled in, you'll feel better, but it might be good to have a little help to jumpstart the process, I'm going to write a prescription for an antidepressant that could help. I can put you on a low dosage to start. Your body may need to break the habit of feeling bad. It's a circular thing. You feel bad emotionally, so your body feels bad. Your body feels bad, so you feel depressed. You see what I'm saying?"

I think of my Dad who I admired so much. I think of all his deputies and my uncle, all who seemed like tough guys. *Cowboys don't take pills.* I also think of the guy that ran into our car, high as a kite on illegal stuff. "Yes, but I don't want to take drugs." I lift my head and meet his eyes to see if my answer made him mad, but all I see is kindness. Even though I'd rather not be talking about this, I have to admit it's kind of nice to have someone who understands how I've been feeling.

"No one's going to make you." He lays his hand on the paper-covered table next to me and taps it twice. "Tell you what let's do. I'll write the prescription and you can think about it. If you decide to give it a try, you'll have it there. But you'll need to give it several weeks before you know if it's making a difference. And I want to know if you start.

"Now, this is something I ask everyone your age. Have you ever had any thoughts about harming yourself?"

They always asked this during the detention center intakes, so I'm used to the question. "I'm not thinking about killing myself, if that's what you mean." I pause a second then add, "But I wish things had gone a different way."

"What way?"

I pick at a spot on my hand. I haven't told anyone else this. "Like I wasn't left behind."

He sets the clipboard under the little shelf with the cotton balls and tissues. "I know things might seem bleak right now, but you have your whole life ahead of you."

Great. A long miserable life. Gee, that's really going to cheer me up. I don't bother to answer, but that doesn't stop Dr. King.

"Did Mr. Murry tell you he and I go way back? We were kids together. I can tell you he's a good guy. Someone you can trust to do right by you. I'm hoping next time I see you, things might be looking up. What you and I talk about is between us, unless I have your permission to tell others. However, I kind of need to tell Mr. Murry some of this, since he'll be taking care of you. But if there's anything you don't want me to tell him, let me know."

"You can tell him whatever you want." Everything is in a *Robert Kelly Morgan* file anyway. Everybody gets to look at it but me. Does that seem right?

"Okay. Let's get him back in here." He scoots his chair away and stands up. "I'm going to have my nurse come in and draw a blood sample."

My skin tingles, and the room gets warm. I blink away the images that appear: *The emergency room. A nurse sticking a needle in an arm. Someone asking, "Who can we get to sign for the surgery?" A kid moaning, no, no, no. Someone saying, "It's going to be okay."* But the kid knew it was a lie. And he was right. It's not been okay one day since.

The images float away as Mr. Murry comes back in. The nurse is right behind him. She's smiling but I'm not fooled. Dracula probably smiled too. "This won't take but a minute. Do you want to stay sitting up or lie back?"

I lie back. I've never liked needles. I follow her instructions to make a fist and feel the needle slide in my arm. It seems a long time before it goes back out. Dracula puts a band aid on my arm. "All done," she says with a little pat.

I stay lying down and feel relaxed now. The worst is over. Even with Mr. Murry standing a foot away, I feel myself getting drowsy, but just then the doctor comes back in, so I sit up.

But he's talking to Mr. Murry, not me. "I'll know more when the lab results come back. His glands feel a bit swollen. The most immediate concern is his weight. Try some protein shakes between meals till he gets a few pounds back on. No surprise given the circumstances, depression is a concern. I know he's been someplace the food options weren't good, but weight loss is very common in depression. I think it's part of the reason he's so thin. I'm going to give you a prescription for an antidepressant. He's not real keen on the idea, but maybe in a few days he may feel differently."

Just when I think he's done with me, I get the next question. "Do you know the last time you had any shots?"

Uh-oh. Maybe the worst isn't over. "I want to say yes."

"You know?"

"No, I just want to say yes."

They both laugh. Easy for them, since they aren't the ones about to get stabbed. Repeatedly. Dr. King asks Mr. Murry, "I don't suppose you have any immunization records?"

"Afraid not."

"Then we'll have to err on the safe side." He sticks his head into the hall, motions to a nurse, then orders up a whole mess of disease names. Each one sounds worse than the last.

I look at Mr. Murry. "I don't like where this is headed."

"I know, but better than getting sick." To add insult to injury he asks the doctor. "Did you include Hepatitis A?"

"Yes, I'm aware that's a problem in your setting."

The nurse comes in with a tray of needles. "I'll handle it," Dr. King tells her. He throws a small white cloth over them.

I flick my eyes to the tray then narrow my eyes at him. "Does that make them go away?"

He laughs. "Psychologically maybe. I'm sorry but it'll all be over in a minute or two then you can be on your way. This first one is the worst so let's do it in the rump. It's going to sting just a bit."

Famous last words. You know it seems like I should have the right to say no, I'm not doing this. But if I kick up a fuss, I'll look uncooperative, not to mention I'll seem like a big baby. I really hate shots. I roll over and tense.

"Try to relax. It'll be less sore afterwards."

I grimace as the needle goes in. I'm such a wuss. I sit up for the next ones.

I hate the preliminaries as much as the shots, the smell of alcohol and the cold swab of the cotton ball before the wait for the needle. Of course, if I was brave enough to look, it would take the guesswork out of it, but I'm not in the mood to be changing my ways. There's three more, two in the left arm and one in the right.

The doctor is cheery about it all even if I'm not. "All done. That wasn't so bad was it?"

I just stare at him.

He laughs. "I withdraw the question." To Mr. Murry, he says, "He may run a little fever tonight. Give him a couple of Tylenol, if needed. On your way out, schedule an appointment for about a month from now. I want to see how he's doing on his weight. I'll call you if the bloodwork turns up anything."

Mr. Murry hands me my new jacket. I'm more than ready to get out of here. I knew the day was going too good to last.

SAM

24

Driving away, I'm mulling over Mike's concerns about the boy's physical and mental health. A few minutes later, I broach the antidepressant subject but get resistance.

"Are you going to make me?"

"No, it's your decision. But there's no shame in needing a little medical help to feel better."

He's looking out the window as if something fascinating is out there, so I drop it. We've had a good outing and I hate it to end on a sour note. "Let's go to the library and you can get some books. There's only so much reading about The Village a person can stand."

He brightens up like I said I'd take him to Disneyworld. It's a small-town library, but it's new and done up with the latest trends: a fireplace with easy chairs, large windows, colorful artwork. It's spring, so the round front table has gardening books on display with a little sign on top saying *Dig In*.

The older lady at the desk—her name tag says Doris—is happy to assist. She explains a minor can have a card, if the legal guardian shows a county driver's license and agrees to sign on their behalf. I'm not a legal guardian, so I'm ready with a half-truth but no need, when I sign she doesn't blink at the different last names. Probably assumes I'm the stepfather. Or maybe she doesn't care. How many people try to illegally get a library card anyway?

Doris hands Kelly a paper card. "The real one will be mailed to you in about a week. You can check out three books on the temporary card."

He thanks her, throwing in a "yes, ma'am," and they have a nice chat about some favorite authors. She tells a long rambling story about her daughter that has me bored to tears, but Kelly listens politely. By the end of their conversation, I can tell she's completely smitten. Those manners and smile are a lethal weapon.

215

Doris leans over and whispers he can have five books if he'd like. If delinquent kids only knew how far they could get if they didn't slouch, grumble, and say "yeah" all the time. They'd get away with a whole lot more.

"I'll hurry," he says to me.

"Take your time. We just need to be back by four if you're going to be there when Mr. Galloway comes."

I linger around the newspapers and keep an eye on him, but not because I think he'll run out the door. His anxiety has been on display all day. He's continually trying to gauge my reaction and react accordingly. The doctor visit was rough on him. Here, for the first time, he looks at ease and I can observe him being himself. He doesn't look at any books for teens. His fingers graze the books on a shelf dedicated to mythology, and he pulls a few out to read the backs. The psychological report wasn't wrong. It's plain to see the boy is intelligent.

On the drive home, Kelly holds his books in his lap and at least half a dozen times pulls the library card out to look at it. I get it, something that's his with his name on it. I realize I'm making an internal switch. He's becoming Kelly, not the boy or the kid. I give myself a little mental shake. Tomorrow, I'll go back to my mostly administrative duties. My spread sheets, budget, personnel evaluations, supply requisitions. I'll turn him over to the other staff, and our interactions will be limited.

When we arrive at The Village, I see Galloway arrived early. He's sitting on the front porch scribbling on a yellow legal pad. Kelly's all smiles as his lawyer walks down to meet us at the bottom of the steps. "Hi, Henry"

"Hey there, sport, whatcha got?"

"Clothes." Kelly turns to me as I hold up the bags as evidence. "And books from the library. Look, I've got my own card."

"Super." He tugs on the sleeve of Kelly's new jacket. "You look pretty spiffy. Nice haircut."

Over the top of the boy's head, Galloway looks at me with a shit-eating grin. He's entirely too pleased with himself, so I shove the bags into his hands. "Here. Make yourself useful." I turn to Kelly. "Get some drinks out of the fridge for you two." Galloway smiles as Kelly springs up the stairs and goes inside.

We linger at the bottom of the concrete steps where the lawyer continues to grin, this time right at me. "Shut up, Galloway," I say.

216

He holds his hands in front of him, the packages dangling from his wrists. "Hey, I got nothing but nice things to say. In twenty-four hours, he's a whole new kid. You got any other openings? I have a couple of nineteen-year-olds coming down the pipeline I'd like to send your way; that is, if minimum security applies to people who robbed someone with a gun." He sighs. "They are both alumni from McGee. I wish they could have had a place like this back when."

"Might not have changed anything."

"We'll never know. They'll still have decades of prime crime years ahead when they get out."

"Depressing thought."

"My boss tells me to think of it as job security." He gives a little smirk. "But hey, I'm good at my job."

"It's a pretty slick stunt you've pulled off, but don't get too cocky. This is just day two. A lot could go wrong."

"Please let me have my warm fuzzy thoughts. I don't get many."

"You're on the client's side. You must get accolades."

He shakes his head, "Are you kidding me? Most of them think it's my fault if they get shipped off no matter how overwhelming the evidence or how extensive their criminal history."

Kelly appears at the door with the drinks, so we quit our conversation. I go in the kitchen and find Gene putting groceries away. Apparently, he thinks getting three different kinds of cereal yesterday wasn't enough and returned for more kid-friendly food. He faces me with a bag of potato chips in one hand and a bunch of bananas in the other. "Hey. How'd the day go?"

"He was fine. Pathetically grateful for everything he got. I felt like I'd donated a kidney. He wasn't too happy at the doctors, of course. Got zapped with blood work and a bunch of shots. Mike wants him to think about going on an anti-depressant."

Gene leans against the counter. "Lordy. Are we set up to handle all of this? Eating issues, depression. They should have put him in a juvenile center."

"I don't know. Despite the obvious need, none of the juvenile facilities I worked in ever had qualified mental health staff. Plus, Kelly just spent the whole day in the community with me rather than sitting in a cell. Anyway, doesn't matter what we think. The USS Juvenile sailed without him."

Thirty minutes later, Galloway appears and holds out his hand. "Mr. Murry, a pleasure. Take good care of my client."

I shake his hand and look at the boy. Kelly meets my eyes and doesn't immediately look back down which is progress. "I think we're going to get along just fine." I give the lawyer a half-ass smile. "And if I ever need an attorney, I'm calling you."

I glance out the window as they say their farewells. Galloway gives the boy a hug. Good. The kid needs to know he has someone going the extra mile for him. He's not going to have anyone else.

In the evening, once again, I bring him back to this building after we eat. He seemed kind of tired, and I figure, what's one more night? Tomorrow, for sure, I'll pass him off to staff next door. And besides, like yesterday, he's soon asking to go upstairs for the night.

"Sure. You'll need to get up earlier in the morning to go to the stables. Mr. Hicks is meeting with us about your work assignment. He's particular about who works with his horses, so he wants to talk to you before making a commitment. Don't be offended if he's kind of gruff. Mr. Hicks likes horses more than people."

Kelly's collecting up his books. "Believe me, I get that." He swipes his arm across his brow where there are beads of sweat.

I give him a longer stare, then beckon him with my hand. "Come here a second." He looks half-afraid of me, but complies. I peer closely at him. Gene joins us and I say, "He looks a little flushed."

He asks the boy if he can feel his forehead and Kelly nods. His eyes are on Gene as he places his hand with the practiced air of a father. "He does feel a little warm. Shots can do that."

"Won't hurt to give him a couple of Tylenol before bed. Wait here," I say to the boy. I grab a couple of pills and a glass of water, and Kelly dutifully swallows and hands the glass back. "Okay, head on up."

He walks a couple of steps away, then stops and turns sideways. I wait to see what's on his mind.

He swallows and acts like he's going into confession mode. "Thanks for today. It was the best one I've had in a long time." He immediately turns back around and starts walking up.

"You know, I learned something today." I call after him, as he stops on the third step and turns back to me. "I never knew what I was missing not shopping at Goodwill."

A flash of a smile. He heads ups the stairs, and I make sure he gets up there okay before turning away. Gene gives a tap on my arm. "Good job. He looks a lot more comfortable around you."

Truth is, I'm more comfortable around him. He's such a strange mix of vulnerability and resilience. Here's a kid who took care of himself for a year, but gets excited about a library card. Who escaped from a secure facility, but smiles at cereal boxes. I can tell this kid has a zeal for life that's warring with sadness. *And depression.* With kids, that diagnosis is nothing to take lightly. Tomorrow, I'll see if I can convince him to try the meds for a while.

Hours later, I wake with that groggy sensation of being awake without knowing why. The clock by my bed says 2:48. I reach up with my hand to straighten the monitor and stare at it intently for a few seconds, like staring hard enough will improve my hearing. All's quiet so I turn over and try to go back to sleep. A minute later, I toss the covers off, cursing at myself for being neurotic. I'm not going to be able to go back to sleep till I eyeball that boy.

At the top of the stairs, there's enough light for me to look in his bed and see he's not in it. He must be in the bathroom, that's probably what woke me up. The door to there is open. I don't see him, but it's dark. "Kelly?" No answer.

I massage the wall in search of the light switch and flick it on. My eyes scan the bedroom and most of the bathroom since the door is open. I stride in there and with one motion, yank back the shower curtain. No kid. *Shit! Where is he?* My eyes sweep the room and land on the window. The clasp is twisted to the open position. I know I locked it when I prepared the room for him. *No. No. No. He couldn't be that stupid.* With both hands, I pull it open and mentally brace myself for the worst as I look down.

Thank God. No little body down there. My feet thud back down the stairs.

I must have sounded like an elephant so no surprise, Gene's door opens. "What's going on?"

"I can't find the damn kid."

"Oh no. Surely not." He comes into the hall, shutting his door behind him.

"Finish checking this floor, okay? I'll look downstairs."

I race through the first floor, flicking off the alarms to the outer doors, then look around the outside of the building. How could he have gotten out? I guess he was smarter than I thought. And a better liar. All that promising not to run and I actually believed him.

Once back inside, Gene asks, "Any luck?"

"No." *Fuck!* "Well, I said this would happen, didn't I? Stupid little shit. He's in a world of trouble now." I report escapes to local law enforcement. It's an automatic transfer to secure custody, but if I could find him, maybe I could avoid all that. I'm furious at the kid, but madder at myself for caring so much. And damn it, I feel betrayed. Now isn't that stupid?

Gene grabs my arm. "Calm down, Sam. Go check the tracking screen."

"Yeah, right. I'm not thinking straight."

As soon as the screen comes up, his tracking device is blinking in the building. I grimace. "Christ, he must have cut it off somehow."

Gene looks over my shoulder. "I went up to his room after I'd finished on the second floor and looked for it. I didn't see it anywhere."

"He probably threw it under the goddamn bed." I go still as the words leave my mouth. I raise my eyes to Gene's. "You don't think …?"

Racing up the two flights of stairs and into his room, I go down on one knee to peer under the bed. There he is, curled up by the wall with a blanket under his head, sound asleep. I sag with relief, then roll to my butt and sit there with my hands around my knees and take a deep breath.

Thank God.

Gene followed me up. "He's here," I say.

Gene leans against the wall, out of breath. "I'm getting too old for this job."

I take a deep breath and peer under again. "Kelly," I say quietly. No response, so I try a little louder. "Kelly!" He doesn't budge.

Damn it! I reach under the bed and as soon as I touch his arm, I can feel the heat radiating off him. I lay down on the floor—*Hell, I'm getting too old for this too*—and reach my hand to his forehead, a repeat of a few hours ago. He's hot as a firecracker.

"Gene, he's burning up."

"Can you grab him?"

"I think it'll be easier to move the bed, then pull him out." We slide the bed enough out of the way to allow me to bend down and scoop him into my arms. His head rests in the crook of my elbow. There's a cut on his forehead, the dried blood runs down the left side of his face. How the hell did he do that? Must have nicked it on a nail sticking out under the bed.

I look up at Gene's concerned face. "His shirt is sopping wet. He sweat right through it."

Kelly's eyes flick open, but there's no alertness there. A whimper and a whisper, "Don't let them get me."

Gene has pushed the bed back in place and turned down the covers, so I can lay the boy on the bed. He reaches over to join the forehead testing party. "Yeah, he's really hot. I have a thermometer, want me to get it?"

"If you don't mind going up and down these blasted stairs again."

A snort. "I'll manage."

I rummage in the drawers and get one of the newly purchased T-shirts. As I peel off the one he's wearing and replace it with a dry one, he finally seems to look a bit more alert. Gene returns with the thermometer and gets the boy to open his mouth, so he can slide it under his tongue. We sit in complete silence until Gene pulls it out, glances, then holds up the evidence. "It's over a hundred and three. What was in those shots?"

"Hell, if I know. I'll get more Tylenol."

It takes some doing, but we manage to get them down Kelly before he promptly goes back to sleep. Gene brings in a cold washcloth and bathes the boy's face, then gently lays it across his forehead. He's sitting on one side of the bed next to the boy and I'm on the other.

I shake my head, and whisper, "This is a fine mess."

One side of Gene's mouth turns up. "I shouldn't have said retirement was dull. What now?"

"Go back to bed. I'll sit up here awhile, if for no other reason than to make sure he doesn't end up back under the bed. I may lie down across the hall later."

"Okay, call if you want me to come spare you." Gene lightly pats the boy's chest as he stands up. "Can't get a break, can he?"

After he leaves, I pull over the rocking chair and settle into it, watching the boy's chest rise and fall. I have to agree with Gene, the kid deserved at least a few good days. I'm just relieved he's still here.

When an inmate takes off on us, I'm usually more hacked off than anything else. It messes up my statistics and causes a ton of paperwork, but I don't take it personally. This time however, when I pictured this naive boy on his way to an adult prison, I had a complete moment of panic.

I shudder to think of him there where the threat of violence is always at hand. One look at him, and the prison staff would probably haul him off to segregated housing, where he'd be locked in a cell twenty-three hours a day for his own protection. I hate to even think about what that experience would do to this kid. Hell, what it does to any kid. I've never gotten over my shock that in corrections, people can legally do things to children that a parent would get arrested for. If I locked my son in a closet and did nothing but feed him three times a day, child protection would be all over me, but the state does it with total immunity.

An hour later, I move across the hall to stretch out on the bed. I go to sleep, hoping he'll be better in the morning. One thing's for sure, my plans to hand him off to someone else ain't happening anytime soon.

SAM

25

By daybreak, Kelly's fever has dropped some, and we get him roused enough to walk downstairs with Gene behind and me in front to be sure he doesn't take a tumble. I set him back on the couch like yesterday. He won't eat, but he drinks a little of a soft drink before he rolls over and sleeps all morning. He refuses any lunch and by afternoon, it's obvious he's truly sick. This has to be more than a reaction to the immunizations.

Around two o'clock, he abruptly sits up, doubled over and holding his middle. He isn't going to make it to the bathroom so I grab a trash can. What little food he has in his stomach comes up, followed by a yellow stream of bile. All that effort getting him to eat has been for nothing.

Should we go to the hospital emergency room? I really don't want to. Well, this is what old friends are for. I call Mike and am told he's off today, so I call his cell. As soon as he answers, I begin my rant.

"The boy you saw yesterday is really sick. He has a high fever, just threw up, seems like he can barely move. Do you know the hassle I'll get trying to explain his situation if we go to the hospital? Anyway, I'm blaming you. He was fine till you saw him."

Mike gives a chuckle. "You've been blaming me for things since elementary school. I'm at my kid's ball game. Soon as it's over, I'll head out there. Let me check the office and see if the lab results from yesterday's blood work are in."

It seems an eternity passes before Mike arrives. "Thanks for coming. You can join some small tribe of doctors that still make house calls or get a certificate or something."

Proving he's as much a smart ass now as when we were both ten, he says, "I prefer money."

Mike pulls a chair over to the couch and sits down. "Hey, Kelly, bet you didn't think you'd see me again so soon, huh?" He picks up the boy's hand and checks his pulse. Kelly's eyes flick open for a second, but he doesn't speak and closes them again.

"Let's have a look at you and see if we can get you feeling better." I have to admit, Mike has a good bedside manner.

He goes through the customary routine, listening to his heart and lungs, taking his pulse and blood pressure. After he's done, he winds up his stethoscope. "I did get the results from yesterday." He reaches under the boy's chin. "I was suspicious about these glands. He's got mononucleosis. Combine that with his general poor condition, and we've got a pretty sick pup."

I ask the dreaded question, "Should he be hospitalized?"

With the most energy I've seen all day, the boy's eyes open with a look of panic. Doesn't take a genius to figure out a hospital isn't a happy place full of sweet memories for the kid.

"They can't really do more than you can, and this is no quick fix. I'm going to give him something that will hopefully improve his discomfort, but he's going to be weak for days and will need restricted activities for much longer. The biggest concern is the spleen, so I'll need to monitor that. Otherwise, keep up the meds for the fever and joint pain, hydration and nourishment, or hospitalization might become necessary. Lots of patients go off their food."

I scowl. "Well shit, we were just getting him to eat half decent."

"I'll make a list of what you can pick up at the drugstore. He takes pen to paper, scrawling in that way doctors do. "Here's what you need." He turns back to the boy. "Okay, Kelly, I'm leaving now so I can't torture you any more today." Mike gives his arm a gentle squeeze. "Hang in there. I'll call and check on you tomorrow."

I walk Mike to the door as he clues me in a little more about Kelly's condition once we're out of earshot. "Thanks for coming."

"No problem." He grins. "I give special consideration to all new parents."

I frown at him. "Ha, ha."

When darkness falls, I carry Kelly up to his room.

"You sure you got him?" Gene asks.

I give a little snort. "It's not like he weighs anything. I could juggle him if I wanted."

I stay across the hall again and check on him a couple of times during the night. What a mess Bonnie has gotten me into. I decide to call her tomorrow. She can get her ass out here and play nurse with us.

Hmmm, Nurse Bonnie, now there's a thought. I picture her in a nurse's outfit. *Oh, yeah.*

In the morning, it's back to the couch to try and get some fluids and nourishment down him. Despite our best efforts, we have little luck. I can barely keep him awake. When I try to get him to take a drink, he turns his head. "Tired," he whispers.

I force myself to be mister bad guy and put on my best authoritative voice. "Here now, none of that. You've got to drink." I force him to half-sit, but he still turns his head away.

Now I really feel like the parent of a toddler. I look at Gene and say louder, "Let's take him on to the hospital." That does it. He opens his mouth for the straw and takes a drink. I get a couple of sips down him, but he goes back to sleep mid-drink with the liquid dribbling down his chin.

We try a couple of more times during the day and have no success. Frustrated, I call Mike. I think I know where this is headed. "I'm having no luck getting him to drink anything much less eat anything. I've begged and threatened. I'm running out of options."

Mike is quick with his response. "Take him to the ER. I'll call ahead and let them know you're coming. That'll help grease the wheels, but you may still have some problems explaining the custody and payment information."

"I know," I groan. "I'm calling the judge and getting his help expediting this." After all, he owes me.

Reaching Judge Nolan isn't easy. I go through three people until I get one to understand I need him now, not later. Number One and Number Two say he's on the bench and can't be disturbed. Number Three tells me she'll take him a note. I pace around the room for the next five minutes till the phone rings.

"Murry."

"This is Judge Nolan. I'm afraid to ask what's going on. Did he run off or did someone hurt him?" Obviously, Number Three was sparse with the details.

"No, but he's very sick. The doctor wants me to take him to the Med Center.

I'm worried about getting him seen and his possible admission. I'm not sure with a minor how to go about it."

"Yeah, they won't like it. I get calls from time to time authorizing medical care on kids that Children's Services take there before they go into foster care. I'll meet you to sign paperwork. Are you going now?"

"As soon as we can load him in my car. Should be there in about an hour."

"Okay, call me a few minutes before you get there, and I'll head over." He gives me his cell number.

"Great. Thanks." I'm grabbing my jacket and keys as I hang up. I inform Gene on the run. "The judge is meeting us at the hospital."

"Do you want me to drive?"

"I don't think so. Just help me load him into the car. I need you to hold down the fort here. This is probably going to take a while. I'll call you later."

We go back to the unmoving boy. Now I wish I hadn't used the hospital as a threat but no matter, he doesn't wake up. I wrap him in a blanket and pick him up. I point with my elbow, "Grab the pillow, will you, Gene?"

The beautiful weather of the past few days is gone. There are no rules for March; anything can happen. It's been a dull, menacing day, with overcast skies and times where the wind whips up and turns the early spring leaves upside down. It's cranking up again, with a bite to it.

I cradle the boy to my chest while Gene opens the back door of the car. Bob Morris, one of my COs, is standing at the bend of the driveway with about ten of the inmates while they prepare to go out on a work project. Needless-to-say, all eyes look our way. I take great pains not to knock Kelly's head putting him in the back. Once he's situated, I head out. Pulling up next to Bob and the guys, I roll the window down.

"Hey, I'm on the way to the ER. I'm likely going to be gone the bulk of the day. Check with Gene on coverage, if you would."

"Sure." He leans over and glances in, his eyes getting that look adults do when they see a sick child, doesn't matter the circumstances. "Poor kid."

The inmates are giving me approving looks. Many of them are dads, maybe good ones, maybe not. But they know the kid is one of them, so they have a connection regardless.

I'm over the speed limit most of the way but get forced to a slow crawl during the winding four miles along the river. As luck would have it, I get behind a slow-moving farm wagon, impossible to pass on these roads as its backend waffles one way then the other. I'm drumming my fingers on the steering wheel and gritting my teeth in frustration until the road straightens out enough, I can get around him.

I glance repeatedly over my shoulder for any movement in the back. Kelly's face looks like he's dead-but-breathing. For just a moment, I entertain the horrifying thought that he could die. *Oh man, he doesn't deserve that.*

The best distraction from morbid thoughts is to get mad at someone, so I silently cuss the jail staff. They should never have let this boy get in the shape he's in. Then I focus my fury on Children's Services who should have found a good foster home for him and none of this would have been set in play. And why couldn't the grandfather have been someone who wasn't a class A asshole? I'd be sitting in my office right now ordering supplies instead of … *dammit!* This time it's a fucking camper with an "I ♥ the Smokies" bumper sticker.

Ten minutes out, I call the judge. I get one lucky break and see a car pulling out of a parking space close by the ER entrance. I carry Kelly in, and a well-dressed man's eyes go straight to us. I've never met him, but it's gotta be Nolan. I gratefully turn the admission over to him and take a seat with the boy in my arms.

Once Nolan works his judicial magic with the hospital folks, he walks over to me. We skip any formal introductions. "You made good time," he says.

"I drove like a bat out of hell except for the damn curves."

The judge looks at the boy in my arms. "Poor kid." That seems to be the thought of the day. Hell … of the week. "What's wrong with him, do you know?"

"Mono. A bunch of shots might have jumpstarted this. Doc said it's probably been percolating awhile. Jails are hotbeds for all sorts of diseases. The kid's in such bad shape, it's hit him hard. I saw on the jail records he'd been in the infirmary several weeks ago. Probably started then." I shift the boy in my arms and pull up his shirt exposing his jutting ribs. "Did you have any idea?"

"*Jesus.* No, I only saw him once before sentencing. Much as it pains me, I guess we have to credit Galloway for doing whatever it took to get him out. His inclination was right; the kid's in bad shape."

I look over at admissions and quietly ask, "What did you tell them?"

227

The judge lowers his voice. "That he's a ward of the state. I let them presume foster care or else it might complicate things."

"Good thinking." Otherwise they might want us to follow prisoner protocols and that could get ugly. I'll have to straighten the payment stuff out eventually, but I'll worry about that later. A nurse materializes, then an orderly who rolls up a gurney. Down the hall we go until they park us behind a curtain, pulling it halfway closed. I expect Nolan to take off, but he stays with us.

A doctor in green scrubs strides in with a little nod to us. He leans over the boy and peels back his eyelid with his thumb, shines a light in that one, then the other before he murmurs to the nurses, who murmur back. They peel off the boy's shirt. Here in this setting, Kelly looks even thinner, every rib bone pronounced for all to see. Two nurses give me the icy eye. More murmuring. They slip off the rest of his clothes and put on a hospital smock which the doctor pushes aside as he completes his exam.

A nurse slips a needle into the top of the boy's hand and tapes it down. She grabs a plastic bag of fluid and efficiently attaches it to the silver rack by the bed, before running a narrow plastic tube to the needle in Kelly's hand. As one nurse puts fluid into him, another arrives to take it out, filling several vials with his blood. Finally, they talk to me, letting me know they're admitting him but reassuring me he's not in any imminent peril. He's a lot of "D" words including "dehydrated" and "depleted."

Within minutes, we're standing by his gurney in the hallway of the pediatric ward while they do the last of the room preparation. A little gray-haired lady, the poster child of hospital volunteer grannies, smiles at us and puts a teddy bear in Kelly's bed.

I stare at her in surprise, but with a grin she anticipates me. "Everyone thinks these are for toddlers, but you'd be surprised how many teenagers want one, although most won't admit it. They say they'll give it to a younger sister or brother." She winks as she walks away.

Judge Nolan and I stand together under this colorful animal wall mural with Kelly on the bed beside us, his new, fuzzy-faced friend looking up at me accusingly, like somehow this is all my fault. Our eyes meet—the judge's and mine, not the bear's—and all I can say is, "Shit."

Nolan shakes his head. "Yeah, one for the memoir."

It's a good thing the judge stuck around, because as they're rolling Kelly into the room a policeman and a hospital social worker corral us in the hall for a "little discussion." Great, now I'm about to go on the child abuse registry. A young teen, skin and bones, with a big cut and bruise on his head; I'm not surprised someone rang the alarm.

The judge gives the cop the abbreviated story. I'm out of trouble but the cop still needs to fill out his report and goes into Kelly's room for pictures. The boy has rolled over on his side with his cheek resting on the top of Teddy's head.

The officer looks up at me. "You're kidding."

"Not what you were expecting, huh? Me neither."

He shakes his head, takes his pictures, then leaves.

The IV must be working it's magic because Kelly is stirring. I lean over, say his name and can see him coming to the surface. His face shifts, his lips move, then finally his eyes open. He looks lost, so I quickly go into reassurance mode.

"Hey there, Kelly. I brought you to the hospital but nothing to worry about. Everything's okay."

His eyes scan the room and I can see the panic starting to build. His voice is an urgent whisper. "Don't leave me here."

"I'm staying right here, Kelly. As soon as they say you can be discharged, we'll go back. Together." He opens his mouth, but before he can say anything else, I motion to the judge. "Look who came to see you."

Nolan moves next to the bedrail. "Hello, Kelly. I wanted to make sure you were okay."

Kelly doesn't look reassured. His forehead furrows with worry. "Please don't send me somewhere else."

"I won't be doing any such thing," the judge says. He tilts his head in my direction. "I think you've made a good friend here."

The boy takes a shallow breath, scanning the IV bag and the needle in his arm. His eyes go from my face to the judge's, then back. "Will you promise me something?" His voice is barely above a whisper, but his eyes are intense.

I look at Nolan and decide to speak for both of us. "We'll sure try. What is it?"

"If I die, will you make sure I go back to Wyoming? I don't want to be buried here all alone."

Nolan's hand, which had been absentmindedly trailing across the fake-wood headboard of the bed, stops. It's been an emotional few days with two straight nights of bad sleep. I'm tired and my defenses are down. There's a little ball in my throat and it takes a moment to speak.

"Nobody's going to die."

He gives me this look like he's thinking, *you poor fool*, before he whispers, "People die all the time."

My eyes flick to Nolan then back to the boy. "Hey, kid, nobody's dying on my watch, got it?"

There's the faintest glimpse of a smile. "Okay."

It's an awkward moment. I take hold of the bear and sit him up, attempting to lighten things up. "Looks like another friend dropped by."

I expect him to make a face but never mess with volunteer grannies. They know their business. Without a trace of embarrassment, he slides his hand across the bed to the bear and pulls him close before laying his head on him and closing his eyes. Two seconds later, he's sound asleep. I reach up and turn off the overhead bed light, casting his face in shadows.

Nolan nods his head to the hall, and I follow him out. He runs his hand through his hair then turns to me. "I'm completely freaked out. My mother told me to go into accounting. I should have listened. Numbers are far less emotional."

I shake my head. "I don't know, I got pretty upset when my accountant told me I wasn't getting a refund this year."

He laughs. "He's going to sleep for some time. How about we hit the cafeteria and I buy you a cup of coffee?"

A nurse comes through pushing an IV setup, so I step back against the wall. "I'd love the coffee but have to stay here."

Nolan looks back toward the room and gives a half laugh. "He can barely raise his hand; he's not going anywhere."

"I know, but leaving an inmate unsupervised in a hospital is a big no-no."

He nods. "Right. I should have thought of that. It's just hard to think of him as an inmate, especially here in pediatrics," he says, as he taps the friendly looking giraffe on the mural flowing down the hall. "So, have you been cussing me out ever since I sent him to you?"

"Pretty much." We both laugh, but I get serious. "Hey, it's good you insisted."

The judge, to my everlasting gratitude, fetches me a cup of coffee before he heads out. I promise to keep him up to date.

The rest of the day crawls by. Kelly sleeps. Nurses come and go, taking vitals and switching out IV bags. I find yesterday's newspaper and reread it before deciding to make one more call. Ziegler answers on the first ring.

Her voice is fast and clipped. "I've had a good day, so please don't ruin it for me. He isn't gone, is he?"

"Not to worry. He's lying here a few yards away from me. But I want a full refund for giving me damaged goods. He's sick as a dog. We're here at the Med Center."

She drops the attitude. "Oh, no. What's going on? Is he alright?"

"Get over here when you get off work and I'll tell you all about it. And fetch me some dinner. I'm stuck here and starving. Oh, and make sure you bring a dessert. You owe me that much."

I can hear her smile over the phone. "Yeah, I guess I do. I'll be there in a couple of hours." I hang up the phone and smile.

Things are looking better.

SAM

26

Other than standing for brief stretching and a few steps here and there, I'm pinned in place. I watch the people going by in the hall. In addition to the parents, there are volunteers, church groups, and sports teams that come to visit the kids and provide entertainment. You can feel the love.

Hurting kids, caring adults—sure, I get that—but I can't help but think about kids in detention facilities who are some of the most traumatized kids on the planet. Kids who watched one parent kill another. Kids who had their bodies sold for sex. Kids who live out of a car and get locked up for being truant from school, because they're too embarrassed to go in dirty clothes. No one's visiting them. No one is wrapping them in love. I bet most of the people in this town don't even know where the juvenile detention center is.

The only bright spot in the day is dinner with Bonnie. She blows in with two large bags in her hand and in thirty seconds has taken command of the room. She brings Chinese and eats with chopsticks, using them in an expert manner.

"Show off," I tell her, but she just smiles and loudly clicks her sticks together. Then she freezes and casts a guilty glance at Kelly.

"It'll take more than that to wake him," I assure her.

Her face softens and she lowers her voice. "Poor kid." She glances into the hall. "All these parents visiting their kids, and all he has are corrections people."

"Yeah," I say. "I had similar thoughts."

She reaches for an egg roll and drops it on her plate. "I hate he's sick, but maybe it's a blessing in disguise."

"What?" I ask, "So he can't run?"

"Well, there is that. But when I worked at Longview girl's facility, there were kids who would have nothing to do with any adult till they were sick or hurt. It was a chance for us grownups to step up and show them not everyone is out to hurt or take advantage of them.

"I remember one girl who avoided me like the plague. One night when I was making rounds, I found her on the floor with a blanket. Her bed was wet, so I sent her to the bathroom to change while I put clean sheets on her bed. When she got back, she looked at me with big eyes and said, "You made my bed." I just nodded, wished her good night, and walked away like no big deal. After that, she'd comply with every request I made. She'd even tell me little jokes. Sought me out. Sometimes a crisis can be an opportunity."

I glance at the sleeping boy and frown. I'm not looking to bond, even though I admit the little cuss is growing on me. I just want him to get well. Till then, I'm stuck with him for the foreseeable future. It's all Ziegler's fault, of course, but it's hard to be mad at someone who's pulling a pecan pie out of a bag.

She reads the box top as she opens it to slice our pieces. "Eight hundred calories a serving." She gives a big sigh and proclaims, "A moment on the lips, forever on the hips," but I notice she digs into her piece with relish. I don't know what she's worried about. She looks *great*. I like a little meat on the bones. And her curves are held where they belong by toned muscles.

The night nurse comes in and with a grunt at us, goes over to take more blood from Kelly. How can he get well if they keep draining him? The other nurses have been very nice, but this woman has a sour expression. However, in fairness, if nurses are like correctional staff, she may have worked double shifts and be too tired to be smiley.

She jams a needle in Kelly's skinny little arm, and I see a slight grimace appear on his face. She frowns, retracts the needle, then jabs it back in with gusto. I involuntarily wince. This time, a little sound comes out of the boy's mouth.

In two seconds, Bonnie has abandoned dessert and is standing by Kelly's bed where she looms over the five-foot-three nurse. She puts one hand on her hip and with blazing eyes says, "Would it kill you to be a little more gentle?"

The nurse looks up in surprise and says, "His veins have collapsed." But I notice this time, when she pulls out the needle, she's less abrupt and casts a watchful glance at Bonnie as she leaves the room.

After the nurse goes to find her next victim, I look at Bonnie's still narrowed eyes, and grin. "I always knew you weren't a nice girl. It's one of the things I admire about you."

She walks over to pick up her plate and polish off the last of her pie. With a slight smile, she says, "Sometime, maybe you can tell me about those other things." She starts packing up, carefully sliding the pie back into its container. "I've got to run an errand, then my bed is calling."

I gesture to the hospital chair beside the boy's bed. "I guess that's my bed for the night. I'll be stiff as a board by morning."

She laughs and reaches up to pat my cheek. "Builds character."

I grab her hand, pull her to me, and give her the kiss I've been wanting to plant on her since that day she showed up with Kelly. Her arms come around my neck. If not for having to stay here, I'd be following her home, and she knows it too. She brushes her thumb across my lips and gives me a big smile before making her departure.

Kelly has a good night. He sleeps non-stop and a little color comes back into his face. My night, however, is lousy. Between the uncomfortable chair and the steady stream of nurses, I only catch a few winks. I'm worried I'll end up here a second night, but late in the afternoon they discharge the kid. He's pronounced stable even though he still barely opens his eyes. I'm given medicines and a boatload of instructions with the priority to get food and liquids down him. Great. Like I was so good at that before.

Winter has struck back today. No snow, but otherwise it feels more like a crisp January day than March. The cold air hits us outside the hospital doors causing Kelly to wake a little, enough to look at me and take it in when I tell him we're going back. He's asleep again almost as soon as I lay him down on the back seat.

I'm anxious to get home to some decent food and a shower but hit rush hour traffic. I crawl through town, happy I don't have to battle this every day like most of these people probably do. Just when I think I'm home free, there's an accident on US 68 that has traffic backed up for miles. It's dark by the time I turn on The Village road.

Gene meets us to help with the doors. I pick up the boy and as we start toward the building, there's a slight movement in my arms. I stop and look down to see the boy's eyes gazing up at the heavens. It's a clear moonlit night, and out here away from light pollution, the sky is brilliant. I stand still a minute, because

I realize this is the first time in a long time he's been outside at night.

I shift him a little, so his head is slightly elevated. "When you get to feeling better, I'll take you up there to that hill," I say, pointing with my chin, "where you can get the best view. But you'll have to be up to walking. I can't carry your butt that far. Something to look forward to, huh?" His eyes find mine, but I can't read what's in them. Hope? Or just more despair? He closes them, and his body gets heavier. One arm drops off his side and hangs loose. Gene tucks it back next to the boy's chest and we head in.

In the morning, it's back to the couch. It's crunch time. We've got to get some food and drink down him. Gene fetches a sports drink and a protein shake. I try to hold Kelly's head up, but he isn't helping. I worry the couch will once again be drinking more than he does. I'm getting frustrated, but we are *not* going back to the hospital.

"Okay, let's try this." I scoop him up and cradle him on my lap, like you would a toddler. His head falls back on my chest, but it's supported so gravity will be on our side. "Come on, the first sip is the hardest."

I'm just about to go into threatening mode, when he allows me to get the straw in his mouth and takes a pull. He rests after the sip, as if he just lifted two hundred pounds, but slowly he takes five more before stopping. "Okay, rest a second. You're doing good, just a little more." And like that, I alternate between cajoling and encouraging until he drinks half of each bottle.

For the next several days, I go about my business with him in tow. He can't even go to the bathroom on his own, so I can't leave him alone for long. We have a staff meeting next door, and I haul him over and lay him on a bunk till we're done. At night, I take him back up to his room and continue to sleep across the hall in case he needs me during the night. When I picked him up this morning to take him downstairs, he wasn't really awake. I'm sure he wasn't aware of his arm wrapping around my neck.

I'm reminded of the school experiment where kids are given a ten-pound bag of flour and they're supposed to take it with them wherever they go. The point, of course, is to make being a parent seem like the heavy burden it is, discouraging them from becoming one too early. I'm not sure what this experience is doing to me. The times I do have to leave Kelly with other staff, I find myself lecturing them to make sure they get him to drink enough. "Call me if he won't,"

I say. "I told you to give him his medicine at two o'clock, didn't I?"

The staff listen carefully. They nod. I see them smile when I walk away.

KELLY

27

Lifting my eyelids seems like a huge effort. I try to figure out the right muscles to do it and quit about halfway through. Words are too heavy to get out of my mouth. Even my bones ache. I must have been cursed at birth. Just when I get to someplace that seems okay, I'm knocked off my feet. *Again.* Sometimes I wonder if I'm ever going to get beyond all this.

I'd sleep all the time if they'd let me. Mr. Murry busted me my first day for lying, but he lied about not forcing me to eat. He picks me up in the morning and takes me downstairs and back up the stairs to bed at night. I want to say it's humiliating to be treated like I'm two years old, but if I did, I'd be the one lying again. My secret is I like it. I want to know someone is really here and when I feel his arms around me, I know I'm really here too.

I master drinking, then food comes back into my life. At first, it seems like a trick. With my eyes closed, I open my mouth for the straw, but instead it's a spoon. Applesauce. I want to revolt, but it's already sliding into my stomach. Maybe it's not so bad after all. At least I didn't have to chew.

The next go-around, the spoon holds mashed potatoes. It seems strange moving my jaw up and down. Chewing is like running a marathon and the swallow, especially the first one, like pole vaulting. One big push to get it down. I eat because I know I need to in order to get stronger. I eat because I know Mr. Murry wants me to.

I wake during the night and realize it's storming. Rain smacks against my window. There's a brilliant lightning display with a few big boomers then rolling thunder. I enjoy the light show. Once the loud claps are finished, the rumbling is like a lullaby. I drift back off to sleep.

I wake to birds singing. Out of habit, I pull the covers up around my head. Morning is generally not a good time for me. For so long, I'd wake up sick to my stomach, like my mind knew I was somewhere I didn't want to be. Then memory would kick in, letting me in on its dirty little secret that I was locked up. After that, the sick-in-the-stomach feeling would be joined by a knife-in-the-gut pain that would travel up to my heart and lungs.

Today, the memory arrival isn't so bad. I'm here in my nice room. Mr. Murry or Mr. Simmons are somewhere close at hand. The sun is streaming in the window, and I can see the leaves, fresh from last night's rain, have taken on a shiny polished green. The storm cleared and it's left this bright and shining morning behind. I'd like to walk over to open the window and let fresh air rush in, but I'd also like to climb Mt. Everest and neither of those things is happening today. Steps sound on the stairs. I count them and know when he's nearing the top. I also know what comes next.

"Hey there, buddy. Good morning. You awake?"

Not wanting to commit, I half raise my eyelids then close them again.

There's this interesting sensation of going airborne without expending any of my own energy. My own version of an amusement park ride, no ticket required. My head is on Mr. Murry's chest, as we head downstairs. I can hear his heart beating. He must know I'm awake because he's talky.

"Just so you know, the nice ladies at the restaurant have sent some of their specialties including pumpkin muffins light enough to float on air. I told them you'll eat several; that way there's plenty for me."

I picture muffins floating all over the room, tumbling in the air, hitting the walls and bouncing off with a little squeak. I smile at the thought. It reminds me of something I once read in a book. That thought nags at me. *Books. Books. Books.*

As I'm being laid on the couch, I figure out why. My eyes fly open. "Oh, no," I try to say, but my voice is so rusty it comes out as a croak.

Mr. Murry is looking at me with a concerned expression. "What is it?"

My voice comes out a whisper, but it's more words than I've put together in some time. "My library books. Are they overdue?"

Mr. Murry's expression goes from concern to amusement. I'm not sure why. There's nothing funny about overdue books. It's one of the cardinal sins of librariness. "Not to worry," he says. "I'll take care of it."

That thought about the books was like a jolt of electricity. It pulses through me like the paddles they use to jump people's hearts on TV medical shows. The room is in complete focus, and I turn my head like it's the first time I'm seeing it. Testing, I raise my hand and flex my fingers. Good to know body parts still work. My stomach is working too. I'm hungry.

Mr. Murry is back with a bowl and a spoon. It's oatmeal. Ewww. Where's the damn muffins he went on and on about? But then I spot something even better. Sitting on the side table is a cinnamon roll. With icing dripping from the top and running down the sides before pooling on the little blue and white plate.

There's a time and place for boldness. I point. "I want that."

"Oh, you want *my* breakfast?" Mr. Murry scrunches up his face like he's deciding the fate of the world. "Alright, I'll let you have it. But … you have to sit up to eat."

He and Mr. Simmons grab a couple of pillows and prop me up. I'll admit, it's nice to see things from a vertical perspective again. Mr. Simmons hands me the plate. Mr. Murry turns and walks away saying, "I'll get you a fork."

Screw that. I'm in no mood to wait. Breaking off a chunk, I stuff it in my mouth, savoring the taste of sugar and cinnamon. It's everything I thought it would be and more. Thankfully, no one put any damn raisins in it.

Mr. Murry comes back with a fork, but just laughs and walks away. My fingers keep getting caked with the icing, but to hell with good manners. I lick it off between bites, sucking on each finger before breaking off another chunk. It takes a long time to eat it, but hey, I've got all day. When the last crumb is gone, I lean my head back on the pillows, stuffed and exhausted. That was great. I can feel the smile on my face.

Mr. Murry comes over and takes the plate. He looks down at me, then smiles at Mr. Simmons. "I feel like we should give him a cigarette."

That makes no sense. I try not to look at him like he's crazy. "I don't smoke."

For some reason, they both think this is hysterical. Mr. Murry is shaking his head, as he takes my plate to the kitchen. I look over at Mr. Simmons. "What?" That just makes him laugh more.

Let's face it, they're both weird, but I like them. I like being here with them. I decide I'm going to start calling them Sam and Gene. Just in my head of course.

They don't have to know.

SAM

28

At long last Kelly seems to have turned the corner. He eats better each day and can now stay awake all morning. He has a trifecta of activities. He reads, looks out the window, and watches me. He tries to be sneaky about it, but I catch him looking over the top of a book or glancing when he thinks I'm not paying him any attention. Not sure what he's finding so fascinating. Each day after lunch, he pretty much goes clunk. He naps all afternoon which revives him enough to make it awake till an early bedtime.

This afternoon my immediate supervisor, Squirrel Thompson, drops by. A long-term bureaucrat, he's reached as far up the totem pole as he's likely to go. And no, his real name isn't Squirrel, but he's gone by that for as long as anyone has known him. We get along. He generally leaves me alone to do my job which I appreciate.

I walk out to the front porch and lean against a pillar as he walks my way. I stick my ink pen behind my ear. "I wasn't expecting you, was I?"

He pulls off his sunglasses, folds them, sticks them in a front pocket of his shirt, decides he doesn't like them there and switches them to the other pocket. For a second he does nothing, but then pulls them out, unfolds them, and puts them back on. Maybe I do know how he got the name Squirrel.

Now focused on me, he says, "No, but I had a meeting not too far down the road and thought I'd swing by to see how you were getting on with that little problem Ziegler foisted on you."

"Hmmm... the little problem is right where he always is this time of day, passed out on one of our couches."

"You don't mean it."

"Oh, but I do. Mono. Bad case of it."

I watch him pull his sunglasses off and this time, he keeps them in his hand as he reaches for the rail and comes up the steps. "As if this whole situation wasn't bad enough. Can I eyeball him? Or you want him to stay asleep?"

"No problem. A bomb could go off and he'd sleep through it."

I hold the door open and he accompanies me to the back porch. The kid likes it out here on nice days. I can see why. The front of this building is on flat land, but here in the back the land drops away. The back porch is up on stilts with trees hugging it all around. It's almost like being in a tree house. Where there's a break in the foliage, you can see the rolling hills all the way to the river.

The wicker furniture has red and white striped cushions that have faded till they look pink and cream. One of the smaller cushions doubles as a pillow. The boy is in what I think of as a classic kid sleep mode, curled on his side with his left arm flung out and his right arm draped across his chest. A light patchwork quilt, with every color known to man, covers most of him with his socked feet sticking out the end.

Squirrel stares down a moment then raises his eyes to mine and whispers, "Sweet Jesus. Maybe you should throw him back into the pond till he gets bigger."

"That's a thought."

Once in my office, Squirrel says, "I know you said he was little, but I pictured a scrawny drug addict, not someone who looks like he's at my grandson's sleepover. I think my Jake is a year younger but has twenty pounds on this kid. What the hell are you going to do with him?"

"Right now, we're just feeding him. In his current condition, he's only one step above taking care of a stuffed animal."

"Where are you housing him? When he's not on the couch?"

I point up. "Third floor. One of the quarantine rooms."

"That's a good idea for now while he's sick. You can move him to the barracks later."

"Hmmm."

He gives me a searching look. "Isn't he taking up a lot of your time?"

"It's not a problem. I can still do business as usual with him parked here."

Squirrel drums his fingers on the arm rest and looks pensive. "He won't be parked there forever." He stretches out his legs. "I'll be honest, Sam, I don't like it. I know I pushed you to take him because we had to stick him somewhere, but now that we've got him, we can explore other options. Besides the drag on your time, he's so little, I'm worried about our liability. I read about a juvenile serving adult time over in Missouri who got raped by another inmate and then hung himself. The state is paying the parents a small fortune after the court settlement."

I lean back and put my feet up on my desk. "Not that I'd let anything like that happen. But hell, Squirrel, this kid doesn't have any family who could sue. I could throw him off a cliff and no one would even know." I don't mention Galloway. He'd care, but I figure he'd approve of me arguing to keep the kid here. Wait, I'm arguing to keep the kid here? I could push Squirrel to find another spot for the boy and get back to the way my life was a few weeks ago. So why am I stalling?

I flick my Bic pen between my two fingers while I nod at my boss. "I thought we had this discussion and there wasn't any place better than here to send him."

"Yeah, nowhere in-state, but I could try working out a deal with another state to house him in one of their youthful offender facilities. It'd cost us some money but probably cheaper than the overtime you'll rack up trying to maintain him here."

I chew on the cap of my pen and think. A facility in another state that doesn't have it out for him. That could work. He'd be with other teens and they'd have a school program. I should jump on it. But then I remember the boy at the hospital. *Please take me back.*

I give a dismissive wave. "Thanks, but let's not burden the taxpayers if we don't have to. I'll keep the overtime in check. It shouldn't be an issue." As the words leave my mouth, I know the only way to keep my overtime in check is simply not to claim it.

Squirrel nods but fixes his eyes on me. "Two years is a long time to babysit, Sam."

Two years with my seventy-eight-pound bag of flour. It does sound like a burden but when I open my mouth to say, "Yeah, see what you can do," it somehow turns into, "I've got this under control." I hope I sound more confident than I feel.

One last narrow-eyed scrutiny from my boss before he says, "Let's see how it goes. Best to keep our options open."

Almost a week later, Kelly is far from up and about, but he's looking better. After days of rain followed by snowflakes for forty-eight hours, we're gifted with a warm and sunny day, a prequel to the season ahead. Spring keeps fighting to arrive and will win out eventually, but this year winter doesn't want to let go.

Kelly is doing his daily window watching. Without breaking his gaze from looking out, he says to me, "This weather is weird."

I laugh. "No native would disagree with you."

He moves his hand up to touch the window. "I don't mind. Wyoming's weather can change on a dime too. I bet you don't get snow in June or July, do you?"

I give a mock shudder. "Heaven forbid. But see what you think in August when you can squeeze the air and have water drops fall out of your hand."

His mouth falls open and he looks wide-eyed at me. I can't help but chuckle. "It's only an expression. But it gets very humid. You'll see."

He sighs and turns his gaze out again. "That's too bad, it sounds like a fun thing to do."

While his eyes are fixated out the window, I can stare at him. The smile is still on my face. He's such a funny, weird kid, and damn entertaining with his little observations and expressions. Those first couple of days it felt awkward having him around, but now it's like he's been here forever. It goes both ways I think. He's relaxed around me and has gotten really comfortable on that couch. I narrow my eyes and give him a good look. Maybe a little too comfortable. That kid I saw on day one couldn't wait to get outdoors, but this one doesn't seem to mind just viewing the world from behind a glass pane. I know he's been very sick, but still...

I keep my tone conversational. "I talked to Dr. King yesterday. He doesn't want you to overdo things but says it would be good to start getting out some. Let me finish up here and we'll go somewhere. A drive or something. How's that sound?"

He glances at me, shrugs, and looks away. "I don't really feel up to it today, maybe tomorrow."

It's like the kid's pilot light has gone out. Just when I decide to push the issue, there's commotion next door and I have to go deal with an inmate's medical emergency. It takes up the rest of the morning and the day gets away from me. The next couple of days, spring showers nix any outdoor activities, but on Thursday the sun pops out and the temperature zooms up into the low sixties. With me monitoring, Kelly was able to manage the steps alone this morning for the first time. After breakfast, he assumes his spot staring out the window. I decide enough is enough. This time I don't ask.

"It's beautiful today. We're going for an off-road drive." I hold up his sneakers in my right hand.

He pulls a face. "I don't know about that. I'm pretty tired."

"You won't be running a marathon. The fresh air will do you good."

He frowns but I pull a chair over and start putting his shoes on, then grab his jacket. He's gone into Vietnam war protestor mode, not actively resisting, but not helping much either. It's like dressing a three-year-old. I stuff one arm in a sleeve, pull the jacket behind him forcing him forward, then stick his arm in the other sleeve before zipping up the jacket. I cheerily proclaim, "There, ready to go."

He's not buying it.

I'd parked one of the all-terrain Gators at the bottom of the front stairs, so I plop the kid on the front seat, sliding him over as I get in behind the wheel. He slumps against the seat with his head down as I drive. I wheel us across the meadows then turn onto the trail that takes us to the waterfall.

It's a particularly picturesque spot, a favorite with the park visitors. I pull up next to the stream, cut the engine, then lean back like I'm at a drive-in movie. After all the recent rains, the water roars over the rocks before pooling into the creek. Virginia bluebells line the stream bank, their blue flowers vivid against the green leaves. Birds are flitting in the trees, unhappy with our arrival, until they settle back into their springtime, nest-building tasks. Flanking the creek, the dogwood trees are in full bloom. The breeze knocks off some petals which drift down like snow. A male and female mallard float down the stream. I couldn't have orchestrated a better showing if I was directing a Disney movie.

Waiting is something I'm good at, so I just sit and enjoy the view myself while sneaking little peeks at the boy next to me. His head stays down initially, but I can see him looking around through the tops of his eyes. Eventually he raises his head and leans it back against the seat.

A wren lights on top of the windshield, bobbing his short tail up and down before raising his head and letting out a loud trill. Kelly's eyes flick to mine and he smiles, while we both freeze in place so we don't scare away our new friend. The bird seems intent on thoroughly investigating our vehicle, bobbing all the way across the front. After he finally flies off, we continue being nature show spectators for several more minutes. I let the boy be the first to break the spell. His voice is so soft, I have to lean over to hear him. "It's like... paradise."

I give a slow nod. "Yep."

His eyes meet mine. "This is the good part of the world." Then he looks down at his hands. "It hurts."

Seeing the pain in those eyes, I can't help wanting to comfort him. Without thinking, I bring my arm around his shoulders. I'm surprised at myself, but after all the carrying and feeding of him, it seems natural. I give his shoulders a little shake, "I know." And I do. I've managed to nudge him out of his cold indifference to life, but it comes with a price. "I wish we could have the good without the bad, but that's the problem with life, it just doesn't work that way."

I give him a little squeeze. "I know you've seen more of the bad than seems fair."

His voice cracks with an anger I've not seen in him. "Life's *not* fair. Not at all. God did a half-ass job. I could make up a whole lot better world." He glances up with a defiant expression, probably expecting me to take him to task for dissing the Almighty.

But I just shake my head. "Well, buddy, it's all we've got unless we quit. You don't strike me as a quitter."

He twists his head to look straight up at me. "I don't want to be."

"Then don't. I'm here to help, but it's got to start with you."

He slowly nods and leans back next to my arm. I find his comfort with me touching. And a little unnerving. A few seconds later, he pulls back and gives me a grin. "Hey, you wouldn't consider letting me drive this thing would you?"

Now we're on safer ground. I poker up my face. "Sure. Slide on over."

"Really?" His face brightens, but he leans his head back looking doubtful.

I thump him on his arm. "Hell no, did you honestly think I would?"

"It was worth a shot." He gives a long-suffering sigh. "Well, in that case, I'm going to start chugging those protein shakes so I can walk down here on my own."

I reach down, turn the key, and start turning the cart around. "God knows I want that. I'm about to throw my back out from hauling your butt around."

As I move the gear from reverse to drive, Kelly sits up a little straighter. "Make it go fast." And to his delight, I do.

KELLY

29

I thought I was dying and my only thought was: *About fucking time.*

When dying seemed off the table, I found being sick was the next best thing. Nothing mattered anymore. There was nothing left to lose. I was happy to let others take care of me, but I agree with Sam. It's time to give that up.

So, I'm crawling out of the hole and hoping there aren't any feet waiting up there to stomp me back down. I pick up the habit of eating again. It's good to have my appetite back, but something else makes a reappearance that's even better.

It's warm enough I can take my afternoon naps on the back porch. I love waking up with the breeze blowing over my face and the sound of the trees outside the screen. I never wake up wide awake. There's a middle world between sleep and being truly awake, and I like to linger there. Eventually, I know I'm awake, but my mind can drift along going in and out till I achieve complete consciousness.

Today I'm just coming out of the lingering stage. There's a swirl of green, the leaves of a branch brushing gently on the screen. I'm enjoying watching the movement when out of the blue, or out of a long-ago habit, I reach into my mind. One of the twigs disengages from the branch, folds itself up into a tiny sliver and scrunches through the screen, coming to rest on the wood frame. I count and on three with a pop, a small figure emerges. The twig has feet and arms with a long leaf for a body and a folded leaf for a hat. He walks in front of me and tilts his head like I'm an interesting specimen. A smile splits my face and I whisper, "Welcome back." With another pop, he's gone.

I roll onto my back and stare at the ceiling where the shadows sway and dance across the white bead board. I can make them take on shapes and personalities and hold conversations. Warmth and strength flood my body, but it doesn't stop there, it channels through my mind. The world, which has been tipped on its side for so long, rights itself and I swear I can almost hear it click into place.

A moment later, I reach for one of my notebooks, the one Sam got me at Target that day that seems a lifetime ago. I flip it open past recent doodlings to the first blank page and start to write. Like an inspired artist who begins splashing colors on a canvas, I fill page after page. The words pour out. It's like they've been waiting for me.

For the next several days I write and write, like I did that time for Professor Hill back at the jail. There's an old oak tree out back next to a plank fence. I am happy I have enough strength to climb to the top rail of the fence and hoist myself up into the tree's branches. Up a few yards, there's a large horizontal limb where I can wedge my back into a crevice and put my feet out like it's an easy chair. It's amazing how different the world can look from a mere fifteen feet up. I like to watch everyone come and go unknowingly beneath me. Well, except for Sam and Gene who know I've claimed this spot. Up here I think about life … about *lives*. It's easy to have more than one at the same time if you want to.

Your body is in command of life one. Getting up, getting dressed, eating— it's got you covered. Second life, your brain takes over, such as when you're sitting in school while the teacher lectures but looking ahead to what you'll do when the bell rings. Or thinking about hitting a home run and rounding the bases. Third life gets exciting. Seeing water drops on a flower, smelling the morning rain, the feel of the wind on your skin. It's amazing all the good things you can find out there, but you have to look for them. I figured out a long time ago, most people don't. But I do. And that's how I got a fourth life. I can make things come to life or take things apart then put them together differently. I can dive into a picture and weave stories together. It's not the kind of magic I'd really like to have, the kind where you chant a spell or wave a wand and make something happen, but it's as close to magic as I think I can get.

I'm grateful to have this ability returned to me, but somehow, it's changed. I've always known my worlds aren't real, but I would sink myself into them to the point I didn't know if minutes or hours had gone by. I used to refer to it as lost time. My Dad would reach over sometimes and swat me with his rolled-up newspaper. *Hey, Earth to Kelly!*

Now I can go there to visit, but I control it rather than letting it control me.

It's like having a foot in each world at the same time. It's not quite as awesome, but I decide maybe it's better this way. After all, I'm not a little kid anymore. A man needs to have self-control.

My dream of being an author is back on the table. After a couple of weeks, I pick up my notebook and read what I wrote. Some things need to be changed, but overall, I like what I've written and when I get to the good parts, I smile like I'm reading somebody else's book. And why not? An author is not just the creator, but the story's first reader.

Someday, I hope others will want to read my stories too.

BONNIE

30

Sundays at The Village. It's my new routine.

Sam and I both know this is about more than the boy, but he's always the main topic of conversation for the first part of my visit. This Sunday, Kelly is enjoying his daily nap, so Sam and I walk down to the restaurant. We get lunch to go and settle at one of the picnic tables. Sam reaches over and helps himself to some of my chips. I let him if for no other reason than I need to save calories for pie. He fills me in on the week's activities—the funny things Kelly said, a drawing the boy did—and while he does, I try to remind myself this is tough-ass Sam Murry.

He waves a chip in the air. "The original idea of merging him into the program with the other men is dead and done. His physical health is going to be an issue for an extended time. We can mix him in on some work assignments, but mainly he'll be with Gene, me, or The Village nature preserve staff."

I chop my lemon chess pie into bite size pieces, scientifically proven to be less calories that way. I know what he says about Kelly's health is true, but that boy wouldn't be going next door to the barracks if he was up to doing a marathon. I know better than to say that, but I ask something equivalent. "So basically, you're an unorthodox foster home?"

Sam's head comes up and I see he's about to vigorously deny any such thing. Then he sighs. "Yeah, I guess that's about it."

"You know adolescents get bored pretty easy. Once he gets his health back, you may have your work cut out for you. Especially as he gets older."

"I know." Sam polishes off the last of the chips and absentmindedly folds the empty chip bag into a flat square. "I just keep picturing him forever as this little kid, I guess because he looks the part. No one would guess he's fourteen. I took him back to the doctor for a check-up. Mike said his weight may have something to do with that. Extremely low body weight can delay the onset of puberty. Mike said he'll be thin for years no matter how much he eats, because with no body fat, his body has consumed itself."

"Like female gymnasts," I say.

"I suppose." Sam starts jamming our garbage in the bag. "Anyway, I'm glad he doesn't know I fought tooth and nail not to take him."

I give him a look and move my foot next to his. "He could find out. But my silence can be bought."

Those dark eyes fixate on my face. "Did you get a room in town?"

"Uh huh. But you know I can't put that on my travel voucher. After all, you've got a place right here." I laugh, enjoying his discomfort. "I know, not in front of the children."

He takes off his sunglasses to fix me with a look. "Not to mention all the cons next door." He's twisting his sunglasses like they're a dish rag. "I have to ask you something."

"Shoot."

"About the kid. I'm obviously not maintaining a professional distance. I've become, I don't know, overly attached or something. I wake up at night and have to go peek in on him to make sure he's okay."

I can see I need to answer this seriously. "You know, I've given this some thought. Obviously, you have to be careful no one thinks anything untoward is going on."

He grimaces. "Christ. That thought will keep me up nights. Good thing we have cameras."

Now I let myself smile. "I'm here to vouch for your quite normal male tendencies. But seriously, Sam, you're human. If I gave you a puppy you had to carry around and spoon feed for weeks, you'd be attached. This is a kid. If he had parents, it'd be different, but he's got no one but you to take care of him. I've seen the way he looks at you. How can you stay detached from that?"

He expels a breath. "Thanks. That's a relief. Maybe when he gets well and calls me a 'motherfucker' a few times, I'll get over it."

I laugh. "Something to hope for. You know I can list lots of folks I've known through the years that are where you are. I knew a social worker who had twins on her caseload. When their parents were found overdosed, she couldn't find a placement for them, so she just took them home. The agency ended up approving her as their foster parent. Later, she adopted them."

Sam's face looks more relaxed and he rests it on one hand while he leans his elbow on the table. "There was a guy with me on the police force that helped a social worker remove two brothers from a bad home situation. It was Christmas so he took some toys to the shelter where they were staying. The kids were so thrilled to see him, he started going every few days. Long story short, he ended up adopting them. I thought he was crazy."

I point my fork at Sam. "Teachers have done it, principals, coaches. In fact, when they're looking for foster homes there's now there's a name for it... *mining*. They look for the parents of a childhood friend, or a teacher, or a coach. I've even seen staff in juvenile facilities take kids home."

A black spider has crawled up between the slats of the picnic table, so Sam gives me a glance. When he realizes I'm not going to chick-out on him, he says, "Anyway, it's not like I'm adopting him. I just want things to go smoothly while he's here. And hey, I never knew you were such a wealth of information on the juvenile system."

Reaching over with the side of my hand, I flick the spider in Sam's direction. "I know a lot of things that might surprise you." While he's busy pushing the bug off his shirt, I reach into my big bag. "Oh, before I forget. I had luck on my covert assignment." I hand Sam a backpack. Kelly's backpack. I'd gone to great lengths to get it sprung it from the juvenile detention center.

He reaches in and pulls out a paperback book, a baseball cap, and a small wooden horse. "Kelly will be thrilled. They give you any grief?"

"Nah, they were glad to be rid of a loose end. But they remembered him." I smile and tilt my drink can at Sam. "The kid who went through the fence. He'll live in infamy."

"You are good! My favorite spy." He grabs hold of my hand and pulls it to his lips, then gets paranoid someone's watching and guiltily let's it go. I laugh and he gives me a sheepish grin. He looks so darn appealing, it's all I can do not to lean across and kiss him.

I purse my mouth and move a strand of hair behind my ear. "Any chance you can take off early today?"

Sam smiles. "Every chance."

SAM

31

On Monday, I find myself whistling and smiling. Sunday nights with Bonnie have that effect on me. And this time, Monday morning too. Bonnie took the day off, so I took another half-day.

I open the screen door and it bangs behind me. We like it loud. Gene is manning the office. I toss my keys on the desk but keep my cup of coffee in my hand. "Everything go okay last night? Where's Kelly? Asleep?"

"Everything went fine. I taught him to play Scrabble and I'm sorry I did, because I lost. I'm blaming it on getting stuck with the Q, but the truth is, he caught on pretty damn quick and you can't believe the words he knows. Apparently, he memorized most of the dictionary while he was in jail. And to answer your other question, nope, he's awake and a happy little camper on the back porch."

I peek around the corner. I can't tell what he's doing but he's bent over the table engrossed in something.

"What the hell does he have back there?"

Gene gives me a crooked grin. "Legos."

"Legos? Those little plastic block things?"

"The very same. Mrs. Adair from the kitchen sent over a big bucket of them. Someone told her there was a little boy here. She took it literally. I was going to give them to one of the staff who have kids, but Kelly grabbed them out of my hands. He's been monkeying around back there with them for two solid hours."

I give a mock shake of my head. "What have we come to? Are we a prison or a day care center?"

Gene smiles and jerks his thumb in Kelly's direction. "Go have a look."

Kelly turns around in his chair as he hears me approach. His face initially looks guarded but at the sight of me, he completely lights up. "You're back!"

You'd think I'd been on a two-week trip. But I find myself smiling at him, too. I lay my hand on his shoulder. "Hey there, what have you got?"

He gives a little smirk. "Assorted creations."

"What's this?" I turn my head and see it's a plastic key about a foot in length.

He's still looking like the cat that ate the canary. "You know how they won't let you have almost anything in jail because they say it can be made into a weapon or a key? Well, I made a key. See, they were right!"

I'd made the mistake of taking a sip of my coffee while he was talking and come close to doing a spit-take. I crack up and Kelly's laughing too. I realize it's the first time I've ever seen him laugh out loud.

I tell him, "Better that than the weapon."

"Don't think it didn't cross my mind. But I was afraid someone," he looks at me pointedly, "might freak."

Nodding my head and squinting my eyes at him I say, "I think you were wise not to."

He rolls his eyes at me. "That's me. Wise."

He looks very content, but I notice him resting his head on his chin and his eyes look droopy. "Did you sleep this afternoon?"

"Not yet. I might lie down a minute. Should I put all this up?"

"Nah. Leave it all out if you want to come back to it. I won't let Mr. Simmons make fishing lures out of them."

"I told him I'd make us some bookends," he says while covering a yawn with the back of his hand. He takes a step and crawls down onto the couch. There's a ladybug crawling on the screen that grabs his attention. I watch his face and see his eyes lose their focus and fall into dreamy contemplation. This is a look I'm coming to recognize. I find myself looking at the bug, noticing how bright the red and black colors are on its back. Shaking my head, I tell myself to get a grip. I slide a chair next to him and put myself into it. "Hey, before you go off to la la land, I have something for you."

He begrudgingly opens his eyes halfway. I reach into my pocket and bring out the little horse Bonnie fetched from the detention center. Those dark eyes go wide and his mouth makes an O as he takes it reverently into his hand. He looks up at me like I just handed him a check for a million dollars and whispers, "Thank you so much."

"You can thank Ms. Ziegler. She's the one who went and fetched it. He was in your backpack which is in my office. You can get it after you get up."

"I will thank her." He lays back down with the horse clutched in his hand inches from his face. Seconds later, he's breathing steadily. I pull the throw off the back of the couch and cover him up before going back to Gene who looks up with a smile. "He still at it?"

"Nope, hit the wall."

"Well, it *is* the longest he's stayed awake in the afternoon since he got sick."

"Yeah, I have to wonder what he has in store for us when he's up all day."

Kelly's health continues to improve. It's time to get him set up with a school program. My own school experience was pretty positive. I played on the baseball team, made decent grades, had good friends, and it was six hours a day I didn't have to deal with the chaos of my home life. But in my professional life, I've grown more cynical about the education system. For a lot of inmates, it's where their downfall began. The school yard fight that results in an assault charge and the kid never meaningfully connects back with his old school again. Truancy charges put kids in detention sitting next to drug offenders they can hook up with when they all get out. Some schools hand out suspensions like candy, even though just one suspension doubles the odds of the youth dropping out. I've known prison guards to drive past the high school and proclaim *job security*. It even has a name: the *school-to-prison pipeline*.

So, I'm pleasantly surprised after contacting the local school system, how amenable they are. Kelly will get homebound services. This is some catch-all category including kids with medical or mental health conditions that prevent them from going to school. Once again, Judge Nolan is pressed into service to go sign the paperwork a parent would normally sign. Soon after, I get a call telling me a teacher will be contacting me to set up the times and days.

I was happy to get all this in motion, especially after I fielded a phone call from Squirrel a couple of days ago. After some general updates, he asked, "How's the kid?"

"Much better."

"Glad to hear it. I have good news for you. I've done some asking around and I've found a boot camp in Texas we could send him to. A place that emphasizes discipline, perfect for kids like him. It's in an open setting and although

255

they generally like kids at least sixteen, they'll take him since he was tried as an adult. They like having a big hammer hanging over the kids' heads. I'll have to pull some strings to okay the funding, but considering the circumstances, I think I can swing it."

I drop my head into my hand and almost groan but catch myself in time. Other than prison or jail, I can't think of a worse place for Kelly. To the general public, the idea is appealing: wayward kids who learn to shape up and fly right. But study after study on the effectiveness of boot camps for delinquent kids shows extremely poor results. The reality is most of these kids, Kelly included, have tremendous histories of trauma. Military discipline and running laps are hardly the way to come to grips with the abuse, neglect, and tragedies they've endured.

Squirrel sounds really pleased with himself, but I think he's becoming a pain in the ass. "That won't work," I say. "The boy's better but the doctor said for the next year there's a danger of a relapse, especially if he does anything too physically strenuous."

It's like I stuck a pin in his balloon. "Well, damn, it seemed like the perfect solution.

I think the perfect solution is for Squirrel to butt out.

On the first day the teacher is scheduled, I don't know who is more nervous, Kelly or me. I have him wait inside while I go out to greet her. Reddish hair, in her fifties is my guess. She looks around with a big warm smile and says, "What a pretty spot. I confess it's been years since I've been to The Village, but I always direct out-of-town guests here." She sticks out her hand for a hearty shake. "Stephanie Knight."

I like her already. "I'm Sam Murry. Thanks so much for coming out."

"Well, it's certainly intriguing. How's Kelly feel about getting back into schoolwork?"

"I think he's happy about it. Of course, I'll stick around the whole time so you don't need to worry about anything. Not that I expect any problems."

"Years ago, I taught in a juvenile detention center. People would ask if I was scared. I'd just laugh and tell them it was the safest place to teach. The one school where you know a kid doesn't have a gun. I'm not worried."

I can tell she means it. She exudes confidence. Kelly comes to his feet as we walk in and I do the introductions. His default with new people is caution, but she's good with him. I decide she looks and acts like everyone's favorite aunt. I can see the boy immediately relax.

I flick on the light switch. "I thought you all could work around the kitchen table. The light's good and it's quiet. Help yourself to drinks in the fridge. Or I can do a decent cup of coffee if you'd prefer. "

"This will do just fine." She pulls out a seat and sits down motioning Kelly to the seat beside her. "Why don't you sit here? It'll be easier to look at the work if we're on the same side of the table."

Within minutes I can tell it's going well. He's looking eager to please. She explains he'll be assigned to actual school classes and she will be the go-between, giving him the assignments from the respective teachers. She passes out testing materials and he sets to work. After they finish, I send him next door to Gene. Kelly shyly thanks her on his way out.

She says, "See you Wednesday," and is rewarded with a smile. As he closes the door, she turns to me. "He's darling. He'll be fun to work with. You might be interested in seeing the school information I got from Wyoming. I highlighted the pertinent parts."

It feels strange looking at these snippets from Kelly's childhood. Words jump off the pages: *Bright and capable, doesn't pay attention in class, advanced writing skills, daydreams, interacts with teachers but shows little inclination toward interaction with peers, inattentive,* and finally, one comment highlighted and underlined: *Suggest clinical evaluation for maladaptive daydreaming.*

I look up. "What's maladaptive daydreaming? I've never heard of it."

She takes a paper clip to the forms Kelly was working on. "It's a weird duck. It means someone daydreams to the point it interferes with their day-to-day functioning. They tend to build their own worlds with imaginary beings set in a unique time and place. Often over time, the imaginary world becomes preferred over the real one. Abused children are more prone to it, but even children with happy childhoods can have it. Some clinicians believe it's almost addictive. It's not a psychosis, because unlike schizophrenia, the person knows their daydreams are not real. One of the biggest indicators is the lack of interest in peers. Kids who do this find real live kids aren't as entertaining as the imaginary people and beings in their minds."

I tap my fingers on the table. "He spends hours writing and drawing."

"Many creative people, artists and writers, are described as daydreamers. It's often associated with being a genius. The Bronte sisters and C.S. Lewis all created elaborate, fantasy worlds. Typically, these kids outgrow it sometime during their teens. Their imaginations remain active which helps them be creative, but they become more interested in real-world social interactions."

She points her finger at the file in front of us. "If you look at the next page, you can see that his behavior in school wasn't a problem, but there are disciplinary reports for truancy. He'd just up and leave in the middle of the school day. He was taken out to be homeschooled at the beginning of fifth grade. This is all old information, but I thought you might like to see."

"Yes, thank you."

After she leaves, I mull over the information. Kelly's mother died of cancer when he was just three. As much as his father must have loved him, how much time and energy would you have for your active toddler when you're caring for your dying wife? I can see how a bright kid might fill the void with his own thoughts.

However, the school truancy is unsettling. Not too many elementary age kids just take off from school at will. He seems to have had the impulse to walk away from anything he doesn't like, regardless of the consequences. But hey, he's older now. Surely he's learned his lesson. Like she said, this is from years ago.

So why does this make me nervous?

SAM

32

As time goes on, we establish routines. Kelly goes to the stables every morning and works with Ed Hicks. The first time I take him, Ed reads him the riot act about the do's and don'ts of the barn, ending with "and if I ever see you with a cigarette within a hundred yards of the stable, you're done."

If Kelly is shy and vulnerable with other staff, it disappears here. He looks like he'd expect no less. After Ed finishes his tirade, Kelly jams his hands in the pockets of his jeans and asks, "Do you want me to clean the tack?"

They stare at each other. Ed has on his mean face, but Kelly isn't fazed. It's a side of him I haven't seen before and I kind of like it. Whatever happens between them, I can tell Kelly passed with flying colors. Some horsey ESP thing. Within days they are thick as thieves. Maybe that's a bad analogy to use in a corrections setting.

Monday and Wednesday afternoons the teacher comes. The other days Kelly works with the nature preserve staff under Brent, the preserve manager's supervisor. Brent was hesitant at first when I asked about letting Kelly work with the preserve staff, but any reluctance he and the other Village folk had quickly disappears once they get to know him. If nothing else, Kelly's lively curiosity and zeal for learning wins them over. He wants to know the names of everything, and soon he can identify a snake, salamander, or bird with the best of them. He soaks up knowledge like a sponge. I heard someone at the door the other day hand something over to Gene for "Sam's kid." I should remind them he's an inmate.

On the days Gene or I are doing the supervising, I let him work with the inmate crews doing maintenance in the buildings or clearing honeysuckle and other invasives out of the forest. He works way past what any child labor laws would allow. I might feel bad about it, but he told me that first day he likes to work, and he didn't lie. I'm the one making sure he doesn't overdo it. Mike's warnings about relapses ring in my head. Even with the work, there's plenty of time for his other pursuits. It's these times I'm aware of the uniqueness of his situation, even if he isn't. If he was a kid living at home, he'd be hanging out with friends, playing on sports teams, and doing the things a normal teenager would do. Here, he isn't allowed to even have a phone.

For most of his recreational time, he's on his own. If the weather isn't horrible, he heads off for solitary hikes. It doesn't seem right for a kid his age to spend so much time alone, but he doesn't seem to mind. I think of the information Mrs. Knight gave me about kids who use their imagination to see life in a different way. I'd read up on it. "World-building" some call it. I can't decide if it's a good thing or a bad thing.

Gene and I, and even some of the other staff, try to do what we can for entertainment. I brought a couple of baseball gloves and we toss a ball on the front lawn now and then. As often as possible, I try and get him off the property. We stop by the library regularly, hit the grocery store and run other errands, or sometimes just get a fountain soft drink from a gas station and drive around the backroads. On rainy days and in the evening, he reads books or writes in his ever-present notebooks. It's nowhere near the life of an ordinary kid but he seems content.

Sometimes when he's gone a long time, I get nervous enough to check his tracking device to make sure he hasn't fallen off a cliff. Often, I see his little dot in the same place. Out of curiosity I go to see what's so damn interesting. It's easy to figure out. From here you can see down into the adjoining property where Edith Casey runs a horseback riding stable. From the vantage point on this hill, I see several rings including one with jumps and watch a lesson in progress. Boring stuff to me but with Kelly's fascination with horses, I suppose it's high entertainment.

So, for the most part, things are going pretty smooth. With one notable exception. Trauma is a tricky adversary, always waiting for a weak moment to raise its ugly head. One night, I wake to screams coming from the monitor and dash up the stairs. By the time I arrive, Kelly's sitting straight up in bed, but he's not really here. Wherever he is, it's not good.

His eyes are glassy and sweat is pouring down his forehead. He blinks rapidly. I've seen this before in others. He's in the midst of a full-blown PTSD episode. I know better than to touch him so I say his name until I can see him start to come out of it. Eventually he focuses on my face, but he still looks confused and traumatized. My heart goes out to him. I can only wonder what he just saw.

"Kelly, you're okay. It's not real. It's over. Look around the room and tell me what you see." There's a pause, but with prompting, he slowly and quietly starts naming the desk, the chair, the curtains, and I can see his muscles begin to loosen. "Now take some deep breaths." I get him a washcloth to wipe the sweat off his face. He complies and when I take the cloth back, he flops down on the bed sideways with his head facing away from me.

I lean over so I'm looking down at him. "You okay?" He nods. I know the answer before the next question but feel compelled to ask it anyway. "Do you want to talk about it?" His head shakes no. That's what I figured.

During the next few months he has two more episodes. Even if he wanted to talk about them, he probably doesn't know what triggers them. It might be a smell, a song, a certain look on someone's face. I hate it for him. I know it's hard to feel truly safe when your mind is trapped in the past. What he needs is trauma counseling but it's not easy to get. I can ask for a psychologist with DOC to come have a look at him, but I'm reluctant.

I used to have a boss who would say, "The more you stir, the more it stinks." For some reason, I like to keep Kelly's placement here quiet. I don't want other divisions meddling into things. You just never know where things might lead. I try and get something set up with the mental health people in the community, but the one therapist who's available doesn't hit it off with him, and Kelly completely clams up. For such a sweet kid, he can be mulishly stubborn, and I know when I'm beat.

KELLY

33

Time moved like sludge when I was in jail, but here, months have zipped by. My father used to say April is promise, but May is achievement. I'm not sure what June is, but I know I like it. There's no other smell in the world quite like fresh cut hay seasoning in the sun. It's a shame it can't be bottled up to be uncorked in January.

June days are wonderfully long. Since I have to be inside at dark that's a major plus. I push the boundary sometimes and receive a few lectures from Sam, but I can tell he's not mad. He knows I'm close enough to make a dash inside before getting into real trouble. A week ago, he came home with a bell—the type where you grab hold of a rope and knock it back and forth against the metal sides. He installed it on the front porch, telling me, "When I ring this, you better get your butt in the building."

I walk miles each day on the trails through The Village's three thousand plus acres. Mainly, I go to the woods. As soon as the tree canopy takes me in and the cool air hits my face, I feel free. And normal. Just a kid out taking a walk. There are no green Department of Corrections signs, no uniforms, and most important-ly, no one is telling me what to do or what not to do. If it wasn't for the monitor on my ankle, there's nothing to mark me as an inmate.

Here, I can still feel magic and look for the smaller world inside the big one. I watch the dragonflies, turn over rocks in the creeks looking for salamanders, or sit quietly on the bank to get a rare look at a beaver or otter. One time a whole fox family appeared to get a drink, the kits tumbling over each other as they played. How I wish I'd had Brent's camera.

He used it the other day and took a picture of me holding a green snake I'd found. He printed a copy and gave it to me. Over the last few days, I've taken it out several times to study it. I decide I look, well, improved, I guess that's the right word. The picture gives me hope. Like I'm living a new life. I'm working on becoming a new person, a better person, than I was. I haven't hit a ten on Dr. King's happiness scale, but I'm happier than I thought I'd ever be again.

My favorite place to walk overlooks the riding stable next door. From my hill at the edge of the woods, I have a good view of the horses and their riders, but they can't see me. I fling myself down and look up as I lay on my back. The sky is clear except for some huge white clouds that throw shade patterns on the ground as they slowly drift across the sun. I smile as one floats across me. At the sound of voices below, I roll over on my stomach and watch the riders with their horses enter the ring. I rest my chin in my hands. My nose gets tickled by the grass. I like grass. I admire it. Cut it off again and again and it just grows right back. Break off a stem and another stem takes its place. Horses love it. If I could live off it too, wouldn't that be perfect?

Speaking of food, I sit up and pull out the peanut butter sandwich I packed. I chew while I watch the riders below. I've come to recognize the owner of the stable. She's in the middle of the ring yelling instructions to her riders. One day a plastic grocery bag floated across the ring and a rider who wasn't paying attention fell off when her horse leapt a couple of feet straight up. I smiled thinking of something my uncle once told me. *My boy, horses are only afraid of two things. Things that move and things that don't.*

The owner is on a roll today, pacing around inside the ring like a circus master. "No, don't get so far forward! Wrong lead, wrong lead. Do you want me to jab your mouth like you are doing your poor horse?"

I smile. It's great fun watching them get chewed out. I've jumped a horse over a log or ditch in my day, but I've never jumped fences in a ring with colorful, man-made poles. When they do it right, it's beautiful to see. I'd like to try even if I got yelled at. I picture myself jumping all of them perfectly and the lady saying, "Great job." Although come to think of it, I've never heard her say that to anyone. Even better, I'd be the first.

A week later, I'm walking over to the riding stable when I'm startled to find a horse on the trail. He still has a saddle and his reins are trailing the ground as he walks. I blink twice to make sure he's not a mirage, something conjured up out of my imagination because I miss riding so much. But no, he's real. I recognize him as the big bay horse from the lessons next door. A great jumper, but one of the harder ones to handle. I've seen him throw in an enthusiastic buck when he gets excited. A couple of unaware riders have come flying off him. Exciting stuff. Then of course, they get yelled at. Even better.

After a minute of cat and mouse, I manage to grab the loose reins. He's a good ways from the farm. I should start leading him back because it'll take a while. They're probably worried about him. Riding him would get him there much quicker. That would be a good thing, wouldn't it? Because what I really want more than anything in this world is to get on him. I can't resist. It's fate. The last time I thought something was fate, I ended up in jail, but I shove that thought away without much effort.

This guy isn't as big as The Village draft horses, but he's tall. I shorten his stirrups and walk him over to a rock to use as a mounting block. As my seat settles into the saddle, I feel the energy from him radiate into my legs. Once we start moving my body takes over. It remembers this. Walking through the woods on horseback is a fantasy brought to life.

Straight through the woods would be quickest, but there's a longer way out around the meadows which allows for trotting and cantering, so I head that way. I fill my lungs with the smell of grass and for the first time in a very long time, I feel exactly like me. No worries, no fears. It's true what my uncle used to say: *When you're on a horse, you borrow freedom.*

Fate must be working double-time today because ahead are three trees that went down in a recent storm, each trunk thirty yards apart and begging to be jumped. Yeah, maybe I've never jumped anything this big, but this horse is a pro, and in my head, I can hear the lady yelling instructions.

My horse gathers himself and I can feel the massive power underneath me as we sail over the first log. After the third, I let out a *whoop*. What a rush! My horse gets excited about it too, and I can feel him readying himself for an I-did-great buck. "Oh, no you don't," I say as I pull his head up and squeeze him forward, nixing any misbehavior. He's still raring to go. Maybe I'll jump those logs again.

And then, I hear a voice.

I jerk my head to the right to see the lady from next door, mounted on a gray, with a look on her face that tells me I'm in trouble. I try to come up with a good reason for why I'm on her horse. If only I'd stayed in the woods. I hope she doesn't think I stole him. Oh man, I could be in big trouble. I flash to the last time I stole something, and it didn't turn out so good. Is there such a thing as unauthorized use of a horse?

My horse nickers at his friend. "I found him loose in the woods." I holler and wince at how completely lame that sounds.

She walks the gray perpendicular to me and yells back, "So I see. Well, don't just stand there, bring him to me."

She's got that kind of voice that makes you want to do what she says, so I start to hurry her way, but see a problem. The lady's walking her horse to where the property barrier of The Village and her land intersects. I stop several yards out.

She walks her gray right up to me. She's dressed in riding pants, black boots, and a bright red riding jacket. Her face is bronze with the look of someone who has spent a lifetime outdoors in the sun and wind, and her eyes are very blue. She pins me with them. "You might as well do me the favor of riding him home. I'll bring you back on my tractor once he's put away."

I slide off him and pull the reins over his head. It's not a move that makes her happy. She's scowling at me now. "What, you have fun on my horse then won't help me out?"

I really, really want to and for a second I think I will. But then I picture Sam's face as my tracking device sets off alarms, and I hold out the reins in front of me. "I'm sorry, I can't." I don't say anything else because the more you explain, the more trouble you usually get into. Juvenile detention taught me that.

She gives me a pained look. "Can't?… Or won't?"

I don't answer but my left foot, of its own volition, touches my right leg where the ankle monitor is attached. She looks at me, looks at the fence boundary, then seems to come to a conclusion. I'm afraid it's the right one, and I can feel my face flushing. Lately, I'd almost forgotten to feel shame but in front of someone from Planet Real World, it comes roaring back, a reminder of how people view the likes of me.

She walks her horse past me and reaches down for the reins. "Alright then, I'll pony him back. What's your name?"

Nothing good can come from this. I toy with giving a false name, but if Sam finds out he wouldn't like me lying. The lady raises one eyebrow like she's thinking, *any minute now.*

"Kelly." I decide maybe it's not necessary to add my last name.

"Well, Kelly, you did some good riding. Can you get home from here okay?"

I nod and she trots off with both horses. I'm left standing alone in the meadow worrying about the consequences. *Why can't I stay out of trouble? What's wrong with me?*

Once home, I climb up in my tree where I feel safest. Sam drives up in the truck and walks inside. Soon after I can hear the distant sound of the phone ringing as it drifts out of the open window. A minute later Sam reappears outside. My heart starts racing. Sure enough, he's looking for me. He stands at the bottom of the tree and looks up, shading his eyes with one hand. "Kelly? Come on down."

Oh, shit.

SAM

34

I get a phone call from Ms. Casey next door. "So, Sam, when did you start incarcerating small children?" She's never been one to mince words.

"Hello, Edith. Is there a problem?"

"I'm just surprised. It took me a minute to put it together. That boy of yours caught a loose horse of mine, and I was about to knock him over the head because he wouldn't walk it over to me on my land. He looked at that boundary line like it was full of land mines."

"Good. He should."

"So what's the deal?"

"You don't need to worry about him, if that's what's bothering you. He's harmless."

I can hear her huff through the phone. "Sam, I may be getting older, but the day I can't handle a ninety-pound kid, two feet shorter than me, I'll hang up my spurs. Where did he learn to ride? He's good."

"Wyoming. How do you know he's good?"

"Because he was on my horse having a grand old time, and that gelding isn't an easy beast to handle."

Shit. I'll kill him.

"Edith, I'll talk to him. I'm sorry if—"

"Don't. I'm not calling 'cause I'm mad. I'm calling 'cause a boy who handles a horse like that might want to come over here for some lessons and try some actual fences. Or will he blow up if he crosses that magic line?"

"Nothing that drastic. I'll have to come and—"

"What's he been riding over there? Surely not Ed's draft horses?"

"No, nothing. But Ed did say I should look for some —"

"What do you know about horses, Sam?"

"Not much, but—"

267

"I'll make you a loan. One less mouth for me to feed for a while, so it's a win-win. I've got an event going on this weekend. Come Monday around noon and I'll show you what I've got."

She hangs up without bothering with any other niceties.

I have to laugh. Did I get to finish a single sentence? Typical Edith.

When I tell Kelly I've talked to Edith, he freezes up. I'd planned a little lecture, but he looks so pitiful I skip it and just ask if he'd like to go over there to ride sometime. I don't tell him anything about Edith's plan to get him a horse for here. I'm not sure how I even feel about that, even though Ed's been pestering me about it too, but when I see Kelly's eyes light up at just the mention of riding, I feel myself caving.

On Monday, I show up at Edith's as instructed. She shows me a "nice little mare." Her words. The horse doesn't look at all little to me. She explains she's not showy enough for hunter shows and too challenging a ride for anyone who isn't experienced, but she's a "good mover." She assures me Kelly won't have any trouble handling her, but I'm not sold. Not that long ago, I was spooning food down his mouth and now we're throwing him up on a large animal that has a mind of its own. What's wrong with this picture?

I see a pinto pony dozing in the shade by the fence. I like the looks of him. His head isn't much higher than the top fence rail, and hey, aren't pintos kind of western? I point at him. "What about that one?"

Edith skewers me with a look so dismissive I feel my shoulders hunch over. The club of people who can intimidate me is small, but Edith could be president. She grabs a halter and says, "We want him to have fun riding, not fall asleep while he's in the saddle."

I go over to stand by the mare and try to look knowledgeable. I reach up to give her a pat on the head. She nips at my arm then stomps a front leg, narrowly missing my foot as I quickly jerk it back. Edith doesn't have the good grace not to laugh.

The next day Edith drives the mare over in her trailer. I've told Kelly the horse is for the tourists because Edith will need her back at some point. Any misgivings I have about putting him up on a horse are erased the first time I see him ride. The instant he's in that saddle, he's transformed. The joy on his face is unmistakable.

KELLY

35

The Village is getting a horse but it's going to be my responsibility to take care of her. Tourists like to see the animals. Eye candy for the field, Ed calls it. But Ed believes all horses should work, so I'm to ride her regularly. Like that's a chore. If it is, give me more.

I think she's beautiful. Her name is officially Palmyra Promise, but her barn name is Ginger. She shines in the sun like a copper penny. Ms. Casey brings a saddle and bridle too. She acts like we've known each other for years. "Warm her up in the paddock. Take her through her paces and let's see what kind of a match we've got."

I mount, then reach down to adjust the stirrups on the English saddle. I walk Ginger in a wide circle to limber up her legs, do a few turns, ask for a couple of halts, then a trot. Eventually, I move her into a canter and do the leads on both sides before taking her back to a trot. Ms. Casey calls me back over. She's smiling and I am too. It's like it's contagious. Even Sam is smiling.

"Okay," she says. "Y'all look good together. Take her out."

I don't need to be told twice. Ginger and I head to the open fields and her ears immediately perk up as she takes in her new surroundings. She prances, eager to go, and I don't make her wait. Easing my grip on the reins, I let her canter then go to a full gallop. The ground flies by underneath me and the wind whistles in my ears. This feels so good. If I died right now, I wouldn't care.

I take her back to a walk and go up to the top of the highest hill. We look at the vista with the lake below. I've stood here many times on foot because it's a great view, but on a horse, there's something that makes it spectacular. I could stand here all day, but Ginger is raring to go, so I head her down a trail into the woods.

Some horses don't make good trail horses, but Ginger isn't one of them. She shows no fear of crossing the wide stream. We wade in, her feet sinking in the loose gravel. I pause her halfway and let her play in the water, pawing it vigorously with one hoof, before putting her head down for a drink. I watch shiny blue dragonflies, catching the sun on their wings, hover over the water then zip off sideways, showing off their speed and agility.

Done with her drink, I push Ginger on, reaching a clearing with a pool of deeper water. There's a huge turtle sitting on a log. I take it as a sign. Indians believe turtles are associated with wisdom and spirituality. My dad told me when turtles appear to you, the message is to remain determined yet serene. Serene hasn't worked for me in a long time but today I *am* determined. The person on this horse right now is who I used to be. I remember him. He was fearless and confident. I want him back.

As if to prove the gods are finally smiling on me, the clouds part and sunlight pours into the clearing. A thrush is singing somewhere and a kingfisher dives with a jeweled splash and comes up with a fish, shakes his feathers and flies away. A heron glides in from somewhere unseen, skimming along the top of the water, its wings outstretched, following a current of air before folding up and standing on the bank in the mud. I'm reminded the world can be a gift. I've been given a second chance and I'm going to take it.

Once back at the barn, I reluctantly slide to the ground then run my stirrups up the saddle before removing it. I replace Ginger's bridle with the halter and hose her off. To reward her and prolong our time together I stand and hand-graze her a little while. I'm reluctant to put her back in the field but eventually run out of excuses not to, so I open the gate and reach up to slide the halter off.

I give her a little pat on the neck. "Good girl, we'll go again soon."

She seems less impressed with me than I was with her, because she immediately walks a few yards away, folds up her legs, and drops to the ground. She rolls from one side to another in the dirt washing away all traces of our ride. I can't help but laugh. She gets back up and does a shimmy shake—the kind where if you're sitting on the horse it rattles your innards. The dust flies off her in a cloud.

I join Sam by his truck. He gives me a grin and says, "You look pretty pleased with yourself."

I can't deny it. After finishing up my work in the barn for the day, I walk down to the creek. Bees are busy working the flowers just below me. A snake emerges from under a rock and starts swimming. It's one of those summer moments when time seems to stand still and I'm acutely aware of every living thing around me. I feel so alive. The Village is my world now and I have moved from simply accepting I'm stuck here, to taking it to heart.

It's like I'm home.

Almost.

SAM

36

A week later, Edith stops by to check on her horse and to set up a time for me to bring Kelly over to her place for a jumping lesson. The boy's out on the mare and she watches him with a smile on her face but then frowns when she sees the pair sail over a small stone wall.

"Stupid me, I should have known he'd find something over here he could jump," she says. "He needs a helmet. I'd never let a student jump eighteen-inch rails without one. The impact of hitting his head if he came off would be like a car wreck."

She doesn't realize how much that analogy hits home, but I feel compelled to say something in my defense. "Watching him scares the devil out of me, but when I said something to Ed, he just shrugged it off and told me some long story about how he used to ride a half-broke mule when he was a kid."

Edith gets a disdainful look on her face that she must have spent years perfecting. "Knowing Ed, that doesn't surprise me. He's never worn a helmet in his life and isn't about to start now. Like I said, the boy should always wear head protection when he's jumping and anytime he's doing more than just trail riding at a walk or trot. Honestly, there are lots of folks who'd never let their kid get on a horse without one.

"I've got a used one here in the back of my truck I'll let you have. It's only about a year or so old. You should replace them after about five because they lose their effectiveness." As she hands it to me, she squints her eyes. "Is the boy going to be here longer than four years? How old is he anyway?"

If this was a juvenile facility, everything about Kelly would be kept confidential. As it is, tried as an adult, it's all public record so I can answer her. "No, he'll likely be released in a year and a half or so. He'll be sixteen by then."

"Good heavens. Well, consider the helmet my contribution to the cause. You

272

know I'm pretty much a hard ass, but he seems like an awfully nice boy to be here under these circumstances, not that I really know the circumstances. I guess he must have done something fairly bad."

I surprise myself by how quick I am to defend Kelly. "He is a nice boy. His being here is pretty much a fluke." I look over and watch him—thankfully at a safe walk now—heading to the barn. "But don't worry, we're looking out for him."

It's the first time in all our long years of acquaintance, Edith touches me. She pats my arm as she turns toward her truck. "Yes, I can see that."

I watch her drive away and look down at the helmet in my hand. I decide to be like all those folks she told me about. I'll make this a mandatory thing whenever he's riding. I know I'll feel better for it.

When Kelly gets back to the building, I call him over. "I've been informed you need to be wearing a helmet when you ride. I've got one for you." When I give it to him, he looks like I just handed him a pile of flaming dog poop.

He narrows his eyes at me and asks, "Can I say no?"

"No, you can't." What's that I see? A little flash of defiance? Don't like being told what to do, do you? Of course, who does?

He holds the helmet by the chin strap with his arm extended. "I don't need this. I've been riding all my life."

"Doesn't mean nothing can't happen. We live and learn. You'll get used to it."

"I don't think I will," he mutters under his breath.

Defiance is edging into outright rebellion. I narrow my eyes and sharpen my voice. "Get used to it, you mean?"

His mouth tightens. "Yeah."

"Well let's hope you do, because you're gonna. Got it?"

No answer.

I take in his sullen expression. "Got. It?"

"Yes, sir," he says. He sounds disrespectful, even if the words are right.

Whenever I see him riding, he has the helmet on so it's Gene that rats him out. "You know when you aren't around, he takes that off? And if you are around, he goes into the woods and takes it off, then puts it back on when he comes out."

"No, I did not. I gave him an order and I expect him to abide by it."

"Did you now? Spoken like a man who has never had a teenager."

"I'll make him wash dishes till his hands fall off."

Gene laughs. "Ah, Sam, he's by nature, or by his circumstances, an obedient boy, but he's fourteen so that only goes so far. Anything else, I might suggest you cut him a little slack but this is about safety, so you'll have to up your game." He pats my shoulder as he walks by. Why is everyone suddenly patting me all the time?

I'm not about to let myself be outsmarted by a teenager, so I make a plan to catch him in the act. I tell him I'm going to town then double back and pull the truck between him and the road. I get out and wait for him. When he crests the hill, he knows he's busted. He sits on his horse giving me a look-to-kill. I give him a not-so-happy-look right back.

"Get off," I say. "You're done for the day."

KELLY

37

"You did that on purpose!" I say.

"Oh, and you didn't wait till I was out of sight before taking off the helmet I specifically ordered you to wear?"

I decide it's best to deflect since that's true. Also, I don't like the word *ordered*. It makes my lip curl. "The one thing I really enjoy, and you want to ruin it for me."

"I'm not trying to ruin anything. I'm trying to keep you from getting your brains knocked out."

My mouth continues to take on a life of its own. "They're my brains. I should be able to do what I want with them." I listen to myself with rising disbelief. "Oh wait, that's right, I don't have any say on anything, do I? Be a good boy. Do what you're told. I'm sick of it!"

"Calm down."

"I don't want to calm down. I'm tired of always being calm."

Sam gives a little sigh. "Yeah, I can see how you might be. Regardless, you'll have to wear the helmet."

He's looking kindly at me now. I hate that more than anything. "And don't be so fucking understanding. You don't know everything." *Is this really me talking?*

His voice gets quiet. "No, I don't. Nevertheless, you have to wear the helmet."

"Arghhhh … fine! I'll walk her back on foot. Happy? Want me to wear this shit-ass hat to do it?"

"No." He holds out his hand. "I'll take it for now. "

It's a dangerous moment and we both know it. I really, really want to throw this blasted thing right at him. Or drop it on the ground and make him pick it up. Maybe give it a kick for good measure. But like a trained monkey, I find I can't do anything but hand it over.

I walk Ginger back to the barn, take her tack off, and put her back in her field. I'm so mad my hands are shaking. I head down into the woods kicking at sticks in my way before picking up a few rocks and flinging them as hard as I can at tree trunks. Really, it's just not fair. I love how free I feel when I ride, with the wind in my hair, and wearing that stupid helmet will change everything. *I hate this place.* Mr. Murry can go straight to hell. I'll go stay in the barracks with the other inmates. I'm sick of being treated like a baby. That'll show him.

When I get to the bottom of the trail, I climb up on a large rock that juts out over the creek and let the clean, silky smell of flowing water fill my nose. I watch the creek cascading over the rocks, busy on its way to the river, which takes it to a bigger river, which takes it to the ocean. It's always moving, going places. I want to be a creek, but oh no! I'm like a fucking-ass pond—stuck in one place, stagnant, with green slime growing on top.

What I'd like to do is stay in the woods all day and hide. I pull my knees up and wrap my arms around them, which pulls up my pant leg enough to expose the tracking monitor. Scowling at it, I hit it with my fist as hard as I can. *Damnit! That hurts!* Oh geez, I wonder if I damaged the stupid thing. No, it seems okay. I squeeze my eyes shut. Crap, I can't even hide.

When I open them again, my eyes zone in on the trail that crosses the creek and heads up the hill and off the property. For the first time since I got here, leaving sounds good to me. To be on my own again, free, without people always telling me what to do. I climb down from my rock and go to the creek. It's not deep except in a few spots where it pools. There's one of those here, about three feet deep. It looks so cool and inviting. I'd love to jump in and cool off. But oh, no, I can't do that either! I can't submerge the tracking monitor in water. No swimming allowed. For a second, I consider jamming my right leg down into the water. Would my little dot vanish? That would be *sweet.*

Instead, I find a shallower spot where there's some rocks I can walk across. On the other side, I start walking up the trail, away from The Village, away from all its rules and expectations. At the top of the hill, the trees thin out until it's just grass. From here, I can look down and see the main highway. It runs east and west, each direction leading to some city somewhere. Every minute or so a car or truck goes by and I'm jealous of those people who can go wherever they like.

If I scrambled down to the road, would someone stop and pick me up?

I sit down so my feet don't do something crazy. I remember Henry's little pep talk right before I left the jail: *You're going to get mad or you're going to get homesick,* he warned me, *but remember to put the brakes on.* Then Sam's face pops into my mind. *Running away is a hard habit to break. Does a promise mean something to you?*

A shadow moves across the ground and I look up to see a red-tailed hawk soaring above me. I lie back on the grass and watch him climb higher and higher, going in and out of the clouds, floating on thermals. I close my eyes. I pray the next time I open them, the hawk will have changed into an eagle, and these green hills will have turned into snow-capped mountains—just like home.

I count to three and open my eyes.

Still a hawk.

Still just hills.

Still no mountains.

SAM

38

Kelly walks the horse away while I toss the helmet behind the seat. At the top of the hill, I stop and watch in my rearview mirror as he stomps off into the woods. Once I get back at the office, I pull up the tracking screen. I don't mind him getting a good mad on—it's probably good for him—but I want to be sure he doesn't do something stupid.

He walks a good bit and the dot quits moving for a while. *Thinking, are you? Or still cussing me out?*

Gene materializes. "Did you catch him red-handed. Or should I say red-headed?"

"Oh, yeah. He was steamed."

"Where is he?"

I point to the screen. "Pouting in the woods. He's been sitting there for awhile."

"How bad was it?"

"Cussing and yelling, and I'm pretty sure I came close to having the helmet thrown at me."

Gene gives a little grimace. "I'm glad he didn't go that far." He taps the screen with his finger. "He's on the move. It's lunchtime. With my boys, that cured a lot of sulking."

I start to laugh and agree, but instead, sober up and lean forward closer to the screen. Kelly's not walking in this direction. I look at Gene. "He's heading up to the top of that bluff, the property line next to Highway 68."

Transfixed, Gene and I stare as the little dot gets closer and closer to the property line. I let out a big breath when it stops moving. A pause to consider the options, perhaps? And how about the consequences? I hope so. Nevertheless, I unlock my desk drawer and reach for my car keys in case I need to blitz out of here. Thankfully, his deliberations are short, and the dot starts to head back in this direction.

Gene whispers, "Good boy."

I'm not so sure *good* is the word I'd choose right now. I scowl at Gene, "You don't think he did that on purpose just to yank my chain, do you?"

Gene laughs and thumps me on the back. "We'll never know. I'm guessing probably not. If he was really trying to annoy you, he's the type of kid who'd go back and forth three times then run in a circle."

I can't help but chuckle. That would be like him. "Now what? I've still got to deal with his direct disobedience and how he acted toward me."

Gene straightens up and rubs his neck. "What's your plan?"

"That's what I'm struggling with. I was so intent on catching him, I didn't think through the next step." I blow out a breath, lifting my eyes upwards. *Heaven, give me strength.* "I guess the most logical consequence is to ground him from the horse for disobeying me about the helmet. I don't know what to do about his little fit. He looked far more shocked at the words he was saying than I was. The jail people said he never gave them one cross word. It's probably the first time in who knows when, he felt safe enough to let loose a little. I hate to zap him for it, but I also don't feel I can totally let it slide."

I put my hands on both sides of my head. "I feel like every decision with him is huge and I don't want to screw it up."

To my eternal irritation Gene is chuckling. "I think you're overthinking this."

I let my hands drop into my lap. "You think?"

"Sure. See how he acts when he comes in. If he picks it right back up, you may need to lower the boom. Otherwise, let him stew awhile. Tell him you're thinking about consequences and will let him know later when you decide."

I'm impressed. "That's brilliant. Spoken like someone with a lot more experience than I have."

Gene nods. "I did have practice. Took the car away from my Jason right after he got his license, when he picked up a speeding ticket. He didn't talk to me for a solid week. Once the week passed, he acted like nothing had happened. 'Hi Dad, how's it going?' Kids. Gotta love 'em." He grabs his jacket. "Well, I'm heading over to pick up the men working on the east side. Let me know how it goes."

I turn off the screen because Kelly will be here soon. I roll my chair back enough to see out the window. My mind drifts to an orientation training for my first juvenile gig. The instructor said kids were sent to us for problematic behaviors, then we act surprised and outraged when they show those same behaviors once they're in our facility. We put them in an even more stressful situation than their homes, but then, let them show any emotion like anger or frustration, and we wham them—like any negative feeling isn't allowed. The instructor invited us to see these outbursts as "teachable moments," a chance to say to the kids that "everyone gets angry, but the key is how you handle it."

The front door opens and shuts. Kelly's steps slow as he passes by my door. Then the pace picks up as he heads to the kitchen. I smile. Gene's right. Let him stew a bit.

In a few minutes, I go join him. He's sitting at the table with a peanut butter sandwich in hand. I rustle around in the fridge, settling on a container of ham salad, which I eat leaning against the counter.

Kelly doesn't look at me when he speaks. "I'm supposed to work with Brent this afternoon." It's both a declaration and a question.

"Go ahead. I've got to go over and meet with maintenance. We'll need to talk later."

He doesn't look at me, finishes, and wastes no time leaving.

The rest of the day he gives me the cold shoulder. Goes out of his way to avoid me. He answers a direct question if forced to, but otherwise doesn't talk to me at all. He caps the day off by going to bed early, the earliest he's gone since his first days here. He makes a big production out of giving Gene a smile and a heartfelt "good night," then turns to walk off without saying anything to me. Just to yank his chain, I tell him good night, which forces a quick, under-his-breath, "night," without making any eye contact.

After I hear him reach the top of the stairs, I give Gene a rueful grin. "Wonder how long he'll keep this up. I guess in the morning, I'll tell him no riding the rest of the week and assign him kitchen duty. That might keep it quiet around here for a little while longer."

Gene gives a little smirk. "Do what you want. I don't care. He still likes *me*."

"Yeah, well, don't think that doesn't bother me, especially since you were the snitch." I point my finger to the top of his head. "Did your kids give you those gray hairs?"

He smacks my hand down as he walks by and snickers. "Welcome to my world."

KELLY

39

Coming upstairs early makes for a long night.

After a shower, I pace a bit, but when I hear footsteps, I run to sit at the desk and open a book. I tense, expecting to see Sam walk in the doorway. I acted awful to him this afternoon. I know I deserve to be punished. But that doesn't mean I like it. What will he do? Any second, I expect to see him in the doorway. I'm relieved to see it's just Gene.

He pulls the rocking chair over and sits down. "So, you and Sam had a little falling out, did you?"

"Did he send you up to talk to me?"

"Nope, came on my own. You know everybody gets mad at the people closest to them now and then. It's only natural."

"We aren't close. He's just doing his job."

"If you think you're just part of the job, you're not as smart as everybody says you are." I lower my eyes. I so want to believe that's true. "And since we're on that subject," he continues. "I think there's something you should know. Sam would skin me if he finds out, so don't let on I told you."

I look up. He has my full attention now.

"You know that mare didn't just show up here."

"She came for the tourists," I say.

"No, she came here for *you*. Sam worked it out with Ms. Casey. She was willing to loan the mare for a while, but when Sam saw how happy you were, he bought that horse with his own money."

My mouth falls open, but words won't come.

Before leaving Gene leans over and squeezes my arm, "Remember, don't tell him I told you."

I'm no longer worried about how Mr. Murry will punish me. I'm no longer mad about how unfair it all is. All I want to do now is make it right.

I sit and think. And think some more. Coming to a decision, I tear a sheet of paper out of my notebook, write, fold it in half, and for the second time today, I disobey a rule. This time, it's by leaving my room after I'm put away for the night.

I quietly creep down the stairs and slip the note under Sam's door.

SAM

40

After a nice long phone call with Bonnie, who darn-it-all seems to find to-day's situation with Kelly more amusing than concerning, I listen to the game on the radio. Baseball season is when I most miss TV reception. Then it's off to the shower. Rubbing my wet hair with a towel, out of the corner of my eye, I spy a piece of paper stuck under my door. Wary, I lean over to get it and flick it open.

I'm sorry. I'll wear the helmet. Please forgive me.

With deep remorse,
Robert Kelly Morgan

I sit down chuckling and shake my head. Crazy kid. I go looking for a pen. When I find it, I turn the note to the back and do my own composing. It only takes a minute. An hour or so later I carry it up the stairs. If Kelly was awake, I was going to leave it without saying anything, but he's sound asleep. One thing about the kid, he's a champion sleeper. I tack it to the molding by the door.

You are forgiven. I propose a compromise. Jumping and anything more than a trot = helmet.
Sincerely,
Samuel Haywood Murry
(Yes, that's really my middle name.)

In the morning, we both act like nothing has happened and the ban on riding never materializes. I remember something else my old training instructor said: *Consequences don't have to hurt. They just have to make a difference.*

SAM

41

Bonnie and I used to have a standing date for Sunday nights, but now she's coming down for the whole weekend as often as she can. Tonight, it's a Saturday night dinner and a movie so I call to make plans.

"Bring the kid," she says.

"Is this a comment on my company?"

"It'll be good for him. Of course, he should be going with a girl or a bunch of friends instead of us old folks, but we're better than nothing."

It's a scorcher. The heat of the day lies like a thick blanket. Not even a hint of a breeze. I track Kelly down to his usual spot on the back porch. He's writing but looks up to say, "Hi." There's moisture on his brow.

I shake my head, "Aren't you burning up back here? Why don't you come into the air conditioning where it's cooler?"

He goes back to scribbling in his notebook. "I like real air."

"Bonnie wants to see the latest comic book hero movie tonight and she's requested your company, if you think you can put up with some AC."

He looks up quickly. I can see the want in his eyes. "Really?"

I tap him on the head with the fishing magazine I have in my hand. "Run upstairs and clean up a bit. We'll leave in an hour and pick her up on the way."

At six o'clock, he presents himself in his best jeans and a navy T-shirt. His hair is damp from taking a shower and his eyes are lit up, excited about this change in routine. I smile to myself at his enthusiasm.

We hit Bonnie's favorite Chinese place for dinner. This is a new experience for Kelly, and he does his usual looking-dubious-at-food thing, but Bonnie helps him make a selection and now he's energetically putting it away. It's good to see him eat like a teenage boy should.

Bonnie has us in stitches with a story about her receptionist and her latest diet. I catch a lady's eye at the table adjoining ours. I can tell she's thinking, *aren't they a nice family.* If she only knew. Some time ago, I told Kelly I'd once been married, and he leapt to the conclusion I was a widower. The poor kid assumes everybody dies. I had to assure him it was nothing that dramatic, merely a divorce.

I don't think much about Amy anymore. We married young and divorced young. When we married, I foresaw a happy-ever-after. But it went wrong fast. By the time we split up, neither of us could stand the sight of the other.

I blamed her.

I blamed my crazy parents for setting a terrible example of what married life should be.

I blamed myself. And I'd never been able to commit since.

I'd been happy enough, at least I thought. I had my work and I didn't lack for female companionship when I went looking for it. But if things started getting too serious, I found some way to mess things up. I glance across the table. I'd done it with Bonnie, sooner than some others, because I figured out early on that I really liked her.

I get up to get a drink refill and look back at the two of them, as I pop my plastic lid back on. Kelly adores Bonnie but not like having a crush. Maybe like having a mom. I guess he doesn't have much experience with that. She teases a laugh out of him. The shadows are gone from his eyes and his whole demeanor is lighter. These last months have been like watching a broken heart be mended. Hopefully, he's beginning to trust life enough to love again.

Maybe I should do the same.

Bonnie waves a chopstick in the air. "We need some ground rules. I get my own popcorn. I need to make that point clear to everyone at the get-go. Do not be reaching. Do not be asking. Get your own."

At the theater, Bonnie dumps half the seasoned saltshaker on her fully buttered, large popcorn. "How can you eat all that popcorn right after dinner?" I ask her.

"Practice. Hands off."

"Fine," I grumble with a wink at Kelly. I get a large popcorn for us to split, with a couple of drinks, then we find seats in the back row where Bonnie insists we go for the extra leg room. I grab a large handful of popcorn and hand Kelly the bucket. I can't help but briefly look his way now and then. He shines with joy at being here. We are here early so the only thing on the screen is some dumb trivia game. Kelly's got his earbuds in, listening to music on the MP3 player he bought a couple of weeks ago.

I whisper to Bonnie, "I'm glad you said bring him. It's like we took him to the beach, or an amusement park, not something as ordinary as a movie."

She takes a peek. "I know. It's pretty cute. You know everybody thinks we're a mom, a dad, and a kid, don't you? It's like we're playing house."

"Yeah, I noticed."

"All these years, I've poo-pooed the domestic life, but I must be getting old. I kind of like them thinking that."

"Did you ever think of having kids? Your own, not from correctional facilities."

"Sure, off and on. Who doesn't? Now it's a moot question. How about you?"

I take a long sip of my soft drink. "I decided a long time ago I didn't want kids."

Bonnie turns a little in her seat to look at me straight on. "Why not?"

I meet her eyes. "I was afraid I'd be a lousy father. I'd been a lousy husband and figured if I flunked that, I wasn't cut out for domestic life." I shrug. "I just didn't see it, didn't think I had it in me to love a kid."

Bonnie's eyes flick to Kelly then back to me. "And now?"

"I think maybe I missed out."

I pause a second before my next words. *Think carefully, Sam. Are you sure you aren't just caught up in the moment?* But tonight, I'm not in the mood to hold back.

"I think I've missed out on a lot of things. So maybe we should think about a more serious relationship."

She stops shoveling in the popcorn and turns to look at me. "I can't believe that line came out of your mouth."

"Yeah, it sounded kind of hokey … but I mean it. What do you think?"

"I think you're crazy."

It's like someone threw a bucket of cold water on me. Is it my timing, sitting here with Kelly right next to us, even if he's oblivious? Or much worse, is it that I've completely misjudged where she and I are heading? I try and come up with

287

something clever to say as a cover up for my hurt feelings, but before I can, she leans into me. "But I'm game. I've come to learn these last months you aren't the complete jerk I always thought you were."

My face splits into a big smile. "I love it when you sweet-talk me."

"Sssshhh." A lady two rows down from us is frowning and gesturing to the screen. The lights start dimming and the screen comes to life with the latest humorous way to admonish us to turn off our cell phones.

Kelly pulls his ear buds out and leans over. "You all are embarrassing me." I reach my arm around him and give him a big squeeze. "Oh, yeah? Are you the etiquette police?"

He squirms away. "Please don't spoil the night by mentioning law enforcement."

I let him go and grab a handful of Bonnie's popcorn over her objection. "Hey," she protests, "what did I tell you about that?" The lady turns around again.

Kelly slinks lower in his seat. "Geez, can I sit somewhere else?"

Bonnie looks around me to give him a grin. "It's okay. We'll behave."

The theater goes dark, signaling the start of the previews, and he settles back with a contented smile on his face. I turn my attention to the screen but in a minute, my eyes flick to my left then my right, checking their faces, registering their happiness, and when I see it, I sit back and sink into my own.

It's as if the gods heard me say that I'd missed out on having kids. I'm getting lots of opportunities to learn what seasoned parents already must know: that worrying about them shortens your life span.

Kelly is going to Ms. Casey for riding lessons. The flat work, as they call it—trotting and cantering round the ring—can get a little boring so I do some strolling. Edith's place has a rich history. There are a couple of old log cabins repurposed for storage, and what looks to be a potting shed. Further down the lane is an old house that's seen better days. Kelly's face lit up when he saw it, and I can just see his imagination going to work making up a story. It does have a certain Hansel and Gretel quality about it.

When Kelly gets to the jumping part of his lesson, I hang closer, partly because I love watching him ride but also because I feel my being there will assure his safety. Which is stupid, of course, since it's completely out of my control. But it's like wearing your lucky shirt to a ball game. You just have to wear it, or you know evil will befall your team.

At first, Edith sets the jumping poles very low and that's fine by me. But when they start getting higher and higher, I put my foot down and say, "No, that's too high." I mean someone has to be the adult in charge. I can't let Edith continue to bully me forever.

Standing on the ground next to Kelly's horse-of-the-day, the two of them whisper a few seconds, then Kelly hands Edith the reins. Leaving the horse behind, he proceeds to jump every one of the poles himself, jogging to each and effortlessly leaping over. To add insult to injury the little shit whistles the whole way around, much to Edith's everlasting pleasure. I slink back to my corner.

So now, as I see him gallop toward fences that are getting *much* higher and *much* wider, I suffer quietly. Edith never acts worried and, of course, Kelly is game for anything. I strongly suspect she could park a car in the middle of the ring, tell him to jump it, and he'd be happy to try.

Then it happens. She stacks up a wall of fake brick squares and sets a pole on top. As Kelly canters toward the fence, I wait for the take-off, that magic moment when Kelly and the horse go airborne. Instead, at the last second, the horse plows both feet into the ground as if to say, *nothing doing.* He stops, but Kelly does not and comes over the horse's head, tumbling head over heels. As hard as it is watching him fly through the air, it's thinking about the moment he's going to hit the ground that has me gasping. All the possibilities course through my head: a broken neck, a severed spinal cord, his head crushed, even if he is wearing the blasted helmet.

Those five seconds take three years off my life. At least.

The landing is as violent as I feared. He hits with an arm outstretched and rolls all the way over before stopping. Dust flies, obscuring part of him from view. But before I can rush into the ring, he jumps up and brushes himself off, completely unscathed. He does, however, look chagrined and Edith shows no sympathy.

"That's what happens when you take your horse for granted," she says.

I have to say something, so they know my nerves aren't made of steel. I holler out, "You all keep this up and I'm looking for a new job." Edith gives me her famous dismissive glance, but Kelly shoots me an odd look. In one fluid motion he remounts the horse. After one more look in my direction, he comes right back to that same damn jump, this time flying over it and successfully landing on the other side.

As if that weren't enough to give me a heart attack, two days later, I see a group of inmates staring up at the top of the barracks building. Of course, that sends my radar into high alert, but I can't imagine they'd be sneaking in booze by helicopter.

I walk over to them. "What's so interesting?" I follow their eyes and spot Kelly halfway up a trellis heading to the roof of the barracks building. "What the hell?"

One of the men speaks for the group. "Some baby bird fell out of a nest. He's putting it back."

I shake my head at them while looking up. "Kelly, get down from there. Now!" I turn to the guys. "What? Did you all egg him on?"

"It was his idea, not ours," the spokesman says. Bad answer. I pin them with a look and they back away. "Sorry, Mr. Murry," a few of them mumble.

Kelly climbs down nimbly enough, jumping from several feet up. He looks downright cheerful which makes me even madder.

"What do you think you're doing?" I demand.

He points up and grins like, *isn't it obvious?*

I put my hands on my hips instead of around his throat. "Do you want to break your fool neck?"

He shrugs. "I was okay. If you remember, I'm good at climbing things."

Unbelievable. I cross my arms. "Funny, but what I recall is that when you go climbing, you get into trouble. Next door, *now*."

This is a day Squirrel Thompson is here going over paperwork with Gene. Thankfully, he quit trying to find places to ship Kelly off to. A couple of months ago, he'd brought his dog along when he dropped by to pick up some things. There's nothing Squirrel loves more than talking about his black lab. The rest of us know to look at our watch and come up with someplace we need to be. Kelly, on the other hand, was an avid listener and was all over that pup. He pet him till I thought the dog's hair would fall off. To cap it off he doodled a picture of the lab which Squirrel seized on to take home. There's been no more talk of boot camps. Kelly has chalked up another ally. I'm not sure if it just happens or it's calculated. Either way, he has a distinct knack for it.

Squirrel and Gene look up as we walk by. By the grins on their faces, I can tell they were watching out the window. I shoot them a don't-you-dare-talk-to-us look. Once in the kitchen, I pull one of the chairs out from under the table, turn it around, then point. "Sit."

"Why?"

"Because I said so." *Did that really come out of my mouth?* I can see Gene and Squirrel off in the next room turn their heads to stifle laughs. I send them a scorching look which doesn't faze them in the slightest.

Kelly continues to stand. "I didn't break any rules."

"Oh, yeah? I'm implementing a new rule. It's called, 'Don't be stupid.' You were stupid so you broke it. Sit."

He rolls his eyes, but his rear end finally makes contact with the chair. It gives me the illusion I'm in command. "Don't move a muscle till I tell you."

My feeling of control is fleeting. The look on his face is somewhere in the no-man's land between condescending and smirking. "What if I need to blink? I read somewhere it takes over two hundred muscles to do it even once."

To think I once believed he wasn't capable of being a smart-ass teenager. I point my finger at him. "Not. Another. Word."

He shrugs and folds his arms over his chest. "Fine."

Oh, he's pushing it!

I give him my most intimidating stare which he counters with a look of complete boredom. I hear a cough from the delegation in the other room. Man, I'm really off my game today. I tell Kelly to stay there till I tell him otherwise, then desert the field of battle and go to Gene and Squirrel.

"You are *not* helping," I say to them.

Squirrel, grinning, waves his hands. "Will you make us sit in chairs, too?"

"Very funny."

"How long you going to make him stay there?"

"Till I'm not mad any longer." I glance back toward the kitchen. "Or till he looks a little cowed."

Now it's Gene who puts his two cents in. "Good luck with that."

I hear the refrigerator door open, then the distinctive pop of a soda can.

I holler in the direction of the kitchen, "What did I say about staying in that chair?"

"I *am* in it. I scooted."

Gene and Squirrel have dissolved into silent laughter. Defeated, I slowly ease into the chair next to them. "I don't know what's gotten into him. Yesterday, I had to pull him out of a cave down by the mill—one that floods after a bad rain. The problem is, he isn't breaking any written rules but he still manages to be bad anyway."

Gene leans over and whispers," I think it's called male adolescence. Remember it?"

"God, yes." I put my head in my hands, remembering. "Once, my brother and I took pallets from house construction sites in the neighborhood. We took the wheels off my sister's training bike, nailed them to the four corners of the pallets, and took it down the biggest hill we could find. No brakes, unless you count dragging our tennis shoes on the asphalt. We also knew how to open a window at the middle school. We didn't harm anything. All we wanted was to play basketball in the gym. This was before security guards, school resource officers, and video cameras were everywhere."

"Nowadays, breaking into that school would get you arrested for burglary at the very least," Squirrel says.

"I know. Back then, if we'd been caught, we'd have gotten yelled at and told not to do it again. Maybe a school suspension at the most. Nowadays, an arrest would be the first course of action. I read where a school resource officer charged kids with forgery for faking a doctor's note. Hell, states now have laws against *disturbing a school*. Students have gotten arrested for burping intentionally. Man, I'm glad I'm not a kid now."

Gene and Squirrel share a couple of their own stories and eventually I lose my homicidal edge. Back in the kitchen, I find Kelly looking unrepentant but compliant. I was ready to give one last lecture, but he gives his most engaging smile and takes the wind right out of my sails. He knows it too. I can see the glint in the brat's eyes.

I grab a couple of sodas. "Take these to the guys."

"Sure." At least he doesn't hold a grudge. He acts like nothing happened.

"Hi, Mr. Thompson."

"Hey there, Kelly. What's shaking?"

He hands them the sodas, leans over and whispers, loud enough for me to hear, "Watch out. Mr. Murry's got a burr under his saddle today."

It's been a bad week. One of the trucks broke down and needed major repairs. The newest inmate's wife snuck him some pills on visiting day, so he wound up higher than a kite a few hours later. I immediately transferred him back to the prison he came from and contacted the police to prosecute the visitor who did the smuggling. Another inmate suffered a mild heart attack. He's okay now, but I had to use overtime hours for staff to be at the hospital with him.

Which brings me to today. Short staffed, I'm helping to supervise one of the work crews near the river, and I brought Kelly along. We're clearing honeysuckle out of the woods and I'm glad to have physical work for a change where I can see the results of my labors. We're close to wrapping up for lunch, so I grab my backpack and pull out my water bottle for a good long drink.

As I'm capping it, out of the corner of my eye, I see Kelly in what appears to be mid-air. At first, I chalk it up to an optical illusion but when I look more closely, something's not right. *What the hell?* I stand up, take a few steps, but then stop with my heart in my throat.

There's Kelly, smack dab in the middle of a fallen tree trunk that spans the width of the gorge—nonchalantly balancing, arms out, walking one foot in front of the other—oblivious to the thirty-foot drop to the rocks and creek below.

I open my mouth to yell but think better of it and snap it shut. Distracting him might lead to disastrous results. With my heart still in my throat, I watch him as step by agonizing step he gets closer to safety. Suddenly, he stops. He's leaning over slightly. *Holy crap! He's spitting and watching it fall!* Finally, he reaches the other side and jumps off, firmly on the ground.

I'm going to kill him. My strides eat up the distance between me and the tree trunk and I'm standing at the edge of the culvert in three seconds flat. Aware now of my presence, Kelly turns and unbelievably, looks like he has plans to repeat the act to come back across.

I put my foot on the end of the tree. "Do. Not. Even. Think about it," I growl.

His eyes connect with mine and it begins to dawn on him that he's in trouble.

Big trouble. I feel a fury I haven't felt in years, maybe ever. My jaw clenches and my head feels like it's going to explode. I've got to be turning purple. Kelly's eyes and mouth are startled open. He backs up a couple of steps. I point to a rock several yards back. "Go to that rock and sit right now. You stay there, do you understand me?"

He goes and sits with his hands clasped in his lap, looking straight ahead, avoiding my eyes. I turn around as Brent comes up behind me. He too looks at the tree and the long drop and cringes, but after he gets a look at my face, I see him cast a sympathetic look in Kelly's direction.

"Don't be giving him that sorry-for-you look. He could have really hurt himself. Or worse."

"I know. Sorry. I'll go get him."

"How?"

He points down a deer trail. "That trail comes out above the gulch. I can cross down there and bring him back. It'll take a bit."

"Great. Go fetch him. Then I'm going to kill him."

I keep my arms crossed and lean against a nearby tree trunk, not taking my eyes off the boy for a second. With effort, I make my voice steady and calm to be sure I don't prompt the kid into doing something rash. Make that more rash. "Stay right there. Brent's coming for you."

Gene sidles up next to me. "Yikes," he says once he reads the situation. "I guess the kid's getting his mojo back."

I give Gene an icy look. "I'd like to take a belt to his mojo."

He opens his mouth to say something, but wisely thinks the better of it, then goes with, "We'll start packing up."

Brent eventually shows up on the other side and collects Kelly. Once they get back, I point to another rock and Kelly takes a seat. By now, our little drama has come to the attention of the other men who toss Kelly sympathetic looks as they file by. Several murmur encouragement, then look like guilty school children when I shoot nasty looks their way. If anyone is getting sympathy around here, it should be me.

I help load the tools in the back of Gene's truck and watch it till it's out of sight before slowly, very slowly, turning and locking my eyes on Kelly. I wait five long seconds before I walk his way. He makes a weak effort to match my stare but can't quite pull it off. His body stiffens and I can tell he's afraid of me, probably the only time since he walked in the door that first day. *Good.*

"Don't look at me like that. I'm not going to hit you. But don't flatter yourself by thinking I don't want to."

I reach down and pull him up by his arm and march him to the chasm. "But you and I are going to have a little chat about your old friend Mr. Impulse Control. Do you remember him?"

No answer, but I didn't really expect one. We stand at the edge and look down at the creek gurgling far below.

"How deep is that?"

"Pretty deep," he says quietly.

"How dumb was it walking across that log?"

"Pretty dumb."

I tilt my head. "You think? You could have slipped. It could have broken in two and just like that," I snap my fingers for effect, "you'd end up with multiple broken bones. That's only if you were lucky enough to live."

I'd cooled off while Brent retrieved him but visualizing again what might have happened fires me back up. My voice gets louder till I'm almost shouting. "I'm going to have nightmares all night because you made a conscious decision to do something completely idiotic with no thought of your own safety, or giving me a heart attack. Are you listening?"

He nods.

I bend down and give him a little shake. "What was going on in your head? I really want to know because this," and I point down, "is the kind of thing where you don't think. And when you don't think, you get in trouble every time. By God, you've supposedly got a good brain, but then you don't use it. I'm going to tell you right now if you ever, *ever* pull a stunt like this again, I'll assign you nothing but kitchen duty for the rest of your natural life. I'll ground you to the building. Do I make myself clear?"

"Yes, sir."

I stop my rant and look at his upturned face and flushed cheeks and rein in my anger. What has gotten into him? It's like he stuck his toe in the pool of bad behavior and decided it feels fine. I look at him closer. Something's not right. He looks cowed but behind that … can he possibly be … pleased? I give up.

"Let's go," I say, waving him toward the truck.

He gets in, puts on his seatbelt, angles his head away. I turn the key and put the truck in gear, looking over my shoulder to back out, when I catch his eyes shifting my way. That little spark of defiance is gone. I'm not sure what's replaced it, but a warning bell goes off.

I put the truck back in park, click off the ignition, and turn to him. "We're not going anywhere till you tell me what's going on with you. And don't you dare tell me there's nothing."

His eyes fixate on about the third button of my shirt. He chews on his lower lip. A fly buzzes through the open window, circles around our heads a couple of times till I wave him out the other side. I resume my staring until dammit, that blasted fly comes back and starts circling again. Kelly gives a little smile. "If a fly is zooming around in a plane, is he flying or is he a passenger?"

I still want to hang him upside down by his heels. I'm not in the mood for riddles.

His eyes fixate on mine, then he says, "I visit the weak but seldom the bold, what am I?"

I lean my head against the back of the seat, sensing we're about to get to it. I pause before quietly saying, "Tell me."

He glances away, but then brings his eyes back to mine before answering. "Fear." Now he plays with his hands, always a tell we're getting to the heart of things. "Better to be brave and stupid than to be afraid all the time."

I nod and ask softly, "What are you afraid of, Kelly?"

He snorts. "It's a long list. Getting in more trouble. What's going to happen to me when I get released. But more than anything..." He turns to look out the window "...you'll leave for another job. Like when you said that at Ms. Casey's."

I shake my head, "I was kidding."

He looks up and to my consternation, his eyes are filled with tears. "But you could. People do it all the time."

All the anger drains out of me. What would it be like to be fourteen and feel you don't have one person on the earth you can count on to be there for you? Who truly cares about you?

Thankfully, this is something I can give him.

Something I want to give him.

Something I never saw myself giving anybody even a few months ago.

I reach my right arm around him to unlatch his seat belt before dragging him across the seat to me. "Listen to me. I'm not going anywhere. When it comes to you, it's not business as usual. I'd do anything for you. I'm in this for the long haul, okay? I expect visits from you and the wife and kids someday when I'm in a nursing home."

He turns into my arms, presses his head against my chest. "Of course, I'd come to the nursing home," he whispers. There's a pause. "What exactly *is* a nursing home, Mr. Murry?"

My throat catches on a laugh. "Nothing I hope I have to worry about for a long time. And you know what? When it's just us, let's go with 'Sam.' Just try not to slip up and say it in front of the others."

He wipes his eyes with the sleeve of his shirt and gives a little smile. "I've been calling you Sam in my head for months." He sits up straighter and gives his mischievous smile. "You'd do anything for me?

"Yeah, I would."

"Would you rob a bank?"

Crazy kid. "Now you're just being a brat. Okay, I'd do *almost* anything for you. All I ask in exchange is a promise to knock off the death-defying acts."

"I promise." He pulls away and twists up to look at me. "Sam?"

"Yeah."

"You should get married."

"Good lord, where'd that come from?"

"You should have kids."

"I kinda have a kid."

"A real kid."

I reach over and pinch his arm. "Hmm. Seems real to me."

He frowns and leans away, rubbing his arm. "You'd be a good dad, that's all."

"You think? Well, while we're being so complimentary I'll tell you something. If I could choose anybody to be my kid, it would be you."

"Gee, a kid with a record? Wouldn't you rather have a football star that makes straight A's?"

"I didn't know there was such a thing. But no, pass. It'd be all downhill after high school. He'd live in the basement, drinking beer till he's thirty, talking about the glory days."

"Okay, try this. A nice straight B, well-rounded guy. Makes the basketball team but doesn't start?"

I scrunch up my face like I'm seriously considering it. "Hmmm. Tempting, but nah, too boring. Sorry, kiddo. Just can't escape it. It's you."

He laughs, "Please don't say 'escape.'"

I crack up. *God, I love this kid.* I almost say it but catch myself. "Put your seat belt back on. All this confessing has made me hungry. Let's get some lunch."

I call Gene and tell him we'll be back in a few hours. Gene must think the worst and says, "Don't be too hard on the kid, Sam."

"I've got it under control."

We grab some food, and on the way back to the car, pass a pawn shop. Kelly abruptly stops in front of it. In the front window are three guitars. He lingers and looks longingly at them. I give him a glance. He's always full of surprises. "You play or just want to?"

"My dad did. He showed me a few chords. I'd like to. It's, you know, a cowboy kind of thing."

"Which one of those looks good?"

He assesses, then points. "The one in the middle."

We go in and with some negotiating, walk out fifteen minutes later with a guitar in hand. Once we get home, Kelly bounds up the front steps and by the time I get inside, he's showing Gene the purchase.

"I'm going to take it up to my room." And with that, his feet pound up the stairs.

Gene turns to me with a smug smile on his face. "I can see I should have worried more about what you'd do to punish him." He makes a look of mock horror. "You're going to make him take up a musical instrument? Oh, the cruelty!"

"Go ahead and have your fun. I took care of the other thing. This was just ... different." I sound unconvincing even to my own ears.

"Riiigght," he says.

Everyone's a smart ass.

KELLY

42

The summer green may be gone, replaced by yellows, browns, and the purple of asters, but it still feels like summer. Temperatures are in the nineties and the humidity is out the roof. I remember Sam talking about squeezing the air till it drips and now I know what he means. Within fifteen minutes of working in the woods, we're all drenched in sweat. I'm not in Wyoming anymore.

School begins and Mrs. Knight and I resume our twice a week lesson times. I'm glad to have her back. She's a rarity in my life. Someone who leaves but returns. They've put me in harder classes this year. Chemistry is mandatory, but it's difficult without a lab. A couple of times, Ms. Knight brings equipment and we do experiments in the kitchen. I like biology because it's the science dealing with nature. And of course, I like anything to do with writing. I get a little thrill each time I see an "A" on the papers I get back from my teachers.

It's funny reading comments on homework and tests from people I've never met. Mrs. Taber, my English teacher, submitted one of my short stories to a regional high school writing contest and I won. She wrote me a nice card and there was a note from the principal too. Shortly after that Mrs. Knight informs me my presence is desired at the school. They all want to meet me. I have mixed feelings. I'd like to put faces with these names, but they know why I'm not sitting in their classroom, so I'd rather stay a mystery. I tell Sam I don't want to go. He stands there a beat, then says, "I'm going to tell you in the kindest, nicest way I can that you are being a total wuss."

Well, that does it. Now I have to go. So we show up one afternoon just as students have been dismissed for the day. I watch doors open and kids flood the halls. Mrs. Knight meets us at the front office and introduces us to the principal. She's much younger looking than I expected and is friendly and nice, complimenting me on my schoolwork and especially on my writing award which she gives to me with a bit of fanfare. It's kinda embarrassing, but kinda nice. We go meet my teachers who thankfully don't look at me like I have three heads, but I still hear the questions they aren't asking. I try to picture myself in a different life walking these halls, sitting in these desks in these rooms.

When we get back to the car, I can see the football team practicing in the field in front of us and clumps of kids hanging out talking in the parking lot. Out of the corner of my eye, I see the sympathetic look Sam tosses my way.

As I buckle my seat belt, I tell him, "Don't feel bad for me. I'm glad I'm not going here."

He frowns at me. "Why? Everyone was so nice."

"It's not that. The truth is I have more freedom during the day than these kids do. School's like a juvenile detention center you leave at the end of the day." I incline my head toward the building. "You did notice the metal detectors, didn't you? Bells ringing, having to stay in a seat unless you get permission to get up, staff doling out punishments. You can't leave the property without getting into trouble. Did you hear the afternoon announcements? *You are released. Students are free to go.* Even the words sound like prison."

Sam starts the car and I wait for him to tell me how wrong I am, but all he says is, "There's good things too. Sports, clubs, hanging out with friends."

There's a question I need to ask, one that's bothered me for some time. "I've never really cared about friends. Does that make me weird?"

He gives me an assessing look and says, "You're fine with adults whether they're in their twenties or sixties. You may just not have much in common with kids your age, especially after all that's happened to you."

I smile and say, "Dad told my Uncle Jack once I had an old soul; maybe that's it."

"Maybe. The other thing is it's only when we're young we get pigeonholed by our age, especially in school. Once we're out, we hang around with people of all ages and nobody thinks much about it."

As we drive out, we pass the girls track team. I glue my eyes on them and their skimpy uniforms. "Of course, there's that."

Sam follows my eyes. "Yeah, sorry. I'm afraid that's off limits for now."

I give a big sigh. "I know. I pretend I'm in a monastery." I take one more, long look at the girls and think about needing to go to my room for a while when I get home.

Just a few weeks ago, the trees that line the field and creek were vivid swirls of yellow, red, and orange, but now, those colors are all gone. The horses' coats have thickened, and we're giving them extra hay. The Village restaurant has a fire pit going so visitors can fix their own s'mores after dinner. I'm not allowed there, but I can see them when I'm working with the maintenance crew replacing bulbs in the streetlights. I think I'd really like a s'more. Hell, I'd just like to sit by a fire. It's these times I yearn to be a regular person again. I try not to feel sorry for myself. At least I'm out here enjoying the fall season after missing the whole thing last year while I rotted in jail.

Staying busy becomes more challenging with darkness falling just after five o'clock. A quick dinner and I'm in for the night by five-thirty. Being inside from dusk to dawn brings the feeling of confinement. If I act annoying enough, Sam gets the hint and takes me out for a walk. Like a dog. I'm reminded of walking Jasper, the Haverly's dog, but now I'm on the other end of the leash.

I spend more time than ever writing. I also do a lot of schoolwork, and it's nice to pretend I'm a regular kid working on his homework. But it's an illusion. A lot of school groups tour the Village. I watch them from a safe distance. My life is so different from other kids my age, and it's too late to ever do anything about it. I picture myself when I get out of here. Alone. But I also picture myself free.

I remember a big old pinto horse my uncle once owned. Even with plenty of grass in his field, he was constantly trying to get out. He learned to open the gate's latch, so my uncle had to wire it shut. He'd jump the fence if any part of the wire fencing sagged. I once saw him pull off one of his escapes. He knew the instant he was free and went into a full gallop, thrilled to be away from fences, halters, and bridles. I could feel his exhilaration.

The holidays are arriving, and the buildings are decked out with greenery and candles for tours. I watch families coming and going from the various buildings. Sometimes, I feel a little stab of jealousy for what they have that I don't and turn away from the window. I'll be glad when Christmas is over.

There are cedar trees all over The Village, so I help Sam cut down a few. One goes in the barracks and one is for us. At first, I don't want any part of it. But Bonnie comes and makes it fun. We were only going to put on lights, but she insists on some ornaments, so we go with a nature theme. She brings fake birds and we hang pine cones and strings of cranberries. Sometimes I love the tree and linger downstairs later than usual to sit in the dark and watch the lights twinkle. Sometimes I hate the tree because it makes me think of past Christmases with my family. After the holidays we put it out for the birds.

As the New Year begins, I think about the fact that I'm now fifteen years old. Fourteen started off as the second hardest year of my life, but things turned around and got better. Next year I'll be sixteen. It's the year I get released. The future is a gaping hole. But one good thing about surviving hard times is you feel stronger.

I'm still here. I've survived. Whatever happens, I'm not going looking for trouble. I remember something my Dad used to say: "You can't always keep trouble away, but that doesn't mean you offer it a chair."

SAM

43

Christmas and corrections, not a happy combo. Every year we engage in a completely unsuccessful attempt to make it something other than depressing. I get grief from my family about not coming to spend the holidays with them, but I can't abandon the kid during this painful time. We're all glad when Christmas is in the rearview mirror.

Typically in this part of the country, true winter doesn't usually arrive till January. This year when it does come, it comes with a vengeance. We break hundred-year-old records. It gets cold. Then colder. It snows. It snows more. I hate these spells because tempers get short and there are fights and other problems. It's what happens when too many troubled people have too much time on their hands. But if the rest of us hate the weather, Kelly is in his element. "You call this snow?" he sneers.

He spends hours outside creating snow formations. My favorite is the snowman that gets built around the mailbox, so it looks like the letters are deposited in his mouth. It's great for morale. The men are so interested in what Kelly is up to that most of the usual bickering is kept at bay. I finally drag him inside to warm up but all he does is moan, "If I only had some skis or snowshoes."

When winter begins giving way to spring, I realize Kelly has been here almost a year. The last twelve months have brought noticeable physical changes. He's grown several inches. He's still thin but looks fit. He's changed from a cute kid to a handsome young man without going through the gawky stage so many adolescents do. The emotional changes are even more dramatic. I don't see pain sitting in his eyes like I used to. He seems happier and more confident.

Henry has been by from time to time to visit. He also looked into Kelly's relatives' estates. First, he checked on the grandfather's in Philadelphia. The old man left all his money to his college. Not a penny for Kelly, his only surviving relative. Granddaddy was a bastard to the very end.

Wyoming is a different story. Kelly was the beneficiary of both his father and his uncle. It's not a fortune but adding both together, it comes to a tidy sum. Without being told all the particulars, the lawyer in Fort Dixon knows Kelly is alive and well. Since there's no immediate need for the funds, they can sit there for now. The trust was set up so that he wouldn't collect until age eighteen, but since there's a hardship clause, he can access the money earlier. Henry told me he's got everything handled and mentioned it's good to know Kelly will have money waiting once he's released.

I flash back to that call from Bonnie that brought Kelly to my doorstep. Back then, I couldn't imagine having a kid smack-dab in the middle of my life. Now, I can't imagine him out of it.

In January a new governor takes office. Both adult and juvenile corrections get new Commissioners. The commissioner of the juvenile division is a former policeman who has never set foot in a juvenile treatment facility in his life and has no clue what he's doing. In adult corrections we don't fare any better. Our new leader has his eyes set on making a name for himself. He's a big law and order talker. That's business as usual, but this time it's not just talk. He's making major changes to the system, all punitive. Every few days some edict comes down about something we have to start doing or stop doing. Programming for inmates is cut back as "coddling law breakers." Visiting hours are reduced and new restrictions on inmate visitation are put in place.

The new administration's idea of work for us Superintendents is constant, soul-sucking meetings. Today, I'm attending a mandatory meeting at a state park where we are lectured for an hour about escapes, even though it's not been a problem. Next is a whole new list of what's considered contraband. I think of Kelly's Legos key and smile. I also do a lot of looking out the window. There's an understanding all state agencies should book their meetings at state parks rather than pay money to private hotels or other rental spots. This has something we don't have at The Village park—a bird's eye view of a lake. I feel my mind drifting out onto the water. I should see if my brother and his kids want to come here and fish with me some time.

I try to come back to attention when the new Director of Operations is introduced. When I hear the name, I stiffen. *Jesus, not her!* Shannon Isaacs. Surely, they could have found someone better.

After we give her polite applause, she launches into her spiel beginning with "I'm sure you are aware of the great changes this administration has made."

If any of us thought they were great, we're keeping it to ourselves. Her lips tighten at our distinct lack of enthusiasm. I look at my watch and inwardly groan at how much time is left before I can bolt out of here. My eyes glaze over when a committee is appointed to set goals and objectives as part of long-range planning. My suggestion would be they get the last five-year plan that was never implemented and blow the dust off it. Of course, they'd have to find it first. I picture the last scene of the *Raiders of the Lost Ark* movie with a huge building holding a vast amount of crates. Probably all full of five-year plans.

During a break, I go to the back of the room for coffee and stand next to the cedar-paneled wall which pretty much dates the building back to at least the 1950's. The clump of people ahead of me are adding creams and stirring, and I wait till they are done before stepping up to get my cup. Bill Richards, a Superintendent at another forestry camp, walks past me. As he passes, he leans in and grins. "Two years more and I can retire, but I think it's going to be a long two years."

I spot the new Director of Operations talking with a couple of others. Blond, nice figure, well dressed in a white shirt, blue suit, corporate sort of way. Not a hair out of place, lots of makeup. Most people would call her attractive, but she's too brittle-looking for my taste. She looks out of place here in this rustic room with its faded green carpet and no-longer-in-vogue, bronze light fixtures.

Shit, she's coming my way. I work hard to have my face look neutral. It takes some effort. There's no love lost between us. She's wearing a contented smile. Knowing you're now the boss of someone you have it out for probably brings that out in a person.

"Hello, Murry."

"Ms. Isaac."

"Until I was appointed as Operations head, I hadn't realized you'd gone into corrections. It probably suits you better than police work."

That's meant to be a zinger. When I was on the force, she was an assistant prosecutor and I reported her for official misconduct on one of my cases. It wasn't serious enough to get her fired, but it's not something she appreciated. I can tell she's not one to forgive and forget. Too bad for her she can't fire me on the spot. I'm protected by the government merit system. The only way she could get me would be to close down the whole facility and get rid of us all.

She purses her lips together. "I'm hoping to visit all the facilities in the next several weeks. Of course, I'll need to see the larger programs first." She takes a sip of her coffee. "I believe yours in the smallest in the state?"

Cute, real cute. A shot at my manhood. I take the high road and ignore the jibe. "Yes, we're a specialty program. Pre-parole specifically for alcoholics."

She shakes her head. "Well, I don't envy you having to deal with some of the worst losers in the system."

I take another sip of my coffee before I say something I might regret. Bill Richards is standing with three other guys I know well. They all look my way like they're thinking *better you than me*. I notice none of them are coming over to try and save me. I shoot them daggers over the top of my mug as I drink, but they all just grin.

Ms. Isaacs, on the other hand, doesn't seem to worry about what she might say. "I'm not sure of the value of some of these minimum programs. These people need to know if they do the crime, their stay will be unpleasant. Swift, sure punishment is what needs to happen."

I can't let that slide. "The certainty of apprehension has been shown to reduce crime, yes, but studies show value in rehabilitation as well. These people will get out one day and might move next door to us. Treating people badly isn't going to make for a better neighbor."

She shakes a hand in the air which rattles all her gold bracelets. "God forbid any of them become my neighbor. And I don't think playing cards and watching TV is teaching anyone a lesson." After that proclamation, she goes on to explain in detail exactly how superintendents should run their programs. Is there anything more annoying than somebody who has never done your job telling you how you should do it?

When she finally quits talking, I go with patronizing. "Hmm, well we're always looking at ways we can improve. Everyone needs to learn from their mistakes."

She gives a tight little smile as she recognizes the barb I just sent her way.

Having left the high road behind, I admit I get pleasure from seeing it hit home. One of her little pals is looking at us with apprehension, but like my buddies, gives us a wide berth.

I get ready to respond to whatever she's going to say about people learning from mistakes, but she doesn't go there. I'm unprepared for her next words. "You have a juvenile in your program, don't you?"

I twist to set my coffee cup on the table behind me, then turn to her, careful not to show any emotion. "Yes."

"You know studies have shown that the younger a person is when they enter the system, the more likely they are to live a life of crime. "

I should just say, "Is that so?" and let it go but I can't. "Those studies also show it's the involvement with the justice system that funnels kids into adult corrections. If you have two identical kids on a low-level offense like shoplifting, but only one gets arrested, he's the most likely to end up an adult offender. The kid that didn't get caught will usually age out of delinquent behavior on his own."

She frowns at me. "You're saying no one should be arrested?"

"Of course not. But we should keep kids in the shallowest part of the system. Employ restorative justice with apologies and community service, hook them into prosocial activities, get them a tutor, a mentor. The moment a kid passes through the door of a detention center, his odds of a lifetime of crime skyrocket. It's the number one causation factor for entering the adult system. Beats out even a poor neighborhood or substance abuse for cause and effect."

Ms. Isaacs isn't impressed with my Juvenile Justice 101 speech. She's someone who never lets facts get in the way of her opinions. "Well, the juveniles in adult corrections are deep in the system. It's too late for them. All we can do is control the future damage."

She takes a step and a shaft of light coming in the window hits her in the face. With a frown, she waves to one of her staff hovering around ready to jump to do her bidding. "Shut those darn curtains," she tells him. There goes the view.

Just when I think she's leaving to go find her next victim, she turns back to me and says, "Actually, we're looking into converting one of the buildings at Central into a facility to house all our juvenile inmates. Put them all in one place. All, except the ones who require maximum security, of course. The ones who would be on death row if the court hadn't put all those restrictions on that." She scowls like it's a shame she can't execute children and be done with them.

I work hard to keep my voice casual. "Central is medium security. The boy with us scored for minimum."

She folds her arms across her chest. I can almost see her mind calculating. "We already have people working on the scoring tool. Just being a juvenile offender in the adult system should garner more points. We see them as a high-risk population. Impulsive, violent. And of course, it'd be safer for them to be isolated from the adults. We don't want any lawsuits."

If I thought she cared about kids beyond the lawsuits, I would tell her how well the youth in question is doing. I would talk about relationships and trust, the importance of continuity, and the damage caused by disruption. I would tell her Kelly's sad story, but I know it wouldn't make a bit of difference. I know her type. All that matters is public perception, budget savings, and her own personal power trip.

Instead, I say, "I'm all for safety. I can guarantee you that steps have been taken to assure the well-being of the youth in our custody."

She ignores that and fires her final salvo. "We'll be closely scrutinizing programs to make reductions as needed. These smaller programs just aren't as cost effective. After all, we're responsible for the management of taxpayer dollars."

Now she's threatening my job, but I refuse to give her the satisfaction of looking upset. "Keep me posted on how that goes, would you?"

Do I see disappointment in her eyes? Was I supposed to beg? I go back to my table and the next speaker begins. I don't hear a word he says for the alarm bells ringing in my head about moving Kelly. *The hell of it is, she could do it.* I tell myself to relax; it's not an immediate threat. But I've worked in this business long enough to know about the whims of central office. They can mess over staff quite a bit if they put their minds to it, but there's no limit to how much they can screw over the inmates. All it takes is one stroke of a pen from someone hundreds of miles away and a man can get moved the next day. And he can't do a damn thing about it. Undergoing specialized medical treatment? Too bad. Family lives thirty minutes away and regularly visit, but we need to fill a bed four hours away? Off you go. If someone shows up with the paperwork to move Kelly tomorrow, there's nothing I could do but watch. I play out the vision in my head and my blood runs cold.

Putting my hand under the table I keep glancing down at my phone, as if just looking at it over and over will make the time pass faster. A headache comes out of nowhere, twin shoots of pain zipping up both sides of my skull. Just as freedom from this torture looms comes the dreaded, "Does anyone have any questions?"

There's one beat of silence. You can feel the mass hopefulness. People start reaching for their things. Up comes a hand. The air in the room collapses. There's always that one guy. He just has to ask one. Not because he needs answers, no, just so the people in charge have proof of his attention. What a brown-noser.

When I'm finally in the car and on the road, I try and call Henry. He's in court so I leave a callback and stress it's urgent. Halfway home, with my head still pounding, my phone rings.

I hear Henry's casual voice. "Hey, what's going on? Does the kid need some money?"

"No. That's not it. Have you been following the new Justice Secretary and cronies in the paper?"

"Yeah, none of us are too happy about the direction things are going. Won't make my job any easier."

"I just left a big superintendent powwow and the new director told me they want to take any inmate under eighteen and put them in a renovated building at Central."

"That's medium security; Kelly scored minimum."

I glance in the rear and side view mirrors and switch lanes. "I don't think they plan on letting that stop them. She was talking about revising the scoring and retroactively reclassifying everyone."

"You know how slow government is. By the time they get to that point, Kelly is likely to be already discharged."

"I know. But do you know what it would do to him if they pulled up in front of the building and said 'Get in'?"

"Yeah, that's a bad picture. Let me talk to Nolan. I'm sure he wouldn't want that to happen. But if we get him out, where would he go?"

My hands tighten on the wheel, but I don't miss a beat. "I'll take him."

There's a second of silence then Henry asks, "Could he stay there if he's not an inmate?"

"Definitely not."

"Could you keep your job if you don't live there?"

I shrug even though no one can see. "Probably not. It may be a moot point. I get the feeling there's a target on my back."

Henry's voice drops and slows. "Look, I'm on my way home. Let's sleep on it and not do anything rash. No point in you losing your home and your job if it's not necessary."

I feel better simply knowing we've got Henry in our corner. And he might well be right; I could be overreacting. "Okay. Sorry, but she gave me the creeps." We say goodbye and I drive home feeling a little better, but the feeling of unease never completely goes away.

The next day Squirrel Thompson calls me. Bill Richards, the superintendent at our other forestry camp just got fired. The whole facility is being shut down.

SAM

44

For Kelly's fifteenth birthday, Gene and I gave him a camera to use to take wildlife pictures. We knew it was the first birthday gift he'd gotten in years. His shy smile told us how pleased he was.

We didn't celebrate his one-year anniversary of arriving here, but we all marked the day. He's come a long way from the kid I carried up and down the stairs. There's a brightness in his eyes, a growing confidence. There's been no further mention about juvenile inmates being relocated or about closing our program here since my unpleasant encounter with Shannon Isaac those couple of months back. I'm starting to chalk up my worries to state government paranoia.

It's a windy, cold Wednesday. Stephanie Knight arrives with her red hair flying around her head. She tries her best to tame it with one hand while clutching books in her other.

"Goodness, that's a lazy wind, as my grandmother would say."

I give her a dubious look. "Lazy?"

She laughs. "Yes, lazy. Too lazy to go around you, so it goes through you."

I chuckle. "That's sounds like a granny saying."

She and Kelly go into the kitchen, assume their regular seats, and get started. I leave them to it and go into my office to make some calls. A few minutes later, a car pulls up out front. I'm not expecting anyone, so I rise and go to the window.

Oh, shit.

It's Shannon Isaac, arriving unannounced and unplanned, which I'm sure is not by accident. My gut reaction is to keep her out of this building, so I quickly head outside. I reach her car as she closes and locks the door.

She turns and gives me the beauty pageant plastic smile. "Mr. Murry. I apologize I haven't made it out here before now."

Yeah, we're all real sorry it's taken you this long. I match her fake smile with one of my own. She and I could get Oscars for all this pretending we don't hate each other. "No problem. You've picked a cold day to come visit. Do you want to see our main building?"

She waves a dismissing hand. She must be wearing at least five gold bracelets. "I'm presuming it's a dining hall and a dormitory. If you've seen one, you've seen them all. And I'd just as soon not have to deal with all the perverts in custody."

She grimaces as a wind gust blows her hair into her face. "I'd like to go over some numbers with you and especially look at budget and staffing ratio information."

Nothing for it, but to take her to my office. I manage to get her inside and close the door. We start pouring over spread sheets. She nit-picks everything to death. Was this medical expense necessary? It's for a heart condition, so yes. Do the men really need work gloves and bug spray? Yes, because we do want work to get done without ripped hands and Lyme disease from ticks. I keep stealing looks at my watch. More than an hour has gone by. Ms. Knight should be leaving soon. I want to send Kelly next door and out of sight.

Isaac looks to be diligently examining overtime expenses. That should keep her busy a while. "I'll be right back. Can I get you a drink?"

She doesn't look up. "No thanks."

I walk into the kitchen where Kelly and Stephanie appear to be wrapping things up, but before I can say anything, Isaac is walking my way. "Maybe I will have that drink," she says.

She takes in the two people at the table and the books stacked there then turns to me, "You have family here?" I can see her calculating how many rules and procedures I might be breaking.

"No. This is Ms. Knight from the county school system. Ms. Knight, this is Ms. Isaac."

With a silent apology, I don't introduce Kelly. He gives me a speculative look, but I think he knows something's amiss. I can hear the edge in my own voice, and he knows me enough to know my face doesn't usually look like this. Ms. Knight is giving me an odd look as well. She nods hello to Isaac.

Like watching a periscope on a submarine pivot to its target, I see Isaac turn her scrutiny to Kelly. Her eyes narrow and her mouth tightens. Kelly's getting to his feet because he's got good manners. She barks out, "Stay seated," like she's reprimanding a bad dog. He blinks and one second later, sits back down. I see a flush beginning in his cheeks.

Isaac has gone into full investigative mode as she zeros in on the teacher. "How many inmates do you work with here?"

Stephanie picks up her pen and rocks it back and forth between her fingers. She takes her time in answering. "I work with *one* student." I think she's shocked by the level of Isaac's animosity toward a kid she's never even met.

"I'm sorry you have to come way out here," Isaac tells her. "I'm sure you have better things to do." Her eyes flick to Kelly who continues to stare straight ahead.

Stephanie stands up and starts shuffling some of her papers. I think she's defying this witch to tell her to sit. "Your concern isn't needed. I find it an excellent use of my time."

Stephanie glances at Kelly but he's being careful to look at no one. I've had enough. I tap him on the shoulder. "Go next door."

He wastes no time beating it out the back door of the kitchen. Stephanie is staring at me, like *what the hell are you doing*? I've never felt so powerless. But anything I do is going to fan the fire. This is no time to let pride get the better of me. She puts her things in her accordion file. "I'll see myself out."

"Thanks. Be careful going home."

With one last quizzical glance at me, she takes her leave.

Isaac uses the pen in her hand to spin around one of the books left on the table. It's advanced English, but I doubt she's impressed. "So, this is the juvenile you have." It's a statement, not a question.

"Yes."

"How often does the teacher come?"

"Twice a week. She leaves assignments for him to work on in between."

"It must be difficult for you to have to provide an educational program for just one inmate."

"Not really."

She pushes the English book away, like having it near might give her cooties. "I'm told he doesn't stay in the barracks."

How does she know that? Jesus, has she really come to check out Kelly and the rest is just a ruse?

She crosses her arms. "He's in this building I take it. Where?"

"On the third floor."

"I want to see."

Once again, I'm leading someone up to Kelly's room. But this time I'm not showing it off. She walks in behind me and her eyes do the three-sixty. I try to look at it with a neutral eye. His room, which seemed so spacious on his arrival, has shrunk as the result of the occupation of an active and inquisitive boy. Binoculars, a telescope, books, his birthday camera, the Lego bookends he made, various rocks, the guitar. Thankfully, everything is clean, and the bed is nicely made. It looks like I enforce some rules, though I know it has nothing to do with me. He likes things neat. I hate her invading his privacy.

She frowns. "Pretty plush for an inmate, don't you think?"

Nothing I say is going to change her mind, but I feel compelled to say it anyway. "When he came to us, he was barely fourteen, about five-feet tall and eighty pounds. We looked at what was safest for everyone."

"Well, he's not five-feet or fourteen anymore. Why not move him over now?"

It's like sinking into a hole. "Because he's doing well and he's still decades younger than anyone else here. It's easier for staff and frees up another bed for an additional inmate." I throw the extra bed space in there, like tossing a bone to a dog, but she's not biting.

She turns to me and in a voice that's only slightly nicer than when she commanded Kelly to sit, says, "Well, I don't like it. Give him a bed in the barracks. It'll do him good to get a glimpse of what his future holds."

Three beats go by while we stare at each other. "Yes, ma'am," I say. She hears the compliance in my voice and seems satisfied.

When she leaves, I go straight over to find Kelly. He's a sensitive kid. I figure he's upset but I often forget that under that vulnerability is a strong core of resilience. He's playing dominoes with a couple of other guys and looks up. "Is the blonde Cruella De Vil gone?"

Despite the fact that's the best thing I could call her, I feel compelled to go into adult-speak. "Show some respect."

"Sorry." His shoulders drop like he's being contrite, but under his breath he whispers to the inmate sitting next to him, "*Ms.* Cruella De Vil."

I give him a stern look, but inwardly smile. If this had happened a year ago, would he have handled it this well? Can he take being moved over here full-time in stride too? Give up the room he loves? The closeness to Gene and me?

Well, an order is an order. I'm going to have to assign him a bed in the barracks.

Later in the day, I sit down with staff and bring them in on the situation. We give Kelly a bunk and put his name on the bedding chart. It's official. He has a bed in the barracks. That's what she said to do, and I did it. No one said he has to sleep in it.

One small problem solved.

If only that was the end of it.

SAM

45

For the next three weeks, I'm reminded of the time a year ago when Kelly was so sick that I carried him everywhere. I'm not doing that now, but I am keeping him on a short leash. I don't leave the grounds unless I take him with me.

This morning, the phone rings and I finish scribbling my name on a personnel evaluation before reaching for it. I immediately recognize Squirrel's voice. "Sam, I've got bad news. A driver is on his way with an order to pick up Kelly."

Damnit to hell. Rage and fear battle for top billing. "When did he leave?"

"Some time ago, I think, but I just found out. He has to be close. I'm sorry Sam. I feel terrible about this. Listen, they are moving him to Central. Scott Jacobs has been put in charge. I'll call him and tell him to treat Kelly with kid gloves. But Sam, he'll have to go in a cell."

"He won't be coming."

"Look, I know you're upset, but don't do anything rash. And especially not anything that'll make it even harder on the boy than it's going to be."

"I gotta go."

My keys find their way into my hand as I'm hanging up the phone. I run up to Kelly's room and grab some clothes, stuffing them in a bag while I make a quick call to Gene. It's one of those exceptionally warm early spring days, so Kelly went with Brent to do bird banding. I speed off in the truck, ignoring the *Watch for Wildlife* and twenty-mile-an-hour road signs. If any bunnies run onto the road today, they're dead meat. I'm keeping one eye peeled for a white Crown Vic. And there it is. From the top of a hill, I spot it turning from the highway into the main gate. I could drive right past him, but stealth seems the better option.

There's a back road to where I need to go. It's rough and seldom used, but usually passable with four-wheel-drive. I slow down, but still rock back and forth like crazy as my vehicle see-saws on the rough terrain. Recent rains have the creek higher than I like, but I gun it to drive across. Just before I'm safely on the other side, I feel the wheels spin in the mud and my forward motion is halted. *Damn!*

I throw it into reverse and try to roll onto the rocks and try again. Just when I think I've got it, the back wheels fishtail, and I'm still short of dry ground. Cussing a blue streak and angling the wheel slightly to the left, I ease down on the gas. I exhale in a gush when the third time proves to be the charm and I'm rolling again.

Kelly and Brent look up in surprise as I drive up. They know I'm not excited about bird banding. And they know I don't usually drive a truck out here. I force myself to slow down and sound calm. "Hey guys, how's it going?"

Brent tries to make it sound like a joke, but I can tell he's half-pissed. "Okay, till your truck scared everything away. What the hell are you doing driving out here? You know the whole front of your truck is covered in mud, don't you?"

"Yeah, sorry. I need to borrow Kelly." They both frown at me again. They've gotten to be a tight little club of two on their nature activities and I'm an interfering annoyance. Brent's winding up his birding net, so I wait for him to look at me. "Kelly and I are going to work on a project."

I watch his eyes get wide. He darts a glance Kelly's way before he says, "I see." Brent is trying and failing at looking nonchalant. "Kelly and I are going to work on a project" was the agreed upon code phrase made during staff planning sessions should "Operation Rescue Kelly" need to be put into effect.

Kelly, thankfully oblivious to Brent's poor acting skills, gets in the truck. I spin a story about needing him to help me pick up supplies, then get lunch, blah blah blah. He chats about his morning. I try to smile and respond without giving anything away. I am definitely multi-tasking. My mind is cataloguing everything I need to do in the next thirty minutes.

We grab lunch through a fast-food window and then I turn on the radio before getting out. "Enjoy the music," I tell Kelly. "I need to make a call or two." He's busy squeezing ketchup packets across his fries and nods absentmindedly.

My first call is to Judge Nolan. I pace up and down two empty parking spaces while it rings. "C'mon, c'mon, be there." I should buy a lottery ticket, because I get him on the second ring. I don't waste time on idle conversation. "It's going down. Like *now*. They're here."

It's gratifying because Nolan asks no questions and makes no platitudes. He gets right to it. "Okay, Henry and Bill are both in court. I'll let them know and we'll get back to you."

I punch the button and start redialing. This time to Bonnie. As I lift the phone to my ear, I see Kelly staring at me from inside the truck. He's getting suspicious or at least curious. I give a little smile and hold up my forefinger signaling *one more minute.*

After talking with Bonnie, everything is set. Now I just have to break the news. It's good news, but once again Kelly's life is going to be abruptly altered without him having a clue that the Fates have been plotting behind the scenes.

Closing the truck door, I grab my sandwich. I take a bite then slurp down some drink. Kelly's finished with his food, so I offer him some of my fries, but he shakes his head. "What's going on?" he asks.

Stalling, I take another drink, put the cup into the truck's cup holder, fold the sandwich back into the wrapper, and stick it in the bag. Taking a page from Kelly's old playbook, I can't stand to think of eating. I fix my eyes on his face as he sits there quietly looking at me. It reminds me of our first day, but he's not that frightened kid anymore. There's strength in those eyes now.

"You remember the lady from Corrections who was here a while back?"

"The nasty one?"

I'm not in the mood to tell him not to talk that way about his elders. "Yeah, her. Here's the thing. They want to take anyone who is under eighteen and put them in a facility up north." I hold up my hand and speak quickly before he can process enough to get panicky. "You aren't going. Everything is in hand. If you remember, Judge Nolan was the one who made sure you came here, and he's totally against having you moved. He's meeting with Henry right now to take care of it."

I reach over and tug on the brim of his baseball cap. "Here's the best part. You'll be done with the Department of Corrections. The judge is going to do a judicial release and the rest of your sentence just goes away—and not just because of this proposed move," I hasten to add. "He knows how well you've done and that you're ready to be released."

Kelly wets his lips before asking, "What does this mean? Where will I go?"

"With me. Henry will have Judge Nolan appoint me as your guardian."

He smiles. "Really? I can leave my room at night now?"

He looks so trusting... and he still doesn't get it. I shift in my seat and lean on the steering wheel. "Well, it's a bit more complicated. You won't be allowed to stay in the building. We'll have to find somewhere else to live."

Now he's frowning. "But what about your job?"

"I'm probably going to be looking for a new one."

He gives me a stricken look. "Because of me?"

I shoot for levity. "Hey, I'm not robbing a bank, but I did say I'd do almost anything for you, didn't I? Don't worry about any of that. I'll need to work some things out and I will."

I watch it all sink in. His brow is furrowed as he tilts his head. His next statement is more fact that question. "We aren't going home."

"No, I packed some things for you. You'll stay at Bonnie's tonight. Hey, this will be the first time in a long time you'll be spending the night somewhere else. Like a vacation, right?"

He just stares at me and says quietly, "I guess." Would I ever think I'd feel so bad telling someone they just got their freedom back? But I understand. It must be deja vu for him. Once again, the kid's been loaded into a car and hauled somewhere he's never been before.

There's an awkward pause while we stand there waiting for Bonnie to answer our knock. That's gone in a flash when she yanks open the door. She grabs up Kelly in a big hug and gives him a loud smoochy kiss on the cheek. "Now I can do this all I want." If that wasn't enough, she grabs me around the neck, pulling my mouth to hers and says, "This too."

Kelly makes a pained face and says, "Please stop."

Bonnie laughs then gently takes his arm to pull him inside. He's quiet once we get in the house. Bonnie says, "Back in a sec," and goes into the kitchen while I hit the bathroom. When I come out, I see him slowly walking around the living room. His hand reaches out to barely graze some yellow tulips in a vase. He looks up as I walk in the room.

"Hey kiddo, what do you think? Fancy pillows and flowers—girly stuff, right?"

He gives me his slow shy smile and jams his hands in the pockets of his jeans. "I haven't been in a house in a long time."

That statement shoots a little dagger into my heart. I make a vow to get him as many normal experiences as I can, as soon as I can. "Well, it's high time you were."

I'm not sure what we're all supposed to do. I guess park here awhile till I hopefully hear back from Henry or the judge. Once more, it's Bonnie to the rescue. She makes us help her plant flowers in her yard. We're all sweaty by the time we're done and plop on the back patio. She brings us out some lemonade. She takes one look at Kelly and says, "We need to get you some shorts."

Kelly never wanted to buy any. I presumed it was because he didn't want the tracking monitor on his leg exposed. He shakes his head and says, "Cowboys don't wear shorts."

Bonnie laughs. "What do cowboys wear in the pool?"

"Cowboys don't swim."

Uh-oh. Something about the way he said that has Bonnie skewering him with a look. "Don't? ...or can't?"

Kelly sees his error. "Umm... well... they don't sink or anything. They umm... just can't go from point A to point B."

Bonnie's eyes narrow. "Well, I know a cowboy that's going to learn." She waves her glass in the air and takes on an expression of false modesty. "Lucky for you, I was a lifeguard for two summers at Camp Trails End."

Kelly flashes me a help-me look. I just grin and look clueless. Today, that's an easy look for me. After we finish cleaning up, Bonnie puts us to work helping in the kitchen. Mostly, we watch her cook. Kelly is completely engrossed, like he's watching an action adventure movie. It occurs to me that over the last few years, he's rarely seen a meal prepared. Anything fancier than a bowl of cereal or toast that's appeared in front of him seems conjured out of thin air. The glories of institutional life.

I decide to bug out as soon as we have our early dinner. There are too many things left undone back at The Village, and darn that Henry, why hasn't he called me back? Bonnie can tell I'm anxious about leaving them.

"He's fine Sam. I got this."

I reach over and brush her cheek with my finger. "I know you do."

I know she does—and I know he's safe—but I feel the ripples from the crazy day and can't unwind. My phone rings within minutes of getting on the road, and I'm glad to see it's Henry. I punch the button. "Talk to me."

"I just left Nolan. We're all set."

When I first contacted Henry about my fears, he talked to Nolan about a judicial release to assure Kelly was kept out of DOC's clutches. Judicial releases are possible if a certain amount of the sentence has been fulfilled. Lots of inmates apply, but relatively few are released because the prosecutor usually has to agree. Most of the time they object. Kelly's prosecutor, Bill Evans, was on board, but only if Kelly's placement at The Village was in imminent peril. With Kelly safe and doing well he saw no reason to rock the boat. Judge Nolan pointed out Kelly's medical care was covered as an inmate, and there was no sense in me losing my job and living arrangement if I didn't have to. But he assured me he'd take care of things if push came to shove.

Despite knowing the legal procedures were a formality of what we'd already planned, I feel a wave of relief wash over me. "Great. Thanks, Henry."

"No problem, I'm happy it's all worked out. There is one thing I need to talk to you about."

"Yeah?"

"Judge Nolan and I discussed this for quite a while. He's not appointing you as Kelly's guardian."

I can't believe my ears. "What? You're involving child welfare? Are you crazy?"

"Not that. Hear me out. Nolan declared Kelly an emancipated minor. If things don't work out, we don't want Kelly to end up back in the system."

A kernel of hurt feelings starts in my gut, and I can hear the resentment in my voice. "What? You guys don't trust me?"

"Don't be offended, Sam. Hopefully, this is the happily-ever-after ending we all want, but this is a change in circumstances for you both. What if you have a falling out and you don't want to be his guardian anymore? We'd be in a mess. This way, Kelly can use his inheritance money to support himself if need be."

I blow out a breath and flick my eyes to the rear view mirror where some butt-head in a convertible is riding my bumper. "Okay. I have to admit I haven't thought this all through as much as I probably should have. I've just wanted to make sure he was safe."

"And you have. But Sam, things will be different when he's no longer in custody. You can't foresee what impact this will have. How's Kelly taking it?"

"Shell-shocked. I hate that his life has been turned upside down in an instant. Again."

"At least this time it's something positive. He's a pretty resilient kid."

"He's had to be."

"I'll get with him to explain this in a few days."

Just before I get back to The Village, I realize Kelly was scheduled to go to Ms. Casey's to ride this afternoon, and I didn't let her know we weren't coming. She's not a person who takes kindly to a lapse in good manners, so I pull in her drive to make amends. I track her to the barn and sure enough get a disapproving look. She makes a point to take a long look at her watch.

"I'm sorry, Edith, but things got crazy." I fill her in on the day's events and let her know having inmates as neighbors is likely coming to an end soon.

"Where are you going to live, Sam?"

"I haven't gotten that far. I'm sure I can find an apartment in town or something."

"Hmm. I might be able to help you out." She points down her drive. "Around the bend there is what used to be the caretaker's house. It's been sitting empty for years, so it needs some work, but it's habitable if you aren't real particular. I could make the rent cheap if you'd do the repairs."

I smile, thinking of the walks I've taken past that house and the peeks I've tried to make through the overgrown shrubbery currently eating the porch and columns. I love to rehab. People, houses, whatever. And right next door to The Village.

"Edith, I can't tell you how much I'd appreciate that. Are you sure?"

"I am. I'm not getting any younger, you know. It would be nice to have someone close by. And I can put the boy to work if he's willing. You want to look inside before you commit?"

"I don't need to. I can't imagine wanting to be anywhere else."

By the time I get home the excitement is wearing off, and the drastic changes coming to my life have hit me like a sledgehammer. The excitement may be gone, along with the moment or two of total panic, but those feelings are soon replaced with a good solid feeling of contentment. I took a kid to heart and he's changed my life.

No more tiptoeing around the edge of my existence. Go big or go home. I got the house and the kid. Now, all I need—no, what I *want*—is the wife to complete the picture.

Back at The Village, everyone wants to tell me all at once what went down during my absence. The driver sent to fetch Kelly was someone they didn't know. He was rude and demanding so they took some glee in toying with him: *Mr. Murry and the boy are in the woods on a work detail. Too bad you didn't call first to let us know you were coming. You can probably find them down by the mill, but no, you can't drive down there. It's just a mile or two hike. What, they weren't there? Well golly, come to think of it, they might have gone to the river. No, there's no road; you'll need to walk it. Yeah, we tried to call him on the radio, but reception is spotty by the water. Sure, you can just wait here. Yeah, I know it's almost five o'clock. Oh, okay, we understand. Come on back tomorrow.*

Later, sitting on the porch with Gene, I let him in on the legal details, the house at Ms. Casey's, and the fact we soon may all be out of jobs. Once we're caught up, we sit and stare across the fields and watch the stars come out. Gene stands up and says what we're both thinking. "Damn, it's weird here without the kid."

I laugh. "Ain't it, though?"

A few minutes later I go inside and listen to the quiet. No radio music, no guitar strumming, no feet zipping down the stairs. I smile thinking about dinner at Bonnie's. The way she laughs. Her singing while she cooks, teasing a smile out of Kelly, throwing flirty looks at me. How did I ever think the life I had here, alone, was what I wanted? I go in and call. I clue Bonnie in on the house but decide to wait till later to talk to Kelly about it. He's had enough changes for one day.

When he gets on the phone, he sounds a little anxious. "How's Gene?" he asks.

"He's fine. He'll talk to you tomorrow."

"You'll be back here by then, won't you?"

"Yeah, I'm just not sure the time. Depends on some things here."

I hear Bonnie's voice in the background. "Tell him our plans for tomorrow."

"Oh, okay," he says. "We're going shopping at the mall. She says I'll need more clothes now." His voice drops secret-agent style, and I can tell he cups a hand over the receiver. "Do I have to?"

I can't help but laugh. It feels good. "Buck up, kiddo. Life on the outside ain't all roses. Better you than me. Take one for the team."

I hang up, reassured all is well. I wish I was with them. For now, I need to deal with things here. There's one more matter of business I expect on the horizon.

I look forward to it.

SAM

46

The first morning at The Village without Kelly in the building is definitely strange. Gene and I, by mutual unspoken agreement, have breakfast next door with the men. Otherwise, the morning is normal enough—going over work assignments, looking at supply sheets, answering questions from staff—but the whole time I keep glancing out the door. I'm thankful I don't have to wait long. I've gotten good at spotting a white Crown Vic from a good distance away.

A small irony, the driver is Steve, the one who brought Kelly here. As he parks the car and gets out, he doesn't look happy. The reason for that unhappiness is getting out of the passenger side. Ms. Isaac has decided if you want a job done right, do it yourself.

It's the one thing she and I agree on.

I stay where I am. Let her come to me. Isaac pushes through the door and struts in, throwing dismissive glances at the few inmates who aren't out on work assignments. Steve trails behind her, looking like he'd rather be waterboarded. She looks satisfied when she sees me present and accounted for. She strides toward me like a bullet, her heels clicking on the vintage linoleum floor. I'm talking to one of the men about his upcoming parole hearing. When she starts to interrupt, I take sadistic pleasure in holding up my hand in the classic stop gesture. "Have a seat. Be with you in a few minutes."

She gives me a look that could curdle milk. She doesn't sit. She moves a few yards away and stands with her arms crossed, one of those well-heeled feet tapping impatiently. When the inmate leaves, I lean back in my chair and stretch my legs out. "Ms. Isaac. Is there something I can help you with today?"

Her eyes narrow to slits. She knows I'm screwing with her. What she's trying to figure out is why I've suddenly grown a pair. She tosses a white envelope which lands on the desk in front of me with a sharp slap. "Here's a transfer order.

This driver is here to move Robert Morgan to Central. Where is the juvenile?"

To prolong my enjoyment, I slowly pick up the envelope, pull out the form, push down on one of the three folds, then up on the other. It's amazing what a production can be made of something simple if you put your mind to it. I read with a studious expression on my face like I just learned to read. Reaching the end, I look up and say, "Huh." I watch her mouth thin and her eyelids lower as I crumple it up in my fist. "No can do."

Her mouth is twisting into an ugly shape. "Look, Murry, quit the games. Produce the inmate. That's a direct order."

I put on the blankest face possible. "Can't."

"And why not?"

I look around the room like maybe a boy will appear. "He's not here."

Her voice gets emphatic. "Then. Get. Him."

I give my best teenage shrug. Don't say Kelly's not taught me anything. "Can't."

Everyone in the building is zeroed in on our little drama. Staff listen but pretend they aren't. The inmates don't bother pretending. They're watching with grins they make no attempt to hide.

Isaac, exasperated and acting like my IQ must be below that of a rock asks, "What do you mean, you *can't*?"

"He's gone."

"Gone? Did he go AWOL?" I can't help but notice the thought of Kelly escaping seems to perk her up considerably.

I shake my head. "Nope. Got out the old-fashioned way. With a lawyer. Released by the court based on his successful rehabilitation. Good news, huh? It's always nice, isn't it, to have a successful outcome? That's what we're all about, right?"

She stares at me. I can see the wheels turning in her nasty little head. "When did this happen?"

I smile as I reach over and drop her official form in the garbage can. I'm so happy I no longer have to take her bullshit. "Recently. Shame you came all this way for nothing."

If looks could kill, I'd be a dead man. There was nothing I could have done but hand Kelly over, if he were with us. There's nothing she can do to him now that he's gone. And she knows it. What she can do to me, that's a different story. But frankly, I don't give a damn.

She jerks her purse strap higher on her shoulder. "I don't like your attitude, Mr. Murry." I give her a sympathetic look. Some might call it condescending.

"I know."

PART THREE

~

The Homecoming

KELLY

1

The days have already started to fade into darkness sooner. The smell of the flowers in the meadow grows stronger. The first stars appear in the sky. Nighthawks are swooping above me. I wish there were still fireflies, but their time for the year is gone. I was so amazed when I saw them during my first summer at The Village. There's a Continental Divide for fireflies. You only see them in the eastern United States. I decided they were the closest things to magic on the planet. Imagine making up a story: *See, every summer these little insects rise from the ground and fly up into the sky. Then they light up and blink!* It would sound like far-fetched science fiction. Let's face it, nighttime is way more magical than daytime.

I love the night. One of the best things about being free is just walking out that door into the darkness. I think for a minute about the guys I was with back at the jail. I guess all of them are still locked up somewhere. I wonder how long it'll be till they can stand outside on a beautiful night and see the moon and stars. I feel sorry for them. I know I got lucky.

I look back at *our* house. Sam's and mine. And soon, Bonnie's too. They're getting married in a couple of months. I can see them inside, laughing and flirting. There aren't any curtains on the windows, except in the bedrooms, where old sheets are nailed up. Our beds are air mattresses. We live sort of like we're camping out. That's because of all the work we're doing in the house. Painting, making the floors shine, and lots and lots of cleaning. We had to work on the kitchen first. Bonnie insisted on it. The payoff is now she can cook for us when she's here on the weekends. During the week, it's mostly take-out although sometimes we eat next door at The Village restaurant. I kind of enjoy that, knowing it's no longer forbidden to me.

Sometimes we stop by afterwards at Sam's apartment to pick up things. It still looks like he's living there. Sam says that's the point. He still uses it during the day when he's working. Ginger lives with us at our new place and unless the weather is terrible, I ride her over to the Village each day after Ms. Casey runs out of work for me. Now and then, I go up to my old room. It's strange seeing it so empty. It makes me remember my first day here.

It's a Saturday, so Bonnie will be spending the night. Sometimes during the week, if the house is particularly dusty or smelly because of some work that's been done, we'll stay at her place. Sometimes, the house doesn't seem that bad, but Sam thinks we still need to go to Bonnie's. He seems happier the next day for it.

At first it felt kind of weird having a woman staying in the house with us after all my time of living with just men. We have to put the seat down on the toilet and Bonnie gets on me for drinking from the milk jug and sticking it back in the fridge. But it doesn't take long for me to get over it. She's so funny for one thing. I like watching her make Sam laugh. And I love watching her cook. Did I mention she's good at it?

There's another thing I hadn't planned on. For the first time, I miss my mom even though I don't remember her. Or maybe I feel the loss of not having a mom at all—of never getting to experience what so many people take for granted—like having someone tell me the blue shirt looks better or who puts flowers in a vase on the table or who gives me one of the mixer beaters to lick off the choco-late icing. Come to think of it, kind of like Bonnie does.

Sometimes I can't help but pretend we're a real family. When we go out to dinner, the waitress will say things like, *are you ordering first or is your mom?* They don't know we're just three adults.

Henry explained the whole emancipated minor thing to me. It means I could live on my own, like if I was eighteen. The most common way to be emancipat-ed is if you marry. If you do that, you're considered legally an adult regardless of your age. Marrying at a young age seems pretty dumb, but I guess you get rewarded for your stupidity. I fit a rarer category because I have the money from my inheritance to support myself. I'm like child actors and teenage sports stars who are allowed by the court to live separately from any guardian. After spend-ing these last few years as an inmate, it's weird to think I could walk out the door if I wanted and live alone. Of course, I'd need a way to go somewhere and someplace to live and all that other stuff. When Bonnie sets a plate of brownies down in front of me, it doesn't seem like a good idea.

Even with helping out Ms. Casey and working on the house, I have lots of time for writing. It's fun to play with characters in your head and live another life other than your own. People might even pay you for it. Books have made a huge difference in my life. In stories, the main character never has it easy, but when everything seems beyond all hope, the story can dramatically change and everything work out for the better. The characters usually go on to do great things. Maybe, just maybe, that's what's happening here … in my life.

I'd like to go on to do great things.

SAM

2

Time is an interesting concept. For the prisoners who live here, time is always on their minds. While they are here, in many ways, their time stands still. For a long time, my time was that way too. Days more alike than different. No big changes. Nothing all that notable.

I thought it would stay that way.

I thought I liked it that way.

Sometimes, it's good to be wrong.

For the last several months, time has gone into overdrive, the result of so many changes. One of them is the gold band on my finger. I was relieved Bonnie wanted the wedding small and simple. We got married at The Village and had the reception in one of the old barns. The rafters were hung with twinkling white lights that flowed out the large doors and onto a huge stone patio. Kelly helped climb up to wrap the mini lights around the barn's big beams. He *is* a good climber. "Practice," he says to me. "Lots of practice." And of course, he was my best man.

"Hey kiddo," I told him during the wedding reception. "Without you, this never would have happened."

He didn't miss a beat. Stared straight at me and said with mocked seriousness, "The lengths I'll go to bring two people together."

He looked sharp in his suit and tie. I made him go with me to the mall to buy it, but promised him ice cream if he was good. He grumbled, but it was all for show. I think he enjoyed the wedding, but I'm also sure he was glad when it was over. He'd have to be deaf and blind to be oblivious to the curious looks and whispers people threw his way. Some knew his story; others couldn't figure it out. Who is this kid living with Sam and Bonnie?

My personal life is great, but work hasn't been so good. We're told there's a temporary hiring freeze on new staff positions. That's a clear sign they're looking to close us down. With apologies, several of my best staff gave their notice. I understand. They have families to think of and need to be sure of a paycheck. To provide staff coverage, Gene and I work lots of overtime and everyone else ends up working double-shifts.

The only reason we can get by is that we're not getting new referrals to fill the beds of the inmates that get paroled or serve out. Another clear indication we're on the chopping block. The inmates aren't dumb. They know something is up. With all the uncertainty, there have been more problems, of course—arguments that sometimes become physical fights. Even Kelly's absence has had an effect. It's flatter here without him. He was like everyone's kid, which made it seem a little more like family here.

Waiting for the final axe is the hardest part. The invisible hands that pull our strings are hundreds of miles away and they aren't telling us anything. It makes for a tense situation. At the end of the day, I'm more than happy to take the very short drive home. Ms. Casey hired Kelly, so he's kept busy with the horses. After dinner and on weekends, we all work together on the house. I learn to hate old wallpaper with a passion. There must be four layers of the stuff on the walls. The house has the original wood flooring, but it all has to be sanded and refinished. It's hard work, but satisfying, and a good antidote to the stress of my job.

Tonight, after knocking off from stripping woodwork, Bonnie and I sit on the front porch with a beer and watch darkness come. I'm so pleased that Bonnie is loving living here as much as Kelly and I do. The kid's at the barn putting horses to bed for the night so we have some time to ourselves. I remark on how he seems to have taken everything in stride.

Bonnie curls her legs under her and says, "Yes, I suppose so."

I frown. "You don't sound very sure."

"Well, it's just that he does here pretty much what he did at The Village. He works all day, he reads, he writes, he rides."

I take a swig of my beer while I mull over what she says. "And what's wrong with that?"

She rests her elbow on her chair and leans into her hand. "He's not getting to be a normal kid. He doesn't have one friend his age. He doesn't date. Never goes to a concert or any typical teen activities. The only time he gets to leave the property is with one of us. It's like he's still incarcerated."

I get what she's saying. Well, hell. I hadn't thought about it that way.

Bonnie swats a mosquito on her arm and continues. "In a way, I wish we could talk him into going to school, instead of just doing the on-line degree thing. Too bad Ms. Knight can't be involved now that he's no longer in custody. But if he *did* go to public school, it could be a landmine. Since he was tried as an adult, there's no confidentiality. His inmate info is available if anyone went looking. Some rotten kid could plaster Kelly's mugshot all over social media."

The conversation has got me anxious. She's right. Kelly needs some normalcy. Suddenly, I get an idea and sit up straight in my chair. "You know what? He needs to get his driver's license. That would be a good first step toward the normal teenager thing. He wouldn't be stuck here all the time. Maybe we could even get him into some activities he could drive to and meet other kids, like … I don't know... like guitar lessons... or maybe tennis?"

Bonnie gives me a surprised look. "You're okay with him driving?"

"Yeah, why the hell not? He'll be turning sixteen before we know it." I pause a moment. "Okay, it does make me nervous, but he's more mature and responsible than many kids his age. On a provisional license he can only drive during the day anyway, so there's some safeguards already built in. We could pick him up a decent used car."

Bonnie gives a half laugh.

"What's so funny?" I ask.

She trails her hand down my arm. "Just us talking about him having a car. The very thing that landed the three of us together in the same place."

I take hold of her hand and give a snort. "Yeah. In our line of work, who knew our lives would do a one-eighty on account of a car thief?"

KELLY

3

I curl up under the blanket for a few more minutes reluctant to leave my warm bed. Yesterday was eventful. I passed my driver's license road test. In this state you can get your learner's permit at fifteen. Fourteen days later you can take the driving test and if you pass, you get a provisional license. You aren't allowed to have anyone under eighteen in the car unless you're with an adult, and you can't drive when it's dark, but I don't care about any of that. Hey, I'm very law abiding.

I hadn't even thought about driving. Sam brought it up. The day I passed the written test, Sam drove us toward home but instead pulled into The Village gate. He got out and told me to drive. I was happy to oblige but once I slid behind the wheel a strange feeling came over me. My hands gripped the wheel so hard my fingernails dug into the tops of my palms. My relationship with cars has been complicated. All of a sudden, it didn't seem like such a great idea after all.

Sam leaned over, put his hand around my neck and gave a squeeze. "Just like riding a horse, buddy. You get back on, right?"

It was the perfect thing to say. I took a deep breath and grinned. "Right, and remember you said that since you're along for the ride."

He gave a look of fake horror. "Oh yeah, I forgot that part."

I look at my bedside table where my license is safely inside my new wallet, one of the gifts I got on my sixteenth birthday. Next to the wallet is my phone. Outside in the driveway is my new used car, bought just a few weeks ago.

All of us went on the buying trip to get the car. Good thing, too, because even though I can drive one and obviously, hotwire one, I don't have a clue about the working parts. Sam opened the hood and asked questions about services the dealership might have performed as well as inspections and warranties. He examined the tires. All four looked the same to me. Now, show me a horse and

I know what I'm looking at. My uncle used to say: *One white leg, buy him. Two white legs, try him. Three white legs, pass him by.*

Once he'd gone over the mechanical details, Sam gave me a little nudge. "Well, whadya think?"

I snapped back to attention. "I like the color."

Sam gave me one of those condescending looks like, *really?* I tried to think of something better to say, but then Bonnie rescued me by opening the driver's door. "Let's get to the important stuff. How many cup holders are there? Is there a place to put sunglasses?" Then Sam gave *her* that *really* look.

Anyway, we bought the car.

It still seems odd to have a phone. They're major contraband in any correctional facility. A huge no-no. Bonnie was excited to get one for me, but I wasn't that thrilled. It sort of seems like an ankle monitor you carry. She launched into showing me all the things it can do, and I'll admit I was impressed. It's just that I don't have anyone much to call or text. The only people near my age are the teenage girls who come for riding lessons. They giggle non-stop and say "awesome" every three seconds. I'd be willing to overlook that, but if I got friendly with one of them, I can see problems.

I picture me going to pick her up. I stand there with her father, waiting for her to come down the stairs. Do girls still come downstairs like in the old TV shows? Anyway, my hypothetical date's dad might say: "Well, there son, tell me about yourself. Where do you go to school?" Me: "I don't. You see, I was in jail and then a correctional facility, so I never went to public school. Is Sarah about ready to go, you think?" Dad: "There's the door. Don't let it hit you on the way out." End of story.

I hear noises downstairs, so I get my ass in gear, get up, dress, and head to the kitchen.

Sam's reading his newspaper. He lowers it a second and looks at me over the top. He asks, oh so casually, "Any plans for the day?"

He's toying with me. He knows I'm driving into town for the first time on my own. I need to pick up some vet supplies for Ms. Casey. Not that she really needs them *today*, but it's as good an excuse as any. I throw myself into a kitchen chair, banging my knees on the table leg which sets everything wobbling. I reach out to steady Mrs. Butterworth.

Sam shakes out his paper and tries to get under my skin. "Maybe you're too hyper to be driving today."

Bonnie bends down and kisses the top of my head. "Leave him be. He's just excited."

I sneer at Sam, "Yeah, leave him be."

Sam gives a fake scowl. "You guys are always ganging up on me."

Bonnie winks at me and pours more pancakes into the skillet. Good thing, because the ones on my plate aren't going to last long. The pancakes sizzle. Sam gets another cup of coffee and the steam rises from his cup. The kitchen window is up, letting in a breeze that frees a few daisy petals from their vase. I hear Ginger give a beseeching whinny from out in her field.

Life is almost too good to be true.

A week later I wake to the unmistakable sound of geese on the wing. They sound like little yipping dogs getting closer and closer, then farther and father, fading out till it's quiet again. Fall migration is in full swing and they know exactly when to head south. It's my second fall here and I like it even more, because now I know how it works. The color begins to show in the sugar maples, big patches of orange leaves near the top of the trees. In the full sun, the poplars down by the river shine like gold. It's too early yet but when the red maples decide it's time to show their stuff, they'll look like fire.

I open my eyes enough to tell it's a sunny morning. This time of year, you get two seasons every day. Even though it'll be in the eighties later this afternoon, the morning is nippy, and I want the extra blanket at the foot of the bed. I reach with my toes and flip it up to where I can grab it. My feet are closer to the end of the bed now. I've grown a couple more inches. I'll never be as tall as Sam, or probably even Bonnie for that matter, but at least I don't look like a little kid anymore. Now that I'm sixteen, that's a good thing.

My bedroom has three windows, even better than my room at The Village. I love my room. I love this house. We worked on it for hours and hours, days and days, after we moved in. Bonnie would cook her special brownies and crank up the oldies while we scraped and painted. Each time we get done with a room, I imagine the house going, *aahh, thank you.*

Sam gets a lead on some old doors we could use that would be historically accurate. I go with him to help load if he decides to buy them. He gets out and shakes hands with some guy then walks back over to me. The sun at its late afternoon angle pours into the car. Sam sticks his head in the window. I look up at him from the book I'm reading and have to squint. His baseball cap half blocks the sun, casting shadows into the car. His face is wreathed in light.

With the flat of his hand he gives the car door a double tap. "I won't be long. Stay in the car."

Stay in the car ... stay in the car ... stay in the car. Those words echo in my head.

As he walks away, I get a little light-headed. Despite the warmth of the sun, my body goes cold. The sun, the shadows, those words. The scene out the car window starts to recede, switching from hills to mountains, green bushes to waving grass bending low in the wind.

Dad and Uncle Jack get out of the car. I want to come too, but Dad sticks his head in the window, and says, "Stay in the car." His Stetson hat blocks the sun streaming in the window, casting shadows on the dashboard. "Understand?" I nod. Banner looks disappointed to have to stay too, but he lies down and puts his large muzzle on my leg. I absentmindedly pet him, while I watch my dad and uncle stand on the bluff and look down the road.

We were on our way home from hiking. Dad heard on his radio that his deputies were in pursuit of some crazy driver involved in a hit and run. The guy was headed our way going north while we were going south. Dad parked on a hill above the road where we'd be safe while he watched for the guy to come by and then radio his deputies.

At first, it's exciting being a part of police work, but my initial excitement of being on a stakeout quickly wears off. Now it's just boring.

I drum my hands on the dashboard and look around for something to do. In a few minutes I think maybe Banner might need to use the bathroom. I look at him hopefully, but he's flipped over on his back snoozing, so I guess the answer to that is no. But maybe I need to. Yes, I'm sure I do. It's not disobeying if I have to get out to go to the bathroom, right? That'll be my story anyway.

I quietly open the door, slide out, and head a short distance to where there's a bunch of rocks. I've been reading a book about Stonehenge and decide to make a replica, so I start stacking the rocks into little piles. They look cool. I don't notice that everyone has returned to the car until I hear the exasperated voice of my father. "Kelly, get back up here right now." Uh-oh. Uncle Jack gives a little snort and his voice to dad carries over to me, "Like you thought he'd listen to you."

I rush to stack the last rocks to complete my project as I hear the doors slam shut. There's engine noise which is confusing because it's the opposite direction from our car. I jerk up to a standing position then freeze. Coming right at me is a navy-blue sedan. There's an American flag license plate on the front bumper. I can see the man inside wearing a backward baseball cap. He sees me too and his eyes get big. He yanks the wheel to the right then everything goes in slow motion as I realize with growing horror where the sedan is headed. Banner is sitting on the back seat looking out the window at me. He has his happy dog look with his tongue hanging out. His brown eyes are bright and questioning, like can I come out there with you? I have my eyes fixed on him as that guy's car rams into ours. There's the sound of metal ripping apart. Debris comes flying at me and I fling up my left arm to block it ... pain ... dust in my mouth ... I'm on the ground ... blood running into my eyes ... I can't see ... I don't want to see.

The walls of Sam's car slowly come into focus. Sounds filter back into my brain. Sam's voice gently urges, "Kelly, Kelly, it's okay. It's not real. Look at me."

I feel a surge of fury at Sam. It was real. As real as me sitting here right now. I could smell my dog, hear the wind, feel the roughness of the rocks in my hand. After all these years of remembering nothing about that day, I remember everything.

I'm not the "miracle survivor" that everyone always told me. I wasn't even in the car. Now I know why God cursed me all those years. Now it makes sense. I deserved it. It was me. I'm the one who killed them. I'm not just a car thief.

I'm a murderer.

KELLY

4

Over the next few days, I operate in the same detached way I'd spent those early days at boarding school after Dad and my uncle died. My body goes through the motions of getting up, getting dressed, brushing my teeth, but it's like I'm watching from above. Only riding makes me feel any better, so I work poor Ginger to a state of exhaustion.

When the disconnect lifts, I go from a white fog of nothingness to a red haze of anger. It consumes every waking hour and haunts my dreams. I once had despair down pat, but this anger is overwhelming, and I don't know what to do with it. I try to decide who I hate more. I start with everyone who up and died on me then move on to all the people who have wronged me over the past five years. Most of all, I hate me. I'm the bad kid that didn't do what his father told him and got everybody killed.

I used to think Sam and Bonnie hung the moon, but now everything they do is irritating. One time, when Sam reached over to do that thing where he pulls on my ball cap, I flung my hat off and walked away. I spend most of my time out of the house or in my room. Why am I even living with these people? They aren't my family. I don't want to talk to them. I don't want to even be around them. And most of all, I don't want them to know I'm not who they thought I was. *God, if they only knew what I did.*

One morning, Sam captures me coming down the stairs and tells me to come with him on an errand. I resent the fact he tells me what to do, but old habits die hard and I obediently follow. That's part of the problem. I'm living with the person who had me under his control, who monitored my movements with an ankle monitor. *My keeper.*

I know the errand is a sham when Sam reaches over to turn off the radio. "How about we talk? We haven't done much of that lately."

I shrug. "There's nothing to talk about."

"Come on. Don't give me that. I'm concerned. What's wrong? This isn't like you."

I glance over at him then look out the side window. There's a little stab to my heart. I had met his eyes and no message had been exchanged. The lines of communication, the special secret wire that was all our own is broken. I broke it. *Just like I break everything.* But instead of despair, there it is again, this unexpected fury boiling up in me. I don't need him. I don't need anyone. "Maybe this is just like me."

Sam stares at me a few seconds before he says, "What, so all this time you've been faking? I don't believe that."

I continue to stare out the window. "Believe what you want."

Sam puts his right arm on the back of my seat and pauses a few long seconds before saying, "Okay, what I believe is that something's eating at you, but you won't tell us what it is. Or maybe you don't even know. Was it something about that day we went to get the doors?" His hand comes down on my shoulder. "I think it might be a good idea to see someone, a counselor. We could all go."

I fling his arm away. "I'm done with all that. I don't need anyone inside my head." I glare at him. "Anyone." I let that sink in, then add. "I can figure things out for myself. I'm not a kid anymore. Back off."

I see his hands tighten on the steering wheel. He's starting to look pissed. *Good.*

He looks at me and there's anger in his eyes. "Yeah? Then quit acting like one! Walking around biting everyone's head off, skulking off to your room, skipping meals again, worrying everyone. Even Gene called asking what's going on. Basically, you're just being a little shit, and I'm getting real tired of it. The whole world doesn't revolve around you, you know. You think I don't have any stress right now, closing down the program and watching staff lose their jobs? Watching the men in the program get hauled away to wherever someone decides they want to stick them?"

Guilt piles on top of the huge mound that already presses on me like lead weight. *Sam's right. I am a little shit.* For a split second I want to tell him everything. He's the one person in the world whose regard I most treasure. But it's because of that regard, I can't say it.

343

I shrug. "Yeah, well I wouldn't sweat it. That's their problem."

With a sound of disgust, Sam turns his attention back to the road. I look out the side window. We don't say anything else. When we get home, I get out of the car and walk toward the woods. I can feel Sam's eyes on me, but I don't look back.

Tonight, I fell asleep, only to wake up just after three in the morning tossing and turning. Throwing the covers aside, I sit up and put my head in my hands. I feel tired but know sleep isn't going to come, so I pull on jeans and a shirt. Minutes later, I'm standing out under the glittering stars. I look up at the full moon. The sturgeon moon. The Indians named it that because this time of year the fish are fat and prime, ready to catch and dry for winter. Change is in the air. Birds have turned their music duties over to the crickets and cicadas which are in full song.

I walk down to see Ginger. She's standing there half asleep with her back leg cocked. She lifts her head when she sees me. Looking into her warm brown eyes, I feel comforted. I lean into her and run my hand down her sleek neck taking pleasure in her warmth and closeness. "Don't worry girl, we aren't going riding this time of night, but maybe we'll go soon." I tug on her forelock as thoughts form in my head. *Or maybe we won't.*

Standing here in the night, I revel in the feel of real freedom—of being on my own, doing what I want without having to be accountable to anyone. I want more of it. Why the hell am I here? This isn't who I am. This isn't the center of my universe. That center is over a thousand miles away, and now that I think of it, nothing is stopping me from going there.

I feel energized for the first time in weeks. *What have you been waiting for?*

Excited, I practically run back to the house and throw some things into bags. I write a note and on my way out the door, prop it up on the kitchen counter in plain sight. Easing the car door open, I toss my bags on the back seat. When I turn the key, the ignition sounds loud, but it doesn't matter now. As I move the gearshift, I take a last view of the house. We spent a whole day cutting away the overgrown bushes to expose it. The new paint shines in the moonlight. It looks quiet and peaceful. I feel a catch in my throat, but again there's that little voice in my head.

Yes, it's nice ... but you don't belong here.

Anyway, they'll be better off without me. They're married now. I'm just this kid they feel pity for and got stuck with. I'm just in their way. I ease down the drive without giving the car any gas. The house disappears from the rearview mirror, then the driveway, then the front gate, until there's not a part of it to be seen behind me.

I taught myself not to want things I can't have, so I've found little to want. I've made no major decisions, drifting along where the tide has taken me. People have told me where to go and I go there. Now, at last, I get to do what *I* want without anyone or anything getting in my way. Well, I guess there is one thing in my way. I only have a provisional driver's license, and I'm not supposed to be driving at night.

For a second, I think, who cares? What are the odds of getting caught? But I chicken out and turn into The Village and park just inside the front gate until darkness begins to lift. When the first orange and gold of morning touches the horizon. I turn the ignition, shift the gear into drive, push down on the accelerator, and head west.

BONNIE

5

I see Sam sitting at the kitchen table with a cup of coffee in his hand as I come down the stairs. One of the best things about married life is having coffee ready for me first thing in the morning. Coffee I didn't have to make. Morning isn't my favorite time of day, but I manage a "G'morning" through a yawn as I reach for a mug. "Is Kelly already up?"

Something about the expression on his face pings an alarm. I wonder if they had a fight. Kelly hasn't been great with me lately, but he's been far worse with Sam.

Last night, Sam and I were sitting on the back porch talking about Kelly's recent change in attitude, while Kelly saw to the horses. Sam was looking glum but tried to make a joke of it. "Is there a pod in the basement? What alien stole that funny, sweet kid and left this mean little brat behind?"

I brought him a beer and opened a bag of potato chips before trying to give him some perspective. "Think about how Kelly's past might play into this. He's had all this trauma but for so long he's had to keep it bottled up because he's not felt safe enough to deal with it. Even though he had a good year with you and Gene at The Village, he was an inmate. Now he's free and everything is supposed to be swell, like none of the bad stuff ever happened. It's not realistic. Now he's sorting all those emotions out and it's a painful process."

Sam looked at me after my little pep talk. "I know. I know. It's just easier said than done sometimes. Especially, when he says such nasty things. It's like he's purposely trying to get on my last nerve." There's a little pause. "It's like he doesn't even like me anymore."

Ah, now we were at the crux of it.

"Just give him some time," I said. "He's a smart kid. He'll figure it out. Just try and be patient."

I guess last night's pep talk didn't last long.

"Did you all have words this morning?" I say, pouring myself some coffee.

"Nope. Not a one." Sam leans forward and sets his cup on the table "He's gone."

It takes a second for those last two words to fully penetrate my caffeine-deprived brain. "What do you mean 'gone?'"

Sam tosses a piece of paper on the table. "Gone, as in packed up and drove away. He left this." I pick it up and read:

Dear Sam and Bonnie,

Thank you both for everything you've done for me. I'm sorry for how I've acted lately. I think I just realized it's time for me to move on with my life and let you two get on with yours. I wish you nothing but the best.

Kelly

Okay, so now my brain's fully engaged. I let the note drop to the table. "*I wish you nothing but the best*? What a crock! He calls himself a writer and that's the best he can do? Now what?"

"What can we do?" Sam shakes his head. "He won't answer my calls. Should we try to find him out on the road and drag him home? Contact the police? What would we say? 'Hey, we've got this kid we have no legal hold over and he's gone?' That'd go over big." He puts his elbows on the table and spins his cup in his hands. "He's emancipated. We have no legal right to try and make him stay if he doesn't want to."

The anger I felt when I read the note drains away. I ease into the chair next to my husband. "Oh Sam, he doesn't know what he wants. Where do you think he's gone?"

He pushes his cup away. "Where else? The land of milk and honey. Wyoming. Maybe he's right. He's acted awful lately. Maybe it's for the best."

Sam's usually so in control, and he's trying mightily to put on a good show of it, but this is a real blow to him. I hate to see him hurting. "I don't believe that, and you don't either. But hey, maybe it's what he needs for a little while.

347

Some time to lay the ghosts to rest. We know there's no such thing as stepping back into your old life, but he doesn't. He's young enough that he still believes he can."

I shift from the chair to his lap. He wraps his arms around my waist and leans into me. "Yeah, I know. I'm just second guessing myself. I should have offered months ago to take him back there to visit, but I've been so busy with closing down the facility, the house, looking for a new job. I should have pushed the counseling harder, but I thought he'd snap out of it."

Leaning back, I scowl into his face. "Well, if we're going to play the blame game, I could jump in here with things I should have done too." I place my forehead on his. "Mad as I am at him, too, I'm going to worry about him."

"Me too. But he survived on his own when he was twelve. He's sixteen now. He's not stupid. He'll be alright. And surely, despite all this, he knows if he needs us, he just needs to call. I am going to call Henry to let him know. The kid's more likely to take his calls right now than ours."

"That's a good idea. We'll wait him out. He might have already come to his senses and be on the way back." Sam gives me a smile, but I can tell he doesn't believe it. I don't really either. I give him a quick kiss and stand up. "I'll fix us some breakfast."

After Sam leaves for work, I look at Kelly's note lying in the middle of the table. I fold it in half and stick it in a big bowl where we keep our envelopes and stamps. I think of Kelly driving alone across country and say a little keep-him-safe prayer.

It's going to be a long day.

KELLY

6

It's about a twenty-hour trip to Wyoming minus eating and napping in rest areas. I crank up the radio and sing along, stop for snacks and later to get lunch, happy to be by myself with no expectations, no need to answer to anyone. Free at last. When I'm almost to Wyoming and night is coming, I get some dinner through a fast food window and decide to treat myself to a hotel room for a shower and a real bed.

Having money doesn't mean it's easy to find a place to stay. *Sorry son, you have to be eighteen.* On my third try, I get a room. A bored and distracted clerk runs my credit card and barely glances at my driver's license before handing me a key. A legal stay at a hotel. This is a first for me.

I walk down the hall looking at the doors for the room number. Out of nowhere, I feel a little nauseous. I flash to memories of walking down long corridors with guards, waiting to see which door they'd stop at before I was locked in. I seriously consider going back out to sleep in my car. The only thing that stops me is how badly I need to go to the bathroom.

Once I'm in the room, I relax a little. I think I can do this. I know I need to try. Going to the window, I yank the curtains all the way back. That helps with my claustrophobia although it's not much of a view: a rooftop at the front of the hotel and the parking lot. The window is purely for light; it doesn't open.

I use the bathroom, then stretch out on the bed and stare at the ceiling. I use one foot to push off my shoe and repeat for the other side. I become aware of the bump in my pocket and pull out my phone. There are missed calls from Henry and Sam. Texts. Voice mails too. I put the phone on the nightstand.

To drown out the noises from the other rooms, I turn on the TV and watch the Weather Channel. Out of habit, my eyes are drawn to the southeast where a slanted "80s" falls across five states. There's laughter and the sound of a door closing in the hall. It makes me feel alone but I remind myself this is what I've wanted. I go to sleep watching tornado chasers in Kansas.

In the morning, I wake when I hear a shower running next door and voices in the hall. Excited about the day ahead, I dress quickly and leave the room. I'm definitely *not* eating the breakfast buffet. Old memories threaten to swamp me. For one second I have the overwhelming desire to call Sam, but pride stops me. I feel better once I get in the car and hit a drive-through McDonalds to get a cinnamon roll.

Two hours later, with a growing sense of excitement, my eyes feast on the scenery. *I'm going to be home. Home at last.* It's cold and sunny with the Wyoming blue sky of my dreams. At each familiar landmark my anticipation ramps up. There's the Tindall's ranch. *The Welcome to Fort Dixon* sign, the feed store, now with newer gas pumps out front. Before I know it, I'm turning onto Main Street. I drive up and down it three times before parking across the street from the Sheriff's office. I sit and stare at the scarred wooden door.

I can remember the exact time I last walked out that door, the day before the wreck. My Uncle Jack had come to pick me up in his truck because Dad was going to be working late. I'd been watching out the window from inside and yelled at Dad, "He's here. See you tonight." I'd run out the door and gotten into the truck, happy to be going with my uncle out to a neighboring ranch to look at a horse he was considering buying. Almost like a vision, I can see the boy that had been me. I feel pity for him. I want to warn him about what's coming, but there's nothing I can do to help him. I sit there for a long time before driving on.

For the rest of the day, I visit the places that used to mean something to me. Well, almost all of them. I'm putting off the most important one a little longer. It's like I'm wading in the shallow part of the pool and saving the deep end till I can swim better.

I drive past the elementary school. The second window from the end is the library, where as a kid I sat at the table in the corner under that window with the books I'd checked out. I get out of the car and walk the perimeter of the city park where I once played baseball. There's a vivid memory of riding my bike with my baseball glove hanging from the handlebars. When hunger strikes, I grab a late lunch at our one and only pizza joint. The lunch buffet has almost the same menu, but now TV screens are mounted on the walls.

Finally, I drive out into the countryside, park, and get out where I can feel the cold wind on my face. Hiking to the highest point I can find, I gaze at the vista. It's as beautiful as I remember, yet it seems surreal that I'm here. Evergreen trees give way to waving grasses against a big blue Wyoming sky. How I wish I was on a horse.

I shiver but not with excitement. I'm freezing. My jacket is thin. I've lost my cold tolerance after my years further south. I'm going to need warmer clothes if I stay here. I mean, because I *am* staying here.

Back at the car, I crank up the heater. Suddenly, I'm worn out. I need to find a place to stay and get some dinner. It's like the clock has turned back to my survival years, where the biggest concerns are a roof and some food.

I go to a gas station where I buy peanut butter crackers and a Coke for dinner. While I top off the tank, a car pulls up next to me with two girls and a guy all about my age. I glance over. Would I know them? At some time, I might have sat in class with them. They check me out too. It's a small town and all the kids know each other, so I guess I'm a curiosity.

The girl with the long blonde hair smiles at me. I find myself smiling back. Then the guy she's with steps into view and he is definitely not smiling. The girl says something and laughs at the other girl before they head into the convenience store. The guy left at the car twists open his gas cap without taking his eyes off me.

My gas pump kicks off. I replace the nozzle, trying to look casual about it, before driving away. I look back at the kids in my rearview mirror. Maybe I'm a little jealous. They look so carefree, like they don't have a worry in the world. But maybe I feel a little superior too. I feel older and wiser. I know what they'll probably find out one day. Life can be tough.

My next stop is a crappy old hotel on the west end of town. My dad used to call it Sin City. He got called here routinely to break up fights and pick up drunks. It looks exactly the same as when I lived here. In a way, that's comforting. The man at the front desk glances at my ID and gives me a look but accepts the cash when I hold it out. I put in an extra twenty for insurance. He folds it in half, stuffs it in his pocket, and hands me the key.

"Third room from the end."

On the way to my room, I pass a vending area and buy more cheese crackers, chips, and cookies along with a Mountain Dew. All the major food groups.

It's an old-fashioned motel: one level, doors opening onto the parking lot. I push open the door to my room and crappy proves to be the right word to describe it. I wrinkle my nose at the musty smell. Flowered wallpaper, too faded to hardly tell what kind of flowers they are, is peeling off the wall. The bedspread is so thin I can see the pattern of the blanket underneath. However, I've certainly slept in worse places and hey, the window opens. I let the cold air pour in for a few minues. I can take everything else, if I can just get rid of the smell.

I get an odd feeling, like I shouldn't be here, like Dad might show up and haul my ass right on out of here. I sit in a plastic chair next to a nightstand and eat my cookies. Then I move to the bed. The springs creak as the mattress sags. I shift my weight and they creak again. I can only imagine how loud the sounds in this room must be when people are doing the activities this place is known for. A truck pulls into the parking lot and I hear the laughter of a man and woman, obviously drunk. I listen until they go to a room close by, but thankfully not the one right next to me.

Once again, I revert to the Weather Channel. I smile as the map of Wyoming appears. Eventually, I get bored with hearing the forecast for the fifth time and turn it off. I guess jail has pretty much ruined TV for me forever. Maybe a long, hot shower would feel good.

Five minutes later, after a lukewarm shower that quickly goes cold, I throw on sweatpants and a T-shirt and get into bed. I open the book I bought at the gas station. Cars keep pulling up and people seem to be going to the same room. Every time the door to the room opens, I hear loud music and laughter. It's going to be a long, noisy night. But hey, what matters is I'm free. I have a car. I have money to buy food and clothes or anything else I need. And most importantly, after five very long, very hard years, I'm back where I should be.

The next day dawns clear and cold. It's back to the gas station to buy junk for breakfast and eat in my dining room, otherwise known as my car. There's one major task on today's agenda and there's no sense putting it off any longer. My heart thumps when I turn on to Salt Creek Road. I focus my eyes on the horizon. *Please, please, please. Let it be there.*

And it is. Some rich person didn't buy the land for a second home and tear our cabin down to put up some ugly monstrosity. It's like a mirage. How many nights have I dreamed of being here, and now that I am, it doesn't seem real.

As I get closer, it looks smaller and run down. One of the porch rails has torn off and there's a big hole in one of the window screens. The new owners have done a lousy job of taking care of the property. It's that irritation that makes me brave enough to drive right up and park in front of the house. No car or truck in sight, but that doesn't mean no one's home.

I'll tell them the truth. I used to live here and just want to see the old place. Wyoming has the distinction of the most gun owners in the nation. I half expect to see a rifle barrel slide out the door and hear the distinctive crack of it being cocked and readied for business, but the only sound I hear is the whistling of the wind.

I didn't come this far to turn around. As Sam says, go big or go home. The irony of that thought doesn't escape me as I walk onto the front porch and knock on the door. No one answers. I go for broke and walk over to peer in one of the front windows. The window is dirty and there's a bad glare, so I cup my hands and press my nose against the dirty glass to see into the room.

There's a lag between what I'm seeing and how my body reacts. Every muscle tightens and my breathing quickens, causing my breath to condense on the window. I wipe it with one hand and look again to make sure I'm not going completely nuts. The beating of my heart ricochets up to my ears. *Oh. My. God.* There's my father's favorite chair, our bookcase along the wall, and my copy of *My Friend Flicka* sitting on the coffee table. I turn and lean against the window as my mind tries to grasp this new reality. Or is it the old one?

Henry's face appears in my brain. *Your father left everything to you.* Money, yes, but I never dreamed the house hadn't been sold. It's been five years. I reach over and try the doorknob. Locked, of course. Slowly my brain clears to the point I can think again. With a thudding heart, I walk to the end of the porch and lift the fourth floorboard. The key glints in the morning sun. With shaking hands, I pick it up and clutch it in my fist as I close my eyes.

The last time this key was touched was by my father. I want so badly to feel the connection, for it to feel like more than just a key. With a deep breath, I insert it into the lock like it's a magic keyhole and I'm about to enter another realm. The door creaks open. Sunlight pours in from behind my back, giving the effect of a three-foot landing strip across the room. And I'm the one who's landed. *Home.*

Once I step in and close the door, however, my excitement mixes with dread. Am I ready for this? A flood of memories engulfs me as I move across the living room, trailing my hand along the back of the old leather sofa. My eyes note every little detail, landing on the hutch that once belonged to my grandmother. *Come on, come on.* My hands tremble as I pull open the bottom drawer. Yes! The photo albums are still there. I pull out the one with the red cover and open it to the first page. My parents smile up at me.

I gently touch their faces with my finger. So many times over the past years, I couldn't quite conjure up their faces. Now, it feels like I have them back. I'll get copies made and put them in lots of different places, so I'll never lose them again. I flip through a few more pages then put it gently back in the drawer. I'll look again later.

The light from the windows bathe the wooden stairs in sunlight as I slowly walk up to my room. My bed's made, the brown and cream bedspread pulled up tight over my pillow. Someone else must have done that. I rarely made my bed. It hadn't yet been institutionalized into me.

There's not much in the closet. I'd taken most of my clothes to Philadelphia and watched my grandfather throw all of them away, like somehow if he dressed me better it would make me a worthier person. I pull out the top middle drawer of the dresser that used to hold my childhood treasures. One glance at the old pocketknife my Dad gave me for my tenth birthday, and I shut it with a resounding *thunk*. I've seen enough for now. Too many memories fighting for attention.

Downstairs again, I try to gauge how high my courage meter is. Resolved, I head into my father's old room. His clothes are in the closet. The white shirts have a tinge of yellow. On top of his bureau is a hairbrush with several dark hairs sticking out of the bristles. I hold them gently between my thumb and fingers. This part of my dad is still here. It's an amazing thing.

There are loose dimes, nickels, and quarters in a red bowl. Dad tossed his spare change there before hanging up his pants at night. Sometimes he'd forget to empty his pockets and I'd hear the coins rolling across the wood floor and him cussing. He'd holler for me to crawl under the bureau to get the ones that had lodged against the wall. I'd make a game of it, rolling them back out to him which he always found funny no matter how many times I did it. I wait to feel the familiar pain this kind of thought brings, but this time all I feel is a warm rush of memory and I find myself smiling.

Back outside, I stand on the porch a minute and take in the view. I try to come to grips with this sudden change of fortune. I'm not sure I could have taken another night at the Downtowner. Just when I needed it, my ship has appeared. I get to have my home back. It seems an unbelievable stroke of luck. Like I've been handed a gift, even if I don't deserve it.

I need to run out and get a few provisions. There's a high clean wind sweeping across the plains, tumbling the clouds across the sky. A high wind always exhilarates me. I breathe deeply, taking in the smells of earth and pine I've missed so badly. I lock up and go to the car. In town, I pass the gas station and pull into the parking lot of Becker's Food Center. I load up on drinks, bread, cheese, soup, peanut butter, doughnuts and frozen pizza. *The power's not on, you idiot.* I put the frozen pizza back and buy candles, matches, and a flashlight as well as a few cleaning supplies.

Once I return to the house, I put the groceries away and go on a cleaning blitz, happy to have a purpose and the physical work. Before dark, I light some kindling in the fireplace and feed it larger wood as it roars to life, just like Dad taught me, then I heat up a pot of soup on the edge of the flames, rotating it to heat it on all sides. Inspired by my success, I use a cast iron skillet to make a grilled cheese and then enjoy my feast, finishing it off with a whole row of Keebler's vanilla cookies. After dinner, I pull blankets and a pillow off the bed upstairs and put them on the couch as I scoot it closer to the fire. I open my book but decide Abraham Lincoln was better at reading fireside than I am. I give it up and stretch out, watching the flames flicker and burn.

I have to keep wrapping my head around this. My head is resting on *my* pillow. I am sleeping in *my* house. *I am home. Home at last.* I feel an overwhelming desire to tell someone. Someone who would understand how monumental this is.

Throwing off the covers, I walk into the kitchen, using furniture to guide my way in the dark. I retrieve my backpack from the seat of a chair. After I jump back into the warmth of the sofa, I unzip the pack and take out my little wooden horse. I set him carefully on the side table next to me and ask, "Can you believe this? Isn't this *amazing*?" I take his silence as agreement. Like me, he's traveled far and has been through rough times, but he's come home too. When I lie back down, I enjoy watching the shadows of the fire play across him, almost giving the illusion that he's moving.

I fall asleep but wake up hours later, cold, trying to burrow under the covers for warmth, before giving up and rising to build the fire up again. When I went camping with Dad and Uncle Jack, I always slept through till morning. How young and dumb I was! I must have thought that fire just lasted all night on its own. Now I realize one of them must have gotten up to keep it going. Now there's no one to take care of the fire … but me.

In the morning, the sun of the last two days is gone, replaced by low, gray skies so I don't rush to get out of bed. I eat a cold breakfast then stand in the living room with my hands laced behind my head surveying my kingdom. It's time to do a little de-creeping. I bag up most of Dad's old clothes. On impulse, I put on one of his favorite jackets. Maybe it's my imagination but I can still smell Dad's Old Spice deodorant mixed in with the smell of musty closet. It looks more like a coat on me, but it's warm and I decide to keep it. Most everything else goes in the bag. Once I lost everything, so none of this stuff matters. Possessions are meaningless unless they serve a purpose. Or the person who wore them is still around.

The heavy sky gives way to a cold driving rain. The water isn't working so I can't flush the toilet. I stand on the edge of the porch and pee from under the eaves watching the rain wash it away. When I need to take a dump, I'll have the choice of a bucket in the house, squatting outside in the open and pouring rain, or driving into town. I haven't a clue how to get the power and water turned on. I decide I might call Henry and ask him. Maybe as my lawyer he can call and get the legal details worked out. It seems very adult to say *I'll call my lawyer*. For the first time in my life, I feel like an adult—an irony since the law decided it was okay to treat me that way at thirteen.

The rain eventually stops. I start hauling the garbage bags to the front porch so I can take them somewhere to donate. On my second trip, I see a car turning in the drive. It's tan, a sheriff's vehicle. I knew this could happen, but even so my heart starts thumping. The old fears are always waiting for a chance to jump out. I consider running into the house and slamming the door shut, but no, that wouldn't be too smart.

I walk down the steps making sure to keep my hands in view. As he pulls up and stops, I give a little wave and try to look as non-threatening as possible.

I thought it might be someone I know, but I don't recognize him. He's fairly young, upper twenties I'd guess, with sandy hair and a wary expression.

I put on a smile and try my best to look wholesome. "Hey."

He's checking me out but sounds friendly enough when he speaks. "I'm Deputy Garrett. Did you stay in this house last night?"

"Yes, sir."

"Who are you here with?"

"No one, it's just me."

He nods his head. "You know this is trespassing, right? This house doesn't belong to you."

I squint one eye and tilt my head. "Well, actually, it does."

His mouth gets that tight look. He thinks I'm messing with him. "What's your name?"

"Kelly Morgan."

I count *one, two, three,* then watch him put it together. "Wait … you're his son?"

"Yes, sir."

"I presume that's your car. Could I see your license?"

"Sure. It's in the house."

He follows me up the steps. At the top stair I look over my shoulder at him. "Would you like a Coke or something?"

"I could stand a drink."

I know he's just agreeing to check me out, but now that my initial fear has receded, I'm happy to entertain. Besides, this is the most conversation I've had with a living soul in days. He follows me to the kitchen where I open a door to the back screened porch, grab a couple of soft drinks and hand him one. "Actually, all I have are Cokes. No or-somethings." I smile at my weak joke.

He smiles back then pops the tab. "Coke works. Interesting refrigerator you've got."

"Yeah, I know. The power's not on so the back porch is my cooler for now."

He takes a sip and considers me. "How old were you when … "

He trails off but I know what he wants. "Eleven."

"I was in the Army at the time, but my mother sent me newspaper clippings. A horrible thing." He shakes his head. "I'm sorry."

"Yeah, it was." I'm pleased I sound so casual. I grab my wallet off the kitchen counter and open it to the ID. He gives it a glance and hands it back before asking, "So who is your guardian?"

I have nothing to show I'm emancipated and know from my experiences trying to check into hotels, it's a hard sell. I give a name. "Sam Murry, but he's back east."

The Deputy's brow furrows a bit. "He knows you're here?"

I feel a childish urge to cross my fingers. "Yes."

"You're pretty young to be way out here by yourself. And without utilities." I can tell he's not thinking highly of my guardian. He takes another drink. "Did you all have a fight or anything?"

"No, nothing like that."

I stand while he considers me. "I think I need to talk to him. Do you have a phone?"

Oh shit. "Yes." I try to stall. "Sometimes he's hard to reach if he's working."

"Give it a go. Tell you what, put it on speaker."

No getting out of it. I dial the number. It rings, it rings again, then Sam picks up. "Hey, Kelly."

My pulse speeds up at the sound of his voice. I act like I just talked to him this morning. "I need to tell you something."

"Shoot."

"I, um, came out to my old house, just to, you know, see it again. I figured it had been sold but it hadn't. It's been sitting here pretty much like the day I left … with, you know … um … our stuff in it." I chance a look at the deputy. Geez, this is awkward. How many *you knows* can I put in one sentence?

There's silence for a few beats. "I'm sure that was strange. You okay?"

I get a little push in my gut. Sam, always thinking of me. "Yeah, I stayed here last night." The deputy is listening patiently. "Someone called the Sheriff's office, so Deputy Garrett is here with me right now on the speaker and wants to talk to you about, you know—*Jesus, there's another one*—me being here and all."

The deputy leans in. "Hello, Mr. Murry."

"Hello, Deputy Garrett."

"I wanted to be sure you were aware of Kelly's whereabouts."

"I am. I wasn't keen on the trip, but he felt the need to go."

I admire the half-truth. *Thank you, Sam.*

The Deputy tilts back his hat. I remember my Dad used to do that. "The thing is there's no utilities on here at the house. It's getting pretty cold tonight. I'm not real comfortable with him being here alone in these circumstances."

Sam says, "I can probably get his utilities on from my end. I have the credit history they'll want, but I'm sure it won't happen today. Kelly, can you go to a hotel till then?"

I don't want to, but I'd better play along. "I'll go back to where I was the first night."

Deputy Garrett asks. "Where were you staying?"

"The Downtowner."

He scowls at me then aims his voice at the phone. "That's a real dive. I wouldn't let my worst enemy stay there."

I get defensive. "It's the only place that would take my payment." I'm beginning to get nervous. "I can just sleep in my car tonight."

"No!" Both Sam and Garret say it at the same time. It's irritating, but it works out because now they've bonded.

The Deputy nods at me. "Tell you what, why don't you come stay at the office tonight? You know it, right? The same couch that was probably there when you were a kid is still sitting in the hall. Or if you aren't too particular, you can use one of the cells." He laughs.

If he only knew.

But here's the thing, the idea of going to the office has appeal. I haven't been brave enough to stop by yet, and this way I'd have a purpose beyond just sticking my head in to say hello to whoever I'd still know.

Sam's voice wafts out of the phone. "Kelly? How's that sound?"

I look at the Deputy. "Are you sure that would be okay with everyone? Does Betty still work there?"

"She sure does. We couldn't run the place without her. She'll be happy to see you. Just come on in, late this afternoon. You can eat dinner in town after you drop your stuff off."

Sam speaks up. "Deputy, would you make sure to get my number from Kelly? And would it be too much trouble for you to get the utility numbers for me and call me back?"

The two of them talk, grownups taking over and making plans for me. Just like old times.

"Kelly, I'll call you back after I've made some calls." This is Sam-speak for *you better answer your phone this time.*

"Okay."

"Alright." There's a change in his voice. "Bonnie says to tell you 'hi'. We miss you."

Out of nowhere, I get a lump in my throat. "Tell her 'hi' for me. Bye." I hang up and look down for a moment to rally my composure. The Deputy is looking at me with a calculating expression. He reaches into his shirt pocket and pulls out two cards. "Here's my number if there's any problem. Write your number on this other card for me."

I do as he says and he tells me, "Okay then. I'll see you later today."

Around four o'clock, I stuff some things in a bag and head into town, parking across the street in the same spot I did a couple of days ago. This time I can't chicken out.

Opening the door, I'm struck by how little the place has changed. Deputy Garrett stands by a file cabinet and gives a small wave but doesn't speak, looking over at the desk. I follow his gaze and there's Betty, the receptionist/dispatcher for as long as I can remember. There's more gray in her hair but she doesn't look too different. She's on the phone. She gives me a quick glance while she finishes her conversation. I stand and scan the room and wait, glad to have a minute to get my bearings.

She places the phone back in its cradle and turns to me. "Hello there, honey, what can I do for you?"

I just smile at her. Her eyes go wide. "Oh, my goodness! Kelly, is that you?"

I nod and she pushes out of her chair and races across the room to envelope me in a hug. She smells liked the lavender talcum powder she always wore. For some reason, that smell brings Dad back, like I expect to see him walk into the office at any minute.

Finally, she pushes me back while still holding my arms. "Let me look at you! Oh my, you're all grown up. Oh, it's so good to see you. You don't know how many times I've thought about you." Her face crumples a little. "I still miss your father."

"Me too." I remember my manners. "How are you?"

"Oh, I'm fine, fine. My mother passed away about a year or so after you left and Hiram wasn't too long after. I miss them both but they're in a better place now."

"I'm so sorry."

"Well, life goes on as we both know."

Deputy Garrett takes that as his cue to come forward. "Hey, right on time. You want to stow your stuff over here?"

I set my belongings on a table and laugh. "That really is the same couch." I loved it when I was a kid. It's all fall colors of orange, brown and gold with a repeating image of a rustic wagon perched next to a water mill with pheasants standing nearby. Now I see that it's truly hideous.

Betty walks over and touches the bottom of it with her foot. "The good news is that fabric is going to last forever." Her mouth turns down. "The bad news is that fabric is going to last forever."

Deputy Garrett grins. "Let's just say the budget hasn't improved any over the years. I'm working till nine tonight then Max Tevis will take over. You can shut the door, so he won't keep you up. There's a small TV in the break room if you want."

"Thanks. I'll be fine. I appreciate you letting me stay."

Betty gives me another hug. "I'm so glad you're here. Golly. I have to go over to the church tonight or I'd take you out to dinner. We'll do it another night soon."

"Sure. I think I'll go down to the diner."

She answers the phone as it rings again. I wave goodbye as I head out and walk down Main Street. Halfway down the block is the downtown diner where my father and I ate the bulk of our meals. I'm disappointed when I don't recognize anyone. I ask the waitress about Mrs. Humphrey.

"Oh, she retired last year. Sold the place to my aunt. Another Coke?"

"Yes, please."

I order a bunch of food. I'm hungry and it's a nice change from the gas station and my fireside cooking. Someone left a copy of the Fort Dixon Messenger, our local paper. I scan the front page and turn to the city/state section. The headline at the top catches my eye, "Wyoming Needs Juvenile Justice Overhaul." Under a picture of the Wyoming Boy's School it reads, "Wyoming leads the nation in the number of youth incarcerated per capita. Advocates argue many of the youth are low level offenders who shouldn't be there." Not that I don't care about this stuff, but I just can't go there right now. I toss the paper aside. The things I never knew when I lived here. Wait a minute … I *do* live here.

The waitress comes back and I ask, "Could I get one more piece of pie?"

She smiles. "Of course." As she walks to get it, she says over her shoulder, "You're a good eater."

I grin to myself. Now that's a new one.

After I pay, I take another walk, but it's getting cold, so I head back to my ugly sofa for the night. When I see Deputy Garrett, I say, "I'm sorry. I should have offered to bring you something back."

"Thanks, but I already ate. In the morning, you can get us all doughnuts. We don't mind the policeman and doughnuts jokes. Mr. Murry told me he used to be a cop, so you probably know about that."

I keep my face neutral. So he's talked to Sam about utility numbers and I wonder what else. I try to read his face to see if there's any change in his attitude toward me. I've grown more comfortable with my ex-con status, but this is one place I just couldn't stand people knowing. It'd be so embarrassing, not just to me but to my father's memory. Thankfully, I'm not picking up on any vibes.

I grab a book and go in to claim my spot. Deputy Garrett brings in his replacement to meet me, then he leaves. I read till I'm sleepy then turn out the light. I used to take naps on this couch when I was little. I'd listen to Dad working. That memory should bring me pain, but it doesn't come. I find myself wishing it would.

Instead, I think about Sam. Hearing his voice today makes me realize I miss him terribly. My head gives a little involuntary shake to dispel the thought. It seems disloyal to be missing Sam when I'm here in the place that was my father's. I should only be missing my Dad.

A few days later, I have heat and water and get settled in. There's rain and a cold wind so going outside isn't inviting. A good day for writing. I take a seat at the table, smiling to myself. I'll be a cowboy Hemingway, alone with my pen and my thoughts. After all, Hemingway lived and died in Idaho, right next door to Wyoming.

An hour later, I get up and pace around the house. I haven't written anything, but I've doodled a picture of an eagle flying among clouds. I grab a piece of blank paper and decide I'll write one paragraph within the hour—a short-term goal, just like Mr. Hill taught us back in his writing class at the jail. Yeah, that should do it. An hour later, I have three crossed-out sentences. A quote by Abraham Lincoln pops into my head. *If you give me six hours to chop down a tree, I'll spend the first four hours sharpening the axe.*

This hermit thing might not be working out so well. I decide what I need is a friend, but I don't have a clue how to get one. I give up trying to write, drive into town, and pop in to say hi to Betty. As usual, she's on the phone but is in the process of hanging up.

"Hi there, sweetie."

"Hi. I don't want to interrupt your work."

She pushes her glasses up onto the top of her head. "I wish that was work. That was Irene, over at the church. She begged to head up the fall bazaar for years. We let her, but boy, are we regretting it now. If you give her a penny for her thoughts, you get change. She calls me on every little detail. Well, just last week …"

For the next five minutes I learn more than I ever wanted to know about the goings on of the ladies over at Porter Memorial Methodist Church. I'm saved only when her phone rings again. As she moves to answer it, she motions with her hand to a decent sized cardboard box sitting on a table in the corner. "A package came for you."

Back at the car, I toss the package into the back seat, rather harder than necessary, and take a long, scenic way home. I crank up the music and drive and drive. My own theft aside, I can understand why stealing a car is the number one juvenile crime. It's not only freedom, it's a great diversion from stuff you don't want to do or think about.

Once home, I slam the car door and head into the house. My steps slow going up the porch. Cursing myself, I turn around and go back to the car and get the damn box. I hold it on my hip while I fish for my keys, then once inside, set it on the table. No, it's more like I bang it on the table. I scowl at it and leave it holding court there for the rest of the day.

Just before dark, I pace by it a couple of times. Of course, I think of that damn *Castaway* movie. I never believed that anyone could be stranded on an island for years and not open that last package. Maybe Tom Hanks had great impulse control, but I am not Tom Hanks.

I turn on a lamp then I use my car key to slice through the tape, and then peel back the left flap then the right. Reaching in, I remove some of the newspaper balls. There's two notes on top with my name on them which I push aside, and on the top is a metal tin. The smell of chocolate wafts up when I open it. Bonnie's famous brownies. I stand there jiggling my right foot for a few seconds, then put the lid back on and toss it in the garbage can. Unfortunately, there's more food where that came from, including a jar of blackberry jelly. I groan.

Back in the summer, Bonnie and I spent an hour picking blackberries over at The Village. We paid a high price for those berries when we woke up the next morning covered in chigger bites. They itched like crazy. As I lathered on the calamine lotion, I remember hollering, "We do not have this problem in Wyoming!" I mean those suckers were everywhere. Apparently, Bonnie had the same problem, because she grabbed the bottle out of my hand and headed to the bathroom. As she closed the door, she said to Sam, "Do *you* know where those little buggers went? Let's just say invasion of privacy doesn't cover it!"

I find myself smiling at the memory. Really, I can't load up the garbage can with all this. Throwing away the jelly would be a victory for the chiggers. And it's a sin to throw away food when there are starving people in the world, right? I look at the tin of brownies sitting on top of discarded white notepaper in the garbage and grab it. In less than four minutes, I've eaten all but five of them. I rustle through more of the box. A jar of honey from The Village's beehives, this year's 5K Village run T-shirt, some books, and a picture of Ginger with a bubble drawn below her mouth asking, "Where are you?" in Bonnie's handwriting. Now, that's *low.*

I don't want to read the notes, but impulse control remains AWOL. Bonnie's is mostly light-hearted, filling me in on the weather and local events. She does a little chiding, of course. *You know there's this thing called a phone, don't you? I can tell you how it works if you've forgotten.* Only at the end does she get serious. *Sweetie, we miss you and think about you every day. Your room is right here waiting for you. And so are we. Love, Bonnie.*

My right foot goes back to jiggling. Might as well get it over with. I open up Sam's note and my eyes do a fast skim, like that way, maybe his words won't touch me. Only a few phrases pop out: *Didn't mean to upset you. We can work anything out.* But then my throat tightens and I don't want to read anymore.

I set their notes back on top of the box, close it up, and push it under the table before getting a drink and a pack of peanut butter crackers to chase down the brownies. I walk over to look out the window but it's getting too dark to see outside so all I see is my own reflection. No longer do I look like the kid that used to live in this house. The guy I'm looking at is taller, older, and more serious. Closer to a man than a child, I decide. I'm not sure how I feel about that, but maybe that kid is another person I'm missing.

I pull up a chair and turn out the light, so I don't have to look at him anymore. Now I can better watch day give way to night. The whole horizon is red. The sun slips down and the sky goes gray. Sometimes I think I've spent half my life staring out windows. I should have learned a lesson from the Castaway movie and left that package unopened.

Why don't they just leave me alone?

The next morning, my mood hasn't improved. I give myself a little pep talk. I have everything I need. Silence, solitude, a refrigerator full of food, a well-lit room and a window with a wonderful view of the mountains. This should be my personal heaven, but there's a major flaw I didn't foresee, much less plan for. No use trying to fool myself any longer. I'm lonely. And Betty just isn't doing it for me.

I'm constantly distracted and restless, unable to concentrate long enough to write a decent paragraph. I find myself doing research, doodling pictures, everything but actually moving forward on the book. I read once that struggling to write is like being stuck in quicksand. The more you struggle the more you sink. Please, someone, throw me a rope.

This whole situation is outrageous. Me, a stone-cold loner. Marlboro Man, without the cigarettes. Me, who has secretly regarded my aloneness as being somehow superior to people who need others. Me, who has ignored my peers since childhood, now dying to have a friend to call up and hang out with.

I remembered eavesdropping in the hall while my father met with a teacher. The teacher was saying, "His grades are fine. I'm concerned about his social isolation. He simply doesn't seem to care about the other kids. He's smart, funny, and these kids know and accept him because they've been together since kindergarten, but they've given up trying to do much with him. He'd rather sit alone at lunch with a book. Does he play with anyone after school?"

I only caught snatches of my father murmuring his reply: "… We live pretty far out of town … He has a dog …"

There's a few people in town I know enough to talk with a few minutes about the weather or the high price of milk. I'm a pro at being a casual acquaintance. I go to a store just to look at a pretty girl that works there, imagining having dinner with her, going to a movie. When she gives me a look that might be of interest, I practically run out the door.

During the day, most kids my age are in school. I find the one place where other kids go. The town's tattooed and pierced juvenile delinquents gather to play arcade games in the back of the hardware store. It's sobering to think I feel more kinship with them than the kids at Fort Dixon High School. The feeling is not mutual. They take in my clean-cut appearance and decide I'm of no worth. Joke's on them. I've probably served more time than all of them put together.

I figured I'd be asking for trouble if I kept going there. Sure enough, one day one of the older guys with a mohawk and a bad case of acne, cigarette dangling out of his mouth, starts mouthing off at me. He walks by me and "accidentally" bumps my shoulder. At that moment, Deputy Garrett walks through and the guy melts back into his buddies. I quit going after that. Last thing I need is trouble.

Opening the kitchen cabinet and refrigerator, I go scouting for lunch. There are five foods in the house if you count the ketchup. I heat up spaghetti sauce from a jar and pour it over the leftover spaghetti from last night. It's the fourth time I've had it this week. After a long boring afternoon, I have to get out of the house. Just before dark, I drive to where I can park, then walk up in the hills. At the top of the ridge, I stand and see my house down below, standing all alone.

I hear my nylon jacket whooshing in the wind and zip it up so it'll stop. There's always wind in Wyoming. Sometimes it bellows, sometimes it murmurs, but it's always blowing. Tonight, it's edging toward bellowing, whipping tears into my eyes. More tears come and the world becomes a blur.

I look up at the rising moon and blink back the hot tears. For all these years, Wyoming has been a shining beacon of happiness, of safety, of the life that used to be mine and the one I could have in the future. And now, here I am with everything I wanted and I'm miserable. I just never dreamed "home" would become a place I don't belong.

I stand rooted to the spot, looking at the vastness of the landscape. I picture myself as seen from above—a small, dark figure, all alone. Okay, I tell myself, don't overreact. It's just an adjustment period. Like when I got out of jail and everything felt so strange and unreal. That went away. This should pass too. I just need to wait it out. I stand until my eyes are dry and the cold night forces me to move.

The next day when I can't get words to move from my head to the paper, I busy myself by looking through the dictionary at words that could one day be used in some future book. I decide this is related to writing and is therefore a good use of my time. I had a dictionary at the jail for a whole week as my only book, so I know a lot of words, but then I come across *saudade*. That's a new one. I smile and play with it; only two letters different and it would be *sausage*. But when I read the meaning, I sober up. It's described as a deep emotional state of nostalgia or profound melancholic longing for something that's absent and is not likely to ever return.

Shit. Even the dictionary is out to get me.

I shut it and set it aside.

SAM

7

It's a crisp clear night. Just before heading for bed, I stand on the front porch and take in the full moon and stars. I can't help but wonder if Kelly's looking at the same moon two thousand miles away. It helps to think we might be sharing this.

Darn his little hide. I thought maybe by now he'd come to his senses and at least break radio silence. He never calls, and when we try to call him, all we get is voice mail. Bonnie came up with the idea of the care package, but that didn't get a response either. Patience, Bonnie keeps telling me, patience. I know she's right but it's hard just to sit and wait.

My phone rings at 5:30 in the morning with the news that the Department of Corrections bus just pulled up in front of the main building with transfer orders on all the remaining inmates. By the time I throw on some clothes and get over there, they're already loading the men into the bus. The mood is grim. A few of the men have had this kind of thing happen to them before at other facilities when DOC showed up out of the blue and moved them. They even have a term for it: body-snatching. The staff feel like they've been body-snatched too. We're given the option of applying for a transfer to the nearest prison or resigning. It's an easy decision for me. I quit.

After a bit of time off, I'm now looking for a new job. Once again, I feel the call to work with kids but the idea of marching them in lines in a detention center holds no appeal. I want to catch them earlier. How different things could have been for Kelly if more services had been in place, especially good foster homes for teens.

On a lark, I apply for the local directorship of a private agency that provides therapeutic foster homes. Of course, I need to study up, particularly on what "therapeutic foster care" is since I have no clue. I learn it's like foster care on steroids. The kids are placed in a family—that part's the same—but a caseworker is available twenty-four/seven and works intensively with the kid and the foster parents. "Whatever it takes" is their motto. Having a problem with your fifteen-year-old foster son at three in the morning? Call the caseworker. Kid gets a job but needs a bike so he can get to work? They get him a bike. The kid receives everything he'd get in a residential setting—individual and group counseling, recreation, health care, education—but he gets it in a home setting surrounded by people who care about him. What's not to like about that? It's intriguing.

Before I leave for my job interview, I read over the brochure one more time. A picture of the staff is on the back. They all look young and social-worky. An ex-cop, ex-adult corrections guy is probably the last thing they want. But what the hell, if nothing else, my curiosity will be satisfied.

The office is appealing. Bright yellow and orange colors, lots of pictures of kids on the wall: laughing at an amusement park, splashing in the waves on a beach, dressed up and going to the prom, standing in front of college welcome signs. Nice.

I'm collected by the lady doing the interview and get a tour on my way to her office. I meet and shake hands with some of the staff, all of whom are dressed in jeans. I feel out of place in my suit. I smooth down my dark blue tie and think of Henry and his outlandish ones. They'd fit in here. My interviewer, Margo, looks to be near forty, has short dark hair, a firm handshake, a ready smile, and a take-charge manner. I like her right away. She grabs a bottle of water from the little kitchen area and offers me one. I hold up my hand. "Thanks, but I'm good."

She starts with the standard interview questions and I give the usual canned responses. Out of the blue, she drops the usual patter, leans back, and gives me a serious look. "I guess you know your application is not typically what we get when we advertise this position."

Okay, I can be honest too. "I'm surprised you called me."

"It's a sad fact, but often people who get fired for misconduct in the adult corrections system turn right around and find employment in the juvenile system, so we do get a little paranoid about your kind of applicant. I might have tossed your application aside, but your reputation preceded you."

I lift an eyebrow. "How's that?"

"Stephanie Knight. She's the teacher for one of our kids. Somehow, she got wind you'd applied and sang your praises. Said you'd done wonders with a boy you had at your facility who came from the adult court."

"That's misleading. He wasn't a difficult kid." After I say that, I think, *while he was an inmate.*

She shakes her head. "Others might not agree with you. There are other things you'd bring to the table. You have experience in managing staff. Budgeting and all the administrative details. And I think you'd be good with the foster parents. They sometimes roll their eyes when a twenty-four-year old caseworker tells them how to manage their kids. *You,* they'll pay attention to."

I give her my best lopsided grin. "Well, I am big."

She laughs, "You jest, but that's a plus since we work with lots of teenage boys, and especially since our newest client is the Department of Juvenile Justice. There are some states—Oregon and Kentucky among them—that have used foster homes for delinquent kids with good results, but it was a hard sell here. Initially, they told us, "Oh, you can't handle *our* type of kids."

I lift my eyebrows. "I can't say I'm surprised to hear that. So how did you win them over?"

Margo chuckles. "Sheer luck. DJJ got in a bind when they unexpectedly had to shut down one of their facilities. Out of desperation they sent us some of those kids. I think they just thought they'd buy some time while they pursued a contract with a different private residential agency. They were so sure the kids would bomb out. Well, guess what? Most of the kids did great.

So—almost like a dare—they started sending us some tougher cases. When those kids were successes too, we proved our worth. Of course, not every kid succeeds, but almost without fail we can do a better job than a residential setting."

Margo stops to wave hi as a couple of teenage girls walk by. I give them a wave too, which sets them to whispering and giggling. I nod at Margo. "Sounds great, but there *are* some truly dangerous kids out there."

She uncaps her water bottle. "Sure, some kids have to be behind a locked door for public safety." She takes a drink and twists the top back on. "But look at any study and you'll see the results for residential settings aren't good. Oh sure, kids often improve while they're under roof, but the problem is the gains in an artificial setting often can't be maintained when they go out in the real world.

Group settings can't provide the most important thing. Know what that is?"

I feel like the guy called on in class who doesn't know what to say, but thankfully, she doesn't expect a reply. She answers her own question. "Every kid needs at least one adult who is a trusted, committed parent figure. You can talk about education, vocational training, anger management therapy, but the bottom line is: it's all about relationships. You must have consistency over an extended time period to get that. Shift care—that constant rotation of staff—just doesn't cut it.

So, where do kids turn to get their relationship needs met? To the other kids, of course, and that's not a good thing. Putting a bunch of messed-up kids together is a recipe for disaster. What they didn't know going in, they learn before coming out. In therapeutic foster care, we generally only have one or two kids in a home, so you don't have that problem." Margo reaches for her water bottle again with a rueful grin. "Sorry, don't mean to lecture, I'm just real passionate about what we do."

I smile. "I can see that." I think of a certain fourteen-year old-boy who formed a relationship with a trusted, committed parent figure. Not that he's around at the moment to receive that benefit, the little twerp. I shove that thought aside and say what I know. Heck, what I've lived.

"I agree with everything you say. It's hard for kids to care about others, or even themselves, if they don't feel anyone cares about them."

She uses her water bottle as a pointer and aims it at my chest. "Bingo. And even if no one cares about what's best for kids, they should care about the costs. You can put a kid through an ivy league college for what it costs to incarcerate them. Foster care may not always be cheap, but it's a fraction of the cost."

By the time I leave Margo, I know the Army needs people like her as recruiters. I'm more than ready to enlist for a tour of duty. A week goes by with me checking my phone every thirty minutes. Just when I'm about to give up hope, I get the call. The job is mine. I'll start in three weeks.

I'm excited about the job, but I don't feel right planning to work with other kids until I solve the problem with my own kiddo. Every day for the past couple of weeks, I've been chomping at the bit to get to Wyoming. Only because I have Deputy Garrett's boots on the ground, have I been able to resist.

Just when I decide I can't resist any longer, I get the call from the Deputy

I've been waiting for. "He's looking kind of sad and lonely. I think it's time you come fetch him."

We talk another minute before I hang up and fill in Bonnie. I turn and look out the window. It's been hot and dry, feeling more like summer, than early fall. Ginger, out in her field, is standing in the shade dozing. She's gotten fatter since Kelly up and went. He left her in his dust, just like the rest of us. Ironically, now that I'm called to action, I feel unsure of myself. Maybe Kelly was right, maybe I don't really know him.

Bonnie squints her eyes at me. "What?"

"Should I do this? Maybe it's wrong. I'm not even officially his guardian and I'm not his father."

She gives one of those over-the-top, long-suffering female looks with the rolled eyes and a heavy sigh. I know what she's thinking. *Men are such idiots.* But she tries to be slightly more diplomatic. "Oh Sam, of course you are. It's just that you're both too pigheaded to say what each of you needs to say. Have you ever told him you love him?"

I hem and haw.

More eye rolling, then she waves her hand at me. "Well, go on, get going. Go get our boy."

The next day, I'm in the air looking down at fly-over country. I rent a car at the airport and start driving unfamiliar dark roads, getting to Fort Dixon well after midnight. I know better than to get a room at the Downtowner and follow the recommendation of the guy at the gas station for the best hotel in town which isn't saying a whole lot. But it's reasonably clean and quiet which is all I require. I'm tired and need to get some sleep, but I keep running scenarios in my head of the best way to convince Kelly I still know what's good for him.

The next morning, it's a crisp dawn, icy around the edges, and fifty degrees cooler than back home. I slept in longer than I meant to. There's not much left on the breakfast buffet, but I grab coffee and a muffin while glancing at the TV screen. Clouds will soon be rolling in. There's even mention of snow. What? At this time of year? Yikes. I must have made a face because the guy next to me, who is also grabbing a late breakfast, laughs and says, "Hey, we routinely have snowpack on the ground into June." To his amusement, I express my sympathies.

As I'm driving through town, I see the sheriff's office. I have the address of Kelly's house, but it'd be nice to have some additional information. This is rural America so they must give directions like we do at home. Something along the line of: *Turn on the road with the old blue shirt hung up on the fence pole.*

I luck out and Deputy Garrett is there. I extend my hand. "Hi, I'm Sam Murry. I've come to get my kid … I hope."

He gives me a firm shake and I feel his eyes sizing me up. "You don't think he'll go willingly?"

"I'm optimistic we'll come to an understanding."

The Deputy smiles. "He's underage. I could help you pop him in the car if need be."

I don't try and explain about the emancipated thing. I smile and shake my head. "Tempting. But I'm afraid it would be a case of winning the battle but losing the war."

"Did you think he'd come home by now?"

"I hoped, but I'm not surprised he hasn't. Probably some adolescent pride at stake. Above and beyond everything else, though, there're lots of ghosts here."

"Yeah, I feel for him. He seems like a nice boy."

I think of all the *pretty nice kid* comments I heard when Kelly was on his way to me years ago. "He is. I was hoping you could tell me how to get out to the house. I tried GPS and it gave me that line about unmapped country roads."

"Sure. It's not that hard. I'll jot it down. And there's someone you should meet. He walks me into the break room where a woman is fixing coffee.

"Yo, Betty, this is Kelly's guardian."

We exchange niceties, then the Deputy wishes me luck and leaves the two of us alone.

Betty offers me a cup, but I shake my head. She cups hers in both hands before saying, "I hope you've come for Kelly. It was so good to see him, but he sure doesn't need to be here all alone. He's had hard times, I can tell."

"Yeah, he has, but he's a great kid."

"He always was. Such a cute little tyke. Rob completely adored him."

"So do I. I'm going to go get him."

"You do that."

The drive is beautiful, if not somewhat bleak compared to where I live. I follow the directions and park in front of a rustic cabin. I'm relieved to see Kelly's car parked out front. Before I can fold out of my insanely small rental car, he's opened the door.

A pang goes through me at the sight of his face. Past images of him flash through my head: The way he burns like a candle in the wind, his extremes of joy and grief, his excessive remorse for small sins, his soft heart over a baby bird fallen from its nest, the way he looks at the world that pulls you in.

I've missed you, kiddo, I want to say. *I truly have.*

It doesn't look like the feeling is mutual. His face is impassive, leaning toward a frown. So much for the fantasy he'd light up at the sight of me.

He cuts right to the chase. "What are you doing here?"

I go for the light touch. "Oh, I was in the neighborhood and thought I'd drop in. Mind you, it took a hell of a long time to get to the neighborhood, but hey, here I am."

He continues to stare at me, playing with his hands, his eyes shooting daggers.

I pocket my keys. "Can I come in? It's in the seventies at home and I'm turning to ice out here."

He frowns but moves aside. I blow on my hands as I step into the warmth. I wasn't kidding. I'm freezing my ass off.

The place is sparse. It's obvious that just men used to live here. None of those little touches that women always add, like pillows, candles, pictures, and knick-knacks. He watches me look around and I wonder if he resents me invading his father's space. And damn, if I don't feel weird about it. Being in his childhood home is strangely moving. I picture him here as a little boy sitting at that table eating dinner, lounging on that worn-out couch, legs dangling over the arm.

He jams his hands in his pockets. It's such a familiar gesture, I smile, but all he says is, "I'm not really set up for company."

"Yeah? This is nice. It was a beautiful drive from town to here."

"Why are you here?"

Okay, we aren't interested in chit-chat, I see. "I wanted to see how you were."

"I'm fine. I told you that on the phone."

"Okay, well I'm here. Do you want me to just turn around and go back?"

Henry once told me that a good lawyer never asks a question he might not like the answer to. This surely fits that category.

Kelly doesn't say 'yes.' He doesn't say anything. But the look he's giving me says, *sure, the road's that way.* If I didn't know him so well, I might be hurt, but this attitude is too over the top. It's not like we had a big fight or huge falling out. We've talked cordially on the phone. This whole stern demeanor thing has to be about his internal demons, not about me. *What happened to kick this all off?* I'm determined to find out.

As I walk slowly around the room, I can feel his eyes on me. I'm reminded of those days when he was on my couch, always trying to look at me without me knowing it. He's breathing quicker now and biting his lip. *C'mon kid, let me in.* I make an overture. "Could we go get some lunch or something?"

"I'm not hungry."

Man, he's really making this hard. So much for the subtle approach. I walk over to the table, pull out a chair. "Surely, you can at least give me a drink."

He points the pencil in his hand to the refrigerator. "Help yourself."

You're really working overtime at being a brat, aren't you? Fine. I can play that game too.

Opening the refrigerator door, I make a production out of it. I move some drinks around on the shelf. Take one out, frown, put it back. Get another. Pop the top. Slowly take a sip. Give him a smile and get a frown in return. *Game on.*

"We miss you, you know. Thought maybe you were missing us too."

He looks to the side and slouches against the door. "Not really. I've been busy."

Oh, you little liar. "I thought maybe I could help you wrap up some things here, then you could come on back home."

His finger idly traces the molding on the door. "This is my home."

"I understand. I think everyone feels that about where they grew up. But home is where your family is. It's not good for you to be here by yourself. We've been worried."

"I can take care of myself. You don't need to worry. No one's holding you responsible. Besides, you aren't my family." He looks away. "Someone killed them." His voice chokes on those last words.

375

Yeah, this is about grief. That's the thing about trauma when you're a kid. You can block it all out in your mind, but the body knows. It's programmed into the brain, waiting to surface the moment something triggers it.

I take another sip to fortify myself. Mentally, I apologize to the poor Deputy who I have to throw under the bus. "I stopped by the sheriff's office to talk to Deputy Garrett. I told him I'd come to bring you home. He had agreed to keep an eye on you till I came."

I give him a glance. Oh yeah, his face has flushed to red and his body has gone rigid. He crosses his arms and his eyes go to slits. "So what, you have spies? I'm emancipated, or have you forgotten? Are you saying you're going to try and force me back?"

I shake my head. "Absolutely not."

Something flashes in his eyes. "Oh … well, good."

"Nope, if you don't want to come back, I'm not going to drag you. Can't really." I hold up the real estate brochure I've been holding in my hand. "We'll just have to come here."

He looks like I just said that I can sprout wings and fly. "What the hell do you mean?"

"Just what I said. This is nice country. Kind of cold, but I guess you get used to it."

He's giving me such a shell-shocked look, I want to laugh. *Didn't see that one coming, did you, kid?*

"You can't leave everything and come here."

"Sure, I can. Lost my job, remember? And Bonnie's looking to quit hers. She can't stand working for DOC anymore either."

I lean back casually in my chair and start flipping pages. "I guess we might want to bug out during January and February when the snow is three-feet high. Of course, we all need to be here in December for Christmas. Hey, I bet there's some great ski places, am I right? Bonnie would love that."

Kelly's voice is rising. "I don't think you understand. I don't want you here."

"Really? Hmmm. Too bad. Good thing it's a free country, huh?"

His right foot is jiggling on the floor. He crosses his arms. "You told me if I went my own way, you'd let me. You remember that? Did you lie?"

"I do remember." I tilt my head to the side and grimace. "The thing is, I did kind of fib. I *might* have meant it at the time. Maybe I thought I could. But I find I just can't let you go, so you're stuck with us whether you like it or not."

I strive to keep a conversational tone and look down as I keep thumbing through the booklet's pages. "You know why? We need you." There's a moment of silence before I look up from the brochure. I meet his eyes and hold them. "We love you. You don't walk away from the people you love."

There's a second where I think Bonnie was right and that's all he needed to hear. But no, his lips curl down. His hands knot into fists. Here we go.

"Well, I sure as hell don't need you. What I *need* is for you to leave me the fuck alone! Get out of my life. I never asked for you... for either of you." He takes a step and backhands my drink off the table. It rolls and gurgles, leaving a stream of dark liquid flowing across the wooden floor.

I decide to stand up for my own safety's sake before pushing on. "Oh, maybe you don't need us right this minute. But you will. You'll need someone sitting on your side of the aisle at your wedding. To give a best man speech that's total-ly humiliating. And heaven knows, you'll need babysitters for your kids when they're driving you crazy."

His nostrils are flaring. "You think you're clever, don't you? You don't really know me. Stay out of my life. Stay out of my *state!*"

I can be a real butt-head when I put my mind to it. "Oh, so now you own Wyoming? I don't think so." I hold up a page. "Look at this." I read, "*Three-bed-room cabin. Rustic and charming.* Hey, isn't that just down the road from here?"

He reaches over and grabs the booklet out of my hand and flings it against the wall. "You're really an asshole, you know that? You think that's funny? You're just making me mad!"

I raise my voice to match his. "Yeah, well you *should be* mad. You got screwed. That doesn't make you mad? It sure as hell makes *me* mad! But the one thing I'm not doing is leaving."

There's one long second of silence before he kicks the chair I'd been sitting in across the room and grabs his car keys and jacket on the way out the door. I watch as he gets in his car and slams the door shut with force, before taking off at a fast clip down the long drive.

So now comes the nerve-wracking part. An angry teen with a car—never a good combination. But its daylight and he's stone cold sober. The roads are lightly travelled so I send up a little prayer that he'll be okay and will calm down soon. Then I plop down on the comfy old couch. Kelly's little wooden horse is on the coffee table staring accusingly at me.

I reach over to tap him on his nose. "That went well, don't you think? Yeah, you're right, I should clean up that mess on the floor."

KELLY

8

I stomp on the accelerator and don't let up until I'm a few miles down the highway. I slow when I see another car come up on my tail in the rearview mirror. Last thing I need is a speeding ticket. I slow down and after a bit, my thoughts quit churning. I block Sam from my mind and drive. Just the act of moving feels good. It's not the same as riding a horse, but it sure is easier. Just sit back. Relax. And go, go, go.

I do miss riding. I need to see about buying a horse. Why haven't I done that yet? The answer is there at the back of my mind. *Because you really don't plan on staying here so it wouldn't be fair to the horse.* No! I shove the thought away. It's not true. This is my home. It's always been my home. It always will be my home. It's where I belong.

I spot a sign for a town ahead and with a shock, realize I've been driving well over an hour. Damn, I need gas. I keep going until I hit a gas station, fill up, then turn around and head back to Fort Dixon. I try to decide where I should go when I get there. Not home. I don't want to talk to Sam. Maybe he's gone, but I doubt it. He's not going to leave town just because I threw a fit. I squirm a little in my seat thinking about it.

Why did he have to show up out of the blue? *Why don't you admit that part of you was glad to see him?* Okay, maybe I was, I can own up to it. But I'm still pissed off at him. He was such a complete jerk! Who does he think he is? He can't tell me what to do anymore.

Little specks of ice hit the windshield and soon it's snowing hard. I can barely see out the windshield, so I slow way down. I haven't driven in this kind of weather before. I flash back to Dad getting up in the middle of a snowy night, grumbling about having to go rescue *tourons*. That's Wyoming-speak for tourist and moron combined. Thankfully, the snow starts to let up a bit and by the time I

379

get back to town, it's gone from a driving snow to the Christmas card kind—the type where it's falling in large soft flakes, like in a snow globe. A quiet snow.

If I could, I'd go for a hike in the hills, but the roads would be too bad to try. There's the café, but the thought of food makes me nauseous. Just like old times. So I drive around the town in circles. I start with a large one, then smaller and smaller. Eventually, I'm driving the same four streets over and over, circling the one place I haven't been and don't want to go. But I have to. It's way past time.

I park and sit in the car while the snow covers the windshield. Finally, I reach for the door handle and get out. Like I'm headed for the executioner.

Or to court for sentencing.

Or to wait for a cell door to open and swallow me up.

Or for a state car to deliver me somewhere I've never been before.

The place is empty of any other living person. Good. I look around. For a moment the snow has me disoriented. I thought they were here, but no, there should be a little evergreen tree nearby. Finally, after zig-zagging a bit, I find the right place. The evergreen tree is there, but it's bigger. Of course, it is. It's been five years.

Three stones, all lined up in a row. The one on the farthest left is slightly different than the other two which are identical except for the writing on them. Different names, different births, same death. I go to the one on the farthest left first. I have practice with this one.

Kathleen Marie Morgan. Beloved wife and mother. Dad and I came here every Mother's Day. We always brought flowers and I wish I had something to offer. My eyes go to the tree. I remember its name now, a rocky mountain juniper. The pretty little seed cones are bluish. I snap off part of a branch and lay it in front of my mother's tombstone. I decide it looks nice, so I break off two more. Next, I go to Dad's stone and trace his name, so close to my own: *Robert Reilly Morgan.* The snow has covered the ground.

At the funerals, there were those little dirt mounds. And the chairs and a tent and those people telling me how sorry they were and how things will get better with time.

How wrong they were.

Now it's cleaner, emptier, the snow softening all the hard lines. The eagle on top of a neighbor's grave is sporting snow on his majestic head. He doesn't look quite as majestic that way. I imagine him knowing it. I brush off his head and picture him saying, *thanks, pal.* To my surprise, the thought makes me laugh, except the laugh turns almost instantly into a sob. *No.* I clamp it down. I didn't cry the day of the funerals either. I wanted to. I tried to.

But I didn't come here today to cry. I came here to say something. I go down on my knees at their feet. I'm not praying, but it seems a fitting place to be. "I'm sorry. I'm so, so, sorry." My voice sounds quiet, like the falling snow.

No one answers. The snow keeps coming down. I hear a dog barking in the distance and the rumble of a passing truck. The earth hasn't moved. I think about the guy that died in the other car. I've hated him for what he did to them. For what he did to me. He's somewhere under a stone too. Maybe he had a son. Would his son grieve for him after what he'd done? I decide, yeah, he probably would. If he loved him, he'd forgive him. He wouldn't hate him.

I look at the stones and this feeling of complete certainty comes over me: I know they wouldn't hate me either. They knew I loved them. They loved me. You don't hate the people you love. And they'd forgive me, I know they would. I remember all the times my father's arms came around me to comfort me when I was hurt or upset. If he could rise out of the ground right now, he'd do just that, I'm sure of it.

But he can't. I'm all alone now. I look up and let the snow fall on my face. *I don't want to be.* I close my eyes. *I don't have to be.* For the first time, I think about what I can have, what I *do* have, not what I can't.

A memory pops in my head of when I was about eight. There was a stray brown dog that hung out near my dad's office. I tried so hard to lure him inside, especially when the weather was snowy like this. For days and days I'd put food out for him, but he'd only eat when I moved a safe distance away. He'd only get so close and no closer.

My father found me frustrated and crying. "But Daddy," I said. "Why would he stay out here where he's so hungry and cold? I could fix him a warm bed and be his friend, play ball with him. Why won't he come to me?"

Dad cupped my face with his hand and said, "He's too afraid, son. He doesn't know it could be better, so he sticks with what he's got."

I'd thought that dog was pathetic. Now I know he's got nothing on me.

As I get to my feet, I feel the bite of the cold. Back at The Village, the asters, ironweed, and goldenrods are in full bloom. Monarchs will be fueling up on them as they make their way down to Mexico. Ginger will be getting her winter coat, turning from sleek to shaggy.

I head back to the car I left a few hundred yards up the cemetery road, pulling my coat collar up around my frozen ears. My feet pick up the pace, faster and faster. I let them have their way and break into a run, just like I used to do. Only this time it's different.

I'm not running away.

SAM

9

I prowl around the house, shamelessly snooping, paying special consideration to the photo albums I find. It's an emotional experience looking at the kid he was before he was mine. Proof he didn't hatch from an egg the day he arrived on my doorstep. I'd never seen pictures of Kelly's parents. So sad. I carefully put the album back where I found it. I rummage through the kitchen looking for something to eat. I use the bathroom. Twice.

I look at my watch. I get a drink from the fridge and look at my watch. I walk over and stare out the window and look at my watch. I call Bonnie to give her an update, then look at my watch. I call Kelly but it goes straight to voice mail. Why did we buy the kid a phone if he never bothers to turn it on?

Three hours later, if the floor could talk it would be cussing me. My pacing is wearing a hole in it. *Where the hell is he?* Great plan, Sam. Take a traumatized kid and traumatize him some more. Aren't you clever? Where did you get your psychiatric degree? I look out the window for the hundredth time. *Damnit, still snowing.* Christ, outdoor swimming pools are still open at home. How can people live like this? Kelly out there, unpracticed, driving in this mess while he's upset. Maybe I should call Deputy Garrett and have him go look for Kelly.

Just as I consider reaching for my phone, I see his car. I feel a great relief, but seconds later, it switches to anger. *Here you are scaring the shit out of me again.* Emancipation be damned, I've had enough of this. I'll stuff him in the car all by myself. He may be bigger than he used to be, but I can still take him.

My mad disappears at the sight of him walking toward the house. The love I feel for him is so strong, it's like a pain piercing the center of my chest. I think about the first time I saw him, that little kid in those gawd-awful clothes. I didn't want him. I said he'd be trouble and by golly, he was. Glorious, life-altering trouble. I told Gene I hoped we could help him. I just didn't realize how much he would help me. How much he would change my life.

I'm not leaving without him.

I don't wait for him to open the door. No use pretending to play it cool. I pull it open while he's still a few strides away and he walks straight in. One look at his face and I can see the anger is no longer there. They're the eyes I know so well, seeking out mine, gauging my reaction. My need to comfort him kicks into high gear. I reach out to pull him to me, but when I stretch my hand out to touch him, he backs away, so I let it drop. *Careful, Sam. Don't screw this up now.*

I watch him swallow. The action seems to use every muscle in his body. He opens his mouth, closes it, then opens it again. "I need to tell you something." He gives me a lopsided grin, which he has a hard time pulling off. "I'm still a liar..." He swallows again, then whispers, "I do need you. I *love* you."

His face crumbles. Now unchecked, the tears finally come. When I reach for him this time, he doesn't pull away. I fold him into my arms and rest my cheek on the top of his head. I can smell the faint scent of wood smoke on his jacket. Tears turn into sobs. He cries so hard he can barely get air. I try to absorb his pain and my own tears come. For a few minutes, I let him cry, then he allows me to walk him over to the couch. We both sit down, but I leave my arms around him.

I lean my face down to his and quietly ask, "That day when you got so upset? Is that what led to all this?"

Still sobbing, he nods his head and manages to choke out, "I remembered the accident. It all came back." He takes a big gulp of air. "I wasn't in the car. I was supposed to be. I'd been told to stay but I got out."

I shake my head. "Buddy, that just means you survived. What's the difference if you were in the car or out?"

He struggles in my arms. "No, no, you don't understand!" He raises his head to look at me and I can see the anguish on his face. "It was my fault. The guy would have missed the car, but when he was surprised to see me standing there he swerved. They're dead because of me. I should have stayed in the car... if I'd just stayed in the car!"

His head drops, but I gently raise his chin. My mind races with possible responses. I'm going to have one shot at this. I need to get it right.

"Listen to me. You aren't thinking straight. Why else would the guy have driven up there unless he was intent on ramming the car? Maybe he was angling to come in from the other direction. Maybe he intended to jump out at the last minute. But even if none of that is true, it is *not* your fault. *You* didn't get that guy high. *You* couldn't control the actions of a crazy man. Do you want to blame whoever said, "Let's go hiking?" Or who ate breakfast too slow that morning and put you all there at just that time? You can't hold an eleven-year-old child responsible for something as normal as getting out of a car."

His sobbing eases and his eyes latch onto mine. I pull my handkerchief out of my pocket and hand it to him. "Can you see that?" Taking the handkerchief, he blows his nose, making a slight honking sound which makes me smile. I take my thumb and brush away a tear running down his cheek. "You ever hear of 'survivor's guilt'?"

He blows his nose again. "Maybe." It comes out as a whisper.

My hand makes circles on his back. "Let me tell you something, okay? You've been looking at this from a child's perspective. I didn't know your father, but I don't have to, because without a doubt if he had the chance for a last thought, do you know what it would have been?"

He shakes his head, but he's listening intently.

"No? It's so easy. His thought would be: *Thank God, Kelly got out.* He would want you to live your life, to be happy, to find people who love you. And we do, you know … love you."

He takes his sleeve across his eyes, then looks up at me and takes a deep breath. "I know. It just seemed wrong to be with you all... to be happy... like they didn't matter anymore." He starts crying again, but this time it's quieter—less anguished—more of a release. I hold him to me, but don't try to stop him. He's held all this in for so long.

When at last he quiets, I drop my hands in my lap and lean forward resting my elbows on my knees. "You never had the chance of grieving, did you? You were too busy coming to grips with a life turned upside down and inside out. But buddy, you're going to get past this, I promise you. You know why? Because you're a smart kid and a gutsy one too. A kid who climbs trees and skips across gullies, right?" I nudge his shoulder with mine. "A kid who writes books and saves baby birds and knows how to annoy the hell out of me when he wants to, right?" I nudge his shoulder again. "Am I right? Huh, am I? Am I?"

He bumps my shoulder back. "You sure think a hell of a lot of yourself, don't you? A real know-it-all."

"Damn straight. You know what else I know?"

"I can't wait. What?"

"I know I'm starved, and you don't have crap here to eat. Can we leave before we get snowed in? Let's go to my hotel because it's right behind that illustrious Waffle House."

He tries to look offended which is hard to pull off with red swollen eyes. "Hey, don't be knocking the Waffle House. It's our only chain food and we're awful proud of it. Anyway, I have a whole box of granola bars we can survive on."

"I ate them while I was waiting for you to get your ass back here."

"*Jesus.* Remind me to never get stuck in the woods with you. The provisions would be gone the first night. We'd starve to death and they wouldn't find our bodies till the spring thaw."

I grab back my handkerchief and stuff it in my pocket. "I was hungry. Now I'm really hungry."

He looks out the window where it's snowing like crazy again. Then he smiles, the slow, warm one that's his trademark with just a hint of mischievousness. "Can I drive your rental car?"

I smile back. "Sure, it'll be good practice for you."

He narrows his eyes at me, gives me his own superpower look. "You're a terrible liar."

I laugh, hook my arm around his neck and pull him over. I give him a kiss on the side of his head. "Right you are. But tell you what, if we aren't snowed in tomorrow, you can drive me around in your car and show me the sights."

He smiles and nods. "Sam?"

"Yeah?"

"After that? Can we go home?"

SAM

10

It was a fun Christmas. Our first one together in the mostly renovated house. I work out a deal with Edith to buy it with twenty acres of the surrounding land. Enough land for Ginger and Kelly's newest horse, a three-year-old black gelding that has what Edith describes as "spunk." I thought Ginger was plenty spunky enough, but when it comes to horses no one listens to me. Edith has become the grandmother Kelly never had. A rather intimidating one but hey, you can't pick your family.

Or can you?

It's a joy to watch Kelly truly come into his own. The purging of old demons and the strengthening of our relationship bring a new confidence and contentment. There's success on another front too.

Kelly kept a secret. The whole time he'd been at The Village, he'd kept in touch with an author named Dennis Hill, a guy who taught a writing class at the jail. Apparently, something Kelly wrote while he was in jail stuck with the guy. He eventually sent it to his publisher. *A Reason for Gladness* was published and was selling reasonably well—that is, until a celebrity in a nearby town for a basketball game happened to pick up a copy of it at the airport bookstore for his son. On the plane and bored, he opened it and started reading. He loved it. He talked it up in a recent interview and since then, sales have jumped considerably.

Will it hurt sales if people find out it was written by a teenage convict? Maybe. But most of us believe it will only add to the allure. Besides, Kelly will be his own best ambassador just as he's always been. Bonnie and I call it, *The Kelly Effect*.

Because of Kelly and my new job, I've become involved with juvenile justice issues, joining an advocacy group to promote needed reforms to the system. There's a new emphasis on "cross-over youth," kids like Kelly who begin in child welfare and get pushed into the juvenile justice system. They even have a name for it. The foster care to prison pipeline.

I'm not the only one with a new job. Turns out Henry had political connections we never knew. He got appointed to fill a state senate term when the incumbent passed away. Kelly's on his mind too. He's serving on the judiciary committee and is working with others on drafting juvenile justice reform legislation that would eliminate mandatory transfer of youth to adult court. It would go back to the way it used to be with juvenile judges making the determination after reviewing each individual case. Unfortunately, it's likely not to pass. Legislators like to run on get-tough-on-crime platforms, even if it's counterproductive to public safety.

But we can always hope that wisdom will eventually replace fear. Someday.

The one thing I don't fear is that Kelly will become one of those negative statistics. Not on my watch. Not on his watch. There's a quote I've read about these resilient kids—the ones who endure so much trauma but in the end rise above it all: *Some shatter, some bend and stretch, and some resound like a clear bell.*

My kid is ringing.

KELLY

11

Sam cannot break the habit of bringing his work home. Sure, for the first six months or so, it was just files and phone calls. Then one night, he gets a call about a sibling group of three needing emergency foster care placement. Their mother was arrested on a drug charge in a neighboring state and for weeks the kids lived in their rental home alone until Kyle, the oldest at thirteen, was caught shoplifting food. He ended up in juvenile detention because they couldn't find an adult to release him to. Only then does he spill the beans about his two younger sisters, Katie and Kara, ages ten and eight, at the house alone. The foster home that was lined up had their own crisis and pulled out at the last minute, but Sam went on ahead with Bonnie tagging along to pick up the kids.

The authorities said they could wait and get Kyle the next day, but Sam went straight to the detention center so the boy wouldn't have to spend the night in a cell. Sam could have pulled a Mrs. Williams and sat in the agency office with them all till morning, but he brought them home instead. Bonnie cranked up the oldies station and we all ate pancakes at one o'clock in the morning. The girls sat there wide-eyed. Kyle tried to look tough for an hour before falling asleep on the couch. Sam just looked at me and said, "What is it with you guys and couches?"

There was no foster home available to take them the next day either, so they stayed with us another night. And another. And another. Then came the news their mother had died while she was in jail.

People die in jails all the time. They aren't a good place to be.

Fortunately for the kids, the Murry foster home becomes their one and only foster home. It becomes their adoptive home as well. What's more, I decide that emancipation isn't all it's cracked up to be, so my name gets added to the adoption paperwork. I make what I fervently hope is my final juvenile court appearance.

Standing before the judge, I glance at the man next to me and think about my good fortune. How lucky am I to have had two good men love me with a father's love, when so many kids never even have one?

Now I know that my tide turned years ago. It wasn't marked with a big ship rolling in. Instead it came in small waves: Henry walking through that door to save me. Bonnie, who wouldn't back down. Sam, who literally took me in his arms and saved me from drowning in my own despair. Professor Hill who believed in my talent. The corrections officers who bought me candy bars. Pop and Granny Haverly. Mrs. Williams, who I've long since forgiven. All the people who kept me connected to the world when I was so very tempted to give up on it. Maybe it's the human condition but the bad memories fade. It's the love and kindnesses I remember.

The judge makes the adoptions official and Kelly, Kyle, Katie, and Kara all become Murrys. Of course, we think it's hilarious each of our names starts with the letter K. We call it fate. Fate and I are old friends.

I can't say it hasn't been an adjustment doubling the size of our odd, not-so-little family, but it's been worth it. I like being a big brother. Kyle sticks with basketball, but I'm teaching both girls to ride. I'm in no hurry to be on my own, but I make a promise to Sam that I won't be living in the basement drinking beer when I'm thirty.

I'm still working on finding friends my age, but I do have one very good, older friend—I drive over sometimes to have dinner with Henry. Eventually he's going to get my record expunged. Once he does, officially, it'll be like none of it ever happened. Almost.

Ms. Casey began taking in rescue horses and I help her out. Like Sam, I enjoy taking things and making them better. Ms. Casey's niece, Jillian, has flown in from Texas to help out before she starts college this fall. Let's just say the niece didn't fall too far from the family tree.

We had a huge disagreement about an equine training technique. Even during my time as a convict, I've never been cussed out so thoroughly. I listened with a sappy smile on my face, as she called me every name in the book and stomped away. Ms. Casey saw the whole thing, walked over to me, and whacked me on the shoulder with her riding crop. "Don't just stand there like an idiot, go ask her out."

Never let it be said that I'm not good at taking orders. Did I mention Jillian is really smart and funny too? And that she's going to college just an hour away from here?

Besides helping Ms. Casey, I'm working on the sequel to my published book. When I get done with it, the next one is going to be based on my father. I think he'd be pleased. I read somewhere that although musical child prodigies are fairly common, child prodigies who are writers are not. The theory is that only an adult has the experiences, insight, and understanding it takes to be an author. There are several teenage writers that have proven that theory wrong. *The Outsiders*, one of America's best-known novels, was written by a girl who was only fifteen. I sometimes wonder: If my life had gone differently, would I still have become an author?

I no longer dwell on the past, but I'd be lying if I said it still doesn't come back to bite me from time to time. Grief and trauma are like shrapnel that didn't get removed before a doctor stitched you up. They rattle around in your body, not causing any damage most of the time. But sometimes when you least expect it, they push up against a nerve and you feel the pain. It's like *oh, yeah, you're still in there, I remember you.*

There are days that make me terribly sad. As much as I love Sam and Bonnie, at times I both yearn for the past and mourn the loss of what might have been. I become nostalgic for the future that never was. I feel not just my pain, but an empathetic pain for my father, who only got to have eleven years with his son. He didn't watch me become a writer. And we never took that trip to the ocean we had always planned.

The good news is, even though it will never entirely go away, the shrapnel gets a little smaller all the time and I'm experienced enough now to know the painful times will pass. I go for a ride, shoot baskets with Kyle, or if it's a particularly bad spell, I find Sam.

Last night, I got up out of bed and went downstairs where he was watching a late-night ball game. I slid next to him on the couch, and without a word, his arm came around me. I laid my head on his chest and listened to the beating of his heart, strong and true.

Spring, my favorite season, has arrived. With it comes endless possibilities. Right now, it's almost time for dinner, so I hurry to fill the horses' buckets with fresh water for the night. In one of the half-full ones, a bug floats on top, his legs paddling away. He's probably been at it for hours. I wonder if he knows how close he came to drowning. Good thing he kept swimming. With a smile, I tilt the bucket over and watch him hit the ground. After one little pause, he crawls away.

JUMPING-OFF POINTS FOR DISCUSSION

All social "systems" have their pros and cons, good points and bad points, bad apples and angels. This is most certainly the case with the child welfare and juvenile justice systems described in the novel.

- What were some aspects of these systems that surprised or shocked you?
- At what points were you fearful for Kelly of the System's effects?
- At what points were you glad the System was there?
- At what points in the story were you cheering for Kelly and/or Sam to "beat the System?"
- After reading the book, what are some opinions that you find yourself holding about the juvenile justice system?
- What are your hopes for incarcerated youth and the people who serve them?

What social systems or organizations have you found yourself involved with? For instance, a hospital, a spiritual or religious organization, a sports team, or a government entity. If comfortable, share with your discussion group something about your experience—the good, the bad, the ugly, the beautiful.

- What are/were some of the frustrations?
- What are/were some of the triumphs?
- Is/Was there one person, like Sam was to Kelly, that made the experience worthwhile or because of whom your life will never be the same? What was that like? Consider sharing about this "angel" with your group.

AUTHOR'S NOTE

I hope you enjoyed reading *The Car Thief* as much as I enjoyed writing it. It was the first time in my long career of working with at-risk youth, where I could control the outcome, so I made the ending a good one. The characters, of course, are fictional but most everything else in the book is something I've witnessed, including unfortunately, ugly courtroom battles over whether the Department of Juvenile Justice (DJJ) or child welfare had to take responsibility for the child. And yes, this played out right in front of the youth in question. I've seen wonderful foster homes and poor ones; fantastic judges, and ones who seem to hate every kid who appears in front of them; defense attorneys who go all out to do what's best for their kids and some who fall asleep during hearings. In criminal justice so often what happens to you is a roll of the dice. And just so you know, it wasn't a common occurence, but I did see kids bring their teddy bears to their correctional placement.

The impetus for this novel came out of one of my tasks when I worked for Kentucky's DJJ. (And yes, we did have a kid squeeze out through a fence of one of our brand-new detention centers.) I was charged with writing an impact statement anytime a proposed piece of legislation might have "unintended consequences" that would affect us. In reviewing a bill that would automatically transfer juveniles to adult court for certain offenses, I gave several examples of problems that might come up. Most notably, I asked what would happen to a fourteen-year-old who got waived to adult court, finished his sentence while under age eighteen, then had nowhere to go with no parent or guardian to claim him.

The law proceeded as written. I believe the comment made to my concern was "that's not going to happen." Well, sure enough, that exact scenario soon came to be. A boy who testified against two adults was given a one-year sentence and "served out." Just before his release, when the officials suddenly realized they couldn't just turn a kid out onto the streets, we (DJJ) were asked to come get him. Well, no, we couldn't. We had no legal custody and no way to get it. So, I called Social Services who were none too thrilled. They ended up having to file a dependency petition in juvenile court, and just like when an abandoned baby is found on a doorstep, they had to take custody. The point I'm trying to make here is that regardless of what these young people have done, at the heart of it, they are still kids.

My apologies if you agonized over trying to figure out what states Kelly was in. I wanted to make a point about child welfare and juvenile justice systems in general, without getting bogged down in the policies of any specific place. I chose not to put Kelly in my home state of Kentucky because for the most part, it has a progressive juvenile justice system.

Let me brag here a bit: Kentucky's state-wide system of diversion (thank you, Court Designated Workers) keeps low-level offenders from formal court processing, and we are one of only eight states that do not have any youth under the age of eighteen in any adult facility. We have a system of small, treatment-oriented facilities where most kids don't sleep in cells at night, nor do they wear jumpsuits or shirts with DJJ on the back.

Our line staff are juvenile service workers. Encouraged to develop positive relationships with the youth, they aren't there to "guard" youth but to help them through their day. Those juvenile detention center rules and consequences Kelly had to comply with are from detention manuals I've reviewed from other states. Other than the kids in secure detention and the most serious offenders who present public safety issues, most of Kentucky's youth in DJJ facilities are regularly off-campus either doing community service projects or engaging in pro-social activities including hiking and canoeing. You can tell from my book I believe kids need to be outdoors.

It's an exciting time in juvenile justice. Juvenile crime is at unprecedented low and the numbers of youth incarcerated in just about every state is declining. The problem of youth crossing over from child welfare to juvenile justice is beginning to be addressed. There's a growing recognition that incarceration and typical surveillance-type probation show poor results, and that whenever possible, the best treatment occurs in the family and community. States are also realizing that for good outcomes, counseling and support win out almost every time over coercion and control.

Unfortunately, nationally, we still have a long way to go. Many states including Kentucky still put status offenders—kids who've committed no crime—in juvenile detention. There are too many large ineffective juvenile prisons, and too many young people get forced into the adult system. In many jurisdictions, physical and sexual abuse happen too frequently. And there's still way too much solitary confinement, even though we know how damaging it can be to an adolescent with a still developing brain.

During the two years I worked on this book, I looked at every juvenile justice story that sprang from the headlines. In one state, a seventeen-year-old hung himself while locked in solitary at a juvenile detention center. Days later, in the same detention center, a thirteen-year-old was put in solitary and also hung himself. Sometimes it seems we just don't learn.

One thing I hate about these tragedies is that they taint the public image of juvenile workers, the majority of whom work hard every day to provide the best care of the youth in their charge. Furthermore, they do this difficult work usually with very low wages and even less appreciation. Yes, we should value these kids, and as we do, we should also value the people who take care of them and treat them accordingly.

I volunteer in my county's local juvenile detention center. It is a well-run facility and I want to thank the Superintendent and the rest of the staff for the good work they do. If you are inspired after reading this book, please find out where your closest juvenile detention center is. Ask the staff what they need. New games, movies, books, and soccer balls are just some of the possibilities. Even better, see if you can teach an arts class, conduct a writing group, help kids learn to play a musical instrument, or just go out and play basketball with the kids. If it's a good juvenile detention center, they'll be happy to have you.

When the kids find out you are a volunteer, they will likely ask you: "Why did you come here?" Tell them you haven't forgotten them. Tell them you know they are better than the worst mistake they've ever made.

If you want to learn more about juvenile justice in America, these national organizations are a good place to start:

Campaign for Youth Justice
campaignforyouthjustice.org

Coalition for Juvenile Justice
info@juvjustice.org

Juvenile in Justice
juvenile-in-justice.com

Annie Casey Foundation's
Juvenile Detention Alternatives Initiative
acef.org

ACKNOWLEDGEMENTS

A huge thank you to my writing mentor, Mary Knight—award-winning author of the marvelous book, *Saving Wonder*—who guided me through the process and made the whole thing so darn enjoyable. More thanks to Kimber Gray for the amazing layout and cover design. Another big shout out to my friends and Beta readers Cheryl, Christie, Karen, Kathy, Linda, Marcy, Margo, Pam, Steve, Terry, Tracey, and Ward for your help and encouragement. And last, but not least, all my love and heartfelt appreciation to my husband, Geoff, and son, Greg, who could never get on the computer and had to endure almost two years of mostly take-out food. Your sacrifices are duly noted.

ABOUT THE AUTHOR

With an undergraduate degree in Law Enforcement and a Master's in Criminal Justice from Eastern Kentucky University, Vicki Reed has enjoyed a long and successful juvenile justice career. Beginning her vocation as line staff in a juvenile detention center and then as a probation officer, Reed eventually became the director of a private agency, where she opened an emergency shelter for delinquent teens. Later, during her tenure with the Kentucky Department of Juvenile Justice (DJJ), she assisted in the development of a statewide system of juvenile detention facilities and alternatives, removing all youth under eighteen from any adult jail or facility. As DJJ's Director of Classification, she also championed the use of therapeutic foster care for delinquent youth and continued that work later as the regional director of a private foster care agency.

A sought-after speaker, Reed is currently the Executive Director of the Kentucky Juvenile Justice Initiative (kyjuvenilejusticeinitiative.org), an advocacy group seeking, among other things, to eliminate the detention of status offenders and the use of mandatory waiver transferring youth to adult court. When not promoting juvenile justice reform, she spends her time riding her horse Toby and cutting invasive honeysuckle out of the woods of Shaker Village at Pleasant Hill. Reed lives with her husband and son in Lexington, Kentucky, the proclaimed *Horse Capital of the World*. This is her first novel.